THE DUKE'S REFUGE

THE LEEWARD ISLAND SERIES -BOOK 1

LORRI DUDLEY

WILD HEART
BOOKS

Cover design by: Carpe Librum Book Design

ISBN-10: 1-942265-14-X

ISBN-13: 978-1-942265-14-6

To my husband, John,
I'm blessed to do life alongside you.

CHAPTER 1

...Why did you not mention your illness sooner? Must you continue to be so blasé regarding your life?

I'm sending Georgia and your sister on the next ship to Nevis. You may notice some changes in Georgia ...

—From Nora Lennox to her husband Fredrick Lennox in the Leeward Islands

"*M*oor the line!" the captain called out. Feet shuffled above deck, and the echo of male grunts filled the air.

Georgia Evelyn Lennox straightened the skirt of her finest muslin traveling dress. She'd saved this particular pale pink gown especially for the day they would reach Nevis. Now, she adjusted the sleeves with the same care a knight would prepare his armor for battle.

She didn't wear it to impress a specific person, certainly not her father. Pink gowns had become her own kind of chain mail.

1

Her bonnet, embellished with pink silk flowers, transformed into her helmet. And her fan or her frilly pink parasol—her shield.

She slid on her matching pink gloves, hooked her parasol over her arm, and as best she could, inspected herself in her tiny handheld mirror, looking for chinks in the pink armor. Satisfied, she opened the door, but paused on the threshold.

"Aunt Tessa, it sounds as if we might be nearing Nevis. I'm going to climb aloft to speak with the captain. Would you care for anything?"

"Dry land." Aunt Tessa mumbled under the covers.

Georgia chuckled. "I shall do my best."

Aunt Tessa rolled over and pulled the blanket off her face. "I daresay, I'm feeling a mite better today. I merely need a good rest."

"Then I shall leave you to it." Georgia lifted her chin, happy to be free of her stuffy cabin. Aunt Tessa, with whom she'd shared a room throughout the voyage, had suffered from a weak stomach the entire journey.

Georgia did her best to put on a valiant front, but tending to her aunt in the darkness of the poorly lit cabin had allowed her imagination to run rampant. What would she find when she reached Nevis? How close to death did her father lie? How would she care for him? Other than passing the chamber pot to Aunt Tessa for the past five hundred leagues, she had no experience in aiding the sick.

She pressed to one side of the hallway as a sailor brushed past, then she climbed the remaining steps. Warm sunshine spilled upon her face, and she inhaled a deep breath of briny air. The few precious hours a day she escaped above deck kept her sane. She shook the layers of her pink traveling dress, more to allow the air to circulate than to remove any lingering wrinkles.

"Lower the dinghy dead astern!" the captain hollered to the crewmen working the gunwale.

Overhead, the cries of gulls pierced the air, a sign the ship must be nearing land. Georgia's eyes adjusted to the sunlight. Sure enough, off the port bow, a strip of land rose out of the sea to a monstrous peak. Clouds hung low around the mountain, obscuring the top from view. Aquamarine waters shimmered in the light of the sun.

Her lips parted, and she inhaled a gasp. There was not a gown in all of London that captured the sea's spectacular color. Even though she'd been above deck for only a moment, the sun heated her skin, and the humidity drew beads of perspiration from her brow. She opened her pink parasol, flipped it over her head, and strolled toward the captain to wait for an opportunity to speak.

A sailor saluted the captain and rushed off to see to his duties.

Georgia stepped up to the helm. "Is this the coast of Nevis?"

The sea-worn man's leathery skin crinkled at the corners of his eyes. "'Tis Nevis, my dear, and your final destination. We be just sendin' over a few men to chat with the Marshall before we deliver ya over in the dinghy."

Georgia lingered above deck, absorbing the view and sucking in deep, stabilizing breaths. She turned away from the sun, east toward England. She could only pray her father's untimely illness hadn't ruined her chances with the Earl of Claremont. Her stomach flipped with the dip of each wave, and her fingers gripped the end of her parasol to keep her hands from shaking. By the time she'd subdued her riotous emotions, the crew had returned from land, clambering aboard the ship again.

"From the sounds of it, a big storm's abrewin', Cap." A ruddy-faced crewman who'd just boarded approached the Captain. "Accordin' to the Marshall, they've seen all the signs. Sea's been calm as a bowl of soup, and the fish have been

3

jumpin' into the net as of late, but now the breeze has picked up, and you can feel 'em swells rising."

A light breeze ruffled Georgia's bonnet, lifting the tiny hairs on her arms and tugging at her parasol.

The captain glanced at the weather vane and reached for his spyglass. He pulled open the telescope and swung it in the direction of the wind. Georgia followed the Captain's gaze and squinted, but other than a thin strip of white feathery clouds on the horizon, there was only blue sky.

"Let's make this quick!" the captain called out. He turned to Georgia and said, "I apologize, Miss Lennox, but we'll be needing to rush through our farewells. Best of luck to ya in Nevis. Better go below and prepare your trunks. My men will be set to load them when yer ready."

Georgia's heartbeat quickened as she made her way below deck. Soon, she'd set foot on land, away from the smelly, cramped space of the boat. She'd also be leaving its security to face her father. What would he be like after six years? Would his eyes still flash with merriment like they used to?

She gritted her teeth. It didn't matter. He'd chosen to leave. He abandoned her and her family and didn't even bother to write. She was here to aid him back to health and then catch the next ship back to London.

She placed a hand on the blanketed mass that was her Aunt. "It's time to pack our belongings. We'll soon be going ashore."

Aunt Tessa rolled over, and a joyful tear leaked down her lined cheek. The poor thing looked like a wilted flower. Her gray hair hung around her green-tinged face.

Georgia scooted about the cramped cabin and gathered their belongings. After filling one trunk, she knelt to lock it, but her fingers trembled, and the key slid with a clink onto the floorboard.

Aunt Tessa knelt beside her and picked it up. "Here, let me

get that. It's about time I did something useful. Some companion I turned out to be."

Georgia chuckled, more to release the tension welling within her than because her aunt's words were funny.

Even the dim room couldn't hide the compassion lighting Aunt Tessa's eyes. "It's natural to be nervous about seeing your father again after so much time. You're doing him a great service by coming." She smiled and patted Georgia's hand. "I, for one, cannot wait for him to see what a beautiful woman you've become. You're two-and-twenty now. Not the same young girl he left behind."

No, I'm not.

"He loves you Georgia." A weak smile crossed Aunt Tessa's lips.

Georgia forced herself to offer one in return. *If he loved me, he would have stayed.*

As Georgia continued to prepare for their disembarking, Mama's words echoed in her head. *He's dying, and he's alone. He's looking to make amends. It's your duty as his daughter to be there for him.*

But he didn't want her. Someone who loved her wouldn't leave and travel halfway across the world when she needed him the most.

A knock sounded on their cabin door. Two burly men entered without a word and began hauling their trunks above deck. She smiled as Aunt Tessa leaned heavily on a sailor's arm, babbling on about the previous night's horrific rocking.

Georgia's steps slowed. Ready or not, she was about to meet her father. Whether he was still the papa she adored from her childhood or the uncaring man who walked away without a backward glance, without ever bothering to write, she would soon find out.

Utter chaos met them above deck. Men bustled about, sealing the hatchways, covering them with tarpaulin, and nailing the covers in place with wooden battens. Dinghies full of merchandise raised and lowered, and sailors rushed to stow items away in lockers. The captain barked orders, and shipmates bumped into each other in their haste to prepare the sails for hoisting. In the fray, Georgia lost sight of the men carrying her trunks, but the first mate grasped her elbow.

"M'lady, you must hurry. Yer boat awaits."

She struggled to keep up with his long strides.

"Unhand me this minute!" Aunt Tessa cried from ahead.

Georgia bit her lip to keep from laughing as a muscular man scooped up Aunt Tessa and carried her to the rails. The older woman screamed as he dropped her into the arms of another crewman in the dinghy. Even Georgia gasped as her aunt slipped through the air. He then turned to Georgia.

"I can handle this myself." She raised a hand to ward off the sailor. He lifted a brow and had the audacity to grin.

She stepped up to the edge of the ship, leaned down, and held her hand out to the crewman in the smaller boat. She stiffened as the man's hands wrapped around her waist and tossed her onto the wooden seat as he would a jacket onto a coat rack. Her stomach rose into her throat as the boat dropped without warning. She gasped each time it jerked to an incremental stop, her heart thudding like a mallet in her chest.

The boat hit the water with a splash, spraying droplets on her hair and face. Georgia wiped them away with the back of her glove. The oarsmen released a grunt with each row, and sweat slid down the edges of their red faces. The breeze wafted the powerful stench of unbathed flesh under her nose with each stroke. Despite a few warm waves that slapped against the side of the boat, the rest of the trip to shore was uneventful.

Above the surf, the landscape grew larger as the boat approached. It was as if the world she knew changed from shades of gray to full color. The sunny beach contrasted sharply with the dreary, gray backdrop of London. A small group of people gathered around the dock waiting for more goods to be unloaded.

Further up, a tight row of shops lined the main street beyond the harbor. Some were small huts, but most were stone buildings with wooden second stories painted in cheerful colors. Shutters lined all the windows, some propped open with sticks. Palm trees—Georgia knew they were called that only because she'd seen them in books and paintings—swayed in the wind. Her eyes dared to steer higher toward Mount Nevis, looming over the town like a hulking green shadow.

The dinghy reached the breakers, and one of the men scrambled out. The waves soaked his boots and pants as he hefted the boat up on the shore. Another crewman plucked her out of the dinghy and plopped her down on the sandy beach. The soles of her walking shoes sank into the soft sand as she waited for her aunt to disembark. Aunt Tessa's feet barely touched the ground before more men hopped out and pushed the boat back into the water.

A gust of wind tugged at her skirts and bonnet. Georgia cupped her hands around her mouth as she yelled back toward the men. "Shall we wait here for our trunks to be delivered?"

Either the wind or the crashing waves swallowed her question. The men strained against the oars, struggling to haul the dinghy beyond the breakers.

That must be what they planned. She slowly turned to face the island of Nevis.

Dark-skinned men and women, most likely natives or African slaves, took their time loading the beached cargo into wagons and carts. Compared to the hustle and bustle of the boat, everyone on the small wharf ambled along at a snail's pace.

"Be mindful of how you handle that, boy! That freight is worth more than you'll ever be." A round-faced Englishman yelled at a slave bending under the weight of the heavy load. The Englishman mopped the sweat from his brow with a lace-lined handkerchief. He sliced his riding crop through the air, and the boy jumped out of the way, almost dropping the freight in the process.

Georgia turned away, unable to bear witness to what would happen next.

The dinghy approached the side of the ship, and the men hooked the ropes for it to be hoisted up again. The cool wind tugged at her bonnet strings, and she plopped a hand on top to hold it in place. The breeze refreshed her warm skin where the sun beat down, but it rendered her parasol useless.

"Thank heavens we're on land." Aunt Tessa closed her eyes and hugged herself. "I vow I will never set foot in one of those dastardly vessels again." She peered down at her boots sinking deeper into the sand.

Her aunt appeared as if she contemplated dropping to her knees and kissing the ground. Georgia pinched her lips to hide a smile.

"I think I'll go rest on that rock and look for your father. He probably has a carriage waiting for us."

Hiking up her skirts, Aunt Tessa trudged through the sand and plunked down on a large boulder in the middle of the beach. With a drawn-out sigh of relief, she fanned herself.

Georgia shook her head. Her poor aunt had paid a high penance crossing the Atlantic. Hopefully, their return trip wouldn't be as wretched.

The back of Georgia's neck tingled with the feeling of being watched. Slowly, she twisted her head.

A strange man stood fifty yards away in front of an open wagon, his white shirt clinging to his muscular chest and arms. His face was clean shaven, and his brown hair ruffled in the wind. Cream-colored breeches hugged his thighs as he planted a booted foot on a rock. He slung his jacket over his shoulder and scanned the shore as if assessing the chaos. His eyes locked with hers.

Georgia averted her gaze. A blast of wind lifted her bonnet and cooled her hair as she turned her focus back to the ship.

The crew were hoisting the small dinghy onto the deck. Had they forgotten about her trunks?

She scrambled along the beach toward the ship and waved her arms. "Wait! My things. You forgot my trunks. Bring the dinghy back down and send them over at once!"

The men continued to scurry about the deck, and Georgia searched for someone—something—to get their attention.

A loud splash sounded. She scanned the water to see what had fallen overboard. One of her trunks bobbed up to the surface of the clear ocean. All of her blood drained to her feet. Everything in that chest would be ruined. Impossible to restore. Another trunk appeared over the railing and plummeted into the ocean depths. *Her armor!* She screamed and ran to the water's edge. "Nooooooooo! My gowns! My dresses!"

Georgia's breast heaved as if a heavy weight pressed on her. *This can't be happening.*

She ran over to a man standing next to a large freight box, jotting down numbers on a piece of paper, and tugged on his arm. "Please, tell them to stop. Those are my things they're dumping into the water!"

The man turned and watched another trunk slap the ocean's surface, dip under, then re-emerge to bob among the waves. He pulled his spectacles down the bridge of his nose and peered at her, then shook his head. "Sorry, miss, but a storm's brewing. The captain won't stop for anything. See there." He pointed with the tip of his feather pen. "He's raising the sails now. Gonna try and outrun it. Otherwise, he could lose the whole ship to those rocks over there."

He pointed to an outcropping of jagged rocks rising out of the water. A massive wave crashed there, hurling a large spray of white into the air. The seafoam fanned out in a gust of wind.

Two more trunks teetered on the edge of the ship's railing

and Georgia covered her mouth as they, too, fell twenty feet and splashed into the water. Her parasol slid from her fingers as she turned to Aunt Tessa. "Do you see what they're doing? Our things." Tears stung her eyes, and her chest heaved with each gasping breath.

Her aunt sat wide-eyed, staring at the trunks slowly sinking under the water. "My heavens. This is quite unexpected."

~

*H*arrison Beaumont Wells straightened and folded his jacket over his arm. The prim, fashionable beauty standing on the beach, dressed from head to toe in a pale shade of pink, didn't match the description Fredrick Lennox had given of his daughter: a hoyden romp of a girl, unkempt and unpolished, with white-gold hair. Her bonnet covered her head so that he couldn't determine her hair color, but he rejected the sophisticated, gently bred lady as a possibility. Fredrick spoke of his beloved, impetuous, daughter like a son.

She held her shoulders back and her chin high in a regal pose as she watched the men row back to the ship. Her curves narrowed into a tiny waist that was probably no bigger than the span of his hands. Despite the heat, her properly gloved hands clasped her parasol in front of her, but the brisk breeze surely made such a thing impossible to use. She peered at the dock, toward the underdressed slaves laboring to load the supplies for their masters, but then she demurely averted her eyes.

She couldn't be Fredrick's daughter. However, the only other female who stepped off that ship was a matronly one, much too old and frail to be Fredrick's youngest child. He had no other options, so he pushed off the rock and stepped onto the sandy beach. He'd ask the woman outright.

As his boots sank into the soft sand, he watched her wave to the departing ship and call out what he assumed to be *bon voyage*, but the wind swept away her words. She ran to the edge of the water and furiously waved both her arms. His jaw tensed. Had she developed a tender heart for one of the sailors? Some bird-witted chit, thinking she was half in love with a man who had a doxy in every port, was not going to survive on this island.

The woman lifted her skirts and waded into the water. Shaking his head, he muttered, "Lord help her, she's nicked in the nob and halfway to Bedlam."

If she had any sense, she'd give up and come back. The water rose to her knees. The noise from the dock dwindled as other men craned their necks to watch the happenings. She would turn around at any moment.

"Georgia!" the matronly woman's back straightened. "Oh, my heavens, Georgia come back. You'll drown."

Georgia. Harrison's jaw clenched. Fredrick's youngest daughter's name was Georgia.

God, I was trying to do a good deed for a friend. Please, don't let this be difficult.

A wave crashed, the brunt of it almost knocking her over. The weight of her sodden skirts alone would drown her.

None of the men on shore attempted to go in after her.

Harrison stepped to the edge of the water. His boots sank into the wet sand. In his best reprimanding tone, he yelled, "Miss Lennox, come back or the undertow will pull you out to sea."

Maybe his words would scare her into turning around. But she continued to wade deeper.

Blast! If he'd known he was going for a swim, he wouldn't have worn his Hessians.

CHAPTER 2

...I am thankful for the opportunity to travel as Georgia's companion. I could use a change of scenery, for I've rattled round in this lonely mansion ever since Richard's passing.
—*Lady Pickering to her sister-in-law Lady Nora Lennox*

*H*arrison dropped his hat and jacket into a pile on the dry sand. "Miss Lennox," he yelled with the same stern voice he'd use to reprimand his son. "Come back here this instant."

When she didn't even glance over her shoulder, he stepped into the lukewarm ocean. A low growl reverberated in his throat as the water seeped in and pooled in his boots. He'd have removed them if he could, but that process would take too long as the woman pressed farther into the waves. He trudged into the breakers, and the salt water flowed over his knees.

The waves pushed Miss Lennox back, and the sodden material of her dress slowed her steps. He turned sideways as a wave drenched his buckskin pants, changing them to a dark tan. When the swell passed, he pressed forward and easily caught up with her. Her bonnet dangled loosely down her back, and her soaked, golden hair shone in the sun. This was definitely Fredrick's daughter.

"Whoever he was, he's gone now." He glanced up at the ship already miles offshore. "He's not worth killing yourself over."

Her head whipped around. Her eyes widened when she saw him, and she yelled back over the noise of the roaring waves, "Help me save my trunks!"

Harrison, now within arms' length of her, stopped short. *Trunks?* A wave crested, and a large brown object bobbed up and down in its midst. "What are your trunks doing in the ocean?" He knew the answer as soon as he voiced the question. The captain wanted to outrun the impending storm. Harrison had been too distracted searching for Fredrick's tomboy daughter to notice.

She glared at him over her shoulder with frosty blue eyes that could chill even the Caribbean's tepid waters. "How could I understand the deuced crewmen's reasons? All I know is everything I own is sinking to the bottom of the ocean."

She leaned forward as if to swim out to the sinking luggage, but he lunged and grabbed the back of her gown to keep her put.

"Unhand me."

She wriggled and pushed his hand away, but her efforts were thwarted by a hefty wave that crashed over them, pressing her body against his. Droplets of water dangled from her long lashes and dripped from her full pink lips. She wiped the water away with a swipe of her hand.

"Let me go."

"Miss Lennox, you'll drown before you reach them."

She struggled harder. "I will not live on this God-forsaken island without my belongings."

"They're merely things. Let them go. You can purchase more."

13

"No." She shook her head, and droplets of water rained from her hair. "You don't understand."

Another wave crashed. Harrison slid an arm around her waist and fought to keep them both upright.

"I need them. My gowns, my linens, my personal effects, they're who I am." She rammed an elbow into his stomach.

"Ooof." The sound slipped out before he could stop it. He grabbed her face between his fingers and forced her to look at him. "Enough. I'm not going to stand by and watch your foolishness sink you to a watery grave." He scooped her up and carried her squirming body back toward shore. Each step was a struggle due to his water-laden boots and her sodden skirts, but the waves aided his progress as they crashed into the backs of his thighs and pushed him along.

She bellowed scathing remarks into his ear and pounded her fists against his chest, putting him off balance until one aggressive wave almost knocked them under the churning waters.

He pitched forward, and she screamed. Her arms flew around his neck and squeezed for dear life, nearly strangling him. At the last second, Harrison yanked his foot forward and propped himself upright. His lips tasted of salt water, and his labored breathing stretched the lining of his lungs.

By the time he placed her on the shore, his shoulders burned from the effort. Her saturated skirts must weigh fifty stones.

He leaned over to draw more air into his lungs, staring at the sand and his ruined boots.

Slap! Her wet gloved hand slammed against his cheek and jerked his head to the side.

"You had no right. No right."

Harrison shook his head to clear it and stood to full height. Anger roared inside him, but he struggled to rein it in.

She stood before him, chest heaving in quick angry bursts, her wet hair plastered against the sides of her face. She glared at him with a defiant set to her jaw as water droplets streamed from her eyes, nose, and chin. "You could have helped me. I was almost there. A few more yards and I would have had them."

"And then what would you have done?"

"I would have held onto them until they floated me back to shore."

"Or out to sea."

Her lips pinched together. "Someone would have come to my rescue."

"Yes, and that someone was me, for all the gratitude it got me."

She flung her hands in the air and stomped over to the woman still seated on the rock. "Come on, Aunt Tessa. Let's find my father and get away from this lunatic."

Miss Lennox eyed the small dock, but by now most of the merchants had loaded their goods and were gone. "Did you locate Papa?"

The aunt sat up straighter and pulled her shawl back over her shoulders. "No dear, I haven't spotted him."

Still dripping like a sodden flag, Miss Lennox scanned the beach, dock, and road for any sign of her father. She perked up as she spied a dark-skinned man, barefoot with rolled-up pants, his eyes combing the beach. She approached the man. "Pardon me, have you seen Mister Fredrick Lennox, or do you know where I might find him?"

The man spoke in thick island jargon, and Harrison's lips twitched as she reared back. Her eyes widened like two open parasols.

"I beg your pardon?" This time she leaned in and focused intently on the man's lips.

The beachcomber repeated the same sentence, answering her in a mix of creole and Caribbean slang about how Mr. Lennox lived a few miles down the road, out in the bush, which was what the islanders call the country.

Miss Lennox blinked. "Th-thank you," she murmured and scurried back to her aunt with a dazed expression.

"I know the man spoke English," she shook her head as she spoke to the older lady, "but I haven't the foggiest idea what he said to me."

Harrison chuckled under his breath.

"Maybe you could ask the nice gentleman who rescued you? You appeared to strike up a conversation with him."

The drenched Miss Lennox let out a huff, then scanned the dock again, probably praying someone else could be of service. Turning back around, she lifted her chin and marched in Harrison's direction. She stopped directly in front of him and placed her hand at her waist. Despite looking like a half-drowned cat, she glowered at him with an aloof, stately demeanor.

"I beg your pardon. Do you happen to know a Mister Fredrick Lennox?"

Planting his feet, he folded his arms across his chest. "Why, yes, I do."

"Could you tell me where he resides?"

"Indeed, I could."

She waited, but he remained silent.

"Well?"

"Well what?" he asked.

"Aren't you going to tell me?"

"No."

She threw out her hands. "Heavens above, why not?"

"It's not *can* I, it's *will* I tell you, and I'm looking for a thank you first."

"Thank you?" she snorted. "For what?"

"For saving your foolish life."

Her lips tightened into a scowl, and he could almost see her mind wrestle over what she wanted versus what she needed. The noise of the pounding surf continued behind him, only broken by the screech of a seagull. Her arms stiffened into

16

straight sticks by her sides. "Fine. Thank you." Her fingers balled into fists and landed on her hips. "Now, *will* you tell me?"

He quirked an eyebrow, enjoying the two red splotches deepening on her cheeks. "Thank me for what exactly?"

Her eyes flashed, and she grumbled something he didn't hear over the crash of the waves. Harrison bit back a smile. This might be worth ruining his boots over.

She exhaled a long breath. "Thank you for saving my life."

He bowed slightly. "You're welcome." He trudged across the sand and bent over to pick up his hat and jacket. Instead of putting them on, he draped his coat over his left arm and kept his hat in his hand.

"Well?" She dogged his steps. "Aren't you going to tell me?"

"He lives up near Tamarind Bay."

"Can I hire a hack to take us there?"

He pointed to the conveyance near the road. "There's one right there. Go and make yourself comfortable and someone will be by in a minute."

She paused and tilted her head as she eyed him. "Thank you...er...good day, Mister...?"

"Wells, Harrison Wells."

"Good day, Mister Wells."

She adjusted her bonnet, gathered her aunt, and started in the direction of his open wagon. Her wet dress clung to her skin, revealing a nice figure and an appealing sway to her hips. Harrison jerked his gaze away.

Out in the water, an eruption of bubbles surfaced as the last of the floating trunks sank under the water. The wind whipped his jacket, and he hugged it tighter to his body. There were only a few puffy clouds on the horizon, but sure enough, a storm was coming.

CHAPTER 3

…I appeal to you to return posthaste. Ashburnham continues to spread rumors of your demise, to lay claim to your title and lands, and he has access to the King's ear.

—From Lord Liverpool to the Duke of Linton in the Leeward Islands

*G*eorgia pulled herself up into a carriage that, in her opinion, was more of a horse-drawn cart. There was one long wooden bench for the passengers and an open bed, where she assumed her trunks would have been placed. She sat next to the driver's position and adjusted her sopping skirts as her aunt settled in next to her.

Aunt Tessa breathed in the tropical air and admired the surroundings. "Isn't it wonderful to be back on land? Already the air smells sweeter, less briny. And to think we're on an island. How very exciting."

"England is an island," Georgia murmured.

"It's not a *tropical* island. Look around you. Isn't it gorgeous? Have you ever seen such vibrant colors?"

Georgia didn't want to look. She wanted to be back in London.

Aunt Tessa turned to face her. "Lady Dunkin told me the Artesian Hotel has a hot spring that makes the pump rooms of Bath seem tepid. She said its restorative qualities are second to none."

"It can't be that restorative. If it were so, my father would be healed." *And I'd still be in England.*

"That is the first thing we shall encourage him to do. We'll have Fredrick soak for an entire week if that's what it takes." She patted Georgia's hand. "You'll see, your father will be back to fair health in no time."

Georgia gulped back her guilt. Her father lay dying from some God-forsaken illness on this God-forsaken island, and all she cared about was getting her things and sailing back to England. She straightened her shoulders. Why did he desert his family to come to this disease-infested place? If he had stayed in England, he wouldn't be in this predicament. Would he? She stared down at her folded hands and tried to quiet her thoughts. Death was the ultimate price to pay for one's sins. Did Papa deserve that?

The carriage tilted as the driver climbed up. She donned her most dazzling smile before turning to him. "Good day, sir. If you could kindly take us to…"

The driver tipped up his hat and eyed her with a crooked smile. "Tamarind Bay?"

"You." It was the only word she could force out between her clenched teeth as Mr. Wells slid beside her and unhooked the reins.

This man, who'd thwarted her from recovering the things that meant the most to her in all the world, she'd no longer tolerate. She crossed her arms. "I'm not going anywhere with you."

He shrugged one shoulder and raised an eyebrow. "Feel free

to ask someone else or to walk. Go about five miles down this road, then take a right. Can't miss it." He jumped out of the carriage and offered his hand to assist her down.

She hated the smug gleam in the arrogant man's eyes. If only the ground would open up and swallow him whole. Raising her chin, she stood and extended her hand, but quickly retracted it. Did she have a choice? Her father had obviously forgotten about her arrival or didn't care enough to send anyone to pick her up. She couldn't ask Aunt Tessa to walk five miles in the hope that these vague directions would take them to Papa's home. And she certainly couldn't leave her aunt here unprotected.

He stood there waiting, watching, with a superior look on his face.

"I presume you are already going in that direction. Correct?"

His eyes never left hers. "You presume correctly."

She lowered back into her seat. "Well then, I recant my decision. We will accept your offer to take us to the Lennox estate." She stared straight ahead, her back stiff as a ramrod.

~

*H*arrison's chest swelled in victory from their battle of wills, but he wondered at his motives. Since when did he harass newcomers—especially of the female variety? It had to be Miss Lennox. Her high-in-the-instep, insolent demeanor irritated him. Irritation. That was it.

Why then had his heart raced when she'd smiled before she realized it was him? He hadn't felt a pull like that since... *Laura.* He swallowed against the pain in his chest. Unlike his beloved wife, this chit had a lot of gall.

God, forgive me for wishing I hadn't fished Miss Lennox out of the ocean.

He pulled himself back into the wagon and grabbed the reins.

Help me see her the way You see her, because right now I'm struggling to find any redemptive qualities.

After a sufficient snap of the reins, the horses lumbered toward home. Had he made a mull of things by sending for Miss Lennox? Fredrick needed family by his side to see to his comfort before he succumbed completely to the ague. Judging by her actions, he never would have pegged *her* for Fredrick's favored daughter. But the way Fredrick's eyes lit up when he spoke of his precious Georgia told him how special she was to him. Maybe Fredrick's memories of her had changed. Or more likely, perhaps, *she* had changed. It *had* been six years since he and Fredrick met aboard the *Aberdeen*. A lot could shift in that time.

He dared a sideways glance at the haughty woman beside him. Even dripping wet, she kept her regal pose. She was beautiful, he had to admit. Long, sooty lashes framed her vivid blue eyes and complemented a small, pert nose. Her full lips even had a slight pout to them, as if begging to be kissed. If she wasn't so high-in-the-instep, he might have fancied her.

He let out a grunt. *That would be the day.*

But his conscience continued to eat at him. Maybe he'd been hasty in drawing his conclusions. Anyone would be snippy and a little crazed after such a long voyage and losing her things. Even though they were only possessions, the stress of the journey could have easily built inside her until releasing through her crazed swim in the ocean.

He frowned and glanced in her direction. She looked downright uncomfortable. Her hands grasped the wooden bench seat in a tight grip as she pretended not to be jostled by the bumps in the road.

Nevis, with all its beauty, couldn't boast of a smooth road on the entire island. As if to make the point, the wagon hit a large pothole, and she fell into his side. She braced herself by grabbing his arm, and he tensed. She quickly yanked her hand away and righted herself.

Yet he could still feel her heat as if he'd been branded. He glanced down, expecting to see a seared handprint. The warmth spread down into his stomach, and he forced back feelings he'd thought long dead.

Miss Lennox sat stiffer than ever now, as though glued to her seat. Maybe he should extend an olive branch.

"I'm sorry about your trunks."

She didn't speak or look at him.

Ah, the silent treatment.

He tried again. "After the high tide passes, we can ride back to port tomorrow and see if anything washed up on shore."

Her head jerked around, and she stared at him with wide, blue eyes. "You think my belongings might still be salvageable?"

Brilliant. Now he'd gotten her hopes up. He fidgeted with the reins. "Perhaps. All sorts of things wash up on shore, especially after a storm. Once, an entire helm of a French warship washed up on the beach."

Her eyes narrowed as if judging whether to believe him or not. Then, with a curt nod, she said, "I appreciate your offer."

Harrison smiled to himself. Maybe he'd made a slight crack in her defenses.

He leaned forward and peered around Miss Lennox to the woman beside her. "I'm afraid we haven't been introduced."

Georgia crossed her arms. "Aunt Tessa, may I introduce Mr. Harrison Wells. Mr. Wells, my aunt, Lady Tessa Pickering, Baroness of Phelps."

He dipped his head. "Pleased to meet you, Lady Pickering."

The woman perked up at the attention. "The pleasure is mine. My brother informs me you are like family."

He nodded. Fredrick spoke fondly of his sister. "How was the voyage? Hopefully you had smooth sailing?"

He directed the question to Miss Lennox, but Lady Pickering spoke up instead. "It was the most horrific experience of my life. If I ever set foot on a sailing vessel again, it will be to send my corpse back to England."

She prattled on about the seasickness, the rocking boat, and the approaching storms until Harrison wished he'd never broached the topic. When he couldn't take any more, she switched to admiring the island's tropical landscape and proceeded to bombard him with questions that he didn't mind answering. What did the island export? What wildlife existed that was different from England? Was there a government? He could barely answer one question before she pitched another.

As Lady Pickering babbled on about the unique foliage, Miss Lennox settled in for the long ride. His curiosity rose as the prim woman battled to keep her wet, drooping gloves from sliding down her arms. At first, she discreetly pulled them higher and glanced his way. He, of course, focused his eyes on the road ahead.

After several more attempts, she gave up and tugged them off in an unladylike manner. She wrung them out over the front edge of the carriage and draped them over the bench to dry. Holding her arms out in front of her, she warmed them in the sun, then tilted her head back and closed her eyes. It took everything inside him not to admire her pretty features while she wouldn't see him looking.

When he'd begun to wonder if she'd fallen asleep in such a ridiculous position, she jerked back upright, folding her slender hands demurely in her lap. Harrison pressed his lips together to refrain from laughing. The woman was an enigma.

CHAPTER 4

...I entreat you to inform the King that I am very much alive. I shall return to London without delay, as soon as I have attended to my business here.

—*From the Duke of Linton to Lord Liverpool*

Somehow, Georgia knew Mr. Wells was laughing at her, even though she didn't chance a look at him, and his humor only inflamed her ire. He had no right to judge. One could be lax on a little propriety, especially after being banished to a rugged island, losing all her belongings to the ocean deep, and being forced to ride soaking wet next to a know-it-all oaf of a man. One would think, with that condescending look, he was the Prince Regent himself. Well, she would not let him fluster her. Instead, she would focus on her looming reunion with her father.

Try as she might, her mind couldn't find a soft place to land there, either. Her stomach twisted in knots thinking about seeing him after all these years. Would he appreciate the changes in her, or would he cast her aside all over again? Old insecurities weaved their webs of doubt. She hadn't been this nervous since her first season. She'd made a cake of herself back then, but she was no longer a naïve hoyden. Never again would she allow people to scoff at her or ignore her presence outright —especially not the overbearing beast of a man beside her.

She fingered the damp muslin of her gown and focused on the passing landscape. The tang of salty air tinged with the sweet fragrance of the island flowers calmed her. Scraggly trees, twisted and bent by the wind, lined either side of the dirt road. The volcanic summit towered over them on the right. Little shanties that appeared barely inhabitable dotted the mountain with wisps of smoke rising out of chimney pipes. On the left, the land sloped off, and if she peered over the tops of the palm trees, she could see a strip of the ocean inlet and another island so near that some of the houses were visible.

"Is that land part of Nevis?" she asked.

"No." He glanced in that direction. "That's the isle of St. Christopher, but the locals call it St. Kitts. Several boats row to her shores daily. If you decide to visit, be careful and go with an experienced boatswain. The currents are tricky between the islands. You don't want to be lost miles out at sea or crushed upon the rocks."

Insolent man—once again, he told her what she should and should not do. As though she didn't have the sense to hire a competent boatswain.

"I will take your concerns for my well-being into considera-tion." She spoke in a syrupy-sweet tone to soften the edge to her words.

He didn't comment further, and they fell back into silence, except for the clopping of the horses's hooves and the murmurs of Aunt Tessa, who'd fallen asleep while still talking.

When she'd had her fill of the scenery, Georgia assessed the man beside her through stolen glances. His boots were Hessians. She could tell by the tassels, but they were worn and not well-maintained. Either he had come from money and fallen on hard times, or imports from Britain were hard to obtain. Her heart sank. If it was the latter, then the traveling dress she wore may be the only gown she'd own until she left this forsaken island. All the more reason to convince her father he'd have better care in England. Maybe they could return on the next boat.

Mr. Wells' cream-colored breeches encased a pair of long, muscular legs, and his right knee brushed against hers every time the wagon jolted. Despite her attempts to scoot over, there wasn't room enough to completely avoid contact, and the intimacy of it filled her with jitters. His frilled shirt was about five years out of style but, once again, made of the finest cambric material. It didn't hide his muscular physique, especially a robust set of shoulders, which filled the expanse of the tailored shirt. His arms rested on his thighs, and his sleeves were rolled up, revealing tanned forearms.

She pulled her eyes away and watched a colorful bird of bright green flit from one branch to another. The animal provided a delightful diversion until a snap of the reins drew her attention back to Mr. Wells' calloused hands. Calloused from what? Fieldwork? Was he a planter or an indentured servant still working off his last remaining years?

With bold curiosity, she kept facing forward but dared to examine his features out of the corner of her eye. His rugged profile reminded her of a granite statue, a strong square jaw that contrasted with a set of full, firmly-molded lips. His angular nose, straight like a pointed arrow, was offset by a pair of heavily-lashed amber eyes. Thick, brown hair, streaked by the sun, curled around the edges, and she was surprised at the sudden urge to run her fingers through it.

"Have you had your fill?"

Georgia jerked her eyes back to the road in front of her. Her cheeks, now hot coals, made the temperature rise from warm to stifling.

"Well?"

A polite man would recognize her embarrassment and let the matter drop. *Actually,* a well-mannered man would never have asked such a question. Ignoring him, she refused to look to her left or right. She instead, tilted her chin a little higher.

"No, truly," his voice purred with confidence, "I want to know how I compare with all the fashionable fobs that prance around London trying to outdo one another. Would I be welcomed into the arms of the *ton?*"

His gaze bored into her until she turned to face him. She crossed her arms over her chest and spoke the truth he so desired. "Why, no, Mister Wells." She forced a pleasant smile. "Your boots are well-made but too worn. Your shirt is of fine material but hopelessly outdated. You might be able to fix all that with a visit to a London dressmaker, but you'd need to invest in a good pair of gloves to hide those calloused hands that blatantly declare you earn a hard day's living."

His burst of laughter threw her completely off guard, but she patiently stared him down until he regained control. "So there is little hope of me reclaiming my place among the Quality?"

She eyed him suspiciously, then shrugged and continued with her honest opinion. "You're fair of face, so what you'll need to do is find a wealthy widow who will be willing to finance a new wardrobe and teach you the ways of the peerage."

His face cracked into a smile, revealing small crinkles in the corners of his eyes and rows of straight white teeth. His laughing gaze held hers, she its prisoner, unable to look away.

"So, you think I'm fair of face?"

"Really?" Her lips pursed. "Is that all you heard of my statement?"

"Oh, no. I'm to understand that the only way I can improve my lot in life is to marry a rich widow, who will love me for my dashing looks, and in turn, introduce me back into society. I got that part, too."

"Dashing maybe going a bit far," she mumbled under her breath. Then the rest of his words sank in. She angled herself toward him. "You said *back* into society. Does that mean you once ran in elite circles?"

His face sobered. "Once."

The solitary word held traces of pain, and Georgia decided not to broach the topic further. They rode in silence until he steered the carriage onto a side road that led up Mount Nevis. The foliage grew dense, and thick vines hung from every tree. Moisture in the air clung to her clothing, keeping it damp, even after the long ride in the hot sun.

"There it is. Up to the left."

A quaint, bungalow-style house with a large, two-story deck peered out from the side of the mountain. The bottom half was comprised of tightly-fitting stones, while the top half had been constructed of whitewashed wood, offset with bright teal louvered shutters. The entire structure could fit inside their London townhouse, but it appeared well-maintained. A strong breeze sent the palms trees waving and the porch rocking chairs swaying of their own accord. The double fans that hung on the porch ceiling spun in tight synchronicity as the shutters flapped against the house.

Mr. Wells pulled the carriage in front of stone steps that zigged and zagged their way up to the main level. Once they'd rolled to a stop, he turned to her. "You should stay in the wagon." His eyes flicked up toward the main entrance "Yes … stay here until I return."

The nervous flock of flitting birds in Georgia's stomach plummeted. "Is my father unfit to be seen? Has his health dwindled so badly?"

His eyes found her face, then lifted back to the window. He rose but didn't look at her as he said, "He's fine. He just …"

Georgia stared, waiting for him to finish his sentence.

"He isn't aware of your arrival."

"He thinks the ship was delayed?"

He glanced back at her and shook his head. She read the truth in his eyes before he spoke the words. "He didn't send for you. I did."

"What?" She rose to her feet as small beads of sweat broke over her entire body. "*You* sent for me?"

"Yes." He jumped down from the carriage and peered up at the house.

She breathed hard as she struggled to quell the anger rising within her. Her life had been turned upside down because this arrogant man decided to host a reunion? "You, sir, have overstepped."

His gaze riveted to her face and a crease formed at the bridge of his nose. "Your father needs you."

White hot flames blurred her vision. "Papa doesn't need me. If he did, he wouldn't have abandoned me." It was bad form to discuss personal issues with a complete stranger, but the waves of pain pounding her chest vanquished her control.

Past hurts and anguish resurfaced. Her voice lowered to a hair above a whisper. "If he cared a wit about me, he wouldn't have deserted me, knowing I'd be forced to live up to mama's expectations. He wouldn't have forsaken me to face my sisters' ridicule alone. *I needed him, and he left.*" She sank back in her seat. Her nails dug into the underside of the wooden carriage bench. "How dare you meddle in our affairs? Take me back. Take me back this instant. This is all a terrible mistake." She forced herself to stare straight ahead, locking her jaw against the hot tears burning her eyes.

Mr. Wells grabbed her chin and twisted her head around to face him. His gaze deadlocked with hers. "Your father is dying. He needs his family. He needs the daughter he remembers and speaks so highly of to be by his side to ease his pain." Mr. Wells examined her eyes as if searching for a redeemable quality. Based on his expression, he found none. His mouth thinned with displeasure, and he dropped his hand. His eyes narrowed and pierced her own. "Weren't you told any of this?"

She leaned back, away from the fierceness of his gaze. "My mother said a letter arrived and that my father was ill, maybe dying." Her voice came out as a hoarse whisper. "I assumed my father sent for me."

Mr. Wells turned away and ran a hand through his wavy brown hair. "I sent the letter and paid for your passage with the hope that you would have a grand reunion. Fredrick never gave me a reason to believe you wouldn't come running here with open arms." His head jerked in her direction, and he leaned in until his face was inches from hers. "Here's what you're going to do. You will pin a smile on your self-righteous face, march up there, and greet your father as a wonderful surprise. We'll deal with the rest later. Am I clear?"

Georgia opened her mouth to tell him exactly what she thought of his demands, but he silenced her with a sharp glare. Instead, she found herself nodding. His hand reached out and half-guided, half-tugged her out of the carriage.

The house loomed in front of her. "You said you wanted us to wait in the carriage while you went inside."

"I've changed my mind."

Aunt Tessa jerked awake as Georgia alighted, seemingly oblivious to their entire conversation. "What a darling house. Look at the rocking chairs on each porch. We shall have some splendid afternoons there sipping tea." She held her hand out for Mr. Wells, and he assisted her down. "Why, Georgia, isn't this wonderful. What an exciting adventure. Nevis is nothing like England at all." When Mr. Wells released her, Aunt Tessa daintily clapped her hands, and her face beamed her excitement.

Georgia wondered about her aunt's enthusiasm. Was she expecting a fun sightseeing trip? Or had her life been so tedious out in Essex she considered a change, any change, to be desirable?

Mr. Wells stepped aside and gestured for Georgia to lead the way up the steep stone staircase. He'd paid for their passage. Why would he do that? The fare for crossing the ocean cost a handsome amount. By the looks of him, it would set him back at least a half year's wages. How could he afford it?

Her fingers clenched into fists. This islander was responsible for her humiliation. Because he unwittingly intervened where he shouldn't have, she would be forced to face her estranged father. Because of the arrival of his letter, she'd missed the Earl of Claremont's proposal and her one opportunity to prove herself to her mother and sister. Because of him, her entire trousseau now lay at the bottom of the Caribbean Ocean.

A complete stranger had ruined her life.

CHAPTER 5

...I assure you, my intention was not to mislead you or demonstrate a lack of concern for my life. I neglected to mention my illness to spare your concern, and for my own comfort, for I disdain pity.

—*From Fredrick Lennox to his wife, Nora Lennox*

Papa hadn't asked her to come.

Georgia wasn't certain how she did it, but one foot continued to move in front of the other. She gritted her teeth, concentrating on what lay at the top of the stairs. She was about to see her father after six long years. He didn't know she no longer fished or hunted or idolized him. He didn't even know she'd traded in her boy's pantaloons for gowns and dresses.

Would he recognize her? Would he be proud?

She fluffed her skirts. The parts that had dried were stiff from the salt water. So much for saving her best gown for this moment. She must look a fright—her dress ruined, her coiffure askew. She adjusted the square bodice of her dress, but the action didn't quell the exposed feeling. Her armor was chinked, leaving her vulnerable. Her heart pounded, and her breath seemed in short supply. Old self-doubt rushed in, whirling and rising into waves of panic until she was once again the tender age of six and ten.

She had thrived in her father's shadow. He was her world, her source of strength, and he'd walked out, leaving her alone to stand against her mother's and sisters' disappointment. She remembered the pivotal moment all too well.

～

SIX YEARS EARLIER

*W*ater squished in her shoes as Georgia raced through the stone courtyard to the back entrance of the kitchen. The wind fluttered her braids out behind her like raised banners. She skidded to a halt at the servant's entrance and held up the largemouth bass that dangled from the fishing line clutched in her hand. It had to be a fifteen pounder at least.

She had done it. She'd caught Old Willy, the prize that had eluded her father and her for over two years. Tingles formed in her stomach as she imagined the look on his face when she showed him. A wide smile spread across her lips, and a giggle escaped. She flung open the door, but she only made it three steps.

"Miss Georgia." Their housekeeper, Nellie, stood at the entrance to the kitchen, plump arms crossed over her chest and a large wooden spoon sticking out from underneath. "Don't you dare track mud all over this house." She shook her head. "Look at you, just look at you."

Georgia glanced down at her muddy knickers and soaked shoes, then wriggled her toes. "He nearly dragged me under, Nellie. He was that strong." She held up her prized fish. "I caught him, though. He never saw it coming. I sat so still for so long, and dangled my worm right above his head. He took one little nibble, then snap—swallowed the whole hook."

Nellie squished up her nose. "You smell like a marsh. I thought your mama told you to stop wearing boy clothes. You're getting too old for gallivanting around so. You better go to your room before Mrs. Lennox sees you. I'll have Mary draw you a bath."

Georgia's head rolled back, and her shoulders drooped. Nellie leaned in for a closer inspection of her catch and whistled. "That is one good looking fish. I may need to change the dinner menu. It appears we're going to have bass tonight."

Georgia beamed. "Papa's going to be so proud of me. I can't wait to tell him we're eating Old Willie for dinner. Where is he, Nellie? I've got to show him."

"Mr. Lennox is in his study, but to warn you, your mama is in there with him."

Georgia dashed down the hall and slid to an abrupt stop when she reached the study. The door was open a crack, and she could discern the rumble of voices inside as those of Mama and Papa. She slipped back behind the door and peeked between the hinges.

Her mother stood facing out the window with her arms wrapped around her midsection. The fabric of her burgundy gown shimmered in the sunlight. Her father's cravat had come undone and hung loosely around his neck. He propped his hip on the corner of his desk and crossed his arms over his chest.

"I can't put up with this charade, Fredrick. Tongues are wagging. I can hardly hold my head up anymore."

He slapped his gloves over his knee. "What exactly are people saying?"

"That you and she…" Her voice trailed off.

"There is no she. There is only you." He pushed off the desk and moved to her side. He placed his hands on her upper arms.

She whirled around and stepped back, knocking his hands away in the process. "Don't play innocent with me, Fredrick. God knows the truth of it. You were found in…in…a compromising position with that…that light skirt!"

"It's not what you think. People are making this out to be something it's not."

"And what are they supposed to think? What am I supposed to think?"

"I want you to believe me."

"I believed you the first time."

He shook his head. "That was a long time ago. I admitted my mistake in being alone with her. Nothing happened."

"So, I'm to believe nothing happened then and nothing happened now. What kind of a fool do you take me for?"

"Nora." He reached out to her.

"Don't touch me. I never want you to touch me again." She turned her back on him.

He moved toward her. "Tell me what to say. Tell me what to do. I'll do it."

"There's nothing you can do to change things." She whispered the words, but the jerk of her father's body showed he had heard it.

"You want to live as strangers."

"The girls and I can move to the city while you live in the country, and when it's necessary for you to be in the city, we'll go to the country."

"I won't do it, Nora. I cannot stand by and watch you live a life without me." His eyes pleaded with her for understanding. "Besides, the girls need their father."

Her mother emitted a strangled laugh. "You mean Georgia needs her papa. You don't pay the other girls any attention."

"I love all my girls. George … Georgia is different. She's special in her own way."

"Because she's willing to behave like a boy doesn't make her one."

He ground his teeth. "I know she's not a boy."

"Well, she dresses like one to please you, and you encourage it. Is that why you turn to other women? You crave a son so badly you'll raise someone else's by-blow so you can fish and play catch with a son? Is that it?"

"Don't be ridiculous."

She whirled back around. "Am I?"

"Yes."

"Georgia will be a laughingstock, her coming out is only a couple of years away. Right now, she doesn't even know how to wear a dress, because you let her run around in boys' pantaloons. You've ruined her for polite society."

"She will be fine."

"She won't be fine. I won't be fine." She jabbed a finger in his direction. "None of us will be fine with you around."

"You truly feel that way? You want me to leave?"

"Yes." Her voice reverberated with pain.

"No, Nora. Please, don't do that to us."

Her face contorted with anger. "You did this to us. Live your life, but leave me be. You asked me what you can do, and I'm telling you. If you have any love left for me, you'll leave me alone."

The blood drained from her father's face. For a long moment, he stood frozen in silence.

Georgia held her breath while her mind screamed, *Papa, don't leave. Don't leave me.*

"Nora, you are my world. I will do anything to right this wrong, but don't ask me to live like a stranger. My heart won't be able to withstand having you near but not being able to hold you—to love you."

Mama closed her eyes as if that could shut out his words.

"Don't ban me from your life."

"Fredrick, if you don't give me space, then I will come to

resent you and hate you. Is that what you want?"

His body tensed as if she'd struck a nerve. With a curt nod, he turned on his heel and stalked out of the room.

Georgia opened her mouth to call out to him, but no words came. Maybe he'd look her way, maybe if she told him about Old Willy... She felt the cold rush of air as he passed, and grimaced when a flash of daylight blinded her. The front entrance opened and closed behind him. Tears stung the backside of her eyes, and her lower lip quivered.

Crash!

A glass shattered against the far wall. Georgia gasped. Shards of fine crystal littered the plush Axminster carpet, and an amber liquid dripped down the wainscoting. Her mother's head twisted toward the door.

"Who's there?"

Georgia stepped back into the shadow and squeezed herself tight against the wall. She searched for a means of escape and considered running, but her mother rounded the corner in seconds.

"Georgia Evelyn." Mama latched onto her ear and pulled her out of hiding. Georgia winced in pain, her fingers tightening around her fishing pole.

"Were you eavesdropping like a lowly servant?" She let go and put fisted hands on her hips. "Young ladies do not press their ears to the cracks of doors." Her mother's nose wrinkled in disgust as her eyes traveled over Georgia's form. "What are you wearing? And what ... My heavens, you smell like a fish market." She leaned in and pointed her finger at Georgia's chest. "I've had quite enough of this, Georgia. It is time you acted like a lady. You are not a boy. No matter how badly your father wants you to be one, you aren't, and won't ever be. I want you to get that through your head." She reared back. "Now go and clean up immediately."

She stepped aside, allowing room to pass, and Georgia didn't hesitate. She scurried back down the hall, wanting to get as far away from her parents as possible. Her mother's voice rang after her. "And make certain you wear a dress. Do you hear me? A dress."

Georgia ducked around the corner and into the kitchens. Her mother rarely came there. Something ricocheted off her back, and she jumped in surprise. Bile rose up in her throat as the swinging fish, still dangling from her line, bobbed around her. Her eyes followed the string up to the rod and down to her hand. Her fingers still clutched the fishing pole. She let go and jumped away as if it were a poisonous snake. The rod thumped against the stone tiles.

Nellie leaned back and peeked her head around a large steaming pot of water. "Your bath is almost ready…" Her eyes narrowed. "What's the matter? Your face is whiter than the wash bucket."

"Take him back for me, Nellie."

"Take who back?"

"Old Willie. Put him back in the pond. Maybe he'll come to life. Maybe there's still a chance. Maybe…" Her throat closed up tight, and her voice became a whisper. "Please Nellie, hurry."

∾

PRESENT DAY

*M*r. Wells' hands caught her waist, and Georgia sucked in a shallow breath. She didn't realize she'd teetered on the edge of the step until he steadied her. He withdrew his hands, and she continued her slow climb. *Her father never sent for her…* She turned around and fought to catch her breath, even though it came in rapid gulps. She couldn't do this. She needed to go back.

"What if he doesn't want me here? What if he doesn't

approve of me?" Only after her ears heard the words did she realize she'd said them aloud.

A gentle touch lifted her chin, and she blinked twice at the transformation. A pair of tender brown eyes filled her vision. She wanted to melt into the sweetness of their depths. His spicy scent, laced with a hint of coconut, wafted around her, and his broad chest loomed like a protective wall. She resisted the desire to cling to his strength.

"Georgia, believe me. He wants you here. Give him a chance. Open your heart to him. *Please*. He needs you, and I think you need him too."

She nodded, liking the way her name sounded on his lips. She wanted with all her heart to believe his words. *He wants you... He needs you...*

She snapped out of her reverie and stepped out of his reach. What did this man know? If her Papa loved her, he would never have left. If Mr. Wells knew anything, he'd never have wasted his money to bring her here. Foolish, foolish man. Besides, how dare he be so forward to use her given name, without her permission?

She spun on her heel to face the painted blue door in front of her. With a quick pat to make sure her hair was in place, she raised a hand and rapped soundly on the wooden panel. *Let's get this over.* She needed to put space between her and Mr. Wells as quickly as possible, even if it meant facing her estranged father. He reached past her, turned the knob, and swung the door wide. She gritted her teeth and braced for an altercation.

The door opened to a microcosm of English society. Georgia didn't know what she'd expected, but despite a few differences —like the tiled floors, the large circling ceiling fans, and the pops of bright colors—there were all the comforts of home. She stepped into the small foyer with a round baroque table in the center holding a bouquet of exotic flowers. A curved staircase on the right led to the second floor, and beyond that, a wide-open door led to a peach-colored salon. Through an archway to the left was a room with two walls lined floor to ceiling with books. A buxom African woman stepped into the foyer from the salon and stopped mid-way across the floor.

"Why, Mista Wells, I was wonderin' who was knockin' on the door." She spied Georgia. "Child, you must be Mista Fredrick's daughter. Lovely, absolutely lovely. Come on in."

Georgia's kid boots wouldn't move. As Mr. Wells brushed past her, he caught hold of her elbow and pulled her through the entrance way.

"Let me introduce you to Hattie." He yanked on her arm, and she bumped into his side. His eyes narrowed on her, and she immediately forced a smile. He shifted to peer behind her.

"Lady Pickering, Miss Lennox, I'm pleased to introduce our housekeeper and the best cook on the island, Harriet Drury. Most of us call her Hattie. And Hattie, this is Fredrick's sister, Lady Tessa Pickering, Baroness of Phelps, and his daughter, Miss Georgia Lennox."

Hattie bobbed a small curtsy, then waved a hand in Mr. Wells' direction. "You'd be sayin dat cuz yer wantin' a slice of my banana bread."

"Is that the delicious aroma I smell?" He smiled a stunning, white smile that shone against his tanned skin. The transformation did funny things to Georgia's insides, as if she'd swallowed a bag of live, fuzzy caterpillars. She forced herself to look away and study the flowers on the table.

"You know it is. I made it for you and Max."

"Ah, Hattie, you own my heart."

Hattie belted out a hearty peal of laughter that shook her belly. "Naw, it's not yer heart I own, it's yer stomach."

Mr. Wells chuckled and, to Georgia's astonishment, opened his arms wide. Hattie pulled him into a big embrace and squeezed the man tight, rocking him from side to side. She'd never witnessed such familiarity with the servants. It only solidified the notion that Mr. Wells, despite his suggestion that he'd once been among the Quality, was a servant himself.

After releasing him, Hattie stepped in front of her and put the palms of her hands against Georgia's cheeks. "Let me get a good look at ya. Why, ain't she a lovely thing?" Her warm brown eyes peered into Georgia's face. "Mista Fredrick is gonna be beside hisself with joy."

Hattie gave one last squeeze, pressing Georgia's lips together into a big pucker, before letting go. She shifted to greet Aunt Tessa with a big smile and enfolded both her hands in hers. "What a surprise and a pleasure."

"The pleasure is mine," Aunt Tessa said. "But I'm a little out-of-sorts—all that rocking to and fro. I would like to rest and freshen up a bit before seeing my brother."

"Right this way." Hattie ushered her toward the stairway.

Mr. Wells glanced around. "Where are Fredrick and Max?"

"Oh, dey in the billiard room, playin' cards," Hattie said over her shoulder.

"Who's Max?" Georgia asked.

Hattie turned, with an exuberant smile. "Dat be Mr. Harrison's son, fine boy and a proud papa." Hattie shooed them with her hands. "Go on now and show yerself. I can't wait to see his face when he sees you."

She shooed Georgia with her hands, and Georgia had no choice but to follow Mr. Wells through the book-lined study toward the billiard room.

"You'll discover things are less formal on the island." He tossed the words over his shoulder. "People aren't as stuffy as they are in England."

She peeked back to find her Aunt and Hattie chattering as if they were newly found friends. Aunt Tessa glanced up and said, "You go on. You and your father need some time alone. I'll be down later."

Mr. Wells slid into the billiards room, but neither of the

figures inside appeared to notice. Georgia followed, but froze in the shadow of the doorway. Her father sat at a round mahogany table and peered over a fanned hand of cards at a young boy. Memories of her father's face—as he kissed her good night, as he helped her reel in a big fish, and as he sat with her curled in his lap during thunderstorms—ran through her mind. Her heart compressed like a folded fan.

He appeared the same but different. His hair had grayed and thinned on top, and the faint lines that crinkled in the corners of his eyes when he smiled were deeper and permanent. His eyes, however, still held that sparkle, like the sun reflecting off a pool of water. His fingers pinched a card, but then changed to another. His brow furrowed as he considered his next play. A slow, confident smile spread across his lips, and he laid down his next card.

He seemed in good health, even if his usual lithe, muscular shape was a little thinner, and his cheeks a bit more hollow. He still retained his dashing good looks. His skin was tanned, which only brightened his smile. The most noticeable change was in his clothing. Her father had always dressed impeccably. Even on a fishing excursion, Beau Brummel would have taken his recommendations on proper outdoorsmen attire. Now, he wore loose-fitting, informal, apparel—no jacket, no cravat, no gloves.

Did he not keep a valet? Was island life so rustic that he'd been reduced to peasant clothing? Her eyes flicked to Mr. Wells, who had leaned against the wall, his feet spread, arms crossed over his chest. A crooked smile hung on his lips as he watched her father's interaction with his companion. She leaned closer to the edge of the doorway, until her head practically rested against the door's frame, to get a look at the small boy sitting at the same table as her father.

She didn't have much experience with children, but the boy looked a similar age to her oldest nephew, Calvin, and he was probably seven … or eight? Or was he ten? She had no idea, and what did it matter, anyway?

A mop of light brown hair hung in this boy's eyes, and he brushed it away with his forearm. Freckles dotted the bridge of his nose and cheeks, and his gaze held her father's. A self-assured, thin-lipped smile grew across his face, and a pair of faint dimples appeared on each cheek. As he lowered his cards, his chest puffed up, and his dimples deepened. Even though she couldn't see the boy's cards, she smiled at his cocky demeanor.

Papa let out a whoop and reached over and tousled the boy's hair. He winked at him, and pride radiated in a warm glow over his face.

Georgia's smile faded as an acidic twinge of jealousy seeped into her veins. She'd once been the proud recipient of such looks from her father. She'd see them whenever she'd reeled in a large bass by the lake. Now this boy—*yes, a boy, w*hat her father had always wanted and would have easily traded for one of his own daughters—basked in the glory of *her* father's praise. Her toes curled in her shoes.

Papa definitely didn't need her. He'd replaced her. With another man's son, no less, even though she was his flesh and blood. The room grew stifling under the layers of her damp traveling dress. She needed to leave. She and Aunt Tessa would go straight back to the pier, even if they had to walk. They could rent a room and wait for the next ship to arrive, headed for anywhere as long as it left this island.

She couldn't watch the exchange between her father and the boy any longer. Tears stung the backs of her eyes, but as she turned to leave, a firm hand grabbed her arm. She sucked in a breath at the fierce scowl Mr. Wells pinned on her, but recovered quickly. With a haughty lift of her chin, she narrowed her eyes and was about to yank her arm away, when a voice called out.

"Georgia?"

CHAPTER 6

...Can it be so? Did mother truly banish Georgia to the Leeward Islands? While our days are filled with endless amusements, luncheons, soirees, and shopping trips, Georgia shall be toiling and tending to our ailing father. Guilt eats at me, but of the four of us, I must admit, Georgia holds the best constitution for the endeavor.

—*Eleanor Hart to her younger sister, Frances Morgan, in Dublin, Ireland.*

*G*eorgia turned slowly, using the time to regain her composure. Her father stared at her as if he'd seen an apparition. Hope and fear warred a tumultuous battle within her chest. She parted her lips to say something, but they only quivered. She willed her feet to step forward, but they wouldn't budge.

"Georgia?" Bracing his palms on either side of the table, Papa rose and scooted around it to get a clear view.

She regained enough control to nod her head the slightest bit, and it was all the encouragement he needed.

"Praise God in Heaven. It's my girl. It's Georgia." He waltzed over and scooped her into his embrace. He squeezed her tight, as though he never planned to let go.

A lump formed in her throat and unwanted tears threatened to leak out. The relief of his joy over their unexpected reunion overpowered her anger, and she melted into her father's embrace.

"Princess. I can't believe it's you." His voice strained with emotion.

A sob tore from her throat, and she clung to his jacket. He still smelled the same, like cedar from their clothes chest. She remembered nights as a small girl when she'd been frightened. He'd sit with her in the rocking chair, and she'd breathe in his comforting, woodsy scent until she fell asleep in his arms. How had she forgotten that special memory?

When he finally pulled back, tears were running down both their faces.

"Let me get a look at you." He held her out at arm's length and peered down the bridge of his nose through a pair of thin wire spectacles. "I almost didn't recognize my girl. You've grown into a beautiful woman, like a caterpillar to a butterfly." He shook his head with a slight whistle. "Who would have thought my little ruffian would turn into a lovely, sophisticated woman. Your mother said it couldn't happen, but I knew one day my little bud would bloom into a perfect flower."

He glanced back at the entranceway. "Is your mother...?"

Georgia shook her head. "It's only me...and Aunt Tessa."

"What a wonderful surprise." He grasped her hand and led her over to sit on a sofa near the table. He drew out a chair and gestured for Mr. Wells to join them. "I assume, Harrison, that you are behind this?"

Mr. Wells didn't reply, merely smiled as if enjoying his friend's happiness.

"I owe you everything, my friend."

Harrison shook his head and relaxed into the chair.

Papa glanced back at her. "You've already met my friend and colleague, Harrison Wells, and this is his son, Maxwell." His hand gestured to the boy, who was standing awkwardly beside the table.

Maxwell put one hand across his stomach and another behind his back and presented a formal bow, so low that his hair flopped forward. He observed her quite seriously until she acknowledged him. Then, he resumed his seat and said, "I can read, and I can count to one thousand."

She blinked, not certain how to respond. Yes, she had nieces and nephews, but she'd had little interaction with them. Usually, they were shuffled off by a nursemaid or governess to do heaven knew what.

Her father patted the boy on the head. "He's a bright one, that's for sure." Then Papa sat next to her on the sofa. "I still can't believe my eyes. I'm so grateful you're here. How was Mr. Wells able to steal you away from your mother, midseason no less?"

The glimpse of sheer joy in her father's eyes caused Georgia to flounder. "He—ah—he wrote that you were ill."

He sighed. "I'm afraid these old bones battle with the ague, but I still have life in me yet. I'm not going anywhere until it's God's time to take me." He shifted in his seat and leaned in closer to Georgia. "Your mother wrote that this season you've set the town on its ear, but haven't settled on the man you want yet. Is that the truth?"

Her mother still wrote Papa letters?

"I figured some handsome gentlemen would have snatched you up and walked you down the aisle by now. I should have known you'd have your own mind and wouldn't settle for any old dandy."

"Well, there is someone." Georgia glanced at Mr. Wells, before dropping her eyes. "He's an Earl." She picked at some invisible lint before meeting her father's gaze. "Lord Claremont was about to propose before I received the letter and found myself aboard the *Aberdeen.*"

"Claremont?" Mr. Wells quirked a brow at her. "The Earl of Claremont?"

Georgia bestowed him a polite smile. "The very one."

Mr. Wells snorted.

She narrowed her eyes. What did he mean by that?

"Well," her father piped in, "I'm certain he's a fool for letting you go."

Seizing the opportunity, Georgia took her father's hand. "That's the problem. He didn't know I was leaving. The night of the Carlson's ball, Lord Claremont promised to speak to mother the following day, but she insisted I set sail immediately and not wait for the next ship to arrive. I had a footman deliver a note informing him of what transpired and a forwarding address for correspondence. I'm certain Julien—er...Lord Claremont—is beside himself anticipating my return. The poor dear is probably a regular visitor to the docks every day awaiting my arrival."

"He's a regular visitor to the docks all right."

Georgia's gaze snapped to Mr. Wells. Now, what did he mean by that?

Her father cleared his throat and patted her hand. "I'm sure he misses you, princess, but I do hope you'll stay and let my weary eyes enjoy my most precious treasure for a while."

Her heart warmed at the familiar endearment. His eyes struck her as so hopeful, so happy.

"Of course." Needles of guilt pricked her chest, but she'd have so much to lose if she didn't return posthaste to London. "Maybe you should think about returning to London where you could receive better care? Dr. Cowper could treat you." She leaned in. "He still owes you from the last hand of cards. You can collect his debt in treatments."

Her father laughed. "I forgot about the few pounds he still owes me. He's lucky I don't play for money any longer."

"If you come back with me, you and Mama might be able to reconcile. I know she still loves you. I find her staring at your portrait in the hall all the time. I believe she's softening. Time heals all wounds—that sort of thing." She hesitated, gathering her courage before she whispered the words that, once out there, would leave her exposed. "You could be my Papa again."

Her father's gaze dropped to the floor.

Georgia's stomach twisted, but she kept going. "Franny, Eleanor, and Ann all desire to see you. You could meet your grandchildren."

A spark lit in Papa's eyes, but then the glimmer fizzled.

She scooted closer. "You could take them for pony rides and go fishing." Her pitch rose as the words seemed to pour out of her. "Franny and Eleanor both have sons. You've always wanted a boy, and now you have them as grandchildren."

She held her breath and silenced the niggling of guilt.

When he lifted his eyes to hers, the pain etched in their depths squeezed her heart like a press.

"Georgia, your mother and I love each other very much, but there is a gulf between us that is wider than the Atlantic Ocean. As much as I want to be with you and your sisters, I had to do what I thought was best for our family. I promised your mother I wouldn't return until she sent for me. Can you tell me with all honesty that your mother has asked me to come back?"

Yes. Her lips parted, but the small one syllable word—she *so* wanted to be true—refused to fall from her tongue.

His lips wobbled before lifting into a lighthearted smile. "Plus, you can't return until you receive word. What if the earl's already sailing to you? The last thing you want is to sail past each other on the Atlantic."

She hadn't considered that. Julien could right now be navigating the seas. She pictured him standing at the top deck railing of the ship facing into the sunset. He'd be fiddling with her engagement ring in his pocket and willing the boat to sail faster because he couldn't wait to be in her arms — the same passionate way he held her in the garden the night of the party.

"...and your sisters?" Her father's voice penetrated her memories. He touched her arm. "Georgia?"

He stared at her with a smile as if awaiting an answer of some sort.

"I apologize. I was woolgathering."

"I inquired about your sisters and your mother, but where are my manners. You must be exhausted from the trip. Let me call for Hattie. She shall show you to your room and get you settled in. Rest, and then you can enlighten me on everyone's affairs and all the latest happenings in London."

He stood, and everyone else followed suit.

Mr. Wells bowed. "Max and I will also be leaving. I'll send Hattie in on my way out."

They said their farewells, and the minute Mr. Wells left, Georgia sagged in relief. The man exuded tension. His mere presence tied her in knots.

∼

*G*eorgia awoke to the bright sun spilling in the window. She rolled over and buried her head deeper into the pillow. Which servant had decided to draw the curtains so early? They should be dismissed immediately. She squeezed her eyes shut and tried to fall back to sleep, but a strange niggling from the recesses of her mind alerted her something wasn't right. Her room usually smelled of tea and roses. Now it held the aroma of clean soap, salt, and fish? She flipped over and lurched awake.

Gone were her French drapery window curtains made from heavy silk and taffeta. Gone were the rich mauve painted walls and ornate hand-carved moldings. Gone was her thick Persian rug. Instead, she lay in a teak bed with light cotton sheets. The walls were painted cream, and a light flowy fabric draped the windows, rippling in the breeze. A gilded mirror hung over a teak bureau, the only piece of ornate furniture in the room.

Nevis.

She fought down the panic that had plagued her since the day her mother told her she'd be traveling. This was Papa's home, and she was far away on a forsaken island. Yesterday, Hattie had shown her to her room to rest. She remembered lying down to clear her thoughts for a moment. She must have fallen asleep and slept the entire night away.

With a whimper, she flipped the covers back. Yes, she was still in the traveling dress from yesterday, and now it was hopelessly wrinkled. A low groan gurgled in her throat. It was her only gown. The rest lay on the ocean floor. She pressed her palms over her eyes.

A light tap sounded on the door, and Georgia dropped her hands. A slender African woman slipped into the room. Her smooth skin reminded Georgia of a creamy cup of cocoa. Her hair was braided in the tiniest braids she'd ever seen and then wrapped up on top of her head and tucked in a cap. Her long lashes curled back up toward her eyelids, revealing a set of wide, deep brown eyes. She didn't say a word, merely kept her focus on the ground.

Georgia waited for the woman to speak or go about her duties, but as the seconds ticked by, Georgia grew impatient. "What is your name?"

"Jenneigh, mum." She bobbed a curtsy.

"Are you to be my lady's maid?"

"If it pleases you, mum." A timid smile lit up the woman's face. Being a lady's maid could be a step up for her.

"Are you a relative of Hattie's?"

"Yes, mum. I'm her niece."

"Wonderful, so you probably know a lot about the island, my father, and the happenings around the house?"

Jenneigh nodded.

"And you can inform me about the people on the island, what they do and their associations, like Mr. Wells for example."

The girl bit her bottom lip but, seemingly eager to please her new mistress, nodded.

"Splendid." Georgia smiled. "We're going to get along famously." Jenneigh could be useful. Georgia noted the empty wardrobe and let out a sigh. "Unfortunately, there may not be much work for you. All of my trunks, with all of my gowns, have sunk to the bottom of the ocean."

Jenneigh's countenance fell.

"Are you good with hair?"

Her chin lifted. "Yes, mum. I'd be much pleased to help you with your hair." She stepped forward. "I can freshen your dress a bit too."

Jenneigh did just that, and then pinned up Georgia's hair. The girl giggled with delight as she ran her fingers through Georgia's long blond locks. She had quite a flair for coiffures and neatly piled Georgia's hair in a cascade of curls on top of her head. With a satisfied smile, Georgia admired the work, and Jenneigh beamed with pride.

Georgia slid on her gloves. They'd been cleaned and washed overnight. Also, someone had polished her kid boots.

After getting directions from Jenneigh, she headed downstairs to the breakfast room, where she found Aunt Tessa and her father enjoying plates of eggs and ham. They each had a cup of steaming coffee and what appeared to be a gigantic pink orange. When he saw her, Papa rose from the table.

"Good morning, princess. I take it you slept well?"

She nodded and drifted to the sideboard, where she placed a bit of egg, a slice of ham, and a half of one of those gigantic oranges. She chose a seat across from her father.

"I hope you found the accommodations adequate?" Papa settled back into his chair. "I know Nevis doesn't have all the luxuries of London, but it's not that far behind. Sometimes, I find the relaxed pace of the island much more enjoyable."

"Indeed, I slept like the dead." She smiled and ate a bite of eggs.

"Your Aunt Tessa was catching me up on all the happenings back home."

Georgia swallowed. "You still call London home?"

"Of course." His brow furrowed. "It's where my family lives."

She bit her tongue and scooped another portion of eggs into her mouth.

"Shall I have Hattie scramble a few more eggs for you, my dear?" Aunt Tessa tilted her chin toward her and blinked twice. The expression always reminded Georgia of a bird.

"No, thank you."

"You must try the..." She turned to Fredrick. "What do you call these again?"

"Grapefruit. They're native to the Caribbean. The island's shaddock fruit crossed with some orange trees the Spanish brought over."

Aunt Tessa spooned out another bite from her half. "You eat it like this, see?" Then she pushed the portion into her mouth.

Georgia imitated her Aunt's actions, but her mouth puckered, and her eyes screwed up tight from the bitter-sour taste.

"Oh. I forgot to mention you should sprinkle it with sugar first."

Georgia wrinkled her brow and pushed the plate away. "No, thank you."

Her father observed the entire exchange with an affectionate smile, as if he were quite content to sit and watch her eat all day. Georgia placed her hands in her lap. "So, what did Aunt Tessa tell you about London?"

He chuckled. "It appears to be much the same as when I left years ago. The Quality looks down their noses at the Gentry and American new money. The Gentry does its best to rub noses with the Quality and somehow make it into their elite circle, while the Americans thumb their noses and say, 'We don't need you.' Which steams both the Quality and the Gentry."

"It sounds as though you miss it?" Georgia eyed him, curling her lips into a sardonic smile.

"Ah, not the social climbing, but I do miss my family." He patted her hand. "Tessa explained that Franny now lives in Ireland since her husband became a diplomat to the British Consulate, which I already knew. That my oldest grandson has eyes for a beautiful French opera singer, which I didn't know, but neither does his mother." He issued her a quick wink. "Eleanor has blessed me with my seventh grandchild, which I did know, and Ann, in about six months will bless me with my eighth, which I didn't know. I also discovered yesterday that my youngest, hoyden daughter has grown into a beautiful out-and-outer, and has caught the eye of the Earl of Claremont. Who could, at any moment, come barging through my door and demand her hand in marriage."

Georgia blushed at the mention of Julien and covered her smile with her napkin.

"Good morning." Mr. Wells strolled into the room and grabbed a plate from the sideboard. He proceeded to heap on eggs and ham, and then he slid into the open chair next to Georgia.

Georgia's fork hung in midair, a bit of egg dangling, as she stared at the man who had the nerve to casually walk in and sit down as if this home were his own. She put down her fork and turned to her father, eager to see his outraged expression. Instead, her father greeted Mr. Wells with a friendly smile.

"It's a lovely morning, isn't it, Mr. Wells?" Her aunt fluttered her fan and beamed in his direction.

What happened to decorum? Shouldn't Aunt Tessa be outraged? Instead, she smiled at him over her fan like a courting girl.

"Beautiful red-streaked sunrise this morning. Last night's squall didn't turn out to be as big as anticipated but, by the look of that sky, the next storm brewing will be the whopper."

She didn't remember hearing any thunder last night, but she could very well have slept through it. Her stomach sank. "Does that mean they tossed my trunks into the sea for no reason?"

"Some storms plow through, others simmer awhile and gather strength." Harrison held his cup out to the footman, who filled it with steamy coffee. "If the captain didn't put some distance between his ship and the bad weather, they may not survive. Even though the rain hasn't started, the sea has turned wild and dangerous." He consumed a big bite of eggs.

Still irritated, Georgia muttered under her breath, "Do you live here?" At least she thought it was under her breath, until he swallowed, swiped his napkin over his mouth, and turned to face her.

"Fredrick asked Max and I to join him for meals, and it's become a regular habit."

Georgia nodded and reached for her teacup, hiding her embarrassment behind its rim.

⁓

*H*arrison ate another bite and leaned back in his seat so he could drink in the beauty seated beside him. Dried off and well rested, she looked angelic with a crown of golden curls pinned up on top of her head. Her alabaster skin now had a pink tinge that heightened her cheekbones. Whether the color came from their sunny ride yesterday or from the embarrassment of getting caught with such a sharp tongue, he couldn't tell.

Fredrick's gaze wandered around the room. "Where's Max?"

"He's seeing Hattie about some treats." Harrison sipped his coffee. "And showing off his new friend."

"A new friend?" Fredrick's eyebrows arched above the rims of his glasses.

As if summoned, Max ran into the room. "Uncle Fred. You gotta see this."

Georgia's face grew taut. He'd expected her to be annoyed by his presence. In fact, he got a good chuckle this morning merely thinking about her indignant reaction when he strode in for breakfast. And she didn't disappoint, but he hadn't expected her reaction toward Max. She watched his son with wary curiosity, as if she'd never been around a child before. He also noticed her stiffen when Max called Fredrick "Uncle." For all her haughtiness, she appeared threatened by a mere boy of eight years.

Max ran to the open window behind Georgia and whistled. A large bird flew onto the sill. Its head was covered in blue feathers, its back green, and its underbelly a bright red. Georgia twisted around in her seat for a better look.

The bird opened its beak and squawked.

Georgia jerked backward with a loud gasp, bumping into Harrison's shoulder. Max stared at her with bright eyes and said, "It's all right. He doesn't bite. Look, he's tame." Max turned to the bird and said, "Say hello, Oscar."

Oscar opened his black beak and let out a loud squawk. Georgia leaned back over the chair's arm until her head almost rested on Harrison's chest. He inhaled her scent. She smelled like the springtime breeze that had wafted the fragrance of the rose garden through the windows of his country house in Kent.

The bird tilted its head, studied her with one eye, and squawked, "Hello."

Georgia flinched as if bitten. Her position exposed the soft, graceful curve of her neck. Harrison folded his hands against the temptation to trail his fingers over its smooth surface.

Max flipped Oscar a bit of biscuit, and the bird snatched it out of midair. He gobbled up the treat and shuffled his weight from one foot to another as if anxiously awaiting another.

Lady Pickering clapped her hands, and Fredrick said, "Well, I'll be."

Max held up another treat. "Now, say Max."

"Hello."

"No, not hello. Say, Max."

"Hello."

"No, you dumb bird, say Maaaaax."

"Maxwell," Harrison's sharp voice called out. "Mind your mouth."

Max's head dropped. "Sorry, Papa."

Oscar let out another squawk, followed by, "Dumb bird."

Aunt Tessa's mouth dropped open, and the room fell silent. She closed it with a snap and then released an inelegant snort. That was all it took. Fredrick threw back his head and let out a contagious guffaw. Harrison couldn't hold back either, and soon, they were all rolling with laughter. Everyone but Georgia, who chuckled, but kept a wary eye on the parrot as if it might bite off her nose.

Max flipped Oscar another biscuit. Satisfied, the bird flew off into the trees.

As the laughter died, Georgia righted herself. Harrison cleared his throat and wiped the palms of his hands down the side of his thighs. "I have work to do, but I didn't forget about riding over to the pier to discover what washed up overnight."

Georgia perked up at the mention of her lost items. "Yes, my trunks." She surveyed her aunt and father. "Aunt Tessa and I shall be ready to leave shortly." She turned with a jaunty tilt to her chin and a devastating smile.

He blinked at its brilliance. Georgia was using her charms on him to make certain he didn't back out. Being away from London must have left him susceptible to feminine wiles. He stood and jammed his chair back under the table.

Lady Pickering waved her hand. "No, no, I'm staying. These old bones are done being jostled about. I've traveled too much lately. I'm going to stay right here and enjoy the warm air."

All eyes turned toward Fredrick.

"I'm afraid I'm a bit overly tired from all the excitement yesterday. I won't be of much service riding out."

"Jenneigh will have to come then."

Her father shook his head. "Today is caning day, and everyone is needed in the fields. Even Hattie and Jenneigh will go out to help."

"But I'll need a chaperone."

Her father smiled. "You'll find the rules of society are less strict out here." He turned to Harrison. "And my friend here knows he has a Higher Power he must face if his intentions become less than honorable."

Lady Pickering, her voice eager with enthusiasm, said, "Fredrick and I are going to have tea on the porch overlooking the ocean. He mentioned that, now and then, you can spot a whale jumping." Her face radiated her excitement. "Imagine, a real whale." She waved her hand again. "No more travel for me. You two run along. Mr. Wells, I trust you're an upstanding gentleman and my niece is in good hands?"

He nodded. "Of course, Madame." If he laid one finger on the self-righteous chit beside him, God would surely strike him dead for hypocrisy. Both Fredrick and Lady Pickering continued to watch him with the same sparkle in their eyes, and suddenly the entire conversation seemed strange. Were they up to something? They appeared eager to send Georgia off unchaperoned.

"Very well then," Lady Pickering continued. "You may go."

"But Aunt Tessa—"

"Don't dawdle. The man is obviously ready to depart."

Harrison stared at Fredrick, who shrugged, and then at Georgia. At least she had the decency to flash him an apologetic look.

CHAPTER 7

....Let us not dismiss the fact that correspondence from the Duke of Linton has been sparse, and may have been forged. Upon inquisition, the Captain of the *Aberdeen* spoke of a pirate raid. The duke's seal may have fallen into wrongful hands. If this holds true, then it is my duty to save the ducal title from being usurped by an imposter.

—*From the Viscount of Ashburnham to the Prince Regent, George IV*

*H*arrison leaned back against the wooden seat as he and Georgia bounced along the dirt road. Once again in close proximity, he was struck anew by her appearance. Her alabaster skin reminded him of the first snowfall back in England. Fresh and clean. Yet, he'd already glimpsed the controlled fury boiling under the surface.

His own hands and forearms were tanned from the tropical sun. England seemed like another world, yet here they were sitting side by side, socialite and provincial.

Maybe he should brush up on his polite banter? He racked his brain for a suitable, yet enjoyable, topic for such a female.

"You've got your cap set for the Earl of Claremont?" he asked. "What do you plan to do as a countess?"

He watched her eyes light up. "Oh, the typical. Plan menus, oversee the staff, host parties, and the like. I may even join a committee to build a hospital, or an orphanage, or something."

"Is yours a love match?"

"We are the match of the season." Her tone suggested he should know this already.

"How so?" He bit back a smile. Baiting her was too easy. *God, forgive me.*

She glared at him as if he was a simpleton. "Because we come from good families. He's from the Greenhill line. His father was an earl, and his first cousin is of royal lineage. Even my sisters are jeal—er—approve."

Fredrick had mentioned a sisterly rivalry. Was this match more about proving her worth to her sisters, or for status, or love? He'd paid for her passage. He had a right to understand her need to rush back. So he dug deeper. "Being the match of the season doesn't imply a love match. What is it you see in the earl? What's his best quality?"

Her mouth opened, but nothing came out. Her long lashes blinked over aquamarine eyes. She floundered for something to say.

"His...um...the way he, ah..." her words faded into silence, which only seemed to enhance the clip-clop of the horses's hoofs and the twitter of birds flying from tree to tree. Even the distant waves crashing on the shore could be heard in the interim.

"He's handsome, and—and he says such sweet words of flattery." She paused. "Oh." Her chest puffed with pride as if about to announce Claremont had singlehandedly defeated Napoleon. "He seats a horse well."

Harrison couldn't hold in the laugh bubbling in his chest.

She rounded on him. "Truly, it's none of your concern."

He struggled to get his laughter under control. "Merely making conversation."

"Then you should stick to pleasantries or...discuss the weather."

"As you wish." He peered up at the sky. "Looks like the weather's going to be hot and humid today with a chance of a blustery sea squall." He turned in her direction and flashed what he hoped was a spry smile. "Of course, that's the usual forecast around here."

Her lips drew into a tight line as she pivoted on the wooden seat to stare off to the side.

He stifled a chuckle, and they continued in silence until Harrison pointed inland. "See that little stone steeple above the tree line? That's our church where Reverend Clark preaches on Sunday. During the week, it's the schoolhouse where I teach the local children."

Georgia turned to face him. "You're a schoolmaster?"

He chuckled at the incredulity in her voice. "Indeed. I also own and maintain the sugar plantation next to your father's, but when the old schoolmaster passed, I saw a need and felt a nudge from God to fill it."

"How old was the schoolmaster when he passed?"

"Eight and twenty."

"Eight and twenty?"

"By old, I meant previous. The poor man died of consumption, too young for my tastes."

She nodded and turned to face forward, but not before he caught the horror on her face.

He berated himself for frightening the woman. "People die in London too. You just didn't always hear about it in the upper circles. Here on a small island, everyone knows one another, and news spreads quickly."

Her eyes narrowed. "How do you know about the upper circles in London?"

"How does one not? Even we *lowly* islanders still hear all about London gossip." He emphasized the word lowly to see if she'd protest, but she only shrugged.

"How many children do you teach?"

"Six free children and about five slave children. The latter are sporadic. Some come if their masters allow, others sneak over to the schoolhouse when they can or to my cottage house late at night, where I teach them to read by candlelight."

Her eyes clouded, and her pink lips briefly parted. "Isn't that dangerous? Couldn't you find yourself in trouble for teaching slaves to read?"

"Why, Miss Lennox, are you concerned for my welfare?"

She crossed her arms over her chest and shifted her gaze in the other direction. "No, I'm concerned for Maxwell's."

Harrison grimaced. Max was safe, safer here than with the riffraff in London, where innocents were shot in the streets. An all too familiar pain slashed his heart. Here the islanders knew each other and looked out for one another. True, there were a few rotten apples, but they couldn't hide on a small island like Nevis.

Her accusation rubbed him like a burlap bag. He enjoyed teaching, enjoyed seeing the children's eyes grow wide with excitement when the combination of letters finally switched from symbols to meaning. Also, there was nothing more important to him than ensuring Max received a proper education, even if it meant teaching the boy himself. Max learned history and arithmetic with the free children during the day and aided his father at night helping the slave children trace their letters.

But Miss Lennox's concern wasn't unfounded. Somehow she was perceptive enough to sense the unrest brewing on the island. The landowners' livelihood relied on the work of slaves. It didn't behoove them to have their property educated. Unfair as it may be, the more dependent slaves were on their owners, the less likely they were to revolt or run away. During the six years he'd lived on Nevis, tensions had mounted. The land wasn't producing as it had in the past, and the sugar crop brought in less profit per pound. Landowners pushed their slaves harder and harder, and scuffles erupted on multiple occasions.

When he'd first arrived on the island, slaves worked his fields hired by the last overseer, but it never settled well with his spirit. He couldn't treat people who were made in God's image as property, so he gave the slaves their freedom and paid them wages to work. So far, God had blessed him in this decision, for the sugar cane thrived on his small plot of land.

It impressed him that Georgia so readily noticed the political tension regarding slaves. There was a mind underneath all that beauty. Hopefully, her awareness was a sign that Great Britain understood also. A month before he sailed to Nevis, England had outlawed the slave trade, but unfortunately not slavery itself.

Georgia continued to ask questions regarding the island, but he couldn't shake his thoughts to give more than terse monosyllables. Eventually, she quit trying to converse, and they rode the rest of the way in silence. They passed sugar cane fields with large reeds swaying with the breeze, clustered huts of slave villages, and other settler homes that dotted the outskirts of town.

Occasionally, he glanced at her, but she appeared oblivious to the lack of conversation. Instead of pouting over his inconsiderate conduct, she studied the people they passed as they drew closer to town. Most were out working in the fields, while some sat on the porches of their single-room houses staring back at the white woman who rode with the schoolmaster. He figured her small, elegant nose would be wrinkled in disgust as they drove through the shanties of the impoverished section of town, but instead, her head was tilted, her gaze steady, as if curious about their way of life.

They pulled up to the pier where no boats remained docked. The fishermen were still out at sea—another sign that a storm was brewing. The islanders knew well that fish practically jumped into the nets before a storm.

Harrison watched the palm trees bow their heads and wave their leaves as a bluster of wind swept up the sand. Whitecaps dotted the sea, and large waves smacked the beach like the slap of a gambler's hands on the table, pulling its winnings back toward the depths. He pulled on the reins and jumped down to tie the horses to a hitching post. The wind filled Georgia's bonnet like the sail of a ship.

"Do you want to stay here while I look for your trunks?" He raised his voice a bit so she could hear over the roar of the crashing waves.

She shook her head, and he helped her down from the wagon.

As they hiked the path to the beach, Harrison frowned at the dark clouds forming on the horizon. The storm was approaching faster than anticipated. They had better make this quick.

~

The tang of salt hung thick in the air, and Georgia's kid boots sank into the soft sand, impeding her walking and slowing her pace. They rounded a tuft of seagrass, and a small African child banged into her skirts. He deflected off her and kept running.

Behind him flowed a pink chemise tied about his neck, flapping in the wind like a cape. Her mouth opened, but no sound came forth as the child darted up the path. Another child followed, looking like a pink Christmas tree with a petticoat tucked up under his armpits. Not just any petticoat—*her petticoat.*

"My things," she whispered. Her heart twisted, torn between rejoicing that she'd found her belongings and horror that children were using her undergarments as playthings. Her voice rose to a shrill octave. "Stop!"

They kept running and didn't look back. Georgia glared at Harrison, but the man wasn't paying attention. He shielded his eyes with his hand and stared in the opposite direction down the beach.

Georgia grabbed her skirts to chase after the lads, but more giggles drifted from behind her. She whipped around to find four children laughing and digging through her washed up trunk. It had sunk in the moist sand where the water ebbed and flowed.

"No!" she shrieked and frowned at her pink gowns floating like jellyfish in the surf. Some lay strewn across the beach.

"Unhand my things." Georgia charged toward the group, grazing Harrison's shoulder in her haste. All four boys glanced up from their scavenging and stared with wide, unblinking eyes at what must appear to be a crazed woman racing toward them.

"Put them back. Put all of them back." Her voice cracked from the strain of yelling over the breaking waves.

Several of the island children tensed as if to flee, but stopped in confusion when she paused and snatched up a pink garment from out of the surf.

"Don't move." Her eyes dared them to disobey her command as she shook out another dress and folded it over her arm. Ocean water splashed around her ankles and re-soaked her shoes. Wet garments weighed heavily on her arm, which she held out to keep from ruining her walking dress. With her other hand, she lifted her skirts so they wouldn't get drenched.

"Take that off right now, young man," she demanded of a boy dressed in her gown of chiffon and lace. He glanced at his friend, who had a pair of her pink unmentionables on top of his head like a nightcap.

Instead of answering, they grinned at each other and burst into loud fits of laughter.

Clenching her fists in frustration, she turned to another boy wearing her bonnet. "Put them back." She gestured wildly toward the trunk. "Put them *all* back."

One boy shrugged, pulled the bonnet off his head, and tossed it into the trunk. The one wearing her dress snatched the bonnet back up, put it on his own head, and giggled as he batted his eyes. Georgia tried to yank it off him, but he got it off first and held it away from her. She lunged, but he tossed it to his other friend, and they all started to laugh.

In a plea for help, she scowled back at Harrison. He stood a good ten feet behind her, his arms crossed over his chest, and his mouth twisted up in a half-smile.

She would strangle the man with her petticoat. Her hands shook with a fresh surge of ire. *She would stuff him into her trunk and toss him out with the surf.* "How dare you stand there and laugh? Any gentlemen would understand the seriousness of the matter, but you, sir, are no gentleman. You stand there while gowns that easily cost more than a year's wages are ruined. These are my things—the only clothes I have to wear on this horrific island. They're ruined, and you think it's funny. You're as bad as these boys." She jabbed a finger behind her, where the lads stood. "No, I take that back. You're worse because you should know better." She impaled him with a look that should have iced his veins, and she reveled in a small spark of satisfaction when his smile faded.

He started toward her, but curved to protect his boots as a wave licked at them. A mass tumbled nearby in the surf, and he bent down to pick up the swirl of pink fabric left at his feet. Wringing the water out of it, he held it up for all to see. His face paled, and the material slipped, almost landing back in the water. Beneath his tanned face, he turned a vivid scarlet. His fingers clutched her silky chemise undergarment.

66

Clearing his throat, he crumpled it into a ball and thrust it into her chest as he neared. She opened her mouth to issue a scathing remark, but he stopped her with one questioning eyebrow. Instead, she pinched her lips into a tight line.

"Boys, listen up. You might think you've found lost treasure, but these things are Miss Lennox's. Put them back right now, and I'll make certain your mamas don't learn you've been snickering over ladies' unmentionables."

All four boys straightened at once and started pulling the clothes off. They placed them back into the trunk, and three of the lads took off running as soon as Harrison paid them a nod.

One boy lingered, however. She noted the redness of tears brimming in the child's large brown eyes. He still clutched one of her evening gowns of soft superfine to his chest and gently stroked it as if it were a baby doll.

"Please hand over my gown." She held her open palm out. His hand stilled, and tears slid down his cheeks.

Harrison's fingers touched her shoulder. "Booker, my friend, you don't want to give up the dress?"

The boy shook his head and his face crumpled. He cried into her gown.

Harrison stepped around her and wrapped the boy in his embrace. When the child's sobbing began to diminish, Harrison crouched down until his face was level with Booker's. "What's the matter?"

The boy gazed up a Georgia, and her heart clenched at the depth of sorrow etched in his face. His gaze flicked back to Harrison, and he sucked in a shaky breath.

"Mista Wells, I don't mean any harm. I wanna put the dress back, but my hand won't let me. I thought we found it, so it was ours and…and…" Tears sprang to his eyes once more. "And my mama has been awfully sick of late…awfully sick." He let out a choked sob. "I wanted to give it to my mama, so she'd have somethin' nice"—he inhaled a stuttered breath—"for them to bury her in."

A gasp escaped Georgia's lips. The poor boy.

Harrison's head jerked around. His eyes narrowed on her, suggesting that he misconstrued her reaction. He turned back and placed his hands on the boy's shoulders. "I'm sorry, son, but the dress is Miss Lennox's, and her things mean a lot to her. You'll have to give it back."

The boy nodded and, with another sob, dropped the dress into the trunk.

"Wait." She reached into the trunk and pulled out the luxurious material that, in itself, could have purchased food for the child's family for a month. She held the dress in her hands. It was the one she'd worn the night Julien almost proposed. She bit her lower lip and slowly held it out toward Booker. "Please, give it to your mama."

The child's face brightened, but then his brow furrowed, and he shook his head. "It's yer dress. Grandmamma says we don't take nothin' from nobody."

"How tall is your mama?" she asked.

"She's 'bout up to yer chin."

"Oh, well then, you must take the dress."

He crossed his hands over his chest.

"You see, the dressmaker cut the dress too short." She held the gown up to the length of her body but folded the material in the middle to make it appear shorter. "It will never fit me. I was going to pass it on to my maid, but maybe we could trade for it?"

The child's shoulders slumped. "I don't got nothin' ta trade."

"Oh, but you do. I collect shells. I've only read about conch shells, and I've always wanted one for my collection. Find me a nice big conch shell, and the dress is yours."

Booker's smile was all teeth, and he scurried off on his mission.

Harrison crossed his arms over his chest and sent her a side-ways glance, but she didn't miss the relief in his eyes. "You have a seashell collection?"

Georgia straightened her shoulders. "I do now."

A smile flashed across his face, but it was gone as fast as it came.

Harrison nodded toward the trunk. "Let's see what we can salvage from this mess. When Booker comes back, he can help me move the trunk to the wagon."

Though her gowns were wet and soiled, such finery should hardly be called a mess. Did he have no regard for nicer things? Though his clothes were worn, at one point, they were finery. One would think he'd appreciate their value.

But then she glanced around and released a rush of air. Most of her dresses *were* torn or ruined beyond repair, and the ocean continued to beat them upon the sand and rocks. A low moan escaped her lips, and her shoulders drooped. He was right. It was a mess.

Harrison bent over and tucked another soggy dress into the crook of his arm. Georgia followed suit, gleaning what could be saved. Now and then, Harrison would clear his throat, wave his hand at an item, then turn and walk away. She glared at him through narrowed eyes, but after several instances, she gasped and lurched forward to snatch up the material. He'd been saving her further embarrassment by allowing her the privacy to pick up her undergarments. Despite his thoughtfulness, she flushed every time he signaled her.

"Do you pack your suitcases by color?" Harrison wrung out the last garment, a rosy pink day dress. "Should I expect tomorrow to find your green apparel littering the shoreline?"

Georgia righted herself after folding a damp gown and placing it into the trunk. She speared him with a look which she hoped said, *We are on fragile ground, don't irritate me further*, but he didn't appear to notice.

"It's either that or you only wear the color pink?" He wrung the sea-water out of another day gown and held it out toward her.

She snatched it from his fingers. "I fancy the color pink. It's a feminine color."

He raised a single eyebrow. "Doesn't that get boring, wearing the same color day in and out?"

She cradled the gown like a doll. It was the walking dress she'd worn the day in Hyde Park when Julien first spotted her. The zephyr material matched the same pink color of the foxglove flowers that grew along the path they'd strolled.

Georgia stroked the soft material. A man couldn't understand the importance of pink—especially not the likes of Mr. Wells. Pink had transformed her from a ruffian child into a sophisticated woman. The color gave her the confidence to face society. Whereas others may see the world in black and white, she saw her world in blues and pinks. Her tomboy childhood spent with her father was blue—calming, safe, and peaceful, but disillusioned. Her present was pink—feminine, accepted, and sanctioned, but contrived.

"I've got one," shouted Booker as he ran toward them carrying a large conch shell over his head. He skidded to a halt at her side and held the shell, pink side up, to show her. "It's in perfect condition, and listen." He raised the object to his ear, and his grin encompassed his entire face. "You can hear da ocean. Clear as day."

He held it up to her ear, but she couldn't tell whether the sound came from the shell or the waves crashing behind her.

"It's perfect. You have earned the gown." She accepted the shell and passed him the dress. "I hope to one day see your mother wearing it—about town," she clarified.

The boy's eyes clouded. "I dunno how to thank you. Mama's gonna laugh with joy."

She gestured to the trunk. "Before you run off. Do you mind giving Mr. Wells a hand carrying this?"

The boy nodded.

She held his treasured dress while he and Mr. Wells carried the waterlogged trunk and placed it in the back of the wagon. Harrison thanked Booker and off the child ran, all smiles, in the direction of home. Wet pink superfine waved like a flag from his arm.

Georgia and Harrison exchanged smiles, and he gestured toward the wagon. His warm hand slid under her elbow to assist her up.

~

"*H*o there!"

Harrison froze and released Miss Lennox. His jaw clenched, but he turned around and tipped his hat. "Mr. Rousseau."

Edward Rousseau approached with long strides as his eyes surveyed Miss Lennox from under inverted V-shaped brows. His lips twisted up into a smile like a rat catcher's ferret, ready for a merry rodent chase.

"Good day, Wells. Fancy seeing you in this part of town. Aren't you supposed to be teaching lessons?" Rousseau tipped his hat.

"We break on Saturdays."

Mr. Rousseau didn't acknowledge his response. His eyes met Georgia's with an eager glint. "Wells, I believe an introduction is in order."

A surge of heat burned Harrison's ears and around his collar at the subtle insinuation that he'd forgotten his manners.

God, help me see him the way You see him, because my fingers are itching to plant Rousseau a facer.

With a tight smile, Harrison offered a stiff bow. "Miss

Lennox, let me formally introduce you to Mr. Edward Rousseau, the owner of the Artesian Hotel." His eyes leveled on the other man. "Mr. Rousseau, may I introduce Fredrick Lennox's daughter, Miss Georgia Lennox."

Rousseau encased her hand in his and bowed. "It's always a pleasure to have a refined lady of the Quality in our midst, especially one so fair. I would love to hear of your voyage and the happenings in London. Island folk must live off bits and scraps of news to quench our appetite for word from our beloved homeland."

A knot formed in Harrison's stomach as the man poured out his platitudes. Georgia withdrew her hand and subjected him to one of her dazzling smiles. Harrison's lips twitched as Rousseau's eyes glazed over, lost in her charms.

He almost—*almost*—felt pity for the man.

CHAPTER 8

...Indeed, our exports of sugar and sugar products did not meet expectations last quarter. However, I shall expend every effort to drive my slaves harder to account for the difference within the next shipment.
    —*From Mr. Edward Rousseau to Mr. Alexander Allan, Director of the British East India Company*

*M*r. Rousseau's lips lingered over Georgia's hand exceedingly long, as if he was considering kissing the top of it. She pulled her fingers away and issued him the same smile she'd used to gain a gentleman's favor during her second season.

The man carried himself well and dressed impeccably, with well-polished boots gleaming. He wore close-fitted buckskins and an olive-green waistcoat of kerseymere—both well-tailored. They had much in common—Quality knew quality. Mr. Rousseau donned clothes in the height of fashion, not from a couple of season's hence like Mr. Wells.

Although, Mr. Wells carried an air about him that was more than the clothes he wore. His wide stance held authority, despite being among someone from a higher social rank. Standing next to Mr. Wells' broad frame, Mr. Rousseau appeared—well—*less*. Even still, Mr. Rousseau could be a beneficial acquaintance.

She took a half step closer. "I would be delighted to satisfy your appetite for news, Mr. Rousseau. I'm certain my father could arrange an engagement for us to talk further."

His neck extended and his eyes locked on her like a fox on its prey, but she was ready for a chase.

"The last bit of news we received was that the Prince Regent had given the Duke of Linton an ultimatum. Either he comes out of hiding, or his title and all his lands will be transferred to Lord Edmund Daulton, the Viscount of Ashburnham. Has the disappearing duke materialized, or shall I be sending Lord Ashburnham a sizable Christmas gift this year?" His eyes flashed, and his voice grew husky. "I find lavish presents a remarkable way to get into someone's good graces."

Georgia fought to keep the wariness from her smile at the mere mention of Lord Ashburnham. Mother had thought Ashburnham to be Georgia's best marital option and pressured her to accept his suit. Georgia's inability to secure a match in her previous seasons only cemented her mother's belief that she needed to marry the viscount as soon as possible.

If this voyage cost her the Earl of Claremont's affections, if Claremont didn't come up to scratch, then Ashburnham would be her fate. After all the energy she'd expended convincing Mama for another season to give Claremont time to propose, she may still end up chained to the shuddersome viscount for life.

A tremor ran through her body as she remembered the way Ashburnham grasped her arm at the Hopkins ball. His long nails, through the silk cloth of his gloves, had possessively dug into her upper arm. The man eyed her as if she were a prize to be stuffed and mounted on his wall. If Ashburnham inherited a dukedom, she'd never find someone of a higher rank to satisfy her mother. Perhaps, Mr. Rousseau might introduce her to some of his prestigious guests. Maybe her future wasn't doomed to be Lady Ashburnham. She couldn't abandon the hope.

"Indeed," she forced a light tone, "His Grace has not yet resurfaced. It may be wise to add the viscount to your gifting list."

"Ah, it is done then. In appreciation of your counsel, may I bestow upon you an invitation to come to the Artesian Hotel for a grand house party next weekend?" He wet his lips. "I shall send over a servant with a formal invitation this afternoon." He glanced at Mr. Wells, then cleared his throat. "To you as well, of course."

Harrison's amber eyes fixed on Rousseau and hardened into granite. A tense muscle in his jaw flexed, and a tight jerk of his head was the only acknowledgment he gave. It seemed Mr. Wells and Mr. Rousseau were not on agreeable terms. Due to social inequality, perhaps? Was Mr. Wells jealous of Mr. Rousseau's elevated status?

"I will be delighted to show you our elite hotel," Rousseau said. "Women of the Peerage often sail across the Atlantic to enjoy the healing qualities of our hot springs and stay at my hotel. In fact, Lady Wentworth,"—his chest puffed—"a close cousin to the Queen, is a frequent guest. But, I must admit, none hold a candle to your beauty, Miss Lennox."

Georgia smiled to produce a dimple in her right cheek. "Mr. Rousseau, you are too kind. I would very much enjoy seeing your hotel. Its reputation precedes itself, even all the way to London."

He straightened and tilted his head with a pleased grin.

She mirrored his movements. "I must admit, the rustic nature of the island has taken some adjustment. It would be splendid to enjoy a bit of home." She splayed her fingers across her chest and offered her coquettish grin, practiced in a way that emphasized her slender cheekbones. "Especially in such good company."

Harrison's gaze veered off to inspect the shoreline as if he'd grown bored. Perhaps she'd laid on the charm a bit thick, but it never hurt to start an acquaintance by gaining the upper hand.

Rousseau soaked her in with a wolfish grin before he cleared his throat. "I must be going." He tipped his hat with his thumb and index finger. "But I look forward to bettering our acquaintance." He backed away a few steps, his eyes never straying from her, before he turned on his heel and headed into the nearby brightly painted general store.

She stifled a giggle at his brazen swagger. Besides the mention of the Viscount of Ashburnham, Mr. Rousseau's brief visit comforted her. Maybe not everything here was strange. He reminded her of the dandies with whom she mingled in London, predictable and willing to bend over backward for a practiced coy smile.

One thing she'd learned from Papa before he left was how to outwit the smartest fish, which, after one botched season, she transferred to outsmarting the Quality. She used last season to study the Ladies of the *ton* as they floated around a ballroom like pretty fish in a pond, every coy gesture, practiced smile, and method of flirtation.

Then, she'd baited the biggest fish, the Earl of Claremont. It was her chance to show her mother and sisters she did belong—that she wasn't a pathetic embarrassment to the Lennox name. Her sisters may have married well, but she would marry better. She had merely needed to reel him in.

Until the letter arrived.

Her gaze flitted to Mr. Wells, and her smile quickly faded. He watched Rousseau's retreating form with a black scowl. Shaking her head, she let out a sigh. There was predictable, and then there was Mr. Wells. With a shrug, she turned toward the wagon.

His hands encircled her waist and tossed her up onto the bench seat. Her lips pinched together at his rough handling, but she didn't bother to comment on it.

He climbed aboard and snapped the reins. The horses lurched forward, and Georgia grabbed the side of the bench to steady herself.

"Tell me the price of the dress."

Georgia snapped her head to the side.

"I will reimburse you." He didn't look at her as he bit the words out through clenched teeth.

"I beg your pardon?"

"The cost of the dress."

"I presume you mean my gift to Booker?"

Harrison snorted and shook his head. "I won't have you holding anything over that poor boy's head. He will not be your personal servant. Name your price."

A wave of fury dripped over her like the ever-present humidity. "I already have. It was one conch shell, and it is paid in full." She turned her entire body to face him. "You don't believe I'm capable of doing something out of the kindness of my heart, do you?"

His jaw tightened. "I know your type. That poor boy is watching his mother die a slow painful death. I won't have you adding to his misery."

"What do you mean, *my type?*"

He fixed her a sideways glance. "Pampered, spoiled, and only out for yourself, flashing a pretty smile here and there to get what you want. I saw you try to manipulate Rousseau with your feminine wiles."

She hadn't done anything that wouldn't be seen at any party hosted by the *ton*. "I don't know what I've done to give you such a poor opinion of me, but considering you've known me for only a day, it's difficult to see how you could make such swift judgments." She turned forward and crossed her arms. "I thought the Bible says it isn't for us to judge. We are to leave that to God. But then again, maybe God doesn't come to this forsaken island."

~

A large gust of wind blasted the two of them as if God himself had put an exclamation point on her sentence. Harrison felt the nudge of the Holy Spirit convicting him.

She is my daughter, and I love her, just as you love your son.

He didn't want to admit it, but Georgia was right. It was for God to judge. The words from Matthew seven stuck in his head. *Do not judge, or you too will be judged. For in the same way you judge others, you will be judged, and with the measure you use, it will be measured to you.*

Harrison let the reins fall slack. He had to release his anger from the encounter with Rousseau. The man tried his patience, but Harrison's toes had curled when she smiled back at the snake. Watching their casual exchange had made his skin crawl as if he'd stepped into a nest of fire ants. It wasn't her fault. She didn't know that the man publicly flogged his slaves within an inch of their lives.

"You're right." He released a breath and gentled his voice. "I judged you unfairly. I apologize."

Silence hung between them for a moment, but he caught her peeking at him. "Don't do it again."

His mouth tugged into a half smile at the haughty way she commanded him. The woman was unbelievable. He'd never met another human being, man or woman, as stubborn as this stiff-backed slip of a thing.

A splatter of rain slapped him on the cheek, and he peered into the ominous clouds above. They appeared so dark, they almost held a greenish hue. *Not good.* He was miles from home, wasting his time on some fool errand for an ungrateful woman.

He'd hoped the storm would hold off, but it appeared they were about to get doused.

He shrugged out of his jacket. "Here." He draped the coat over Georgia's shoulders. "It will afford you some protection."

For a brief second, she hesitated. The stubborn woman was going to balk. Harrison's jaw tightened. But instead of refusing it, she curled her fingers around his lapel and drew it tighter. A sense of smug victory lifted the corners of his mouth, but he wiped the smile away with the back of his hand.

With a nod of her head, she replied, "Thank you."

The dark clouds didn't merely shower, sheets of rain torrentially soaked. The wind whipped up and pelted them with water from all directions. Harrison strained to keep the horses under control with one hand and used his other to wipe the runoff out of his eyes, which dripped from his hair, eyelashes, and off the tip of his nose.

Despite the warm temperature, the lashing wind chilled his bones and caused his clothes to stick to his skin. A shiver ran through his body. He peered at Georgia. Her teeth chattered as she huddled under the jacket he'd given to her when the deluge began. His coat shook as she trembled from head to toe. He had to give the woman credit. She hadn't whined or complained. Without caring about appearances, he reached out and wrapped an arm around her, drawing her up against his side.

❧

*G*eorgia let out a gasp as a vise grip hauled her up against the beast of a man. She protested and pulled away, but he held fast.

Soon the warmth of his skin against her own convinced her to relent. Tears stung her eyes. What had she done to deserve this sort of punishment? Banished to this barbaric island and saddled to this infuriating man, a man who believed he could control her every move. *God, what did I do to deserve...?* She couldn't finish the thought.

Gone was the content little girl, the daughter whose biggest delight was to sit by her father's side. That child disappeared when her papa sailed to Nevis. Maybe Mr. Wells was right. Maybe she was only out for herself. Her father was terminally ill, and all she could think about were her ruined dresses and returning to London.

Hot tears brimmed over and slipped down her cheeks, mixing with the raindrops. She turned toward his chest so he wouldn't see her face. In the protection of his arms, she let her silent tears flow. The warmth of his skin permeated her wet gown. Her breath clouded hot and humid against his chest.

She inhaled his exotic aroma of spiced coconut, and she couldn't think of anything in London that smelled this good. Her fingers rested against the sinewy tautness of his muscles, the thin, wet, layer of his shirt doing little to conceal the powerful man beneath. She trembled, but this time it was not from the cold.

As she lay wrapped in his warm strength, drowsiness weighed down her eyelids, increased by the lull of the rocking wagon. It reminded her of when papa rocked her to sleep in his arms. Back in her early years when she was welcomed and loved. This was what she craved—to be held and protected.

CHAPTER 9

...The storms shake the rafters. I've never seen the like...
—*From Lady Pickering to Lady Nora Lennox.*

*G*eorgia awoke with a start as a gust of wind and a spray of water hit her square in the face. She jerked upright, bumping her forehead into something pointy and hard.

"Ouch. Hold still."

Reality sank in as the warm arms tightened around her. Harrison. Her forehead must have collided with his chin. They weren't in the wagon any longer, but instead, he was carrying her.

She eyed her surroundings to gain her bearings, but the rain blurred her vision. They were moving upwards. Georgia blinked away the raindrops and recognized the steps to her father's bungalow.

"Let me down." She wiggled to get free. "I can walk just fine." A powerful blast of wind assaulted them, and she muffled her voice into his chest. Thunder boomed loud enough to shake the ground, and Georgia's grip on his shirt tightened.

"I'll let you down when we're inside. I can move faster without having to aid you up these treacherous steps."

Harrison ducked his head and turned his back against the wind, pinning her tighter to his chest. She'd seen her share of storms growing up, but nothing compared to the tempest that raged around them. During a small lull between gusts, her protector bounded up the rest of the stairs. She closed her eyes and clung to him like a helpless, scared animal.

The door swung wide as they reached the front entryway, and he barreled through it.

"Thank the Lord. You're back." Papa turned and yelled down the hall, "Hattie and Max, you can get off your knees now. God heard your prayers. They're home safe."

A floppy-haired bullet rushed into the room and wrapped his arms around Harrison's knees, almost knocking the three of them over. Harrison leaned against the doorframe to steady himself.

"It's all right, Max. I'm here now."

Rainwater dripped from their hair and clothing, forming a puddle on the floor.

Harrison straightened. "Step back a second so I can put Miss Lennox down."

Max reluctantly let go and stepped away.

Harrison lessened his hold, and she slid out of his warm grasp. Her legs, still a little numb, wobbled, but he steadied her with his hands. His amber gaze held hers, and she couldn't miss the concern there. To her mortification, heat warmed her body and settled into her cheeks. As the residual warmth from his body dissipated, a shiver ran over her skin, followed by a queer sense of loss.

She cleared her throat, and his hands released her. He stooped down and opened his arms wide and his son jumped into his embrace. Max held on tight and wouldn't let go. Harrison returned the squeeze and kissed the boy on the top of his head. The loving exchange hit a twinge of jealousy, and Georgia's gaze flicked to her papa.

"I'm so glad you're back." Papa smiled and opened his own arms to her. "The storm hit quickly. We were worried."

She hesitated and glanced at Harrison, who watched her over the top of Max's head. Pushing one foot forward, she stepped into her father's enveloping arms. Her own hands remained awkwardly at her side, as though they didn't know what to do. Mama didn't show affection in such a manner, and she only had a vague memory of being in her father's arms. Even that seemed more dream than reality. He squeezed her tight and rocked lightly side to side, not letting go. She raised one arm and patted him on the back.

He pulled back with a glistening of tears in his eyes, then crushed her to him once again. With a chuckle, he said, "These storms are a tad wilder than the ones in London. Eh?"

Georgia smiled and timidly snaked her other hand around to rest on his back. She used to sit in Papa's lap on a rocking chair in the portico. They would listen to rain tap on the roof and thunder crackle in the distance. She'd always been excited when the lightning flashed across the sky, knowing she was safe next to her papa. Here she was once again in her father's arms, but her security felt artificial, like throwing a rug over a hole in the floorboards.

After a long moment, he released her and shooed her upstairs. "You need to get out of those wet clothes and near the fire."

She nodded and headed toward her room. A warm fire did sound wonderful.

Even better was the steamy bath that awaited Georgia, and Jenneigh hung her dress to dry.

"I fear you won't be able to wear this gown again today, Miss."

Georgia frowned as it dawned on her that she had nothing at all to wear.

Jenneigh folded her hands in front of her and stared at the floor. "I have my Sunday dress. You could wear it… ah …. Seein' as you don't have nothin' else."

Georgia sat up straighter in the tub, eyeing the girl to see if she was serious. In London, someone like her wouldn't be caught dead wearing a servant's clothing. If the ladies' maids were lucky, they could hope to receive the cast-off gowns of their employers. But she wasn't in London, and she didn't have a single thing in which to clothe herself. She could either accept Jenneigh's offer or stay in the tub for the rest of the night.

"Thank you, Jenneigh. You're very kind. I would appreciate it."

Jenneigh beamed a broad white smile and disappeared down the hall. When she returned, she carried a Pomona green cotton dress with capped sleeves. The hem was a trifle worn, but other than that, it was a beautiful dress and probably the girl's most treasured possession.

Georgia tried it on, and Jenneigh held out a small hand mirror for her to see. This was the first time in a long while she'd seen herself in a color other than pink.

She fingered the soft material. "It's beautiful, Jenneigh, and though you are of smaller frame, it surprisingly fits." She and Jenneigh were the same height, but the bust was a tad snug. Fortunately, the high waist allowed the rest. "Thank you. I'll take good care of it."

As Jenneigh pinned Georgia's hair into a top knot and pulled loose curls to frame her face, Georgia's mind raced with unanswered questions.

"Tell me, Jenneigh. How is my father's health—really? Since I've arrived, he hasn't appeared ill."

"Oh, praise the Lord, Miss Lennox. It's been a good week. I think yer arrival has lifted his spirits."

"What is a bad week like?"

"When da fever hits, he takes to his bed and hardly eats nothin'. His sweat soaks the sheets, and sometimes he don't know what he's say'n."

Georgia wrinkled her forehead and pulled her mouth into a frown. "It's hard to picture him that way. He seems so full of life right now."

"God willing, he stays dat way."

She tilted her chin up and viewed Jenneigh in the mirror. "Tell me about Mr. Wells."

"God bless 'im. He's a good man."

Georgia waited for her to continue, but only silence pervaded. Jenneigh apparently needed more encouragement, so she asked, "How did he get involved with my father?"

Her voice grew quiet as if she realized she shouldn't be gossiping about her employer. "From what I know, dey met on the ship comin' to Nevis. Took to each other right away. Especially, Mista Fredrick to lil' Max. The boy looks up ta him like a grandpa."

Georgia's jaw tensed, but she hid her annoyance behind a smile. "And what about the child's mother? Where is she?"

"God rest her soul. She went to be with the Lord when Max was nothin' but two."

"Was she sick?"

"Naw, ain't like tat." Jenneigh glanced at the door, then whispered into Georgia's ear. "She wuz killed."

Georgia gasped.

"Mr. Wells don't talk about it much. All I know is he brought his son here to get away from da London riffraff. He didn't want nothin' to happen like that to his boy."

A sprout of sympathy for Max rooted itself in Georgia's heart. The boy had never known his mother. Yes, her mama and she had their differences, but underneath all the layers of disappointment, she knew her mother loved her. Many a night,

Georgia had awakened to find her mother standing by her bed whispering a prayer for her soul. It drove Georgia all the more to marry well, to prove she was worth all those prayers.

A large gust of wind banged the shutters against the house. Georgia jumped, and a jolt of panic surged through her body. The candles flickered and danced in their holders as if laughing at her.

Jenneigh closed her eyes and whispered a short prayer under her breath.

"Does the island get storms like this often?" Georgia fought to keep her growing concern out of her voice.

"We get a few in the fall, but usually not dis time of year. Spring is quiet. I hope it's not a sign of more to come."

Me too. The wind shook the house, causing the boards and windows to moan with displeasure. Would the structure even hold?

"It looks like we might all be sleeping on da ground floor tonight."

"Why? What could happen to the second floor?"

"Yer papa built his house outa stone on the bottom. It's less likely to get broke by the wind and by tings flying around. The second floor ... Well, there ain't nuttin' dat can be done for da second floors whetha dey be made of stone or wood. We islanders know tat wood is easier to rebuild den stone."

A cannon of thunder boomed through the house and shook the rafters. Georgia squeezed the arms of the chair, her voice a mere squeak. "The whole second floor could be destroyed?"

"We pray for da good Lord's protection."

"Could you pray for us both?"

Jenneigh prayed out loud while she calmly pinned each curl. She paid no heed to the howling of the wind and roars of thunder, merely spoke to God as if He sat right beside them.

Georgia hadn't prayed in years. When she had, it was only quietly in church, and she would throw in as many thous and doths as possible to sound official. Now, she silently pleaded with God for His protection.

Jenneigh concluded with an "Amen" and Georgia echoed it.

"All finished. Yer lookin' mighty beautiful. Yer hair shines like gold." Jenneigh passed her the mirror.

As Georgia inspected her hair, her spirits lifted. Her knees may be quaking, but her coiffeur looked lovely.

The raging storm didn't keep Hattie from preparing a hearty meal to fill their stomachs. At dinner, Georgia sat to her father's left, across from Mr. Wells and next to her aunt. The colorful walls were illuminated by candles, their flames flickering each time the wind blew. The light refracted off the crystal goblets, scattering small rainbows about the table.

She spent most of the meal listening with interest to the back-and-forth exchange between Mr. Wells and her father regarding topics ranging from different planting methods to Napoleon Bonaparte's capture and its effect on trade. Often, they paused to get her view or that of Aunt Tessa's. Georgia wasn't used to men valuing her opinion, but she quickly became comfortable and enjoyed offering suggestions. Her father's eyes sparkled, and he beamed his approval of her ideas.

Typically in England, the ladies would retire to another room as to not be bothered by such taxing topics, but her papa asked for them to remain. He refused to be bereft of their company, claiming time spent with his lovely daughter was good for his well-being.

As the evening grew long, Georgia felt herself sitting up a little straighter and adding in a comment or two without prompting. How easy it was to relax and enjoy being herself, respected for her mind and not as some beautiful trinket draped on a man's arm.

Even on a small island, political affairs crept into every aspect, affecting farming, trade, industry, and also teaching. She didn't know the people they spoke of, but Harrison's eyes darkened when certain names were mentioned, one of them being Mr. Rousseau.

At a lull in the conversation, Georgia mentioned their encounter with Mr. Rousseau and his invitation to a ball at the Artesian Hotel.

"Isn't that lovely?" she beamed at her father.

Her father glanced in Harrison's direction, and Georgia followed his gaze. Mr. Wells showed no physical reaction. His arm hung lazily over the back of the chair, and his eyes fixed on the lowball glass held in his fingertips. After downing the liquid and putting the glass on the table, his gaze met Georgia's. His light eyes had hardened to a stormy, dark umber.

"I believe a ball to be just the thing." Papa broke the chilled silence.

Mr. Wells arched a questioning brow in his direction.

"There have been some misunderstandings among the leaders of the community. A little dancing and mingling might relieve some of the tension."

Aunt Tessa perked up. "Oh, how I love parties. Fredrick, with your beautiful daughter present, you won't have a second to talk politics. You'll be too busy fending off all the beaus trying to get an introduction."

Mr. Wells raised an index finger, and the footman rushed over to refill his glass. Georgia thought she saw her father smile, but Aunt Tessa hailed her attention.

"Fredrick told me there's a dressmaker in town, Madame Leflore. I've already commissioned her to come here and take your measurements."

Georgia sat straighter. "There's a dressmaker on the island?"

"This isn't the dark continent," Harrison said with a smirk. "We have dressmakers. You won't have to go around in your privies."

She ignored his comment.

"Georgia," Aunt Tessa patted the table, "were you able to salvage any of your belongings?"

Georgia gasped and half rose, bumping into the table. The fine crystal shook and refracted the candlelight into shimmery waves. She groaned as she sat back down and put a hand to her forehead. "My gowns."

Harrison lurched upright. "The trunk is still in the wagon." His head whipped toward the window, despite the drawn shutters barring his view.

"Oh dear." Aunt Tessa exclaimed as the house shook from a gust of wind.

They were gone. Georgia knew it. All gone.

Harrison's eyes softened, "I'm sure they're fine. The groom brought the horses to the barn. Let's hope he carried the trunk to the barn also."

But she could hear the uncertainty in his words. The trunk was too heavy for one man to carry.

"I could go out..." A crack of thunder followed Harrison's statement.

Georgia shook her head. She couldn't ask that of him, not during such a treacherous storm. He was all Max had. She'd never be able to live with herself if a boy was orphaned due to her need for finer things. She now realized how stupid she'd been to wade out into the ocean to retrieve her trunks. Despite her arguments, she knew he was right. They were only material things. She'd never be able to wear them if she were dead.

She thought of Booker's mother, who would be laid to rest in her gown. At least one would be put to good use.

She sighed. "By tomorrow, all the little island boys will be running around in pink."

A smile stretched across Harrison's lips, and a low chuckle rumbled in his throat.

Georgia pinched her lips together to hide her own smile, which only made Harrison laugh again.

Her aunt cocked her head and blinked as if imagining the scene. "I've always considered blue a better hue for little boys, but why not pink? It is a light red, I guess."

The comment tugged harder at Georgia's restraint. She clapped a hand over her mouth and pretended to cough, but it morphed into a snort. She knew better than to display such emotion in public, and it took everything in her to regain her composure.

After the dishes had been taken away, it was decided that Max and Harrison would stay the night since the storm hadn't quieted. Within a few minutes, they'd worked out the new sleeping arrangements. Harrison, Max, and Papa would settle down in the gaming room. She and Aunt Tessa were set up in an adjoining sitting room. The servants carried in mattresses and readied them, then slumbered near the warmth of the stone hearth in the kitchen. Everyone settled down, and soon she heard the sounds of gentle snores and steady breathing, even through the raging gales and flashes of lighting outside.

Georgia was the only one awake. With blankets pulled up to her chin, she listened to the howling wind and the ocean waves crashing in the distance. Those sounds were becoming familiar, but it was the noise she heard when the wind hit a lull that disturbed her. Each time it occurred, a pit formed in the bottom of her stomach, and her heartbeat fluttered like a caged bird.

The hideous high-pitched squeaking noise split the night air. It sounded part-scream, part-childlike cry, but not human.

Her eyelids shot open, and a tremble ran the length of her body. She whispered, "Aunt Tessa?" but received no response. "Aunt Tessa." She whisper-shouted in her sternest voice, but to no avail.

Her aunt muttered something incoherent, then rolled over, taking the full length of the blankets with her. The damp night air hit Georgia's skin, raising goose pimples along her arms and legs.

The squeaking sounded again, this time from directly outside the window. Georgia slipped out of bed and fumbled to light a candle. It took, and soon the room filled with contrasting light and flickering shadows. Her eyes darted back and forth, searching the dark corners for any movement. She stretched out a hand and shook Aunt Tessa's shoulder, but kept her eyes probing the room. Her aunt swatted at her hand as if it were a bug, then released a loud snore.

Georgia eyed the wash basin on the dressing table but didn't dare wake her aunt with a good dousing.

The squeaking noise erupted again, followed by a crack of thunder. Georgia bolted from the room. In her perilous flight, she collided with something mid-waist, flipped over it, and landed sprawled out across a sofa.

A hand covered her mouth, muffling her scream.

CHAPTER 10

...The island is beautiful, but there are strange sounds that keep
us awake at night, not to mention the storms. The beastly
torrents come on suddenly. I'm told the fever does the same.
Please pray for Fredrick.

—*From Lady Tessa Pickering to her sister-in-law, Nora Lennox*

"Miss Georgia. Shhh." Max's face appeared next to
hers, his eyes wide. He removed his hand from
over her mouth and placed his finger to his lips. "Don't wake
Papa. He'll know the monsters are back."

Georgia sat up, trying to catch her breath. Her candle had
blown out during her fall, casting the room in eerie blackness.
She could feel a small bit of hot wax burning her hand and
hoped none of it had spilled on Jenneigh's Sunday dress. Max lit
a candle next to him and set it on the stand.

"If you're awake, then I can light a candle. Father says I'm not
to keep a candle lit while I'm in bed unless an adult is present."

Georgia nodded, unable to speak. She sucked in a deep
breath and willed the rhythm of her heart to slow its rapid pace.

A flash of lightning illuminated the room, followed by a peal of thunder. Georgia's heart jumped in her chest, and she lunged for Max at the same time he reached for her. She wrapped her arms around the boy, and he clung to her like a baby monkey to its mama. His small frame trembled in her arms.

"Max." She forced her voice to sound calm. "What monsters are back? Do they make that horrible squeaking noise?"

He snickered into her shoulder. "No, silly. The squeaks are the land pike. Hattie calls them squeaking lizards."

"Lizards?" She pushed him back and peered into his eyes. "How big are these lizards? Do they bite? Are they poisonous?" Her grip tightened on the boy's shoulders as she glanced about their feet, expecting one to crawl out and wrap its fangs around their ankles.

"No." He grinned. "They're harmless unless you're forced to eat one. Everyone says they're a delicacy, but I want to spit it out." He stuck out his tongue for emphasis. "Yuck."

"Why do they make that ghastly racket?"

He shrugged. "They just do. Every night, they crawl under rocks and hide in the bushes near the house, sniffing out food. They look like a fish but move like snakes with feet."

Georgia's stomach heaved.

"You sick, Miss Georgia?"

"I need a minute." Georgia waited until the urge to jump up and scream passed. Her father coughed in his sleep and let out a loud snore. The blankets were pulled up to his chin, and his glasses remained perched on his forehead.

A shadow shifted, and Georgia made out Mr. Wells' form. He lay on his side with his head resting on his arm. His tousled hair gave his angular features an even more rugged effect than usual. She imagined running her fingertips down the curve of his strong jaw.

Georgia immediately tore her eyes away. She shouldn't be looking at a man's sleeping form, and why would she even think of doing such a thing?

Another land pike let out a shrill squeal. Icy fingers crept down Georgia's spine, and she waited for her father or Mr. Wells to awaken, but neither of them stirred even the slightest bit. Obviously, they weren't disturbed by the disgusting squeaking creatures outside. Her fingers reached for a book on the end table. Maybe if she threw it at them, she'd gain their attention.

"Please, don't," whispered Max. His stricken face reminded her of Max's frantic remark about not waking Papa, because then he'd know the monsters were back.

"Max," she whispered. "Who are your monsters? They're not like my squeaky lizards?"

He shook his head. She watched his big eyes become overly bright, the flickering candlelight making them appear like glowing pools. His entire body stiffened, and he pulled his elbows in toward his middle. "No. They're big and dark...and they sneak around at night with their booming noises and flashes of light."

Max must be afraid of thunder and lightning, and for a good reason around these parts. She'd never seen a tempest rage like the one carrying on outside. "Do you get a lot of storms like this?"

Max nodded.

"What do you usually do when you feel scared?"

He raised his chin and puffed out his little chest. "I'm not scared. Papa says I'm a man now. Men don't get scared."

A flash of lightning illuminated the room with its eerie, blue light. Max tensed, and his breath held as they waited in silence for the subsequent crash of thunder. This time the rumble sounded distant. Max released his breath, and she felt him relax beside her.

"It sounds like it's moving out to sea," she said.

Max focused on her face. "Does that mean you're going back to bed?"

A wave of sleepiness washed over her, and she stifled a yawn. "Mmmm." She nodded.

"But the land pike are still out there. If you stay here, I can protect you…because…like Papa says, I'm a man now."

Her soft mattress was tempting, but it was also on the floor. How easy would it be for one of those land pike to crawl up next to her while she was asleep? The hair on her arms raised.

She regarded the small, frightened boy. "I believe I could use some protection." She grabbed an extra blanket folded on the side table and wrapped it around herself. Max watched her in silence until she lifted a corner, then he scooted underneath. Another land pike cried out through the lull in the storm. "Maybe you could tell me a story to take my mind off those creatures."

Max shot upright, glanced at his father and then at her. His voice was a whisper when he spoke. "Did you hear the story about the fierce Carib?"

Georgia let out another yawn and snuggled deeper under the blanket. "No. I haven't." Her voice sounded almost as drowsy as she felt. "Why don't you tell me that one … wait." She reached out and pulled Max back down. "Tell me, and try not to move too much."

Max lay back, warming her side. He stared up at the ceiling as he relayed the heroic story, but soon his voice began to trail off. Georgia let her heavy eyelids close, and soon sleep overtook her too.

~

Georgia's sandpaper tongue roved around her mouth, trying to work up some saliva. She lifted her arms above her head and arched her back as she did every morning, but today a jarring stiffness in her neck roused her fully in mere seconds.

Her eyes jerked open, and she stared at the plaster ceiling. Why did her body feel so strange? With a wince, she let her lids flutter closed again. Her hand raised to massage the back of her neck.

That's when she realized she'd slept in this seated position. Ignoring the pain, she lifted her head and reopened her eyes. A pair of snug-fitting cream breeches loomed in front of her.

Confused, her eyes drifted up to a broad chest covered in a loose cambric shirt with a dangling cravat around the pointed collars. Strong arms crossed in front of the muscular chest, and her gaze drew upward. Above a stubbled chin stretched the mocking half-smile with which Georgia was becoming all too familiar.

"Would you care for some tea?"

Mr. Wells' question confirmed her worst fear. He'd witnessed her sleeping with her mouth open.

Her throat felt like she'd munched on cotton. She nodded and looked around for Max, but he was already up, probably tending to that bird of his.

Mr. Wells passed her a cup, and she wrapped both hands around it. The warm liquid flowed over her parched lips and dry throat like a healing balm. She released a satisfied moan, and Mr. Wells' roguish smile grew.

"Rough night?"

She nodded, still not ready to use her voice.

"The storm keep you awake?"

"A little, along with a few other noises I'm unaccustomed to." She cleared her throat to cease the raspy tone.

A deep, throaty chuckle rumbled in his chest. "Don't worry. Everyone's scared of the land pike noises the first night. Nothing to be ashamed of."

She opened her mouth to deny it, but he raised a challenging eyebrow. She shut her mouth without comment, and he threw his head back and laughed. The infectious nature of it drew a reluctant smile out of Georgia.

Unfortunately, smiling reminded her how puffy her eyes were. She could barely see through their half-moon slits. She leaned forward and rubbed her face with her palms. A bad night's sleep was horrible for her complexion. She must look like a bag of potatoes.

But why worry about the way she looked? This was only Mr. Wells. It wasn't like he'd even qualify as a suitor. She pictured herself hoeing a field as the wife of an island schoolmaster/planter, then shook away the image.

He pivoted toward the door as his tanned fingers tied his cravat. She noted their fluid, graceful movement. Funny, he knew how to do it so well. Suddenly warm, Georgia averted her gaze.

"Due to the storm, the roads will be impassable, so your father will be holding Sunday service in the breakfast room. Better hurry or you'll be on the front row."

Was he poking fun at her again? She didn't stop to see, just rose and retreated upstairs.

After washing up and dressing, she sat front and center beside Aunt Tessa, the only seats left in their make-shift sanctuary. Harrison hadn't been funning her about the front row. Mr. Wells, Max, and several servants sat behind her.

Her father stood before a stack of sideways crates as a makeshift podium. He led them first through two hymns. She recognized both from attending Sunday services in London, but they never sounded the way they did today.

Hattie's voice rang out with a soulfulness that raised the fine hairs on Georgia's arms and misted her eyes. The woman sang with such feeling that it seemed like angels might burst through the roof and shine their light her way. Her father and Mr. Wells' baritone voices blended in with rudimentary harmonies, making the music that much sweeter. Georgia joined in quietly at first, the words hitting her like she'd never heard them before. Yes, she knew Jesus had died for her sins, but the song got her thinking.

Were her sins really washed away, all her bitterness, anger, and jealousy wiped clean by his blood? Would Jesus truly leave the other ninety-nine sheep to find her?

She tried to clamp onto the feeling even as the last notes faded.

Her father opened the well-worn pages of his Bible. It reminded her of the many times she'd crawled into his lap as he sat in his reading chair. He'd pause and peer down at her through his spectacles, then begin reading his book out loud for her benefit. She gave herself a mental shake. That was before he'd abandoned her. A mirage.

The warm timbre of his voice ran over her while he read the story of Joseph. When he finished, he closed his Bible with a thump. His eyes shimmered with passion as he walked around the makeshift podium. He perched his hip on the crate and let his leg dangle.

"I love the story of Joseph. The poor boy was thrown into slavery by his own brothers *and* later into jail on a false accusation." He paused, noting each of them. "Most of us would be angry, raving about injustice and wishing vengeance upon our brothers."

Georgia's heart agreed. She wanted to shake Joseph's brothers and scream, "It's not his fault he was their father's favorite." Instead, she held her tongue and glanced around to see if anyone else was equally outraged. The others were listening intently, even Max, but their faces didn't display the injustice that burned in Georgia's heart.

"We may blame God," Papa continued. "Or believe he's abandoned us, but Joseph didn't. He put aside his pride and need for vengeance, and God raised him up to be Pharaoh's right-hand man." Her father patted his Bible and leaned in toward them.

His voice lowered to just above a whisper. "You see, God doesn't waste a hurt. The Bible refers to God as the potter, and we are the clay. I love this metaphor because it reminds me that we are God's masterpiece. He is making us into something magnificent and functional. But if you have ever watched a potter, they have to guide the clay into shape, and sometimes they have to smush it back into a lump and start over. Sometimes, for God to rebuild us into his image, we too first have to be broken."

Georgia swallowed. Being broken sounded painful. How could God do that to His beloved children?

"God isn't as concerned about our comfort as much as he is about our character."

Georgia's pulse quickened, and she sucked in a breath.

Papa then prayed, thanking God for protecting them from the storm and praising Him in advance for what He was going to raise up from out of the rubble.

When the prayer ended, everyone moved the chairs, stacked the crates back in the kitchen, and settled in the parlor. Aunt Tessa cornered Hattie, and the two discussed possible menus for the week. Harrison sat in a chair and read a book. Max called out to Oscar, and to his delight, the bird landed on the window sill and started squawking.

Georgia searched for something to occupy her time and contemplated heading up to the solace of her room to pen a letter to Mama.

A finger tapped her shoulder, and she turned around. Papa held out a square board. "Care to join me in a game of chess?"

Her heart skipped out of rhythm. Play chess with her father? At one time, she would have twirled with joy at the invitation. But would the thrill of spending an hour basking in her papa's attention be worth the inevitable pain from losing him all over again?

Papa's imploring eyes held hers.

She hesitated, wanting to interact, yet afraid. Finally, "Yes." The word fell from her lips.

A broad smile crinkled the fine lines at the corners of his eyes, and with light steps, he ushered her over to the table. He pulled out her chair, and they sat across from each other. A gleeful chuckle sounded from his lips as he set out the pieces. He let her have the first move and observed her every facial expression as if memorizing them.

Georgia studied the board for the best positioning, then moved her knight to block his bishop. Her lips twitched in satisfaction.

"That's the same look a little, white-blond girl with missing front teeth used to give me years ago when she sat across from me just like this."

A smile found its way to her mouth, even as she tried to hold it back.

"You never did do anything halfway." He fingered a rook and examined the board. "When you played chess, you carefully considered each move. Sometimes strategizing five or six moves ahead." He shifted the rook into play.

Over the course of the next few moves, she took his pawn and then his knight.

His smile brightened until a cough rose up from deep inside him. He grunted and pounded his chest twice.

She frowned. "Are you ill?"

"It's nothing. Merely a cough." He positioned his bishop and confiscated her rook.

She swooped up his bishop.

"You used your rook as bait, and I fell for it." He laughed.

"I think you're out of practice." The old familiar teasing rose up inside her as she taunted him with a smile. "Will no one play with you on the island?"

"Ah, at last I gave up playing against Harrison. He made beating me look too easy. I have my pride you know." He winked at her. "Max will engage me in a chess match every now and then, but he gets antsy and is off to play something else before the game is through."

Georgia inspected the board and tapped her lips with her index finger.

"You look so much like your mother. Even sharing the same mannerisms. Nora tapped her lips when contemplating." He sighed. "I'm so grateful to God for the opportunity to spend time with you, Georgia."

A rattle sounded in his chest again. This time he pulled out a handkerchief and coughed into it. Then he cleared his throat. "This is a wonderful day, isn't it?"

Georgia glanced up from the board, his words striking a painful chord in her chest. Was it wonderful, reliving these special father-daughter memories? Need she remind him he was the one who left not her? These moments could have been every day.

Harrison peeked over the pages of his book, and Aunt Tessa stopped mid-sentence and turned his way. The room fell silent.

Her father waited for her response, his eyes more vulnerable than she'd ever seen them.

Georgia broke the quiet with a slow nod. "This is a good day." She couldn't seem to stop the way her heart swelled with compassion. Never had anyone seemed so delighted by her presence. Yet, the hurt of his desertion still lingered.

A smile crept over his face as he returned his gaze to the board. "God is a God of second chances. Here I am, sitting in front of my beloved daughter, whom I never thought I'd see again, and we're playing a game of chess like old times."

He moved his king across from her bishop.

Her queen swept in from the side, taking his king and putting his queen in check.

Fredrick chuckled, the laugh interspersed with a few coughs. "You neglected your queen."

He laughed even harder. "You know what?" he wiped the tears from the corners of his eyes. "Wellington needs to hire you as his advisor. If he'd had you, Napoleon would have been on his knees in half the time."

That drew an easy smile from her. She hadn't smiled often enough over the past few years, unless it was to gain Julien's attention. She missed the smiles and laughter that had flowed so easily between her and Papa when she was young. A warm wave of contentment settled in her midsection like a pelican ready to roost.

Her father's chuckle filled the air. "I'm so proud of my girl. I love you, princess."

Georgia's smile faded. How long had she ached to hear those words again? How many tears had she shed? How many ball-rooms had she entered with shaking knees. trying to make her mother and sisters proud, wishing Papa were there to encourage her, to dance with her? The illusion of what could have been dispelled in a poof. Years of painful hurt flooded into the vacancy. She shook her head and pushed her chair back. "I can't do this again. I will not love you and have you leave me all over."

Silence hung heavy in the room.

Fredrick held his hands up and kept his voice soft. "I'm not going to leave you. I've lived a life full of regret because of my mistakes. I won't do that to us again." Weariness shone on his face. "It will be your choice to leave me this time."

"You say that," her voice shook, "but how quickly you forget. You *are* going to leave." She fingered the material of Jenneigh's dress, wishing it were her pink chiffon gown, and swallowed around the lump in her throat. She raised her chin. "I'm not blind. I see what's coming. I'm going to love you all over again, and then you will die of the ague and leave me, and I'm going to have to grieve you once more."

"We're all going to die, Georgia."

She stood so quick that the table shook and several chess pieces fell over and rolled off the edge. She turned to leave, but he grabbed her hand. "There's nothing I can do to stop that, but I do know there's a time for everything, a time to be born and a time to die, a time to sow and a time to reap. My one regret is that I let fear rule me. Because of it, I didn't get to see you grow into a woman and be the father I should have been for you. I know I hurt you, and I'm sorry." His voice wavered. "I pray someday you'll forgive me."

Georgia's lips trembled, and tears welled in her eyes, but she shook her head. Her voice emerged in a half-croak, half-whisper. "I don't know if I can." She closed her eyes. "Please, don't ask that of me."

Georgia stumbled away, not caring about the disappointed look from Aunt Tessa or the disapproving scowl from Mr. Wells. Only when she reached the solace of her room, did she let the choking sobs loose.

She paced the length of the chamber with her hands balled into fists. Since the day her papa had left, a fortifying anger had fueled her. It allowed her to get up each day with a purpose. Her hatred of her father for leaving drove her to guard her heart against love. Jealousy for the attention her mother lavished on her sisters but not her, motivated Georgia to prove them wrong, to show she *was* good enough to be loved.

And she almost did it. If Mr. Wells hadn't intervened, she'd have made the match of the season with Lord Claremont.

Never would she allow herself to be hurt like that again.

She stopped her pacing and peered down at her fisted hands. Slowly she uncurled each finger until she faced two open, trembling palms. Her heart dropped, and uncertainty hit her with a wave of nausea. She pressed her palms to her stomach and sank into the nearby bed.

What happens if the anger that sustained me disappears?

CHAPTER 11

...Please send word of London and the latest happenings. I'm
desperate for information from home. Dare I ask about Lord
Claremont?

   —*From Georgia Lennox to her friend, Cynthia Orville*

*T*he following morning, Georgia dabbed a napkin at a
spot on her gown where she'd splashed tea. She lifted
the material to inspect it closer. "Please come off," she
murmured to the empty room.

When she'd opened her bedroom door this morning, there
lay her trunk, half filled with gowns. They were still wet, but
each had been wrung out and neatly folded. Most had rips or
water stains, but one bore only minimal damage. After Jenneigh
had pressed it with a hot iron, it was dry enough to wear, and
Jenneigh helped her dress.

The gown was still a bit damp, but she felt more like her old
self. She touched the heavy pink fabric. Once the sun was high
in the sky, she would surely overheat, but it was pink, and it was
hers.

A yawn escaped her lips, and she blinked down at her plate.

She hadn't slept well for the second night in a row. The sound of the land pike taunted her sleep. Their shrill cry sounded like laughter. Maybe they too had overheard the outrageous spectacle she'd made of herself during the game of chess.

She stabbed at a piece of ham. All the more reason to be on the next boat leaving for England, or Ireland, or even Spain. Surely, there would be a ship headed for Europe before the end of the week. She'd find a way to get the rest of the distance home.

Mr. Wells strolled into the breakfast room. A simple cream shirt encased his broad chest, and his sleeves were rolled, exposing tanned forearms. He paused when his eyes rested on her, and she could almost read the words running through his mind. *Can I avoid sitting with her? How could she refuse to forgive a dying man?*

Georgia dropped her gaze, and the seconds ticked by. He muttered a greeting and crossed to the sideboard.

She watched him through lowered lids while he filled his plate. He glanced back, and she quickly grabbed the cream, poured a dash into her tea, and stirred. Maybe he'd take what he needed and leave.

Chair legs screeched across the stone floor, followed by the clink of a china plate being plunked down on the table. No such luck.

Silence loomed between them until her curiosity got the best of her and she peeked over. As if he'd been waiting, Mr. Wells raised an eyebrow and motioned toward her dress.

"Some of the gowns were salvageable?"

She nodded.

"Good."

He swallowed a swig of black coffee and quiet settled again over the room. She racked her brain for words. Should she apologize for her outburst last night or pretend it never happened? Should she choose a mundane topic like the weather? Funny how she could hold hours of lively conversation with any prominent man in London, but here she couldn't maintain idle banter with a schoolmaster.

He rested his coffee cup on the table and turned his head to stare out the window. "After surveying the storm damage, I gathered your gowns up as best as I could. A few hung from the tops of palm branches, so I needed a ladder to get them down. Most were in poor condition, but perhaps Jenneigh can repair them?"

"*You* found my dresses?"

He popped a bit of egg into his mouth and replied with a single nod. She didn't know why she was surprised. The man had twice gone out of his way to retrieve her clothes.

She'd assumed it was the servants who'd gathered them and placed them outside her door, but apparently not. What was Harrison about? Had she misjudged the man? She eyed him skeptically. Did he want something from her? Why was he being so nice?

"Thank you." She swallowed and watched the cream slowly dissipate into her tea. "For … um … my gowns." She dared to peek up at him. "Is there a lot of damage to the house?"

He wiped his mouth with a napkin and shook his head. "No, we were fortunate. Let's pray the rest of the islanders had similar protection."

Leaning back in his chair, he stared at her with a strange, questioning expression. "Why pink?"

"Pink?" she parroted back to bide time. What should she tell him? How much should she reveal to a man she barely knew? Would she even be able to convey its importance adequately?

"Why do you always wear pink? And don't merely say it's a feminine color. Females wear other colors too."

Her sister, Ann's voice rang in her ears. *You're a hopeless case, but if you want to look like a girl, you'll want to wear pink. Pink is a feminine color.*

Georgia had stood before Ann in her muddy overalls, the sound of Papa slamming the door behind him still fresh in her ears. She shifted her feet awkwardly, never more aware of how tawdry she appeared in boys' garb. Not only did Ann appear beautiful, but self-assured. Everything Georgia wanted to be.

For she was not a boy.

Ann raised her chin with a confident smile and tossed Georgia a castoff gown slated to be handed down to her lady's maid.

The dress landed at Georgia's feet, and she bent to retrieve it. Her dirty fingers trembled as she reached out and pulled the dress toward her. She stroked the soft material.

Pink ...

Harrison's gaze measured her in cool silence, waiting for the answer to his query.

Georgia pinched her lips and crossed her arms over her chest.

"What makes a former tomboy wear only pink?"

Her mouth opened, but he held up a hand.

"Fredrick's stories of you always entailed a girl dressed in boy's overalls who spent her days hunting, catching frogs, and fishing for a whopper. What would make a girl like that completely turn the other direction and suddenly become the epitome of feminine wiles?"

Georgia stared at him, shocked by his audacity.

He leaned in, his eyes searching hers. "I need to know if there is a heart behind the ice princess façade you put on."

Anger flared, heating her already warm body and flushing her cheeks. "I don't have to justify myself to you."

She pushed back her chair to stand, but he placed a hand on her arm, waylaying her.

"I ask because the pieces don't fit. It would be easy to think you're an ambitious social climber, but that doesn't line up. Fredrick isn't a blindly devoted father. He sees the faults in his other children, but not in you. So, either you're a conniving actress attempting to capitalize on your father's inheritance ..."

She tried to yank her wrist from his grasp, but he squeezed tighter, stopping the blood flow to her hand.

"Or you've taken husband hunting to the extreme."

The man had taken leave of his senses. What was he talking about?

His eyes speared hers. "Is it an act?" he demanded through gritted teeth. "I want to believe you're capable of the good things Fredrick says about you, but you haven't shown me much."

"What I do is not your concern." She tilted her chin higher and peered down her nose at him.

"As Fredrick's close friend and business partner, I make it my concern."

"I don't have to report to you, nor to my father, for that matter. He lost that right when he left."

He leaned closer. "It's all about you. Is that it?"

"You wouldn't understand."

"Are his stories about you true? Did you follow him around like a shadow?"

"Yes," she hissed. "I dressed like a boy and acted like a boy. There, does that make you happy?"

"It does, yes." His gaze searched her features. "Then why the change? Why did you go to the other extreme?"

"Because I wasn't a boy, and no matter how hard I tried to impress my father, I could never be the son he'd always wanted."

"Did he tell you he wanted a son?"

She wavered. Had he, or did Mama put those thoughts in her head? A collection of memories flipped through her mind, but not one of them was Papa saying he wanted or even wished for a son.

"Fathers have it tough." Harrison's grip lessened on her hand, but he didn't let go. "There's no guidebook on how to properly raise a child. And I can imagine, it's especially difficult for a father of four girls. Fredrick told me having girls intimidated him. He was so afraid he'd break them that he often avoided his daughters, but you were different. You dogged his steps and persisted in getting his attention. So he did the only thing he knew to do. He taught you to do the things he'd enjoyed as a child—fishing and hunting."

Georgia struggled with the meaning behind his words. Had her father truly wanted her? Georgia, not George? Had he loved her all along? She shook her head. It couldn't be. "You can evaluate my circumstances all you want, but you were not there. You don't know my family or me."

"How can I, Ice Princess? You've built walls to keep everyone shut out. So much so that now you're suffocating in your own prison. You can't keep hiding behind pink dresses and a pretty face. You've got to let someone in." His voice softened. "Yesterday was the first time you let the real you take a peek over your walls."

"You don't know—" Her voice cut off, choked out by the worst possible thing that could happen to her at this moment— tears. She didn't want him to see how the pointed arrows of his words struck and hit center target. She studied the edge of the table to hide her emotions, and her vision blurred.

"You need to give your father a..."

A fat tear slipped from her eyes and landed on the fingers that held her wrist.

Harrison glanced at his hand. With his other, he tipped her face up to look at him.

"Blast." He released her wrist, and she turned her whole body away from him. He countered by sliding his chair around to face her.

She squeezed her eyes tight, as if doing so would stop the torrent of waterworks fighting for release. He sat there with his knees lightly brushing the outside of her legs. The slight touch unnerved her, and caused a strange coiling and uncoiling sensation within her stomach. What was he waiting for? Why wouldn't he leave her alone? The familiar rush of anger welled up, and she opened her eyes.

~

*R*elief flooded Harrison when he caught the glint of wrath behind Georgia's despair. Anger he could handle, but tears undid him. A smile tugged his mouth, and he softened his voice to a rolling purr. "There's my girl." The glimpse of angry hurt in her eyes made him think perhaps she wasn't an opportunist.

Georgia's haughty behavior must be a defense mechanism. He saw that now. She was protecting herself from pain. She must have suffered a deep loss when her father left. Harrison recognized it, because he'd built similar walls. "I'll give you credit. You've got fight in you. It's what's gotten you through, isn't it?"

She didn't respond.

"Anger can fuel you, but it won't ever fill you. When it's spent, you'll be left empty." He cradled the side of her face, using his thumb to wipe away the wet track of a fallen tear.

"You don't understand."

"I understand more than you know." He dropped his hand back into his lap. "My wife was murdered."

He paused when her lips parted with a delicate intake of breath.

The words had startled her, but he could tell from her expression that she already knew. His stomach soured, not toward Georgia, but at life in general. All that remained of his vibrant Laura was juicy gossip.

The dark cloud of memories threatened, but he forced himself to continue. Maybe his story could help Georgia. "I wanted revenge on the men who did it. I wanted them to die. They destroyed my life and terrified my son."

She gasped. "The night monsters."

He flinched. "Max told you about them?"

She nodded. "He thought I saw them too, the night of the storm."

Harrison closed his eyes. When would the nightmares stop? "Max had been standing at the window waiting for us to come home. He saw me wrestle with one of the men and heard the shot that killed his mother. Max remembers seeing the dark shadows moving and the loud noise. He's been afraid of thunder ever since." He paused, bracing against the pain that still gripped him.

"What happened to the men?"

Harrison paused. He didn't want to say too much and reveal his identity. Crime was frequent in a large city, but if she recognized the story, then he and Max would no longer be able to live a simple island life. "One died from consumption in Newgate. The other got away, despite the large sums of money I paid to investigators." A bitter laugh rang in his ears, and it took a second before he realized it was his own. "A killer goes about his normal life like nothing ever happened. Yet I walk around with a hole in my heart and constant reminders of my loss."

"Is that why you came here, to escape the memories?" Her blue eyes, no longer clouded with tears, held his own. Concern lined their depths, touching him in a way he didn't want to acknowledge.

"For the most part, yes."

She gently placed a hand over his. "I'm sorry."

Pain washed over him. How could he even consider returning to London, despite the King's summons?

"What was the other reason?"

"I was …" How could he make her understand without revealing who he was? "I used to have a desirable position, and some women were willing to go to great lengths for the security of marrying a man with such a"—he searched for a word —"stable occupation."

"What did you do in England?"

"I..." Harrison licked his lips. "I sort of managed a large estate."

Georgia nodded. "You were a steward?"

"Estate manager, steward, something along those lines." He pulled his hand away. "What I'm trying to say is that I know you've been hurt, but give your father a chance. If you let your walls down, you'll find out how deeply he loves you. Only don't wait too long." His throat tightened. "His days are numbered."

She nodded, but he tried to communicate the urgency with his eyes. "You haven't seen the full effect of the ague yet, but your father fell ill last night."

Her face paled, and he quickly interjected. "It's not your fault. Nothing you said or did caused his relapse. It comes and goes like a storm, but the sickness takes a toll. Don't be frightened when you see him. He'll come out of it. He's a strong man, and having you around has made him stronger. You'll see."

Her eyes widened into two blue orbs, but she nodded.

"I need to fix the damage done to the schoolhouse." His eyes locked on Georgia. "Would you be willing to keep an eye on Maxwell while I'm gone?"

⁓

*G*eorgia's lips parted in surprise. Mr. Wells' opinion of her must have changed over the course of their conversation. If he still believed her to be a conniving actress, he wouldn't leave his son in her care. Would he? Her heart warmed. She straightened, somehow feeling taller.

"Certainly."

"Watching Max isn't difficult. He's fairly self-sufficient. Just keep him safe and out of trouble. He's in the library entertaining Fredrick." He rose and strode to the door, holding it open. "Max?"

The boy bounded through, slid to a halt, and stood at attention. "Yes, Papa?"

"I want you to listen to Uncle Fred and Miss Georgia. Behave yourself." He raised both eyebrows, crinkling his forehead. "You hear me?"

"Yes, Papa." He raced back to the library.

Mr. Wells stood at the door for a moment, watching him. "He's a good boy. The most precious thing in the world to me."

He grabbed his jacket and hat and headed for the back door.

"Mr. Wells?" she called out, not knowing what she meant to say.

He paused, one hand on the knob, and turned back to look at her. "Call me Harrison."

Heat rose in her cheeks. "Harrison, I—um, well—thank you."

"Thank you." His eyes warmed, and the white of his teeth gleamed behind a slow smile. "*Georgia.*"

He left, the door clicking shut behind him, but the way he'd said her name seeped deep into her being. It had flowed over his lips as a half-whisper, as if it had reverence, as if *she* had worth.

Her fingertips tingled, and she re-folded them in her lap. Harrison may be a meager schoolmaster on a small island who irritated her more times than not, but by a mere word, he'd made her feel something she hadn't felt since she was a small girl in braids.

He'd made her feel valued.

She puzzled over it. How could she mean anything to him? He saw her the way most others did. What had he called her? Oh yes, an ambitious social climber.

She sighed. It was mostly true. What he didn't understand was that she needed to marry an earl to avoid betrothal to

Ashburnham, while still pleasing her mother and proving her value to her sisters.

Max's voice from the other room reminded her of her promise. She sipped her tea as doubts crept in. She didn't know how to entertain children. When her nieces and nephews visited their grandmama, the explosion of energy at their arrival and the ensuing chaos usually kept Georgia cloistered in her room until they left. She bit her bottom lip. What would she do with Max? Her mind drew a complete blank.

Had Harrison meant the entire day or merely the morning? She listened to the playful sounds emanating from the next room. Maybe he'd continue to entertain himself as he was right now.

But what if he didn't?

Things were different now. She'd earned Harrison's trust in some small way, but it was still fragile. From the beginning, he'd had such a bad impression of her, and caring for Max was the perfect opportunity to gain Harrison's approval. Which somehow seemed to matter now, much more than it had before.

She couldn't fail at this.

CHAPTER 12

…How I wish you could see the beauty of the island. Glorious colors surround us in bright shades of pink, chartreuse, and turquoise. We are faring well, even Fredrick, but the fever comes on suddenly.

—*From Lady Tessa Pickering to her sister-in-law, Nora Lennox*

"Georgia?"

She was still mulling over ways to entertain Max when Papa called from the other room.

His voice sounded so strained and unfamiliar that her cup slipped from her fingers and clattered on the saucer, sloshing the liquid over the sides. She moved to the door, but her hand froze on the painted wood and refused to budge. She didn't know what she'd find on the other side. She'd never seen her father in any condition other than healthy. In her eyes, he'd always be the robust man who'd taught her to bait a hook and hold a rifle. Her lips trembled at the image of him frail and gaunt.

She mustered her courage enough to push the door part-way open, and she found her father lying on the settee in the library.

Despite the insufferable heat, he lay wrapped in a quilt tucked under his chin. Max sat on the floor nearby, moving a wooden horse in a galloping motion across the rug and making clip-clop noises with his tongue.

"Yes, Papa? May I get you something?"

She inched closer. His entire body shook, even though sweat beaded his brow. She fought down the panic that expanded her chest and made her stomach queasy. Jenneigh said this was typical. Everything would be all right. *Lord, please don't let him die today.*

"Would you like some hot tea?" She hoped he didn't notice the quake in her voice.

"Hattie is bringing tea." He paused and closed his eyes as if regaining strength. How much effort had it taken him to say those few words?

She knelt beside him and put a hand on his arm. It felt clammy and cool to the touch. Just yesterday, he'd stood before her preaching, looking as healthy as a mule. Now, he seemed pale, feeble, and on the verge of death. She gulped down a breath. How quickly and completely the fever had ravaged his body.

His eyes opened, and she glimpsed the familiar twinkle, although weaker than before. "Don't worry so, my dear. It will pass. God still has plans for these old bones." He gestured for her to lean in, and she complied. "I don't want Max to see me like this. These relapses frighten..." He broke into a coughing fit.

Helplessness swept over her as Papa's body jerked with each racking cough.

Water. He needed water. She rose to her feet, but stopped mid-step as Hattie pushed through the door carrying a tea tray.

"Easy now, Mista Fred. Nice n' easy." She set the tray down and lifted a cup to his lips until he took a sip.

After a drink, he continued as if nothing happened. "And I

want Max to remember me as I am, not as some sickly, old man. Take the boy and make a fun day out of it. Just the two of you. It would mean a great deal to me."

Georgia turned to Hattie, unsure whether she should leave her father in his condition.

Hattie nodded toward the boy. "You two get now. I'll tek good care of yer papa. Don't you worry. Breakfast is ready. Have a bite, den be on yer way."

Georgia spurred Max into the breakfast room and placed a bowl of warm oatmeal in front of him. He grabbed a spoon and heaped it full of the light-colored mush.

She sat across from him and watched the boy gulp his food with disgusting sucking noises. Her muscles tensed at the sound. "It's bad manners to slurp down your food."

He issued her a sideways glare. "You sound like Papa."

Georgia peered out the window, all the while racking her brain for ideas of how to entertain a boy of eight years. She hated charades and would only use it as a last resort. She hadn't seen a pianoforte in the house so she couldn't play and have him sing. Besides, she only knew classical pieces. She heaved a sigh. Nothing else sprung to mind.

Max finished his bowl and leaned back in his chair, draping his arms over the sides.

"I don't need a nursemaid to watch over me. I'm a man now."

"That's good because I'm not a nursemaid, nor do I ever intend to become one."

Max delivered a single nod of his chin. "All right then. I'll let you play with me today. What are we going to do?"

Georgia tilted her head and frowned at the insolent child. "What is it you typically do around here?"

A wry smile grew on his lips. "Hunt for land pike."

Georgia swallowed. "Merciful heavens." She crossed her arms over her chest. "That's something you can do on your own time."

"Well, what can *we* do?"

What did boys do? They certainly didn't embroider or discuss the latest fashions. "How about I teach you the dance steps for the minuet?"

He wrinkled his nose in disgust.

"We can play cards," she suggested.

"Nah, I did that yesterday."

"Dress-up?"

He frowned. "I'm not a baby."

Georgia sighed. What did she do at Max's age?

She swallowed as a memory resurfaced of her father's encouraging voice as he taught her how to aim his rifle. It was so vivid, as if she were once again enfolded in his supporting arms. He'd tell her to breathe and say, *You can do all things, but remember, let God lead.*

Max put his elbows on the table and rested his cheeks on the palms of his hands. His blue eyes watched her—waiting.

She wasn't sure if Harrison would approve of her teaching Max to shoot, and she'd have to borrow a rifle.

She sat up with a bolt. "I've got it. Do you have fishing poles?"

Max's face lit. He leapt from his chair and raced toward the door. "I'll go grab them. You get some bread from Hattie." The door slammed shut behind him.

In under ten minutes, they began their trek down the sandy path toward the ocean. Georgia carefully picked her way around puddles, mindful of her boots and long skirts. The tall grass-like leaves of the sugar cane, along with the vast ocean in the background, gave the surrealistic impression that, somehow, she'd shrunk into a miniature version of herself. This must be how an ant felt next to a pond.

Max led the way with the fishing poles bouncing against his shoulder and a large wooden bucket banging against his leg. She followed a few steps behind, swinging a basket of goodies packed for them by Hattie in the crook of her arm. The sun peeked over the top of Mount Nevis, raising the temperature a degree or two.

"My favorite spot is down around this bend," Max said.

Perspiration trickled down the back of her neck. By the time they reached the shallows where the stormwater drained into the ocean, she could have wrung sweat out of the bodice of her gown.

The sun sparkled off the surface, refracting light in all directions, especially after the ocean breeze rippled the water. The bright aquamarine water still stirred awe in her chest. As they rounded a sand dune, what appeared to be a shallow lagoon actually dropped down quite deep. Colorful fish darted among the underwater plants. She scanned the shoreline, now dotted with debris washed up from the storm. Sea turtles dragged their heavy bodies onto the beach, slumping down to rest after battling the waves.

"Grab the bread, and we can use it to catch our bait." Max separated the poles and a small net as she pulled one of the loaves out of their picnic basket.

They both ripped off chunks. Max pierced his with his hook and dangled it into the water. Georgia stood on the bank, neatly folding her hands in front of her. But as she watched him pull out one minnow at a time, her fingers itched to have a try. Instead, she adjusted her bonnet and smoothed out her skirts. Max stood a couple of steps in front of her, his eyes peeled for any movement in the water.

"I can tell you've done quite a bit of fishing," she said.

"Papa and I are great fishermen. One time we caught a grouper this big." He held his arms as wide as they could go. "It was ugly as sin. Its bottom lip stuck out like this." He jutted out his lower jaw and pouted his lower lip.

Georgia smiled at the funny face. "It's nice that your papa fishes with you."

Max lifted an eyebrow and peered up at her. She'd seen his father make the same expression, and a chuckle welled up inside her.

"Aren't you going to fish too?"

She gazed into the water, then down at the length of her gown. Funny, but she'd never fished in a dress before. Dresses were much more cumbersome than a comfortable pair of men's breeches. But she'd have to manage.

Bending down, she removed her boots, rolled down her stockings, and tied her skirts up about her knees. Then she stepped into the clear tepid water and wriggled her toes. Her feet sank into the cool sand until only the tops showed.

"No, stop." Max held his head with his free hand. "What are you doing? You're going to scare the fish away."

"Just wait and trust me. My papa used to fish with me too."

"Truly? Uncle Fred?"

Her lips pressed into a brief frown at his familiar use of the word uncle. She pushed the negative thoughts aside. "Mr. Lennox," she corrected, "and yes, he did."

"He's never fished with me. Said his heart's not in it anymore."

"What did he mean by that?" She grabbed the bread and tore it into smaller pieces.

Max shrugged. "I don't know. Maybe he only liked fishing with you."

She froze, letting the words sink in. Fishing had always been a special past-time for the both of them. "Do you want me to show you a trick he taught me?"

Max nodded.

"Hand me that net."

Max passed it to her, and she waded out farther into the shallows. The colder water rushed over her feet and ankles, reviving her hot skin and drawing the coolness up her body like tree roots moistening its leaves. She crumbled bread pieces all around her and leaned over for a better look.

"When are you going to show me the trick?" he asked.

She stayed his questions with a hand. "Wait a second."

He let out a long sigh as she stared into the water, net in hand. The small waves drifted the bread pieces away. Maybe this was a bad idea. She'd only caught bait in a still lake.

But just as she was about to give up, they came out of hiding. Small brown spotted minnows swam up and poked at the pieces of bread. They nibbled at the bits and, on occasion, nipped her toes. With one sweep, she dredged the net across the water and trapped eight minnows. She held up her wiggling prizes and smiled. "See. Bait."

"Wow." Max exclaimed as she waded back. He pulled down on the net and peered in. "Now we can do some real fishing."

They picked up their things and walked to an outcropping of rocks that jutted into the ocean to form the edge of the lagoon. White, foamy waves curled over the boulders, while others pounded with fists, sending angry sprays of white water hurtling skyward.

Georgia and Max perched on a smooth, black boulder with their backs to the rough surf. After casting their lines, they sat and waited. It wasn't long before the first fish yanked on Max's line. Georgia straightened. The same thrill she'd experienced fishing as a child now filled her chest.

"You've got one." She pointed at the water.

Max pulled back slowly, reeling it in. The fish tugged on the line, yanking him forward a step. Georgia grabbed his shoulders to keep him from pitching into the ocean. Max screwed up his face with determination and pulled harder. A fin splashed out of the water.

"Here it comes. You've almost got it, Max."

He cranked the wooden handle. His small hand jerked back

every half turn. A beautiful fish breached the surface, its scales glistening in the sunlight.

She let out a low whistle. A bluefish as long as her arm dangled from the line. It had to be at least the same size as ol' Willy. "It's a beauty. Probably a ten pounder."

Max puffed out his chest and beamed at Georgia. As he unhooked the fish, Georgia filled the bucket with salt water. She then wrapped the fish in a burlap bag and dropped it in the bucket.

The rush of the catch swirled within her, probably almost as strong as Max felt. He once again readied his hook, and she saw herself as a girl, intent on hooking a whopper. A new fondness for the boy warmed her heart. They were very different people. Max was a young lad growing up on an island, and she was a grown woman who'd lived her entire life on the outskirts of London, yet they shared a common bond.

The vast ocean stretched out before them as they settled back down on the rock. Max hunched his shoulders, but his grip remained tight on the rod.

"This is lovely." Georgia tilted her face up to the sun. "I'm enjoying myself more than I thought I would." She issued him a side glance. "It must be the delightful company."

Max snorted out a giggle. "You're all right, too, Miss Georgia." He shrugged. "You know, for a girl."

She smiled, and a relaxed silence fell between them.

"You haven't had any more nightmares recently have you?" she asked.

"Nah, only the night of the storm."

"Do you miss her?" Georgia wiggled for a better position on the hard rock. "Your mama, I mean."

A loud whoosh of air passed through Max's lips. "I don't remember her. I know her face from the miniature portrait in my room. When I think of her, I get a nice warm feeling right here." He pointed at his midsection. "I guess I miss her, but it's different." He frowned. "My heart sort of hurts when I see other kids with their mamas getting hugs and kisses."

The tug on Georgia's heart almost caused her to miss the tug on her line. She reeled it in, and their attention temporarily diverted to the fish. It was too small, so she threw the sun fish back.

Max settled back on the rock. "Papa says there was a big hole in his heart from when he lost Mama, but God came into the hole and filled it with himself." His eyes met hers. "God filled my hole too. I asked Him to come into my heart."

A hole had opened in her own heart when her father left. It ached...oh, how it ached. Nellie, their beloved housekeeper, had held her whenever the tears came. In those moments of weakness, Nellie would whisper in her ear that she was loved and precious. She wanted to believe the words, but an echo in her mind always questioned, *if he loved you, why did he leave?*

Eventually, she relocated to London for her debut and left Nellie behind at their country house. She'd tried to fill the ache by reinventing herself into the perfect woman, the kind her mama expected her to be, but the pain persisted, even now.

Perhaps she should have brought Nellie along to London. She'd rejected the kind woman's comfort and instead stewed in her bitterness. Had she done the same with God? Did she push Him away too, when He could have helped fill her emptiness?

"I'm going to see Mama in heaven and spend all eternity with her." He peered up at Georgia with raised eyebrows. "That's a long, long time, you know. She'll have enough time to catch up on all the missed hugs and kisses then."

The urge to wrap her arms around the boy almost suffocated her. He'd probably think a hug from a girl was yucky and push her away, so instead, she tightened her grip on the pole.

The two of them fished for several more hours, stopping only to enjoy their picnic. All in all, they reeled in a couple of yellowtail snapper, one small grouper, and an even bigger bluefish. She guessed the second one to be about sixteen pounds.

They headed back to the house, weaving their way back up the path. Each had one hand on the handle of the overloaded bucket, and they often paused to catch their breath. Halfway there, the handle tugged against her fingers, and Georgia glanced back at Max, who had stopped.

He stared into the field. "Shhh." He waved her over with his hand and whispered, "Come closer and be quiet."

She put down the bucket and tiptoed behind him.

"Look there." He pointed to the seagrass. "It's a land pike."

Georgia followed his finger to the thing as it writhed back into the shadows. Its tiny lizard legs flipped a long wide tail behind it. She let out a half-stifled scream and jumped away from the creature. Max slapped his knee and laughed, so wild and free that Georgia had to force back her own mirth.

"You should see your face." He pointed and burst into another fit. "You're so scared of them."

She feigned an annoyed look, then picked up her side of the handle. "Come on. We need to get these back so Hattie can fry them up for dinner."

Max smothered his giggles, picked up the other side, and they started back home.

Hattie stood in the yard hanging the freshly washed sheets out to dry. She spied them and waved.

Max and Georgia picked up their pace, spilling water over the sides of the bucket. They were both out of breath when they reached the house.

"Hattie, Hattie," Max cried. "We caught supper."

Hattie peered into the bucket. "Ooooh, dat you did, child, dat you did. We be having filet of fish tonight."

Georgia met Hattie's eyes. "How's Papa? Any change?"

"He's much better. Dis one passed by real quick. Praise God. He's weak but up and eatin' broth in the kitchen."

"Is Papa here yet?" Max asked.

Hattie beamed a broad white smile and ruffled the child's hair.

"He be dat. He be in da kitchen, sit'n with Mista Fred."

Max pulled on the bucket. "Come on, Miss Georgia. Let's show 'em our whoppers."

Despite the warm weather, Papa sat wrapped in a thick dressing robe, sipping on a spoonful of soup near the hearth. He looked up at them as they entered. Dark smudges underlined his eyes, and his hand shook as he lowered the spoon. He appeared frail and worn out, but his face lit up as they approached. "What have we here?"

Max released his end of the bucket, and Georgia maneuvered so that the water didn't slosh over the sides.

"Uncle Fred, you wouldn't believe it, but I caught a snapper and a bluefish this big." He held his hands out wide, noticeably further than the actual size of the fish she remembered him catching, but she didn't correct him.

In his excitement, Max's words ran over each other, and he barely stopped to take a breath. "Georgia caught an even bigger bluefish and a grouper, but he was small, so we threw him back. She taught me a new trick on how to lure in a lot of bait all at once. You stand in the water, float breadcrumbs all around, wait for the minnows to come"—he swooped his hand through the air—"then slam your net into the water. She's not a bad fisherman." He scrunched up his face. "Being a girl and all."

The men chuckled, and Georgia pursed her lips against a smile.

Max continued. "We caught a total of six fish. Some of 'em we threw back, but Hattie's gonna cook up the rest for supper."

Harrison smiled and ruffled his son's hair.

"Well done, my boy." Her father patted Max's shoulder. "We're celebrating this great catch."

Max held up each fish one by one and beamed with pride.

Georgia, not wanting to intrude on their special moment, stood a few paces back as her father interacted with the boy. Jealousy licked at her, but she kept her smile steady. Max was a good kid and deserved the praise. Why then did her heart hurt? Irrational anger soured her stomach, and she turned toward the door, not wanting to spoil Max's fun.

"Georgia," her father said. "This one reminds me of ol' Willy.'"

Georgia stopped and turned around.

"I wish we'd caught that old beastie. He probably weighs three stones by now."

"I caught Willy." She murmured down to her hands and picked invisible lint off her gown.

"You what now?" Her father twisted in his chair to face her.

Georgia shrugged and peeked up. "I caught Willy the day you left. I brought it in to show you, but you and Mama were fighting."

He stared at her, mouth agape, for a long moment. Finally, in a somber whisper, he said, "I didn't know."

Georgia felt Harrison's gaze on her. She blinked away the tears burning the backs of her eyes, but couldn't look either him or papa in the eye. Not when she was so vulnerable—so exposed. "I tried to have Nellie throw him back, but he'd been out of the water too long. It was too late for Willy, too late to make things go back the way they were."

Sorrow and regret etched frown-lines on Papa's face. A quietness settled over the room. Even Max stayed still. Only his eyes shifted between Georgia and Fredrick.

Finally, her father broke the silence. "I didn't want to leave. Your mama couldn't forgive me, and I couldn't stop loving her."

Harrison sat frozen in his chair, studying her.

Georgia's jaw tightened.

Papa quickly added, "It's not your mama's fault either." He shook his head. "We were both foolish. We should have tried harder. I loved your mother. There was never anyone else. I wish I could have gotten her to understand that. I still love her and probably always will." He frowned down at his hands and let out a sigh. "I wish things had been different."

Georgia swallowed and nodded. "I know that now." She cast a glance at Max and thought of him getting all those kisses and hugs in heaven from his mom. Time was precious. She didn't want to lose another moment with her father.

Her gaze pivoted to Harrison, who gave a gentle nod of encouragement. She sucked in a fortifying breath, walked over to her father, and looked him in the eyes. "I know you didn't want to leave. It hurt to miss you so badly, so I blamed you. Please, forgive me." Georgia put her warm hand over his cold one. "I love you."

Tears reddened his eyes, and his voice broke. "I love you too. I always have. You'll always be my princess."

He placed his other hand on top of hers, and she smiled at him through a haze of tears.

"Let's celebrate." Papa grinned. "Max, go tell Hattie to fix us the greatest meal ever. We're celebrating your fish and Georgia catching ol' Willy."

CHAPTER 13

…Viscount Ashburnham has grown our concerns for the welfare of our grandson, Maxwell. My wife and I request a summons for his return to England so we may ensure his good health with our own eyes.

—*From Lord and Lady Chadwick to the Prince Regent, George IV*

*L*aughter sounded throughout the Lennox cottage as they enjoyed the feast Hattie created. Harrison lounged in his chair, enjoying the banter as Fredrick, Max, and Georgia swapped fishing stories—some about catches and others about taking unexpected swims.

Georgia's bright eyes drew him in as she proudly reenacted how Max had reeled in his biggest fish. Max giggled at her theatrics. A bond seemed to have grown between Georgia and his son. Not once did she accept any of the praise.

Instead, this chit he'd deemed as self-absorbed turned all the attention upon Max and required none for herself. Maybe he misjudged her, but there was no doubt that jealousy had darkened her eyes whenever Fredrick had paid Max attention before. It seemed maybe something had changed today.

Harrison sipped his drink. Georgia laughed at a comment Fredrick made to Max, and Harrison's breath hitched. Her smile accentuated the unique sensual tilt to her eyes. His gaze drifted over her rosebud lips and the straight white teeth they showcased. But it was more than that. There was a natural ease to her, a comfortable grace in her laughter, when she allowed herself the pleasure of mirth. This was a side of Georgia he wanted to see more.

Lady Pickering leaned toward Harrison. "Georgia is a beautiful woman, is she not?"

Harrison cleared his throat and put his glass down. "Outer beauty isn't everything."

"You are right." Lady Pickering folded her hands neatly in front of her. "Georgia is beautiful naturally, but look at the life in her eyes. She's absolutely stunning when she lets her guard down and reveals her true self."

Harrison acknowledged her with the barest of nods, unable to tear his eyes away as Georgia smiled at something Max did. Max repeated the motion, and she giggled. One slender hand shifted to hold her stomach. Her laughter flipped something in his gut, drawing him into a spell.

"You are very fortunate, indeed," Lady Pickering whispered. "Very few people get to see her this way."

The spell broke as he remembered the flirtatious way in which she'd enamored Rousseau. "Because she's usually busy using her feminine charms to turn grown men into lapdogs?"

The woman sighed and preened the ruffles on her sleeves. "I expected you to see past that."

Harrison straightened at the censorious tone of Lady Pickering's voice, and he turned his full attention toward the birdlike woman.

She drew herself up, shoulders back. "Georgia is misunderstood. She keeps up this pretense to protect a very soft heart."

Harrison's brows drew together. "I find it hard to believe the woman who scorned my help after I pulled her out of the ocean, would have a softer side."

Lady Pickering stared him straight in the eye. "You're correct, but it wasn't always so."

Her expression was so serious that Harrison fought the urge to laugh.

"Georgia has placed walls around her heart because so many people have wounded it."

"I know her father left her," Harrison said, "but she has to understand that he believed it was for her own good."

Her eyes narrowed. "She doesn't have to do any such thing. I love my brother, but he didn't understand the damage his leaving would incur. If he had, he wouldn't have left. He thought his disappearance would bring peace to the household. But it left a very vulnerable Georgia alone to defend herself against an overbearing mother and three spiteful sisters."

Harrison drew back at her vehemence.

Her voice softened. "I don't mean to speak ill of family, but Nora never understood a free-spirit like Georgia. The only way Nora knew how to keep her life from falling apart was to take control. If only she'd given things to God and let Him handle it." She sighed. "But sometimes we have to learn things the hard way, don't we?"

"Indeed," Harrison said, though her question was rhetorical.

"Nora was a perfectionist who treated her first three girls like dolls, and each became little replicas of their mother. But, to her dismay, Georgia was a tomboy. She tried and tried to get Georgia to behave, but couldn't. Then to make things worse, rumors began to spread about Fredrick and another woman. Georgia became a daily reminder of Nora's ineptness. Nora's world shattered, and in order to keep what little control she could still exert on her life, she handed Georgia to a nanny and focused her attention on her older girls. Fredrick saw the injustice done Georgia but, God bless him, hadn't the slightest clue how to raise a girl."

Harrison's gaze fell on Fredrick. Harrison, too, wouldn't have the slightest clue how to raise a daughter, but he gave Fredrick credit for trying.

"Fredrick lent his best efforts, and Georgia thought the sun and moon revolved around her papa. She became his shadow, trailing him as he ran the estate, joining him in fishing expeditions, and loading his gun when he hunted. He tried to make up for the lack of her mother's attention, but in some ways, he made the situation worse. Georgia started emulating her father by dressing like a boy, which Nora interpreted as Fredrick lashing out at her for not producing a male heir."

"She certainly doesn't dress like a boy now, so she must have reconciled with her mother."

"Not exactly. When Fredrick left, something snapped inside Georgia. I don't know whether she changed out of spite for his leaving or in an attempt at self-preservation, but she suddenly started dressing like a girl."

"And pink because it's a feminine color."

"Quite so. Her sister, Ann, put that in her head, and Georgia took it to heart. If you could only have seen her before, it would help you appreciate the lengths Georgia has taken. She worked incredibly hard to be accepted by the *le bon ton* and master the fashionable set, down to her walk, her smiles, flirtations, and how to hide her intelligence behind meaningless banter. Her outer beauty also helped polite society overlook her disastrous first season."

"What happened her first season?"

Lady Pickering's thin brows arched. "She was sent out into society like a lamb to the slaughter. Her free spirit was crushed within a fortnight. Georgia was different and polite society isn't accepting of different. Most ladies would have hidden and taken up residence in the country, but not Georgia, she adapted."

"Did her transformation help her relationship with her mother?"

"Yes and no. Now that Georgia dressed as a woman, her mama paid her some attention, but Nora still favored her other girls. Georgia ate up the attention like a starved animal. It became her driving force. She thought if she could out-do her sisters, she could earn her mother's love."

"And to do that she needed to marry well." A muscle in his jaw tensed. "So she sought the attention of the Earl of Claremont."

"Yes, but from your expression, I can see you mirror the same dislike of the man that I feel." She placed a hand over Harrison's. "In my opinion, she began to rely too much on her appearance, and it attracted the wrong sort of gentleman like Claremont. But he's a far improvement from the Viscount of Ashburnham."

"Ashburnham." Harrison spit the man's name like a curse. Ashburnham was the reason the King had summoned Harrison and Max back to London. The unscrupulous wretch was attempting to lay hands on his title and land by spreading rumors of Harrison's demise.

"Nora believes the viscount may inherit a Dukedom and hopes to make an advantageous match by marrying her last daughter off." Lady Pickering slowly shook her head. "You can understand why I jumped at the chance to come here, because I knew it would remove Georgia from her current situation. I'm not certain I've thanked you properly."

She watched her niece, and Harrison followed her gaze. "Don't mention it," he mumbled. His image of a pretentious, fickle socialite merged with the vulnerable woman he'd witnessed today, and the insecure tomboy Lady Pickering described, struggling for scraps of love from her mother.

As if she felt his gaze upon her, Georgia looked up and caught his eye. Their gazes held. Her smile started to fade, so he held up his glass in salute and flashed her a broad grin. Her brows drew together in a puzzled expression before she resumed conversing with her father.

Harrison chuckled. Why did he delight so much in keeping her flustered? If Georgia truly was as her aunt described, he might enjoy discovering the woman underneath the protective façade of pink.

CHAPTER 14

...It appears Lord Claremont's affection for Miss Lennox has waned in her absence. He has reportedly been seen in the company of several ladies, including Miss Cynthia Orville, a close acquaintance of Miss Lennox. It appears Miss Orville has set her cap for the earl.

—*Authored by the Lady L. gossip columnist and featured in The Morning Post*

*G*eorgia's lips pressed together and her nose wrinkled as she peered into the small hand mirror. A light dusting of freckles had sprung up across the bridge of her nose. She scowled at them as if it were possible to frighten them away.

They didn't budge.

With a resigned sigh, she placed the mirror back on her dressing table. She could imagine Max's taunting if she told him she could no longer fish because it was ruining her complexion. A boy wouldn't understand.

She untied her extra wide brim bonnet and tossed it on the bed. Today they'd had a decent catch—a couple of bluefish and a grouper. It had become a daily routine for Max and her to sneak in some early morning fishing before he headed off to school with his father.

Their fishing expeditions had become the highlight of her day. As they waited for the big one to bite, they took turns imagining what they would do if they caught a shark or a gigantic whale, weaving maritime adventure tales to pass the time.

She was surprised how much she enjoyed Max's company. For the first time in a long while, she was able to let her guard down and be herself. When it was the two of them, she didn't have to hold herself so upright. She didn't have to force a demure smile or tilt her head just so. No longer being under her mother's watchful eyes and her sisters' judgmental glances allowed her to relax and be herself.

She picked up her writing pen for the third time that morning. Her hand hovered over the paper until the ink threatened to drip. She should write her mother and sisters, but try as she might, she couldn't decide what to say.

Island life is delightful. Everyone begs for my attention, and I'll be attending a ball this weekend. It's to be a grand affair.

She frowned at the paper.

I've taken back up fishing, and you should see the twenty-pounder I caught from the shoreline.

Georgia smiled at the thought of her mother's face if she posted the latter.

After dropping the pen back into the inkwell, Georgia pushed away from her writing desk. She scooped up her bonnet and pink parasol on her way out of her room. At the parlor door, she paused.

Her father didn't notice her as he sat with the overseer discussing the sugar crop. Papa rubbed his chin, deep in thought regarding some question posed. She didn't want to bother him, so she turned and hunted for her aunt.

She found her enjoying the ocean breeze from a rocking chair on the porch with a round-faced gentleman. The man appeared to be around the same age as Aunt Tessa and spoke with an Irish-lilt as they rocked in complete synchronicity.

Aunt Tessa looked up from her embroidery as Georgia approached. "Georgia. This is Mr. Evan Clark, the local vicar."

Mr. Clark removed his hat and started to rise.

"No need." Georgia waved for him to keep his seat. "I don't mean to interrupt. I'm going for a stroll. Would you care to join me?"

"You go along, dear. I'm enjoying Mr. Clark's company and I'm determined to finish this tricky stitch. I was hoping to embellish some of the new gowns your father ordered with a bit of decorative lace, but there isn't much time. Don't forget, Madame Lefleur is coming this afternoon for a fitting. We are so blessed she was able to accommodate us with such short notice."

Georgia waved as she strolled down the drive. The sand and dirt felt smooth through the soles of her shoes. In London, it would have been improper to go anywhere without a lady's maid or companion trailing behind her. She was always under constant observation and inspection. Raising her arms above her head, she relished an unladylike stretch without anyone seeing. Island life did have a few perks.

A light breeze pushed back the thick humid air and ruffled the pink hem of her skirt. All of her delicate fabrics had been destroyed by either the ocean or the storm, but thankfully, Jenneigh had repaired a couple of her sturdier gowns—a light pink cotton walking dress with short sleeves that didn't over-heat her and a thicker mauve fustian dress.

An avian chorus twittered and chattered in the canopy of trees above her. Rich green thickets covered the ground below, littered with pops of colorful blooms. Tiny brown geckos scurried up the trunks of gnarly trees. As she rounded a bend, the verdant green of the sugar cane undulated in the wind, rising and falling like the tide. In some areas, the cane even towered above her. A low, sweet moan filled her ears, along with a cadenced whacking noise.

At a break in the thick cane, dark ragged men with large crescent-shaped machetes attacked the cane in rhythm. Women in bright dresses stood behind them, gathering the felled stalks into bundles. Their voices joined in a soulful harmony.

A few stopped and stared as she passed, but most continued their work. Georgia fell into step with the workers' tempo, and she lost herself in the untamed beauty of the island. Though she couldn't make out the words, she sang along with the catchy melody, making up her own lyrics.

Rumbling wheels sounded behind her, and she jolted out of her reverie. She turned to see a familiar wagon approaching.

"Miss Georgia," Max called.

A smile tugged her face and she waved at her friend. As the horses slowed to a stop, her gaze drifted to Harrison, dressed in fawn buckskins, a white muslin shirt, and a camel-colored waistcoat. All well-made, though a bit worn.

His strong hands grasped the reins with commanded control. As he stood and rested a booted foot on the wagon's sideboard, his posture exhibited a subtle regality. He'd surely rubbed elbows with nobility. She'd swear on it from the quiet, confident manner with which he held himself, the surety of his self-worth. His caramel eyes found hers, and he raised a mocking eyebrow.

"Miss Lennox, you've become a native."

Make that a pompous, boorish manner. Heat rose in her cheeks. He must have overheard her singing. "Hardly."

Max hung over the side of the wagon. "Come to school with us."

Georgia shook her head. She and children didn't mix well. Except for Max. With him it was different.

"Come on. Please. Papa could use the help—"

"I don't think Miss Lennox would be—" Harrison folded his arms.

"We're teaching them to read." Max tilted his head. "You can read, can't you?"

Georgia couldn't help but smile at the lad. "Of course, I can read."

"Well, all right then. Hop in."

Georgia stood frozen, staring into the boy's pleading brown eyes. She couldn't say no, but she didn't want to say yes. Harrison's brow held a skeptical crease, but he slowly unfolded his arms and offered to assist her up. Her hand, as if of its own will, slid into his. He pulled her up next to him on the bench seat. "The schoolchildren don't bite."

Menacing lout.

He smiled as he snapped the reins.

She glared at him, wondering if he could read her thoughts. Had she gone mad? Why would she accept an offer to spend an entire day with this frustrating man and a pack of wild children?

She continued to chastise herself as Max babbled on about fishing during the rest of the ride.

"Here we are." Harrison reined in the horses next to a one-room stone building. It had a thatched roof and large shuttered windows.

After settling the horses, they all stepped into the school. As Max and Harrison opened the shutters to let in the light, Georgia surveyed the bare room with crude benches for seats and a single wooden podium stationed at the front.

"It's not much, but we make do." Harrison dusted off his hands, then glanced up. "Here come some of the children now."

A fair-haired boy walked in with a smaller version of himself in tow. Georgia guessed the older boy to be about twelve and the younger to be six. The younger seated himself on the front row and the elder in the row behind him. More children filed in until there were nine in all, plus Max. Four girls and six boys.

"All right, class, let's get settled. I'd like you all to welcome Miss Lennox, who graciously joined us today."

Georgia fought the urge to fidget, nervous with all those little eyes honed in on her as they chorused, "Good morning, Miss Lennox."

"Who would like to lead us in prayer?"

Hands shot up all around the room. "Thomas." Harrison pointed at a small dark-haired boy sitting next to Max. "Let's bow our heads and pray."

The boy folded his hands, rested his forehead on top, and squeezed his eyes shut. "Dear Heavenly Father, thank you for this day and for our teacher Mr. Wells and for our guest Miss Len…" He opened one eye and peeked up at Harrison.

"Miss Lennox."

"Yes, Miss Lennox. Lord, help us to learn and be smart and more like Jesus. Bless our friends who aren't here today. Protect our parents while they work…"

Georgia listened to the child's heartfelt prayer. Did everyone here pray to God like He was in the room with them? Where were all the *doths* and *thous*? Could a person simply talk to God?

"And Lord, please, please let the sugar grow. In Jesus' name we pray, amen."

They all raised their heads, and Harrison said, "Well done, Thomas."

Next, they recited the Lord's Prayer from their shared hornbooks. The class all sat perfectly still in their seats, doing as Mr. Wells instructed them. Georgia couldn't imagine her rambunctious nephews and nieces sitting so. She remembered her sister complaining about how their tutors frequently quit without giving notice. Maybe these children were different. All she could do was hope.

"Alexandra, please read," Harrison instructed.

"In Adam's fall. We sinned all."

"Very good," Harrison said. "Now, William."

A thin boy who'd been staring out the window stiffened and turned his attention back to the primer. "Thy life to mend. This book attend."

Harrison surprised Georgia by not commenting on the boy's inattentiveness. He let the words the boy needed to read get the point across in a way that wouldn't humiliate the child.

"Good. Henry, your turn."

After finishing the reader, the children broke into smaller groups. Harrison sat among one group, challenging the older children with harder material. Georgia worked with the younger ones, aiding them with pointers on how to sound out the words the same way her governess had shown her.

After Mary sounded out "Sat-ur-day," she stole a glance up at Georgia with a shy smile and a sparkle of triumph in her eyes. Something blossomed in Georgia's chest, and she wanted to clap her hands with joy.

"Wonderful, Mary. Keep reading."

Who knew helping children learn to read could be so satisfying?

A sneeze sounded outside the doorway. Georgia glanced through the opening and caught sight of Booker sitting against the outer wall listening in. As Mary continued to read, Georgia scooted her bench a little closer to the door, and a little closer, and a little closer, until she was partially in the doorway. She held the book so that all the children could see, including Booker, despite being separated from the other children by a wall. Out of the corner of her eye, she caught him mouthing the words as the other children read, and a couple of times he even mouthed the words beforehand.

After lunch, they conducted the class outdoors. Georgia meandered to the edge of the gathered children, peeking around the corners of the schoolhouse for Booker. She wanted to ask him how his mother fared.

"Booker comes here while his grandma washes clothes." Harrison walked toward her. "But he must return home for chores before his master notices his absence."

Harrison called the children to gather around. They kneeled together in a small circle for a game that involved addition and subtraction, moving flat stones in and out of small cup-like holes dug in the ground.

Georgia opened her parasol and stood behind them in the rose-colored shade. The children divided into teams—boys versus girls. Max scooped up a bunch of the rocks, and the boys cheered, but if her math was right, he missed a play that would have added three more points.

Harrison patted him on the back, then squinted up at Georgia. The sun turned his eyes a warm brown and drew auburn highlights out of the thick waves of his dark hair.

Maybe a little sun could be good for the soul. But that thought went against everything her mother had preached.

"You should join us." Harrison's deep voice rumbled just loud enough to be heard over the children.

She straightened. "I think not."

But the way he continued to peer up at her made her want to hide deeper under her parasol for protection. "Ladies don't crawl around in the dirt."

"It's fun." He shrugged out of his jacket and laid it to cover the ground next to him. He waved her down. "Come on. You'll be sorry you missed it."

Mary scooped up the next round of rocks but couldn't beat Max's score.

"He's on a roll." Harrison twisted to glance at Georgia. "Someone needs to beat him, or you'll have to listen to him brag about how boys are smarter when you're fishing tomorrow."

Georgia chewed the inside of her lip. No, she wouldn't

demean herself. But on the other hand, she didn't relish hearing Max boast. For only eight, he could certainly be a braggart, and his Papa merely encouraged him.

Max picked up another three points. He raised his hands in triumph and scanned the faces to ensure everyone noticed.

Maybe the child needed to be put in his place.

"Oh, fine, scoot over." She snapped her parasol shut and squeezed in between Harrison and Mary. Her arm tingled where Harrison's shoulder brushed against hers. But instead of scooting away, she found herself enjoying his touch, maybe even slightly leaning into him. His tanned fingers splayed within inches of her own, and she imagined how warm they would feel placed over hers.

Max gained two more points, breaking Georgia out of her reverie. She whispered to Mary, who then snatched up three points before Max could grab them. As the score evened, the children's voices rose in excitement until they were shouting over one another. When it was Georgia's turn, she quickly did the figures in her head, then dove for the cup filled with five stones before Max could. He reached for it at the same time, but instead of grabbing rocks, he caught her hand and yanked her into the dirt.

His face blanched, but Georgia laughed and held up the five stones triumphantly. All the girls shot to their feet, jumping up and down and screaming. The boys demanded a rematch, but Harrison shooed them off with the promise of playing again tomorrow.

As the school day ended, Max played outside with the other children. Georgia helped straighten the benches in the schoolroom, and more than once, the weight of Harrison's gaze landed on her. But each time she met his look, he'd turn away and continue working.

What did it mean?

~

*H*arrison scanned the schoolhouse one last time from the doorway. All looked as it should, so he closed the door and turned to the wagon. Max waved goodbye to his playmates and climbed into the back of the conveyance, while Harrison assisted Georgia into her seat, then took his place behind the reins. As they bumped down the lane, he glanced at Georgia. The once prim princess looked nothing of the sort in her soiled dress, complete with a rip in the sleeve from Max's hasty grab for the game stones.

"I'm sorry about your gown."

She stared down at the brown smudges on the pink material. "It appears another dress has succumbed to the island." She sighed and picked at the dirt under her fingernails.

The wooden seat creaked as they rumbled over a pothole. She murmured something indistinguishable amidst the noise.

"I beg your pardon?"

"It was worth it. Thank you."

He blinked at her. "For what?"

"For allowing me to come. I realize you believe me to be self-absorbed. And well…maybe I am to some extent."

He opened his mouth, but she continued before he could comment. "But I enjoyed teaching the children. Their faces were priceless, especially after they read a particularly challenging word." She turned around. "And Max, you have quite the vocabulary for a boy of eight years."

Max popped up beside her. "I know. I already know what ostentatious means."

Georgia shook her head with a smile. "And very self-confident."

"Like my dad." He beamed.

Harrison chuckled, and despite herself, Georgia did too. A

confused Max swung his head back and forth between the two. "What's so funny?" Which only made them laugh harder.

Harrison hadn't laughed this much in ages—at least not since Laura passed. It felt good, as if it were cleansing the corroded recesses deep within.

Georgia settled back in her seat and observed the scenery with a contented smile. "It's so different here."

Her life had undergone quite a change. It had taken him and Max at least six months after they first arrived before they adapted to the oppressive heat, strange critters, and ethnic foods. On all accounts, Georgia had adjusted remarkably well. A twinge of guilt pinched his side. "Do you miss your family in London?"

She didn't answer right away. He watched the range of emotions cross her face—sorrow, frustration, relief, longing. "I do miss them but..." She smoothed the wrinkles out of her skirts and sat up a little straighter. The mere mention of her mother and sisters seemed to cause Georgia to fret, as if subconsciously she were still trying to please them.

Her fingers brushed over a small snag in her dress, and a rush of air passed her lips. Her blue eyes met his, filled with confusion. "It's merely that... things here are so... free. I love my family, and I love London, but sometimes it's..." She wilted into the backrest. "Exhausting."

She closed her eyes and pressed her fingers against her temples.

"Here, people don't presume much," Harrison said. "But in London, keeping up with the role that's expected of you is tedious work."

Georgia opened her eyes and her lips parted. "Exactly."

He fought hard not to laugh at her surprise. He understood more than she knew.

Georgia quieted once again, staring out at the ocean as they rode along.

He should leave her to her thoughts. A glance back at Max showed the boy had fallen asleep in the back, stretched out like a starfish with his hat over his face.

"I made quite a muck of it at first." Georgia stared down at her hands. "I didn't know how to be sophisticated like my sisters. I couldn't even hold a conversation. All I knew to talk about was fishing or hunting." She chuckled to herself. "That didn't go over well with the other young women."

"I can imagine." Harrison pictured the astonished faces of the ladies of the *ton* when, instead of discussing the latest fashion trends, she spoke of the best angler to use. "But the men must have found you refreshing."

"You would think so, but most took their cues from the women and avoided me like I'd contracted smallpox."

"Fickle bunch, the whole lot of them." An ache formed in his chest for the ostracized wisp of a girl. "Your sisters didn't help?"

Her brow furrowed. "My sisters didn't like me much."

"But they're family. What you do reflects on them."

"That's true, but their bitterness overrode it. You see, it was like the story of Joseph my father talked about on Sunday. Jacob favored Joseph, and his siblings grew jealous. Papa favored me. Although my sisters didn't throw me into a well or sell me into slavery, they used my flaws to their advantage. They put me in situations where they knew I would make a fool of myself, and it worked—perfectly. I quickly fell out of favor with the *ton* and was relegated to the status of wallflower."

"Someone of your beauty and lineage wouldn't stay that way for long."

She shrugged. "I used the time to observe the *ton's* interactions. I studied how the women flirted, and practiced it at home in front of the mirror. I listened to conversations and learned what drew the best reactions. I came back the second season and set the *ton* on its ear."

A rush of pleasure and pride filled his chest as if he'd had anything to do with her success. "I wish I'd witnessed that." He bumped his shoulder against hers. "And see, like Joseph you made the best of a bad situation. God will honor that."

"Truthfully…" Her countenance fell. "I didn't like myself. I manipulated people to get what I wanted." Her eyes lowered and a pink flush stained her cheeks. "I still do. God doesn't honor that."

"No, but if you repent. God will forgive." His eyes locked with hers. "You can change."

Just as God was changing Harrison's view of Georgia. He now saw the source of her hurts and the reasons behind her haughty behavior. Georgia was a survivor. To become that way, she'd built thick and fortified walls around her heart. Her eyes searched his as if looking for redemption, but she needed to seek forgiveness from God, not from him.

He halted the horses, and they munched at the weeds on the side of the road. "Georgia, I…" He didn't know what he meant to say. *I'm sorry you've been hurt so badly?*

She would reject his pity, and the walls would go back up, thicker than ever. Instead, he looked at her—truly, looked at her. He found passion in the turquoise depths of her eyes. Georgia felt deeply, cared deeply, and loved deeply, but her wounded heart couldn't take another beating. No wonder she safeguarded herself behind thick armor.

As the sun glinted off her golden head, he wondered what it would be like to step behind those walls, to unleash the passion she bottled up. He shifted to face her, and his eyes dropped to the soft pink of her mouth. He lifted his hand and brushed his knuckle down her cheek.

When she didn't pull away, he trailed his finger across the softness of her lips. She gasped, and her eyes held a swirl of emotion—confusion, timidity, maybe even a hint of longing. One side of his mouth pulled into a half smile. Why did he derive so much pleasure in shocking her?

Like a boat drifting into shore, he leaned in closer.

She jerked against the seatback, jarring him out of the moment.

He stiffened and righted himself. *What had come over him?* He turned forward again and snapped the reins.

They rode in silence until she cleared her throat. "When does the next ship come into port?"

His brows drew together. "Toward the end of the month, give or take a week. Why?"

She reminded him of a panicked child. She wouldn't even look at him. "Lord Claremont might be on it, of course."

Harrison snapped the reins again to stir on the horses. "Of course." He didn't like the bitter quality of his voice.

"Do *you* miss London?" she blurted. Maybe she was trying to rebuild some sort of normalcy.

"Not really."

"You believe the memories are still there?"

He shrugged. "Probably…maybe…I don't know."

"It must have been terrible for you."

"It was."

"I remember when Papa left. At first, I sat in his reading chair and cried and cried. I slept there the first week he was gone, but after a while, that chair became a bitter reminder. Eventually, I couldn't even pass by the study without getting angry."

He'd done a similar thing. He'd wake in the middle of the night, still feeling Laura lying next to him, only to stretch out his fingers over cool sheets. After a while, he started sleeping in one of the guest chambers because he could still smell her perfume in their room. He thought relocating to the country could help him move on, but it didn't. So he packed their things and sailed to this distant island. He'd owned land here, but Laura would never travel this far. Her memories couldn't haunt him here. Or so he'd thought.

"It's why I came here. Friends and family in London believe I should have stayed and preserved her memory for Max, but I couldn't."

He glanced at her, tried a smile. "Death changes you. Everywhere I went I saw flashes of her smile, and every time I closed my eyes, I saw her face, pale and tense with pain before she died."

"I'm terribly sorry."

Her words were a truce of some sort. Kindred pain reflected in the depths of her eyes. "It was a beautiful night, but it turned into my worst nightmare."

CHAPTER 15

...It is a tragic tale. A wife lost in the prime of her youth. The duke driven into solitude by his grief. What many a woman would do for such devotion. I, for one, would dutifully seek his affections for my daughter if he was to emerge from isolation.

—From a match-making mama of the le bon ton *to an acquaintance*

*T*he pain of Harrison's memories festered, and he soaked in Georgia's presence beside him on the wagon, seeking her solace as a healing balm. She didn't say anything, but as their gazes held, the compassion in her doe eyes compelled him to loosen the cork on his bottled-up pain. He opened his mouth, the need inside him overwhelming his good sense. His story emerged in bits and spurts, but soon, the cathartic retelling had him reliving that fateful night.

Seven Years Earlier

149

I was suffocating." Harrison observed the sprinkling of stars struggling to emerge as the sky faded from light pink to blackish-purple. He sucked in a breath and rolled his shoulders to relax his muscles as he and his wife waited for their carriage to be brought around.

Laura laughed, a natural, throaty sound that stirred his blood. "I'd say you were being smothered. If Lady Eastrum's guests had stood any closer, they'd have been wearing your clothes." She smiled at him over her shoulder. "Socializing with you enhances their reputations. I expect tomorrow I'll hear all about how you talked the ear off of Mr. Osgood, or specifically sought out Lord Atwell, when I know very well nothing of the sort happened."

He massaged the back of his shoulder with one hand, then tilted his head from side to side, stretching his neck until it resounded with a satisfying crack. How he dreaded these social engagements.

"It's because you've become a recluse." Laura's voice took on a censorious tone. "If you attended more social gatherings with me, everyone wouldn't be so hard-pressed to gain your attention."

He opened his eyes to the approaching sound of clopping hooves as their team of horses arrived, pulling their carriage up to the steps. The footman jumped down from the rumble seat and opened the door to their town coach. At the moment, the luxurious velvet cushions reminded him of the inside of a coffin.

He needed to move. He needed to breathe.

Harrison released a rush of air through puffed lips, leaned his head back, and peered up into the velvet sky. On a whim, he blurted, "Shall we stroll home?"

Laura fiddled with her necklace and peered down the road in the direction of their townhouse. Couples strolled arm-in-arm as the lamplighters traversed from street light to street light, illuminating the night.

"It's getting dark."

"The sun has barely set." He claimed her hand, and his fingers slid along the satin material of her gloves.

She smiled, and his eyes dropped to her lips. He barely restrained himself from planting a kiss on them, right there with other party-goers strolling around them.

Blushing, she glanced down and rested a hand on her stomach. "Dinner was lovely. Lady Eastrum outdid herself."

"Have you felt any kicks yet?"

She shook her head. "No, silly, it's too early.

"Two little ones in under two years. At this rate, you'll outpace the old woman who lived in a shoe."

She bubbled with laughter. "Because we'll have so many children, we won't know what to do?"

"Don't fret, Your Grace." He smiled what he hoped was a charming grin. "There will be no shoe dwelling if I have any say in the matter."

"Thank heaven for that." She heaved a sigh, and the bodice of her dress swelled. "I've just regained my freedom. All too soon, I'll be showing, and my confinement will begin once more." She tightened her shawl about her shoulders. "A stroll might be just the thing."

"It's settled then." He raised his hand and signaled for their carriage to leave without them.

Harrison pulled his wife closer, and they ambled down the street toward their townhouse. "Have you thought of any names yet?"

"If the baby is a boy, we could name him Simon after my father or George after yours."

He rumbled those names around in his mind. They sounded rather old for an infant, but the baby would grow into them. "And if it's a girl?"

"Jane. I'm taken with Jane."

"Jane." The name rolled off his lips. "I like Jane."

Laura rested her head on his shoulder and picked her way along the cobbled street. The farewells of Lady Eastrum's guests as they disseminated faded into the background.

A candle in the upstairs bedroom window of their town-home meant Maxwell was still up. They'd have time to kiss their son before he drifted off to sleep. A shadow shifted in Harrison's periphery. He paused and squinted through the dim light in the direction of the movement.

"What is it?" Laura's brows drew together.

"Nothing." Yet even as he spoke the word, the back of his neck tingled. *No need to be so paranoid, old chap. This is Mayfair, not the stews.*

He secured his wife's hand in the crook of his elbow and quickened his pace until Laura's breath came in audible gasps.

"Please, slow down. I'm having difficulty keeping up."

He lessened his gait. "Sorry, darling—"

"Well, well, what 'ave we 'ere?"

A man dusted in soot with a scarf covering the lower half of his face stepped out of a side alley. Harrison pushed his wife behind him. As he searched for a means to bypass this stranger, a second scarved man slid out from the shadows and closed in behind them.

Trapped.

Harrison's eyes shifted to the man's hands where the gleam of shiny metal reflected the lamplight.

A gun.

"My man 'as been keepin' an eye on you, gov'ner. Saw you comin' from a fancy party. Figured you'd 'ave some silver pieces jinglin' in yer pocket we can help lighten."

Harrison turned sideways to keep both men in his line of vision, but focused on the one who'd done the talking. "My wife and I don't want any trouble. We'll give you what you want, and then you can let us be."

The leader's eyes hardened, and his lips curled up in a snarl. "You'll be handin' me your purse then."

The shaking of Laura's hands as she clung to his jacket twisted Harrison's stomach. Gritting his teeth, he slowly reached into his pocket and pulled out his purse full of coins. He tossed it to the cold-eyed man, then stepped back. "We'll be going then."

"Not so fast," the leader said. "The lady needs to hand over her jewels."

The other bandit shifted the barrel of the gun to Laura, but Harrison shielded her with his body. He fought the rush of anger energizing his muscles and kept his mind focused. He peered into the henchman's eyes. They shifted in nervous saccades.

This one was scared.

The man was small in stature. He could take him if necessary.

"Everyone remain calm. My wife will hand over her jewels, and then you can be on your way." He appealed to the hench-man's humanity. "Our little boy is waiting for his mama to tuck him in for bed."

Laura held out the sapphire bracelet he'd given her for her birthday and dropped it into the leader's open palm. The man's weasel eyes narrowed on her neck and nodded. "Now the necklace."

Her slender fingers reached back and fumbled with the latch.

The leader's eyes darted up the street. "Give it over already."

Laura's face shone white in the moonlight as she struggled with the jewelry, but her gloves must have been impeding her progress.

"Yer wastin' time. Make 'er give it over." He smacked his henchman on the shoulder, startling him.

The pistol slipped from the henchman's fingers, and he fumbled to right it. Seeing an opportunity, Harrison lowered his shoulder and drove into the man's chest. The gun spun in the air and bounced between the robber's palms. Harrison reached for the weapon as the man lunged at it with both hands.

The gun exploded.

The sound echoed in Harrison's ears. The world fell silent except for the piercing ring. He slapped at the weapon, and it skidded across the cobblestones, but the henchman didn't move. Only his jaw trembled as he stared past him.

Sickening fear shot through Harrison, and his heart froze. He spun around to find Laura sprawled on the ground, blood seeping through the bodice of her gown.

"Laura!" His heart raced into triple time as he scrambled to his wife's side. He pressed a hand on the wound to staunch the flow of blood, but the crimson liquid pooled around his fingers. He gently lifted her head with his other hand and placed it on his lap. Fear filled her eyes as they met his. A fear that nearly squeezed the breath out of him.

"Darling." He brushed a stray lock of hair behind her ear, and his fingers left a streak of crimson down her moon-pale face. "I'm here. Everything's going to be all right." He desperately scanned up and down the street and screamed a hoarse plea. "Help! Somebody, help us!" Where were all the people strolling the avenue only minutes before?

The only reply was the scuffled footsteps of the leader. He reached down to brandish the weapon while his accomplice stood there immobile.

Harrison's gaze dropped back to Laura. The lines of pain faded from her face, softening her features, and her hands moved to her belly. Her breathing shallowed as blood filled her lungs. She couldn't speak, but she mouthed the words, *I love you.*

Tears streamed down his cheeks. "Don't leave me."

But the light in her eyes dulled. Waves of grief inundated him, and a choked moan escaped his lips, "No, God, please no. Not her." He rocked back and forth. "Not Laura." He glanced down through the haze of tears. Her arms were still wrapped around her stomach. As if she embraced their unborn child while they slid together into eternity.

The henchman yanked his scarf down and knelt next to him. Harrison watched the man's chapped lips move, but no sound could penetrate the haze in his mind. A deep scar on the man's upper lip zig-zagged back and forth as finally the words came through. "I-I didn't mean to do it. It just went off. I didn't shoot 'er."

"You fool," growled the leader. "You let him see your face."

A second explosion sounded, and Harrison tumbled into darkness.

It was daylight when he awoke chilled to the bone and face down in the damp earth. His head ached like an ax had embedded in his skull, and his extremities stung with a prickling numbness.

He licked his dry lips and tasted the slimy tang of mud.

"This one's been picked clean already." The small voice seemed to come from beyond a thick fog. "We could get a pretty farthing for 'is boots."

A sharp pain jabbed in his side. "Uff."

"This bloke's still alive," a young boy cried.

Harrison's hands slid through thick mire laced with pebbles. A sense of foreboding loomed, but his brain felt as if the sludge had somehow seeped in, making every thought painful.

He attempted to push himself up. Clumps of dirt and water reeds tugged on the right side of his beard. He lifted his upper body an inch, but his arms were as weak as a newborn babe's. He collapsed back into the muck.

Hands tugged and pulled at him until he was rolled onto his

back. The sun pierced his eyes like knives, sharpening that ax in his head. He squinted at the hovering shadows until one of the figures leaned over him, blocking the sun. Harrison blinked as his eyes adjusted.

Boys. Two skinny lads who couldn't be older than ten stared down at him. Dirt smudged their small faces and caked their overalls. Their pants were rolled up to their knees, and they stood wiggling their bare toes in the slime of the riverbed.

Mudlarks. He'd never expected to encounter the young children he'd often seen trolling the Thames at low tide searching for treasure. Seems they had no qualms about stealing from the corpses, but he wasn't a corpse.

What was he doing in the Thames? Harrison forced himself to remember, and once he did, the crushing pain nearly pressed him back into the mud.

Not his beloved Laura, his beautiful wife. The echo of the gunshot rang in his ears. Flashes of her pale skin and the crimson blood on her lips ripped through his mind. God, why? She'd been with child. They'd just been talking about names. The deep ache in his heart squeezed the air from his lungs.

He closed his eyes, willing himself into nothingness, ready for death's cold grip. His son would grow up without a mother and never know his little brother or sister.

Maxwell. He forced his eyes open as he pictured the boy branding Laura with a sloppy wet kiss before being led off to bed by his nursemaid. He was probably waiting by the window for them to return home.

With newfound strength, Harrison struggled to a seated position and whispered through lips encumbered with mud, "Bow Street. Find a Bow Street Runner."

The boys took off running.

Harrison held his throbbing head in his hands. But no physical pain could hurt as much as the ache in his heart.

~

*G*eorgia gasped, and her hand flew to her mouth. "You were shot? And your wife and child..." Her breath was but a whisper. "I can't imagine. How did you... How are you still alive?"

How? Why was he spared and not Laura? That was the real question, and one to which he didn't have an answer. "I don't know why God spared me. Even though I won't know this side of heaven why God chose to take Laura and the baby, I'm grateful that Max didn't lose both of his parents that night. I can only trust God had a reason, because I should have been dead. Somehow the bullet only grazed my temple." He released a sigh that seemed to hollow out his entire being. "You never anticipate one small impulsive decision setting the tide of life against you."

They sat in silence as the scenery floated past. Georgia leaned against him as if to absorb some of his pain. Like she understood, and in some way, he knew she did. Since telling the investigators, he'd never retold the full account of what happened that night. He exhaled a long breath and released years of pent-up despair. He glanced down at Georgia's small frame resting her golden head on his shoulder.

Would she now recognize his true identity? He cleared his throat. "I appreciate you allowing me to re-tell my tale. Surely, you've heard it circulated?"

She lifted her head, and her eyes were twin pools of sorrow. "Yours is a tragic story. I'm so sorry for what you suffered." She peered over her shoulder at Max's sleeping form. "And Max, my heart breaks for him."

"You hadn't heard it before?"

Her slender brows drew together. "The story is vaguely familiar."

She must have seen his shock for she began to explain further. "Please, don't be offended. Papa and Mama didn't discuss much in front of me, and back then, I was still behaving like a boy and didn't listen to my sisters' silly, girlie gossip. Then, when I had my first season, I became fodder for the tongue waggers. In order to escape their scathing remarks about my behavior, I avoided all forms of gossip. I still find myself wanting to take cover when someone has a juicy tidbit."

He chuckled to himself. *God, you have an amazing sense of humor. Who would have thought you'd send this exasperating, impertinent woman to help heal my wounded soul?*

As they pulled up in front of Fredrick's house, Max still slept soundly in the back of the wagon. Harrison assisted her down from the carriage and walked her up the steep stairs to the main door. "Thank you again for your help at the school."

"I truly enjoyed it." Her eyes reflected genuine honesty.

"If you'd like to come again, we could arrange it."

She smiled, and Harrison felt his breath catch at the beauty of it. "I would like that."

The door swung open, and Hattie's large form filled the entrance. "Dere you are. We've been callin' after you. The dress lady is here for yer fittins."

Hattie shooed Georgia inside to a flurry of activity. As he walked back down the steps toward the wagon, his heart grew heavy with a restless uncertainty. He paused, wondering what God was trying to tell him. No inner voice pressed words into his spirit, so he climbed into the front seat.

A sleepy Max awoke and crawled over the seatback to sit next to him. He draped an arm over his son and pulled him closer.

"Papa?"

"Yeah, son."

"I like Miss Georgia."

Harrison's lips couldn't seem to help a grin. "What do you like about her?"

"I dunno." He let out a yawn. "She likes all the same things I do, and she looks out for me. She lets me take all the credit for catching the big fish, even though she does most of the work." Max turned to face him. "She can't take Mama's place, but maybe Miss Georgia could be my earthly mama until we get to see Mama in heaven? Do you think?"

A tingle shot down his spine. "Well, uh..." He stuttered, searching for words that wouldn't break the heart of an eight-year-old. "We will ... er ... have to pray about that."

"Papa?"

"Yes, Max?"

"I have been praying for it."

Those words pierced Harrison's heart, bringing the sting of hot tears to his eyes. His son wanted an earthly mother, and he'd been praying for Georgia to fill the role. He glanced up into the bright afternoon sky and wondered if God was already working on his answer.

CHAPTER 16

...Though small, the island has many of the amenities you would find in London, and we do not lack. There is even going to be a ball at the Artesian Hotel. It is to be a grand affair.

—*From Lady Tessa Pickering to her sister-in-law, Nora Lennox*

*M*ax's question filled Harrison's thoughts as he stared at his meager wardrobe. He fingered the different fabrics. In London, he'd had closets full of clothing. How had he let his apparel get this bad? He pushed through his everyday wear into the back of the closet and imagined Georgia's face when she saw him at his finest instead of his worn regular dress. One of her genuine smiles would make the effort worth it.

She'd assisted him in the schoolhouse every day since that first. She took to teaching so well that by the end of each afternoon, Harrison would swear she practically glowed.

Today, she'd been especially joyful, but he attributed it to anticipation for the ball. All of the Islanders were abuzz about it. Nevis had many small social gatherings, but every Rousseau gathering at the Artesian Hotel was the grandest.

Typically, Harrison avoided such pomp and stance. Rousseau used the ball as a way to show off his station and the luxuries it afforded him, even if they were ill-gotten off the backs of mistreated slaves. The man was an oily tyrant who thought he was the self-appointed king of Nevis.

Harrison's jaw tightened. The idea of Georgia being paraded around on Rousseau's arm as if she were an expensive bauble was what had made Harrison start digging through his closet for something to don.

He selected a couple of jackets. Hopefully, one would still fit. He hadn't dressed in his finest since...since London. Laura's face appeared before him, hazy in his memory. He could still summon her smile and hear her laughter ringing, but the rest of her faded like the early morning mist in the warmth of the sun. He wanted to grasp hold of her memory, but as always, pain followed in a flash of light and the echo of a piercing gunshot. Her final moments as the light left her eyes were forever etched in his memory. He wiped his hand on his trousers as if he could still feel the vibrant crimson of her blood, warm and sticky on his fingers. Fresh agony stabbed his heart, making it impossible for him to move until it passed. Why would the beauty of her life fade, but the raw anguish of her death remain so vivid?

Harrison shook his head to clear it, forcing his attention back to his clothing. A loose thread hung from a jacket. In his past, such a thing would have been unacceptable. He tugged the string loose and slid his arms into his double-breasted waistcoat. The formal black had grown a bit snug in the shoulders, but the fine kerseymere hadn't faded.

After lifting his collar points, his fingers fumbled to tie his cravat into a proper knot. His valet used to be able to tie it with his eyes closed. Harrison peered into the looking glass, but instead of seeing a sophisticated dandy from the upper echelons of polite society, he pictured Beau Brummell, the acknowledged leader of fashion, casting him a contemptuous eye and saying, "Linton, old chap, do you call this a coat?"

Harrison flicked dust off the shoulder. He was well inlaid. Why had he allowed himself to become so common? Part of him had stopped caring. Who needed fancy clothes to oversee a sugar plantation and teach children? The fickle idols of high society no longer mattered to him. He enjoyed the anonymity of his current life. He savored the privacy. Why then did he now stand before the looking glass, dressed in outdated clothes and longing for something a bit more luxurious?

Max rushed in like a whirling waterspout. "Papa, Papa." He skidded to a stop and whistled. "Wow, Papa, you look bang-up-to-the-mark."

Harrison smiled at his son's awed expression, suddenly feeling like he was prepared to meet with the king himself.

"Are you going to the Artesian Hotel?" Max's voice was breathless with excitement. "Will Miss Georgia be there? Will you dance with her?"

"Slow down. That's a lot of questions."

Max's brows lowered into a frown. He dragged over a nearby chair, crawled on top, and stood up until he was close to eye-level with his papa. His eyes narrowed with an intense gaze. He wiggled his papa's cravat.

"Better," he said, then smiled. "So, what's your plan?"

When did his son turn into a man?

"I'm going to the Artesian Hotel, and yes, Miss Lennox will also be in attendance, along with Lady Pickering and Uncle Fredrick. There will be dancing, but whether I decide to dance is still to be determined."

Harrison gazed at the younger version of himself and ruffled his son's hair. In a few years, he'd be gracing the ballrooms of the Quality. Harrison's brow furrowed. *Or would he?*

Of course, he would. Harrison had written the Prince Regent and explained his situation. Certainly, the Prince would grant him an extension. It wasn't like he'd never planned to return to England.

His anticipation of the coming night dissipated, and his jaw clenched. Heat simmered under his cravat and threatened to spread, poisoning his peace, but he'd not let his anger get the best of him.

God, help me to forgive. Help me to see their reasoning. He knew his in-laws merely desired to see their only grandson, but Max and he had established a life here on the island. His in-laws could travel the Atlantic to visit if they chose.

Instead of writing him to communicate their wishes, they'd sought the ear of the Prince to petition for his and Max's return. Harrison didn't enjoy being threatened. If it had been anyone other than Lord and Lady Chadwick, Laura's parents, the Prince would have laughed at the request. But because of their rank, and his distant cousin, Viscount Ashburnham, spreading rumors about the Duke of Linton's demise, the Prince Regent summoned him and Max to return. He even threatened to give Harrison's lands and title to his blasted cousin if Harrison didn't appear within two months' time.

Even though Harrison requested an extension, there was no way to know whether his request was granted or if it had even found its way to Prince George. There was every possibility the Prince would make good on his threat. Every day that Harrison stayed on Nevis, he jeopardized his son's legacy.

Harrison drew in a ragged breath. There was still time. He needed to make certain Fredrick was well cared for before he left. It was why he'd sent for Georgia. And he hadn't left since her arrival because she'd behaved like she might turn around and sail back to London at any moment.

First she'd been eager to escape back into the grasp of the Earl of Claremont. He remembered all too clearly the earl's wandering eyes and lustful attempts to lure young women into isolated rooms or darkened arbors. Harrison's fingers balled into fists as he considered the rogue laying a hand on Georgia.

He didn't miss the lowered morals of the upper classes. Why did they believe wealth and connections allowed them the right to sin at will? As long as they were discrete, a blind eye would be turned at the frequent romps in the gardens or adulterous affairs among the peerage. Tonight at the Artesian Hotel, he would step back into a microcosm of his old world.

But he was no longer his old self. He was a new creation. *God, get me through this.*

"If you stick with Miss Georgia, Papa"—Max observed him with a pair of serious brown eyes— "she'll know what to do. She's always showing me all that proper stuff. They have a lot of silly rules, but don't worry. She'll help you."

Harrison envisioned the soaking wet and outraged Georgia in her pink dress, pink shoes, pink gloves, and matching pink parasol, her eyes spewing sparks as she stood in the wagon. *I'm not going anywhere with the likes of you.* Oh, yes, she'd help him all right.

He slid his hands under his son's arms, lifted him off the chair, and placed him back on the floor. He grasped Max's small shoulder and pulled him against his side. "That's a brilliant idea. I'll do just that." And he would. If he could focus on keeping the supercilious Georgia off balance enough for her true self to make an appearance, he'd not only survive the night, there was a good chance he'd enjoy it.

~

*G*eorgia's hand rested on the smooth, superfine material of her father's jacket as their open curricle bounced over the cobblestones, then pulled up in front of the Artesian Hotel. He'd been almost giddy throughout the day, anticipating the ball.

Papa's excitement made him appear ten years younger, and he kept glancing at her with sparkling eyes. "My little caterpillar has grown into a butterfly. You have your mother's beauty. I couldn't take my eyes off her the first time I saw her across the room at Almacks. I dragged my cousin away from his dance partner for an introduction." A deep sorrow resonated in his voice. "She has never been far from my thoughts since."

"You truly love her still, don't you?"

"I'll never stop." The sadness in his eyes gave truth to his words.

Georgia never considered how painful leaving must have been for her father. Would she know a love that deep? She didn't expect love from Julien. What Papa and Mama shared was unique. A great love with colossal highs and desolate lows.

His hand gently patted her own, and then they alighted in front of the Artesian Hotel. Her Aunt Tessa followed on the arm of Mr. Clark, who had ridden with them. Georgia had found him to be an inquisitive man, and he had a way of beholding the person to whom he spoke as if nobody else existed in the world. Aunt Tessa had taken to him like a mouse to cheese.

Torches illuminated the surrounding palm trees and the stone stairway leading up to the grand entrance of the resplendent, three-story stone building. Long terraces graced every floor, each lined with windows and doors framed with large blue shutters. Tastefully dressed people littered each level, clustering in groups as their conversations and laughter carried on the evening air.

As they ascended the stone steps, Georgia's chin lifted. She felt her old haughty façade wrap its protective shroud around her, and she tucked herself behind its shelter. She knew too well the pain of vulnerability and had no desire to expose herself again.

Her father presented his card, and two butlers swung the doors wide into an ornate French provincial style room. Chandeliers dripping with sparkling crystals blazed overhead. Elaborate moldings, painted white, outlined the ceilings, and panels of gold mirrors graced the walls reflecting the light and merriment of the room. An oversize portrait of Mr. Rousseau hung on the far wall in between the double French doors to the terrace.

The rich notes of the orchestra floated through the air as dancers brushed across imported marble floors, inlaid with boxes of gold leaf tiles. Some danced in the stiff, formal manner she knew from London, while others rendered a relaxed Caribbean style.

As she observed the revelry, the excitement of a new challenge sent a rush over her skin and spread a smile across her face. The music, the laughter, the elegance—if she ignored the humidity and the smell of the sea air, she could pretend she was in London. This was familiar territory.

As their names were announced, Mr. Rousseau excused himself from a pensive fellow and approached Georgia and her father with a wide smile and open hands. "Welcome, welcome to the Artesian Hotel."

"Rousseau, it is good of you to have invited us. You know the vicar, Mr. Clark, but Tessa, dear, let me introduce you to our host, Mr. Edward Rousseau. Mr. Rousseau, may I present my sister, Lady Teresa Pickering, the Baroness of Phelps."

"Delighted." He bowed slightly.

"And my daughter, Miss Georgia Lennox."

He bowed deeper, but his eyes remained locked with Georgia's. "I've had the pleasure. Miss Lennox and I met in town recently. I must say I was taken in by her charm. It's refreshing to meet such a beautiful, refined lady." He turned to Papa. "It would give me great pleasure if Miss Lennox could apprise me of the latest happenings in London while I give her and Lady Pickering a tour of our grand hotel."

Her father hesitated and scanned the room as if seeking

someone before he replied. "Certainly. But don't tarry too long. I'll miss their company."

Georgia tilted her head and shot Papa a quizzical look. He'd been acting strangely. She hoped his fever wasn't returning.

Mr. Rousseau offered Aunt Tessa one arm and Georgia his other, and guided them into the next room. It too was luxuriously decorated, even more so than some of the salons of London's well-to-do. Every square inch spoke of wealth.

"This is the blue salon, where our guests can entertain, or enjoy a book or a hand of cards. We've imported all the furniture from France. In fact..." He paused beside a gold double-wide high-backed chair tufted with royal-blue velvet fabric that domineered the corner of the room. "This piece was owned by King Louis XIII himself."

"Wonderfully crafted." She watched the way her comment brought on a satisfied glint in his eyes.

They crossed the room, and Aunt Tessa questioned him about the craftsmanship of the large marble fireplace mantel and coffered ceiling. Georgia used the distraction to glance over her shoulder to where couples floated across the dance floor.

"Over here we have the billiards and card room for the men. We won't go in, but I'll let you peek inside."

The thick, spicy smell of pipe smoke encircled her as soon as he opened the door. The room was paneled floor-to-ceiling in rich mahogany. Three hand-carved pool tables filled one end with an array of octagonal game tables at the other. Fine gentlemen loitered around each area. She scanned the faces in the room. Only a bearded man with squinty eyes looked up. The others were too engaged in their activities to pay heed to onlookers.

"You've already seen the grand ballroom. If you allow me to escort you to the terrace, it leads to our famous pump house." He skirted along the edge of the dance floor to the exit. "The house was built in 1778 and has welcomed such esteemed gentry as Lord Nelson, Prince William, the Duke of Clarence …"

As he continued to rattle off a list of impressive names, her eyes skimmed the room. Papa and the vicar had settled into a set of chairs over by the entrance, but she didn't recognize anyone else. She continued to scan the faces of the guests. But then reality hit her, causing her to stumble. She was searching for Harrison.

Mr. Rousseau's grip tightened on her arm, but he forged ahead. Aunt Tessa continued with her questions and didn't seem to notice Georgia's blunder.

Harrison wouldn't attend a party like this. First of all, his dislike of Edward Rousseau was apparent. Plus, he'd find this environment frivolous and petty, not to mention, intimidating for a schoolmaster.

She forced her eyes back to Mr. Rousseau. The man was dressed to impress the dandy set. He wore a double-breasted dark velvet jacket with gleaming gold buttons. His perfectly knotted silk cravat in a deep, claret red contrasted against the snowy white of his cambric shirt. He would blend into any ball-room in London.

Just like Julien. In London, Julien would make the best match of the season. Here, it would be Edward Rousseau. In a way, the two were much alike, with a self-confidence that bordered on pomposity, an appreciation of finery that teetered on obsession, and a desire to be standoffish and gossip about those who didn't belong. If Julien didn't come for her, she could always scoop up the eligible Rousseau. However, a wealthy island gentleman wouldn't impress her mother or show up her sisters.

Would Rousseau make her laugh? Would he love her even when she grew old and wrinkled? Could Julien do those things?

Would he make her feel alive the way Harrison did? But that line of thought would only get her in trouble.

Two young women hovered nearby, and she didn't miss

their jealous glances as Mr. Rousseau escorted her through a large set of French doors. She should have been reveling in the glory of being chosen by someone held in such high esteem, but tonight, she felt...indifferent.

She tapped her fan against her side. Funny, Julien hadn't crossed her mind at all in recent days. Especially since she'd started helping out at the school. Her lips twitched at the memory of all the kids surrounding her. The little ones hugged her, and the older ones fought to tell her what they'd done the night before or what they learned.

Miss Lennox, Miss Lennox. Did you know I can count to two hundred?

Miss Lennox. Last night Mama made plum pudding, and we took it over to the vicar's house.

Their excitement was contagious, and a smile touched her lips. When she wasn't at school, she was catching up with her father or fishing with Max. The distractions were good for her. Sitting around pining away for Julien wouldn't get him here any faster. And if he didn't come or wait for her, then her future was much too grim to dwell upon.

Rousseau's voice prattled on, "Over there is our garden and statuary. I've been told it is similar to the Duchess of Kensington's private garden. We also sit on twenty acres of the best sugar crops in the world..."

She pictured Julien leaping from the dinghy onto the sandy beach and calling for her. *Georgia, I've come to ask for your hand. I've...* He would shake the sand off his Hessian boots with a look of abject horror. Several servants would come running to wipe them down, and Edward Rousseau would fawn over Julien.

Georgia pushed the ridiculous scene from her mind as a light breeze off the ocean tickled the tendrils of hair that framed her face. Rousseau pointed to a Roman-looking structure where the moonlight caught the small ripples off the spring-water pool and reflected hypnotic wave patterns up on the walls.

LORRI DUDLEY

"There's the spring. Its healing waters are world renown and have been known to cure numerous ailments." He gestured toward the stairs. "As guests descend the stairs, they behold the best view of the island, the spring with the gardens and ocean in the background."

Aunt Tessa strolled over to the other side of the balcony and rested her hand on the stone baluster at the top of the staircase. "It is a lovely view."

Georgia moved to join her, but Rousseau's grip tightened.

He leaned an elbow on the railing and shifted to watch her face. His voice lowered to a whisper. "Your eyes remind me of its waters, so blue I want to dive into them."

Georgia fluttered her fan at the compliment and held her smile.

"You look stunning in that dress."

She glanced down at her new gown in a daring shade of red. She'd initially picked out a safe pale pink, but Harrison's teasing voice rang out in her head. *Pink? Why all the pink?* In a momentous decision, like a child handing over her security blanket, she selected the scarlet material.

"The local dressmaker rushed to accommodate me. Most of my gowns were lost at sea."

He took her hand. "How distressing. I would remedy that immediately. I could dress you in silks and satins. You would outshine all of London."

I've heard those lines before. She drifted toward her aunt, pulling her hand from his and tilting her head just so. Then she laughed gaily over her shoulder. It all came back to her readily enough—the poses, the forced laughter, the practiced smiles. "Mr. Rousseau, such flattery will make me swoon."

He scrambled to her side and whispered in her ear. "It is much deserved. A woman as beautiful as you should be praised from the moment the sun rises until it sets. You should be surrounded by luxury."

Aunt Tessa glanced their way and Mr. Rousseau straightened.

What would you say if I told you I baited my own hooks? Georgia's smiling lips wavered. Since when had her pretense become tiresome? She searched for a new topic. "The Artesian Hotel rivals the finest houses in Bath."

"I assure you, it far exceeds the finest house in Bath. I've made certain of it."

She lowered her chin and peered up at him through her lashes. "You have exquisite taste. I wouldn't expect less from a man so impeccably dressed."

The corners of his lips curled into a smile, and his eyes roved over her body as if about to partake in a feast. However, her usual triumph fizzled, replaced by an odd emptiness.

He held his arm out, and his voice rolled with a husky reverberation. "Come, let me show you our prize-winning garden and statuary up close."

No. Not there. Her heart clenched. Just the words brought back another memory—the honeyed scent of wisteria in a different garden, Julien's passionate stolen kisses, and the joy that swelled her heart on that night.

THREE MONTHS EARLIER

*T*he crisp night air cooled Georgia's skin as Claremont guided her down the steps and onto the crushed stone path of the torch-lit gardens. Shadows danced in the firelight and added to the nervous fluttering in her stomach. Feminine giggles and whispered voices resonated from within the alcoves of the tall boxwood hedge that lined both sides of the walkway.

Nothing untoward was going to happen. Lord Claremont

was respectable and about to be her future husband. She just had to get him alone so he could propose.

Her steps felt measured like the tightrope walker she'd seen at Astley's Amphitheatre.

Something snapped beneath her gloved fingers. Blast. She'd broken her fan. Her favorite one.

"This seems like a nice spot to talk." She pointed to a bench situated among potted wisteria vines, somewhat lit by nearby torches.

Lord Claremont hesitated and started toward the darker section of the garden, but Georgia tugged him into a seat on the stone bench.

"Isn't it a lovely night?" She leaned back on her palms and pretended to peer up at the stars.

His voice purred, "It is you who is lovely." He trailed his fingertips down the nape of her neck, the smooth satin of his gloves tickling her skin. Her eyes met his heavy-lidded gaze as he murmured, "So beautiful and soft."

Part of her wanted to lean into his touch. This was it. Anticipation enlivened every pore of her skin, like when she'd been a young girl waiting for her father's words of approval.

Wait for it. He will *say the words.*

Julien's finger stroked her cheek. "Your skin is smooth like cream. Your lips softer than an overripe peach." He leaned in. "You are the most beautiful woman here. These ladies cannot hold a candle to you."

She licked her lips. "But, what do I mean to you…Julien?"

"For a kiss, I would give you the sun and the moon."

His mouth moved closer to hers, but Georgia turned her head. "I don't need the sun or the moon. I'm looking for something else."

"Anything," His lips whispered against her neck. "Anything for you."

CURRENT DAY

*G*eorgia cleared her throat and focused on Rousseau and her present situation. "Actually, I'm quite parched. Perhaps we could partake of refreshments. I'm still adapting to the island heat."

His expression grew tight. "Of course. This way." He tucked her hand in his arm. "We can explore the garden later when the night's cooler."

The words melted off his lips like a rich sauce, and her stomach turned.

She'd barely been away from London, and already she was losing her finesse. She had to keep it together unless she wanted to return to wallflower status.

She tried to remove her hand, but he placed his fingers overtop hers. *Get ahold of yourself. This is your playground.*

As they entered the ballroom, the violin held a lustrous last note before the orchestra rested between sets. The dancers returned to their former groups, clearing a view of the room.

Aunt Tessa excused herself to check on Papa and Mr. Clark.

Across the floor, Georgia's gaze landed on a familiar pair of broad shoulders that made her heart quicken.

Harrison. His powerful frame diminished the rest of the guests until they dissipated in her periphery like fading shadows. She bit her lip to hold back the overwhelming giddiness bubbling up inside. She faltered a step as the imagined shroud weighing her down slipped to the floor, but she quickly regained her footing.

As if sensing her presence, he glanced up from his conversation with the vicar. His eyes locked with hers, and a crooked smile lifted one side of his lips. He dominated the room with his casual elegance, a chameleon of sorts who transformed himself from rural schoolmaster into a prime consort with the upper echelons of society. His charcoal jacket hugged his broad shoulders and narrow waist. His snug breeches clung to his muscular thighs. His smile seemed genuine as he inclined his head before directing his attention back to the vicar.

Georgia swallowed down her riotous stomach, which kept leaping into her chest. Mr. Rousseau followed her gaze and tightened his grip on her fingers. He steered her to the refreshment table and plopped a glass of lemonade into her hand.

"I'm a generous man, Miss Lennox. Unfortunately, on a small island such as Nevis, it is necessary to keep company with all types, even those who'd never grace a ballroom in London." His eyes flicked in Harrison's direction. "I know your father admires Mr. Wells, but I do hope you'll be cautious in your associations with the man."

He leaned in closer until his lips practically brushed the top of her ear. "I cannot confirm specifics, but I have good reason to believe that Mr. Wells was exiled to Nevis by order of the King George III."

Only as much as her mother exiled her. Georgia almost laughed at his insinuation, but bit the inside of her cheek to hold back. She wanted to hear out his ridiculous logic, so she raised her brows and said, "Really? Mr. Wells, the schoolmaster? I noticed the tension between you two. Is that the reason?"

His lips curled into a sneer. "That and the man has stuck his nose into island affairs. He should stay out of politics. He has no idea the labor it takes to run a sugar farm."

"But doesn't he too own a sugar farm?"

"I barely consider it worthy of mention. Wells manages several plots of land on the island for a relative in England, but most of the land is still natural terrain. The farm is a small portion, so he can't comprehend the labor required for a large plantation like Artesian House. Instead, he incites our workers and underhandedly educates the slaves."

"What is the harm in that?"

"You wouldn't understand the affairs of men."

"Oh, but Mr. Rousseau, I'm sure you can put it into simple terms for me." Sarcasm laced her words, but he didn't appear to catch on.

"When slaves are educated, they are given the false hope that they may better themselves. The next thing you know, you have a revolt. Such an uprising could stifle our ability to trade, which would destroy our economy and, in turn, hurt our mother country by paralyzing its import of sugar. Could you imagine, Miss Lennox, having tea time with no sugar?"

Heaven forbid. Georgia's hand tightened around the glass in her hand, and she fought the urge to toss its contents into Mr. Rousseau's impertinent face. Instead, she replied, "How dreadful."

He pressed his fingertips together into a pyramid and closed his eyes as if contemplating something extraordinary. His eyes opened and narrowed on hers with intensity. He pointed at her with his palms pressed together. "Perhaps, you could be of assistance, Miss Lennox."

Her brows lowered. "How so?" She sipped the overly sweet lemonade.

"Your father's close friendship with Mr. Wells may allow you to be privy to confidential conversations." One side of his mouth lifted into a half smile. "Perhaps, you could pass along interesting facts pertaining to Mr. Wells. Anything that might discredit him or diminish his influence. Such information would be rewarded with precious goods from London to replace those you've lost. It may even pay passage to England, if the information proves savory."

She could return to Julien. The thought passed through her head before she could stop it. No, she would never betray Harrison. Besides, it was ridiculous. Mr. Rousseau's suspicions were unfounded. "You're asking me to spy on Mr. Wells?"

"Not spy on him, merely keep your eyes and ears open for me."

She recognized jealousy in his voice, and his eyes shone with malice, but why would he be jealous of Harrison?

Rousseau lifted his glass and gulped down a big swallow.

She didn't trust him, and she didn't like the idea of him publicly humiliating Harrison. Maybe she should keep a closer eye on Mr. Rousseau?

"Let me consider it."

A large smile swept across his face. "I knew, from the moment I met you, that we would get along famously, Miss Lennox."

Uncomfortable under his wolfish gaze, she peered down into her half empty cup. "I should probably return to my father. He doesn't like me to be gone long."

"Of course, let me escort you."

She placed her hand on the smooth, luxurious fabric of his coat sleeve and straightened her shoulders to shake off the tingle of unease prickling the back of her neck. She'd dealt with men of a higher caliber than Mr. Rousseau. She could hold her own. There was no reason to be concerned.

CHAPTER 17

...How did you know you were in love? Did it feel like you'd swallowed live caterpillars? Were you constantly aware of his presence? Did you go to extremes for a glimpse of him and feel elated when you spotted him?

—*From Georgia Lennox (who never intended to post it) to her sisters*

*H*arrison knew the second Georgia walked in the room, knew the same way a planter feels a storm coming. Excitement hung heavy in the air, raising the hair on his arms.

She'd felt it too. He could tell by the way her countenance changed when she spotted him. Sincere pleasure lit her eyes like the luminescent glow of the fireflies that flickered in the underbrush at night.

Then he'd spied Rousseau. The scoundrel carted her over to the refreshment table, licking his chops like the villain in one of the Brothers Grimm tales. Harrison's fingers curled into fists, but he reined his temper in before Rousseau approached. He couldn't stop his teeth from clenching at the sight of the wretch's hand wrapped possessively around Georgia's arm, but he managed to observe them with what he hoped was cool detachment.

"Delightful party, Rousseau. Thank you for returning Miss Lennox. She's promised me the next dance."

Before Georgia could balk, he threaded his hand through her other arm and ushered her onto the ballroom floor. The violins started an up-tempo waltz. His eyes met hers as they assumed the dance position, and it wasn't hard to miss the tempest swirling in their depths at his audacity to claim this dance. But something else flickered under those fringed lashes he couldn't quite figure out—excitement, admiration, maybe awe? He tried to look away, but couldn't seem to pull his gaze from this beauty before him, full of sugar but matched with spice. Harrison's hand came to rest on her lower back, and she stiffened. Her pink lips parted.

"Don't concern yourself." The husky tone of his voice surprised him. "I asked your aunt for permission to dance the waltz."

One graceful brow arched up. "That wasn't necessary," she informed him. "The waltz is danced at Almacks."

"Is it now?"

Things had changed in London since he'd left. The once controversial dance, due to the proximity in which the dancers stood, apparently no longer created a scandal. He drew her close and locked their position in a stance he knew Lady Jersey and the beau mode society wouldn't approve. "Waltzes here in the islands are a little less … refined."

He might have been a little rusty, but he made up for it with gusto as he swept her around the room until her eyes shone bright and her cheeks grew flushed. He'd disliked these events in London, but here on the island, no one thought twice about a schoolmaster dancing with a beautiful high-society woman.

"So, they're dancing the waltz at Almacks?" He noted her

gown as the music lulled. "Let me guess, and now the color red is the height of fashion?"

"No, it's pink."

"Oh yes, I remember." He cast her a knowing smile "Because it's a feminine color. I hate to point it out, but you, my dear, are wearing red."

"It's not red." Her eyes danced, but her face remained utterly impassive. "It's dark pink."

Harrison threw back his head and laughed. A few surrounding couples whispered, probably about his uncivil behavior, but he didn't care.

He leaned in closer to her ear and whispered, "You look ravishing in dark pink."

He felt her shiver, despite the heat.

"Mr. Wells..."

"Please, call me Harrison. Your father has practically adopted Max and me into the family. I believe we can cut the formality now that we share meals together, work together, dance together."

He spun her to the edge of the dance floor as the song drew to a close. He bowed, tucked her hand into the crook of his arm, and rested his other on top of it.

"Harri..." She hesitated, as if her lips were testing out the word.

"Ah, but not Harry." He worked for a cheeky grin. "Harry is what my mother called me when I was in grave trouble. The reminder makes my left ear hurt."

A puzzled expression muddled her blue eyes. "Just your left ear?"

"Indeed. I towered over my mother from age twelve on, but a good ear pull was the perfect height equalizer and mother was right-handed. One tug and I was on my knees pleading for forgiveness."

LORRI DUDLEY

She giggled with an inelegant snort that could only be called adorable. "How often did you hear the name Harry?"

He peered into her gaze. "Quite often." He pointed at his left ear. "If you look closely, you'll notice that ear is slightly lower than the other."

She laughed then, a glorious resounding laugh. She tried to hide her outburst behind her hand, but failed miserably. That was a sound he would hear more of if he possibly could.

"You jest." But then she slowly sobered. Her eyes narrowed in on his face. "No, wait." Her gaze volleyed from one ear to the other. "You're right. One ear *is* lower than the other."

Her eyes were so wide, her expression so shocked, that Harrison raised his hands to his earlobes.

She laughed even harder.

As he realized the joke, he should have been perturbed, but he couldn't summon anything except the warm tightness in his chest. "Now who's the jester?"

His eyes never strayed from her face, but he knew Georgia's hearty amusement would draw unnecessary attention, so he pulled her off to the side of the dance floor to compose herself before others began to stare.

Harrison shook his head, but couldn't subdue the smile stretching across his lips. He must appear like a smitten fool. He snatched his handkerchief from his pocket and handed it to her so she could wipe the tears from her eyes. When she'd finally dampened the laugh to only the occasional snicker, he said, "You should have been an actress."

"I am quite good"—she pinned her lips together for a moment as she quelled another bout of giggles—"aren't I?"

"I wouldn't get too boastful about it." Then she peered up at him with a pair of open blue eyes, shining brightly with residual laughter that made his chest unable to draw breath.

The bold and vibrant red suited Georgia. Pastel pink had fit Laura. Whereas Laura had been gentle and compatible, Georgia

180

was unpredictable and extreme. Similar to this island, she could simmer and rumble like Mt. Nevis, but then bait you with a beautiful sunset and a laughing breeze. Laura would have liked her immensely.

Guilt shot through him. How could he be callous enough to compare the two? Georgia couldn't replace his wife. She couldn't fill the hole left by Laura's loss.

God will fill the hole with Himself. It was the phrase he'd told Max to help the boy through his grief. Now the thought awakened within his own mind. Had he let God fill the emptiness in his heart? Had he ignored the truth and instead clung to the emptiness he felt he deserved?

He stared at Georgia. Could he move past the pain and live a life with another woman? He needed to talk to God about this more, but he couldn't keep his thoughts intact with Georgia's wildrose scent filling his nose and her soft lips tempting him.

He scanned the room, then nodded in the direction of Aunt Tessa. "It appears the vicar and your Aunt might make the match of the evening."

~

*G*eorgia blinked at the change in topic. Was she losing her senses or had Harrison been flirting with her? What disturbed her even more was that she welcomed it. Why would she prefer the attention of a schoolmaster over a wealthy sugar plantation owner? Arrogant men had never bothered her before.

Perhaps her aunt and the vicar were a safer focus. She turned her gaze that way and studied them. Aunt Tessa and Mr. Clark appeared to be competing for her father's attention, each one becoming more animated than the last to convey their story.

A deep ache tightened around her heart. "It's terrible that I never noticed before how lonely she was in London."

Mr. Clark leaned in and listened with rapt attention, and Aunt Tessa flirtatiously fanned herself.

"Once you peek over your fortress walls, princess, you'll discover a whole new world just waiting to love and be loved."

She turned to him. "What walls?"

"The ones you wield to protect your heart." His dark eyes were a rich amber, drawing her in.

She forced herself not to get lost in his gaze. "I don't have walls." But her voice lacked conviction.

He raised an eyebrow. "Yes, you do. For everyone else, you put on an act, but I've seen glimpses of the true Georgia."

She looked away from him, but with a gentle touch, he turned her face back to meet his gaze.

"And you know what?"

She swallowed. A mix of hope and fear warred within her as she braced for his next words.

"She's funny, passionate, and kind." He released her chin. "It's strange, but when you allow yourself to be vulnerable, you can recognize the hurts in others and find compassion." He glanced back at her aunt. "Besides, I don't think Lady Pickering is lonely anymore."

His brown eyes returned to hers and held.

"No." Her voice was barely a whisper. "Not any longer."

"I know you didn't want to come to the island, but I'm glad you did."

"You are?" She hated the childlike hope in her voice. His warm, unwavering gaze pierced through her defenses, and she was transported back to a golden-haired child eager for any kind word to let her know she was worthy of love.

"Indeed."

She watched his lips form the words, and it barely registered that she swayed toward him.

"You've brought the light back into your father's eyes."

"My father?" Georgia stiffened. "Yes, of course."

"He adores you."

She fought to maintain eye contact, even though her chest constricted and a lump formed in her throat.

Her walls didn't feel thick now. Her jaw tightened, and her heart battled against the all-too-familiar ache of rejection. She didn't want to feel ... not like this. She needed those walls.

"He loves you. You can see it every time he looks at you." Harrison's gaze scanned the room, then met hers once again. "There's a ship that's coming to port in a week. I hope you plan to stay—for Fredrick's sake."

Not for your sake?

She eyed him coolly. "I'll stay until Julien sends for me."

His eyes darkened, and whatever had been between them seemed to dissipate.

"Ah, yes, prince charming." Sarcasm laced his words.

"At least I know where I stand with Julien."

"Do you? Will a cad like him stay faithful? Will he still enjoy your company when you're old and wrinkled? Will he love all your quirks? Because believe me, princess, you've got quite a few."

"I don't need to listen to this from the likes of you."

She turned to go, but he grasped her arm. "You're better off forgetting about him and acknowledging the people who truly care about you. The ones right in front of you."

Her eyes blazed. "Are you saying you're one of those people?"

Harrison stared at her. His lips parted, but he didn't say the words.

"I didn't think so." In a whirl of skirts, she left him standing there.

Georgia returned to her father's side and smiled, despite the rush of heated blood roaring through her veins.

"Lovely party isn't it, princess?" Papa smiled at her.

"Quite." She said through tight lips. Harrison had the gall to call her the same nickname moments ago.

"Georgia." Aunt Tessa placed a hand on her arm. "Mr. Clark here has told me what a wonderful thing you are doing by helping out at the school."

"She has a way with children."

Her spine stiffened as Harrison's voice boomed behind her.

"Well, I'm glad she gets to see how normal boys and girls behave," Aunt Tessa said. "No offense dear, but Fanny's and Eleanor's youngsters are wild little terrors. I've found it's best to make yourself sparse when they're around. I wouldn't blame you one bit if you didn't want anything to do with children. Last time they visited my country house, they glued a toy saddle and doll to the back of Fluffy, my poodle. It took my maid four hours to get the saddle off. We couldn't save Fluffy's coat of fur. We had to cut it off, and the dog had to wear sweaters all winter to keep from freezing at night."

A surge of relief ran through Georgia. Until she'd been around the island children, she assumed all youngsters were of such ilk, and Max was the exception. She liked his company. But when she began working with the school children, how amazed she'd been to learn that they were a joy to watch and a pleasure to teach. Even though they could be rowdy at times.

"I hope you're all enjoying yourselves." Edward Rousseau appeared on Georgia's left.

Her father peered at him through his wire glasses. "Jolly time, Rousseau. You do always put on a good show."

"Indeed, quite lovely," her aunt said.

"Miss Lennox, I promised you a look at our prize-winning gardens."

"Oh, I...um." The last thing she wanted was to be alone with the man.

Harrison's hand grasped her elbow. "I don't think that would be wise."

All eyes turned to him. Georgia registered the firm set of his jaw and his commanding glare. Even if he disliked the man so much, this hardly seemed a battle worthy of such vehemence.

A crease formed in Aunt Tessa's brow. "Maybe another time perhaps."

"Ah, but the garden is transformed tonight under all the lights and fullness of the moon. Miss Lennox will be in good hands."

Harrison's gaze became volatile. "She might catch a chill." His words emerged through clenched teeth.

Rousseau picked up the challenge. "The night air is still quite warm."

"Perfect," Georgia said before Harrison could retort. There was no sense in them making a scene. "I've been looking forward to it all evening."

A victorious smile spread across Rousseau's face.

Harrison's eyes met hers with a lethal intensity.

"On second thought, Rousseau is right." Harrison never took his eyes off hers. "Taking in the air would be most agreeable." He then turned to her aunt. "Lady Pickering, would you care for a stroll?"

Now, it was Mr. Clark's turn to be taken off guard. He half-stood and looked like he would offer to assist her himself, but Fredrick stilled him with a hand. "Wonderful idea, my boy. My sister would love to see the gardens. Enjoy yourselves."

Throughout the stroll, Georgia replayed the men's verbal sparring. While Mr. Rousseau boasted about his imports from London and Aunt Tessa babbled on about the vicar, Georgia fought to suppress her rising ire.

How dare Harrison interfere in her life? One minute he melted her heart with his sweet words and laughing smile, the next he berated her like a wayward child. She could feel his eyes boring into her from behind as they stopped to admire a Grecian statue of a scantily clad woman clasping a watering jar near her head. Rousseau explained about the piece and the artist.

"How fascinating. You have a superb eye for the arts." Georgia fawned over him, just like she'd done with all the eligible men back in London. "Very few men are as cultured and refined as you."

Rousseau puffed up at the compliment. "I believe it is my duty to expose the islanders to a new level of sophistication."

"You are very kind." She smiled at him through lowered lashes in a way that she knew displayed the coquettish dimple in her left cheek.

As he guided her to the next statue, his hand warmed her lower back, and his thumb stroked a small path along her spine. Rousseau paused at a marble statue of Cupid and, before naming the sculptor, brushed a stray lock of hair from her face with his index finger. Georgia glanced at Harrison, who'd apparently caught the intimate gesture, for his face hardened into a steely glare that made him look as though he was deciding whether to break the man's fingers or nose.

She turned away as Rousseau led her to the next statue.

"Alas," he continued, "some of the islanders appreciate my efforts, while others do not." He turned to face the statue and pulled Georgia beside him. She peeked over her shoulder at Harrison, but the moment she did, she regretted the look. Harrison stifled a yawn. He met her eyes and lifted a belittling eyebrow that stated, *I know what you're doing. Don't waste my time.*

Georgia returned her attention to the statue of a Roman sentry in full gear. While Rousseau fell for her ploy, Harrison saw through it. In a way, it was a relief. A life with Edward Rousseau would be always pretending, always impressing.

Rousseau's caricature-like qualities emphasized the faults she'd ignored in the Earl of Claremont.

Life would be just the same with Julien. She would forever live a lie. A new level of fatigue washed over her. Her perfect life, the one she'd worked so hard to attain, seemed to be imploding. Was she doomed to a meaningless life of frivolity? Was there more to this life? Was she willing to settle?

God, please don't take away my dream. She didn't want to give up seeing Mama's astonished face when her tomboy daughter became a countess. Mama would have to relent that her imperfect daughter had bettered herself even above her sisters' statuses. Mama would then treat her as she did her sisters—paying calls, planning shopping trips...

"Maybe you could pose for me?"

Georgia jerked back to the present. "I beg your pardon?"

Rousseau leaned in until their heads almost touched and continued in a hushed tone. "I have a sculptor arriving with the next ship." He gazed at her as if she were a plate filled with Turkish delight. "I would love to capture such loveliness for all time. Your replica could be placed in the garden next to the statue of Venus, whom you rival in beauty."

Her mouth fell open. Half the sculptures she'd seen tonight were barely clothed, and he wanted her to pose for him? Certainly not.

A yank on her arm drew her backward, and Aunt Tessa was pushed forward in her stead.

"Pardon my intrusion." Harrison's iron-like fingers clamped on her elbow. "But Miss Lennox and I need to have a private discussion."

Harrison's forceful grip brooked no argument as he propelled her around a hedge, toward a twisted tree with low branches. She might have snatched her arm from him, but something about his vehemence made her want to know what he'd say. He almost pushed her to sit on a branch about bench height, then loomed over her, his chest heaving under his double-breasted waistcoat.

"You are treading in dangerous waters, Georgia. Rousseau is a scoundrel, and you need to stay away from him."

His gaze was so fierce, she had to look away, and a motion beside her offered the perfect diversion. A parrot's sleeping eye opened, and its red, unblinking gaze peered at them. One claw at a time, it meandered down the branch toward Harrison.

She forced herself to turn back to the man. "I know what I'm doing."

"You will disgrace your family if you pose for one of his half-naked statues."

"I'm not a harlot. I won't be posing for him or any other man—"

"Good. We're understood then."

Almost. She had to make him understand that he held no power over her. Even if her traitorous body longed for him to draw nearer. "But I will entertain any man who pleases me, and you will not have a say one way or another. Are we clear?"

Harrison gripped branches on either side of her head. She could feel the tension radiating from his body, and his spicy cologne engulfed her in an intoxicating haze.

"Edward Rousseau isn't your typical admirer. He's not a man who will trail along after you, sniffing at your skirts. He doesn't play by society's rules. He has no scruples."

The bird brushed its black beak next to Harrison's ear and squawked, "Say hello, Oscar."

Harrison didn't flinch. His eyes remained glued to hers. With a wave of his hand, he swatted at the bird. "Go home, Oscar."

The bird backed up the branch but didn't leave.

"Thank you for voicing your concerns." Her voice quivered, and she had to clear her throat to maintain her poise. "However, they are unnecessary. I can fend for myself."

He threw up his hands. "Go ahead try your wiles on him. Don't say I didn't warn you."

She had to show him she was capable. She didn't need his interference. "If you'll excuse me, *Mr. Wells*." Her voice dripped with sarcasm as she stood and attempted to brush past him.

His fingers clamped around her upper arm. "I told you to call me Harrison."

Georgia's knees quaked from the deadly tone of his voice, but she kept her composure. "Very well,"—her voice rang out —"*Harry*."

He released her as if he'd touched a hot stove. She'd barely taken a couple of steps when he called out, "As long as we're understood ... *George*."

She froze. Fury filled her and swept away her snappy reply. She lifted her head and stalked back in the direction of Rousseau and her Aunt.

"Rawack! HarREE!"

A smile twitched on the corners of Georgia's lips. The bird had just tipped the score back in her favor.

CHAPTER 18

...I'm grateful for the barrel of sugar. I'm repaying the gesture with a round of cheddar from Colton's Cheese shop, of which I remember you being quite fond. I must warn you, Lord and Lady Chadwick have appealed to the Prince. A summons is most certain.

—From Lord Liverpool to the Duke of Linton

Oooff! Georgia awoke to the wind rushing out of her lungs as an unruly Max pounced on her, jumping up and down on top of the covers.

"Time to get up, sleepyhead. It's getting late, and the fishing won't be as good. You promised we'd go in the boat today."

"Who let you up here?" Georgia rolled over and encased her head under the pillow to block out the light and Max's persistence. Whatever had she been thinking to agree to such a thing the day after a ball?

"I came up on my own. Everyone is asleep except Hattie and the servants, but they're busy." Max pulled at the corner of her pillow, but she only pressed it harder against her ears.

"It's not proper for you to be in a woman's bedchamber."

"Why?" Max asked.

A flash of pity washed over her. "Never mind." Max didn't have a mother. He didn't know proper decorum.

"Come on, you lazy bag of bones. It's time to fish."

That was it. She'd had enough of the Wells men telling her what to do. With one hand, she grasped the pillow and walloped him with it.

A smile broke out over Max's face, making his freckles bunch together. He grabbed her other pillow, jumped on the bed, and roared the war cry, "Pillow fight."

The white bag of fluff walloped her head sideways, so she attacked his legs and knocked him down on the bed, then tickled him until he couldn't breathe.

"Say I'm the master of the pillow fights, and I'll stop."

"No!"

She tickled harder as he squirmed. "All right, all right," he exclaimed between giggles, "You're the master pillow fighter."

She let him go, and he darted off the bed. His chest heaved as he attempted to catch his breath. He sucked in a large gulp of air. "But, you said we'd go fishing in Papa's rowboat."

An hour later, Georgia found herself being rocked back and forth by the waves in a small rowboat anchored not far from shore. The sun shone high in the sky and bore down on her as if intending to fry her like a piece of bacon. She clutched her fishing rod with one hand and mopped at the beads of sweat that ran down the sides of her face with her sleeve. If only she hadn't ruined her other pink day dress playing that game in the dirt with the school children. She had no choice but to don her last unscathed pink gown, the one made out of a thick weave linen lawn.

Stifling a yawn, she glanced at Max, who was clutching his fishing pole and staring into the water with a determined scowl. Besides a few sunfish not big enough to keep, nothing was biting.

"Max, I think it's time we called it a day."

"Just a little longer. We can't go home empty-handed."

"I think we must admit defeat."

"Please, I can feel one's about to bite. A big one. Pleeeease."

His brows tilted up into an *A* formation, and he peered up at her with an expression that made even the saddest puppy look mundane.

"Fine, but merely fifteen minutes more, then it's time for refreshments in the shade."

His face lit up, and he fumbled to recast his line.

Georgia covered a full yawn with her hand. The late hour when she'd returned from the ball, along with the heat and the steady rocking of the rowboat, lulled her into a trance. Her back and bottom ached from sitting on the bench seat in the small dinghy. She leaned to one side and then another, trying to get comfortable.

She eyed the bow. There was just enough room for her to lie down. It wouldn't be lady-like, but no one except Max would see.

After crawling over the edge of the bench, she settled into the bottom of the bow, seeking shelter from the harsh sun. She folded her legs under the seat, but being able to spread out the tiniest bit felt luxurious. "Holler when something tugs the line, and I'll help reel it in."

She shifted her bonnet so it covered her face. The waves gracefully raised and lowered the boat, reminding her of the waltz she'd shared with Harrison. She relived the dance in her mind, his strong arms holding her, sweeping her around and around the room. He'd looked very distinguished in his formal attire. There had been no padding built into the lining of his jacket, which allowed her to feel the solid mass of muscle rippling beneath her fingers.

There was more to Harrison than an island school teacher. His demeanor and the way he held himself bespoke of quality.

192

Being an estate manager would have placed him on the fringe of polite society, if not closer.

He'd said he left because of his wife's memories, but why did he not maintain the same lifestyle he'd held in England? Could there be some truth to Mr. Rousseau's accusations that he'd been exiled? What could he have done to anger the King so? No, it was more likely that he'd gotten himself into financial trouble in England and escaped to the island to avoid debtor's prison.

Either way, he was here, and there was no mistaking the way he made her heart race.

～

A spray of water doused her face, jolting Georgia awake. Hot rays of sun blinded her eyes, and she squinted against the pain. "What?" She wiped the water out of her eyes. "Where are we? What's going on?"

Another wave crashed into the boat and slammed Georgia against the side. She shot up to a seated position in the bow and held on to the sides with both hands.

"The waves are too rough." Seaspray and tears dripped down Max's cheeks. "I can't row us out of this inlet." He wrestled with the oars and strained against the waves. His pale face was a mask of terror.

"Get into the center to balance the boat," she commanded as she took the oars from him and slid into his position. "What happened to the anchor?"

Max's bottom lip quivered, "I wanted to get a little closer to the inlet. That's where all the biggest fish go. I thought I could catch one then row back out quick, so I raised it."

"You what?" She spun to face the boy.

Tears pooled in his wide eyes, and a sob escaped his throat.

But she didn't have time to worry over him now. She had to

LORRI DUDLEY

get the boat under control. Throwing the anchor back out now would be futile. She'd just maroon them in breaking water.

Georgia strained against the wild sea that spun their boat about like a leaf. Large rocks protruded out of the water on either side. She rowed with all her might, but as soon as she gained some ground, a violent wave would push them back.

A swell pitched the boat to the right, and Georgia pulled away from the rock. Another wave crashed into their side, partially filling the dinghy with water. Her arms ached, and a searing pain shot through her shoulders with each wrench of the paddles. The wooden oars blistered her soft hands, and her soaked bonnet hung in front of her eyes. She tilted her head back and measured the narrow strip of beach between the two rocks. If she timed it right, she might be able to ride a wave most of the way into shore. They'd have to swim the rest. She turned to Max.

"You told me you could swim, but are you a strong swimmer?"

He nodded, eyes as wide as the bright sun.

"All right, we're going to ride the boat in with the next large wave."

"What about the rocks?" His voice quavered.

"I'll use the oars to push off the rocks." She secured her grip on the poles.

A white, fizzling wave loomed behind them. "Max, hold on!" she shouted and started rowing as hard as she could in between the two jutted rocks.

The wave lifted their small boat and tossed it into the air. For a suspended moment, Georgia caught sight of Mt. Nevis, its lush peak rising into the clouds. She even glimpsed Papa's bungalow before the top of the wave curled into the skiff. The stern dipped as the bow lifted, but Georgia kept them from turning over by pushing off the rock to their right with her oar. A loud crack sounded as the bottom half of the oar broke off.

The little boat spun into the left outcrop. The front of the craft crumpled and splintered, and water flooded over the remaining wood. Another wave lifted them, flipping the boat.

Georgia screamed and grabbed for Max as she and the boy tumbled overboard.

The rushing water roared around her ears, pressing her down under the surface as she struggled to orient her position. Where was Max? She'd not been able to reach him before the waves swept him away.

Her lungs burned as she pressed her mouth shut against the salty deluge. She clawed at the sea, kicking her legs to reach the surface, but the heavy weight of her sodden skirts slowed her progress.

At last she breached the water, sucking in a deep breath of salty air. Her arms slapped the waves as she frantically spun in search of Max. Another wave pummeled her from behind, pushing her back down. Something pounded into her stomach.

Max! She wrapped an arm around him and fought with all her might to get to the surface.

~

*H*arrison slowed his horse and narrowed his eyes as he strained to see into the distance. A small boat bobbed among the breakers.

A boat in serious trouble.

"Who would be crazy enough to row into treacherous waters?" Whomever it was, the boat was in danger, and any survivors would need assistance. Digging his heels in, he spurred his horse into a gallop. That area was known for riptides and large rocks that could snap a boat into matchsticks.

He rounded a sand dune topped with waving sea grass and caught his breath. The craft ricocheted off a rock, spun around, and flipped over, spitting its passengers into the turbulent waters. A flash of pink stopped the blood in his veins. He spurred his horse to a gallop. Georgia was on the boat, and if Georgia was there, then...

Max!

He didn't remember leaping from his horse or storming into the water until he was up to his waist in the churning surf. "Max!" He scoured the sea for the pair of them. Georgia's head broke the surface, and she sucked in a loud gulp of air. She struggled, and then her head submerged again. Seconds later, Max popped up where she'd gone under.

"Max!" Harrison plowed through a breaker. His son's pale face rose and fell on the swells. Even at this distance the boy's terror was clear.

Max caught sight of him and screamed, "Papa!"

"Here." Harrison struggled against the ocean's fury. His boots braced against the sandy bottom as the waves repeatedly crashed upon him, soaking his shirt and impeding his forward progress. Max's small arms slapped the water as he struggled to stay afloat. The boy was still at least two wagon-lengths away. Another wave crested, drenching Harrison's hair and flooding his eyes and mouth with salt water. He spit out the briny tang. *Please, Lord. Help me get to them in time.*

Between swells, he caught a glimpse of Georgia's head as she came up for air before another wave crashed over them. Woman and boy disappeared, and his heart stopped. He dove under the frothing breaker. When he resurfaced, Max and Georgia had risen to the surface again and sputtered, but at least their heads were above water. Harrison lowered his face and swam, extending his arms with long, quick strokes and kicking with all his might.

The churning water roared in his ears, drowning out the thunderous beating of his heart. He lifted his head to get his bearings but didn't stop swimming. A thunderous crack of splintering wood sounded as the ocean sucked the already-damaged boat back up against the rocks, pummeling it over and over until debris floated around them.

"Papa!" Max screamed again and fought in Georgia's arms to swim toward Harrison.

She must have heard Max's shout because her gaze shot toward Harrison. A look of sheer relief swept over her features. Then the next breaker washed over them, but Harrison was almost within range. She pushed Max in his direction, and Harrison reached him within a few strokes. His son clung to him like a starfish, and Harrison hugged him tight. "It's all right. Papa's got you."

He turned to find Georgia watching. She didn't see the wave sneak up behind her.

He opened his mouth to warn her, but the wall of water hit her with full force. "Georgia!"

Her eyes rolled back as the water swallowed her whole.

"Max, hold on." His son's arms tightened around his neck, nearly choking off his air. Harrison braced as the same wave walloped them, pushing him back toward the shore.

He searched the water churning around them until he spied a swirl of pink. Reaching under, he felt around until he connected with something soft, then grabbed hold and pulled.

Georgia's head split the water as he yanked her up by her collar. She sputtered and gasped, and he struggled to keep his grip on her without going down himself. Max slid around to his back so he could get a better hold on Georgia. At last she stopped struggling, and he turned to swim toward shore, but her sodden dress weighed a ton and slowed his pace.

The blasted woman seemed determined to swim in her gowns.

At last his feet struck sand, and he struggled to find his balance. Both his son and Georgia were like limp weights as he strained to walk through the water.

Finally, he stumbled out of the sea and dropped both

Georgia and Max onto the beach, then fell on all fours into the soft sand. His lungs burned as he fought to drag in air and catch his breath.

Max rolled to kneel beside Georgia. "Miss Georgia, wake up." He grabbed her shoulders. "Wake up. Please."

Georgia's limp body didn't stir even as Max shook her. A second round of fear surged through Harrison. *God, no.*

He crawled to her and rolled her onto her back. Her lips were blue, her face paler than the white sand beneath them. He grabbed her face between fingers and bent low until his ear hovered above her lips.

She wasn't breathing.

His heart hammered as he flipped her over, turned her face to the side, and pushed with all his weight on her mid-back. Nothing happened, so he pumped harder and harder until he thought he might break her in half.

In a powerful lurch, the sea water spewed out of her. Georgia coughed, and the water kept coming—nearly half the ocean it seemed.

"She's alive." Max danced around them, kicking up sand.

Relief washed through Harrison with such force that he closed his eyes and sank back on his haunches. "Thank you, God. Thank you." He'd almost lost them. *Oh, Lord.*

Georgia coughed, and he turned his focus back to her, helping her to a seated position. With wet hair matted to her face and red-rimmed eyes, she looked weak as a new kitten. But he'd never seen such a beautiful sight.

And he'd almost lost her.

He pulled his hands away, but then they began to tremble so vigorously he had to cross his arms over his chest and tuck them under his armpits to keep Max from glimpsing how shaken he was.

"Papa, you should have seen it." Max's voice gave him a welcome distraction. Something to focus on as he studied his son's flushed face. "The waves were huge. Georgia pushed off the rocks with the oar, then the boat spun."

Anger surged through Harrison, consuming his relief. He rose to his feet. "I don't want to hear another word." He turned on his son. "What were the two of you doing out in that part of the ocean?"

His son's bottom lip quivered, but it didn't diminish Harrison's blaze of anger. "What were you doing out in the ocean at all? You know I don't allow you out without an accomplished adult."

Tears squeezed from his eyes. "I thought it would be all right if Miss Georgia went with me."

"You are never to go near that water again. Do you hear me?"

Huge tears spilled from Max's eyes, pulling on a blanket of guilt that smothered a little of his fury.

"It was my fault," Georgia whispered in a raspy voice.

Harrison whipped around to find her slowly rising to her feet. She looked so shaky, so near death even still, his anger whipped back into full force.

"Of all the selfish, irresponsible"—he began to pace— "to try such a stunt with my son." He scrubbed a hand through his hair. "You can be reckless with your own life." He jabbed a finger through the air at her. "But don't bring my son into it."

"I'm sorry. I'm to blame." Her voice was weak, and her clothes hung on her like rags.

"But, Georgia." Max's voice pitched high between sobs. "I was the one who—"

"I dozed off," Georgia interrupted.

"You what?" Harrison's temper reached a pinnacle. "You fell asleep on a boat, in rough seas, with my son at the helm?" His hands balled into fists. *God, help me not to strangle her.*

"I'm sorry. I—" She paused, and any color that had returned to her face fled. She swayed, then crumpled forward.

Harrison lunged and caught her before she landed face-first in the sand.

Max screamed, then grabbed Harrison's elbow as he hoisted Georgia into his arms.

"She's dead." His son pulled so hard, Harrison almost stumbled.

He shook his head and tried to calm the boy even though his arms were full. "It's all right. She merely fainted."

"She's not dead?"

"No."

Max's tears continued, but Harrison didn't console him, for he, too, fought back tears. "Come on, son. Help me get her back to the house."

CHAPTER 19

...Please make arrangements for the Countess of Claremont and her son, Lord Julien, the Earl of Claremont's arrival within a fortnight. Allowances may be needed if foul weather delays the voyage.

—*From the Countess of Claremont's steward to the Artesian Hotel*

*G*eorgia kicked the sheet off. Her muscles screamed in protest, but if she didn't cool her overheated body soon, she might ignite into a blaze. Her cheeks burned like a hot iron. She put a hand to her forehead. Was she feverish? She squeezed her eyes against the morning sun, and the slight movement caused her skin to ache.

The clock read ten minutes past eleven. *Blast.* She'd missed breakfast and her morning fishing expedition with Max.

Who was she funning? Harrison would never let her near his son again.

A deep sorrow penetrated her heart as if a stint had been hammered in, and now her joy leaked out like tree sap. She ignored the pain as she slung her legs over the side of the bed.

She straightened her shoulders, but the grief and guilt over yesterday's debacle only caused them to slump again.

She sighed and put her face in her hands. Harrison probably wouldn't allow her near Max or the schoolhouse. Fishing with the boy and time with the children had seemed a lovely but unimportant diversion before. Now... she'd had no idea she would miss them this much.

A fresh wave of heat flushed through her, and she fanned her face. Warm and achy...was she sick? Had she, too, succumbed to the ague?

Maybe she'd dreamed it all. Could the entire nightmare have been a feverish delusion? Had she been in her bed the whole time?

Jenneigh slid into the room with her head down and bobbed a curtsy. Halfway through the movement, she peeked up and halted with a sharp intake of breath.

"What is it? What's wrong, Jenneigh?"

The girl's eyes dropped to her hands and clutched her apron. "Never fear, Miss. We have some creams that will help."

"Help with what?" Georgia's hands once again felt her face. Jenneigh didn't need to answer. The truth swept through her like a wave.

"Oh, heavens, no." Georgia jumped up, grabbed the hand mirror, and winced at the sight of her bright red face—brighter than the pinkest dress she'd ever owned. She sank back onto the bed. Yesterday in the boat, she'd fallen asleep, but she had on her bonnet. It must have shifted. *No, no, no. This can't be happening.*

"Aloe will sooth ya skin and take da heat out. Couple days and dat old skin will peel off, and you'll have fresh new baby skin underneath."

Along with a dozen freckles.

A broad smile grew across Jenneigh's face. "I know what will make ya feel better. The dressmaker delivered the rest of your gowns yesterday. I'll show dem to ya."

The new gowns had arrived just in time, for she'd ruined her last salvaged dress yesterday. At least she had one positive thing to dwell upon. Jenneigh helped her dress in a white frock and applied cream to her face.

"Let it set like dat. Ring fer me in an hour, and we'll take it off."

With her face tingling and covered in what felt like a slimy film, Georgia headed downstairs to find something to eat. Hattie had set aside some fruit and biscuits on a plate, which she carried with her into the library.

But the day was too warm to eat indoors. The heat of her skin formed beads of sweat around her hairline. It ran down and mixed with the cream on her face. She fanned herself and moved to the porch where the air was cooler. Papa and Aunt Tessa sat in chairs, rocking slowly under the ceiling fans.

"Good afternoon, princess." Her father grimaced at the sight of her but tried to cover it with a smile.

Aunt Tessa paused her rocking. "Oh, dear, does it hurt?"

Papa rose and pulled over another chair for her.

"Especially when I look in the mirror," Georgia said in a flat tone.

She sat and lifted her face to the cool ocean breeze. The rockers squeaked back and forth, and a wagon rumbled in the distance.

"What a wild day you had yesterday." Her father's eyes softened with concern. "Max told us the whole story. You were very brave."

Aunt Tessa's head bobbed. "We're so fortunate no one drowned."

"It was a miracle." No doubt about it.

"That it was. God was with you. Don't worry about the burn." Papa pointed to his face. "Happens to all of us Northern Europeans. The cream helps. Good as new in a couple of days."

Please, God, no freckles.

She would be scoffed at and teased as bran-faced the moment she returned to London. She probably shouldn't have come below stairs looking the way she did. In England, she would never allow herself to be seen in such a condition, but her room was hot and stuffy.

It's merely family.

Then a flash of motion caught her attention. A carriage.

"Ho, there." The driver reined in the horses at the base of the porch stairs, and a numbness sank over her as Mr. Rousseau's footman, overly dressed in maroon livery, jumped down, lowered the steps, and opened the door to assist Mr. Rousseau down.

Sight of the man jerked her from her stupor, and she scrambled for the door to get out of sight. "Tell him I'm indisposed."

"Good day, Mr. Lennox, Lady Pickering… Miss Lennox."

Georgia froze in the open doorway. She'd been spotted.

She turned as Mr. Rousseau mounted the stairs, carrying a bouquet of tropical flowers. His eyes were focused on the difficult climb as he said in a soft voice, "Miss Lennox, these are for you…" He stopped midstride, hand outstretched as he peered at the sheen on her face. Or maybe it was the bright red showing through the cream.

"Good day, Mr. Rousseau. These are lovely." She said through stiff lips. "Thank you. Now, if you'll excuse me a moment, I'll put these in water."

"Certainly." He averted his eyes and cleared his throat. "Um, take your time to freshen up. It will give me a chance to speak with your father."

She tried to smile, but her face wouldn't oblige under the tightness of the dried cream. She stepped inside, closed the door, and rang for Jenneigh on her way upstairs to her room.

Jenneigh burst in a few moments later with a towel and a pitcher. She made quick work of removing the mask and fixing Georgia's appearance. As much as was possible, anyway.

Georgia's face still shown bright pink, but at least she didn't look like a sea monster. She instructed Jenneigh to put the flowers in water, then descended back downstairs. This time, she greeted Mr. Rousseau on the porch with a smile.

He stood upon seeing her. "Miss Lennox, would you care to take a turn about the yard?"

Mr. Rousseau wasn't exactly a pleasant conversationalist, but he was influential on the island. It would be wise of her to accept. "Certainly, let me get my bonnet." She reached inside, pulled her hat off the peg, and tied the strings in a bow under her chin.

He offered his arm, which she accepted, then tipped his hat to Papa and Aunt Tessa. "We'll return shortly."

When they reached the bottom of the steps, he said, "You'll need to be more careful about the sun." He circled his index finger around his face. "I'd hate for you to ruin your fair complexion."

"I assure you, I used every precaution. It was an unforeseeable circumstance."

"I'm glad to see you're well and about. I heard about your escapade yesterday." He shook his head. "I still cannot believe Mr. Wells would set a refined lady like yourself in a pathetic little rowboat with only his young son to handle the oars."

"He didn't—"

"The man is nicked in the nob." Rousseau talked over her as if she hadn't spoken. "The waters around here are treacherous. How fortunate you weren't harmed." He cleared his throat. "Once you're ... er ... healed. I would be delighted if you'd join me on a real sailing vessel. I have a beautiful schooner. It rivals the Prince Regent's private yacht. Plus, my men will do all the necessary work. We would merely relax and enjoy the day."

"Well, I—"

"Some hesitation is understandable after such a traumatic event, but I'm sure you'll come around with time." He fished into his coat pocket. "Here's the second reason for my visit." He handed over a small stack of letters tied in a bundle. "A cargo boat arrived in St. Kitts, and I was able to send a courier to retrieve mail." His volume rose as a self-important smile touched his face. "One of the perks of making acquaintances with the wealthiest man on the island. It has certain privileges."

She accepted the bundle and fought the urge to sort through them for any correspondence from Julien. Letters from home were scarce and tended to arrive all at once. "Thank you. These are precious, indeed."

"A passenger ship is scheduled to arrive in a couple of weeks. I'm expecting several guests at the hotel. I would love to have your company as well, to help entertain."

She hesitated. Would Harrison approve of her acting as hostess for Edward Rousseau? No, he wouldn't. He wouldn't approve of anything she did anymore, not since she'd nearly killed his son.

Mr. Rousseau's eyes narrowed, and she realized she hadn't answered.

"I…I'll check with Papa and Aunt Tessa." She mentally berated herself for woolgathering.

"Splendid."

They'd completed a circle and now ascended the stairs. She could hear another wagon approaching, but the conveyance wasn't visible yet.

When they reached the porch, he turned to her father and Aunt Tessa with a bow. "Well, I must be on my way."

Georgia glanced over to see Harrison's wagon slow. Her stomach twisted, and she held her breath, but he didn't wave or even tip his hat, simply paused at the end of the drive. Had he stopped when he saw the Rousseau carriage?

Her anger rose, making her cheeks even hotter. Neither she nor Mr. Rousseau may be in Harrison's good graces, but he could at least be polite and acknowledge Papa.

Mr. Rousseau raised her hand to his lips in a bold gesture. "Glad to see you are well. May I pay you a call at a future date?"

She stared over Rousseau's shoulder as Harrison snapped the reins and pressed the team on past their house and around the bend.

"Ah." Her gaze dropped to the letters in her fingers, grateful to be holding them. "Of course, I'd be...delighted."

A broad smile lightened his features. "Very well, then. Farewell, Lady Pickering, Mr. Lennox." He started down the steps, but paused partway and half-turned. "Oh, and Miss Lennox, please keep me informed in regards to Mr. Wells' condition."

Georgia didn't respond, but she didn't need to. She understood what he implied. Mr. Rousseau pivoted on his heel and marched down the remaining steps.

"My, he's a strange man," Aunt Tessa whispered once he was beyond hearing distance.

A trace of doubt flickered within Georgia. *Was Harrison right? Was she treading into dangerous waters?*

☙

*G*eorgia stole to her room and pulled the string on the letters. One from Mama. One from Eleanor. One for Aunt Tessa.

None from Julien. Her heart sank. Maybe Mama or Eleanor would mention him in their correspondence. Maybe he'd boarded the next ship, and their letters told of his coming.

She tore open her mother's missive and scanned its contents. The first paragraph was instructions to make certain she wrote to them often and kept them abreast of her father's condition. Surprisingly, the next paragraph was an apology for sending her off on short notice. Georgia would revisit that part thoroughly at another time. The rest was merely the latest news about her sisters and their children. Nothing in regards to Julien. *Nothing.*

She ripped open Eleanor's letter and skimmed its contents, then started over and reread it.

Dearest Georgia,
I hate to be the bearer of bad news,
but I feel you must be apprised of the compromising
position in which I discovered both Lord Claremont
and Miss Orville at the DeLeruth ball.
If your intentions are still for Lord Claremont,
then you must return posthaste, or I fear
Miss Orville is going to betray you further.
I know she is your friend and this must grieve
you dearly, but it is best to learn of these things through
family rather than the gossip columnists. I hope this
letter finds you well. Please give my regards to
Papa and Aunt Tessa.

Truly Yours,
Eleanor

Her mouth dropped open as the weight of shock pressed in on her. *How dare Cynthia...*

A cry—part-rage, part-pain—tore from her lips as her fingers balled into fists, crumpling the letter. She paced the length of the room.

She'd thought Cynthia was one of her dearest friends. But maybe she'd been like all the rest, conniving, willing to do anything to advance her social status.

Georgia imagined Eleanor's thoughts as she penned the letter. *You overreached, dear sister. Did you really believe an earl would marry the likes of you?* Or Mama's, *See, this is why I have secured the Viscount of Ashburnham's favor. I knew you couldn't bring Lord Claremont up to scratch.*

Fierce, white-hot anger seared through her as her thoughts tackled each other before one could even be completed. Georgia pressed her hands to the sides of her head to keep it from coming apart.

Julien's not coming. He never loved you. The notion pierced her like a gunshot.

Despair swallowed her anger, and her knees caved. She sank to the floor, her skirts billowing around her in an icy, white puddle. The anguish of a young girl in boy's pantaloons poured through her as if she were still running down the hall to the safety of the kitchens, her mind screaming, *Papa, don't leave. Please, don't leave.* Ol' Willy hanging on the fishing pole, thumping against her back.

She'd known all along, hadn't she? Julien wasn't coming for her any more than ol' Willy would come back from the dead. Julien had never intended to propose. He never really wanted her. She'd wanted it so badly, she'd convinced herself of a lie.

Her dream of being accepted by her mother and sisters had already died.

CHAPTER 20

...I'm sorry for our exchange before you left. I should have
given you more time to adjust to the idea, but I feared you'd
wear me down with your refusal. I wish we weren't always at
ends.

—From Nora Lennox to her daughter, Georgia Lennox

*G*eorgia ate supper in her room that night, claiming to
be still recovering from the near drowning. In truth,
the weight of her grief was more than she could
cover up.

Jenneigh came and applied more cream, then helped her
wash it off a couple of hours later. The salve did take the heat
out, and her cheeks faded from a vibrant red to bright pink.
Georgia stared into the mirror and studied the sprinkling of
freckles that appeared across the bridge of her nose and cheeks.
She'd never regain her perfect alabaster complexion.

"Mista Wells and Max came by askin' about you dis
afternoon."

Georgia's breath hitched at the mere mention of his name.
Jenneigh rubbed the sticky gel-like substance over her burned

cheeks. The smell caused Georgia's eyes to water, but everyone swore the aloe gel could work wonders.

"Mmmm," Georgia murmured as Jenneigh coated around her lips. It was a shock that Harrison would think of allowing Max to be in her presence after the other day's disaster. Oh how she would miss their daily fishing trips. It seemed life on the island had taken a lonely turn.

The following day, Georgia forced herself to come out of hiding. She dressed in a deep lavender gown that drew some of the red out of her face—at least she told herself it did. Now she wished she hadn't let Harrison's comments regarding her wearing pink irk her. On a bold whim, she'd selected gowns of other colors, but now she'd give almost anything for a pink dress to boost her confidence.

She had Jenneigh spend extra time on her hair, which she pulled up into a beautiful spray of ringlet curls. Hopefully, her buffer of outward glamor, along with her practiced serene smile, would cover her inner turmoil.

Yet sadness followed her around like a shadow as the morning progressed.

Aunt Tessa commented on her quiet behavior as the two of them sat in the solarium, and Georgia told her about the letter. Surprisingly, she didn't break down at her aunt's shocked face, nor at her look of pity as she did her best to cheer her up. Georgia put on a good show, but she felt like a puppet whose strings had been cut.

"I know it hurts, my dear." Her aunt laid a hand on Georgia's arm. "When your uncle passed, I thought my world was ending, but slowly I found joy again. First, it appeared in the little things, like my morning talks with God."

The words pricked Georgia's curiosity. "You speak to God in the mornings?"

"I speak to God all the time, but especially during my morning cup of tea."

Georgia leaned in. "What do you tell him?"

"Back then, I told him of my pain and loneliness, but now I tell him how thankful I am for you, for your papa, and for my new friends."

A twinge of pain twisted in her chest. "Next time you speak to God, can you ask Him why He would destroy my future hopes?" Her words dripped with bitterness.

Her aunt patted her arm. "Georgia, God wants what's best for you."

That couldn't possibly be true. She turned from her aunt and reached for a book from the side table. She didn't want to hear what Aunt Tessa had to say. The best for her was Julien, but she'd been forced to sail away from him. God obviously didn't give a wit about her. If He did, wouldn't He have answered the one prayer she'd wanted more desperately than any other? If He cared about her, why would he squash her dream?

Aunt Tessa sighed. "Sometimes what's best for us isn't how we pictured it."

Georgia's eyes misted with tears and the words on the page blurred. She didn't want to let go of the dream she'd striven so hard to achieve. Didn't God understand how much work she had put into catching Julien's attention? She could sense Aunt Tessa's gaze upon her, but she refused to continue the conversation.

As the sun rose in the sky and warmed the house, Georgia tried to read, but her mind drifted. Her pain wasn't quite the same as Aunt Tessa's. She couldn't imagine the horrible finality of being separated by death. Her aunt and uncle's marriage might have been arranged, but over time they'd grown to love one another deeply.

Julien hadn't died. However, he *had* rejected her.

Her uncle couldn't prevent his death. He didn't leave Aunt Tessa on purpose.

Not only had Julien chosen not to come for her, he had chosen someone else over her.

Georgia closed her eyes to hold back tears. Why would God destroy her dream of marrying well? Why would He take Aunt Tessa's husband from her? Why did He take Papa from her as a child? And why would He take Papa from her a second time just as she started to let him back into her heart this time? Everyone here acted as though his days were clearly numbered.

The indoor air suffocated her as she fought down a fresh surge of tears. Another drop of sweat cascaded down the side of her face, and she slammed her book shut.

Aunt Tessa peered up from her embroidery. "Some fresh air might do you good."

The idea had merit. A brisk walk along the beach might clear her jumbled thoughts. She grabbed her pink parasol, the last intact pink item she owned, and picked her way down the path to the shoreline.

The ocean breeze cooled her flushed face and gently tugged at her parasol. The waves lapped at the shore, quite different from the ones that had tried to drag her under a couple of days ago. Maybe she had more in common with the island of Nevis than she'd originally imagined. Its beauty was alluring, but upon closer inspection, it was conflicted, untamed, and misunderstood.

She veered off the beach to the path that led up a hill. Before her stood a stunning view of St. Kitts, sitting only a canal away. The crystal waters and the lush greenery of the island eased her nerves as she weighed her options.

She could scurry back to London to try to salvage whatever she could of her relationship with Julien. It would entail paying someone to row her to St. Kitts to obtain passage on a ship bound for England. It meant leaving her father in his moment of need, and she would likely never see him again. Max would be hurt by her departure. And Aunt Tessa would have to end her blossoming romance with the vicar to act as her chaperone. If Georgia did return to London, there was no guarantee that Julien would even choose her.

And if he did, would that truly make her happy?

On the other hand, if she stayed, Cynthia would wring a proposal out of the earl. Georgia's sisters and mother would chastise her for once again failing to capture a husband. And when she returned to London, without any alternative, Mama would force her to marry the Viscount of Ashburnham.

She could avoid her mother and sisters and public scrutiny by remaining here in Nevis. But eventually, her father would succumb to the ague, and she would need to find a husband to support her.

There was Edward Rousseau. He could be a decent match. He was from money and held a prominent position in Nevis. True, he wasn't titled, but her chance for a title had passed—or *sailed* might be a more apt word.

Mama would be disappointed. Not a splendid match, but acceptable. Would Rousseau's boastful nature wear on her? How long before she grew bored with his flaunting lifestyle? Could she live that life?

A thought slipped in, stilling her as she stood on the rocky bank overlooking the ocean. *Did she appear the same as Mr. Rousseau? Did others see through her pretense? Did they see the pathetic woman beneath her façade, the woman desperate for their acceptance?*

The sea swelled, and white foam sprayed as the waves slammed against the rocks below.

Harrison seemed to see through her. There were moments when all the pretense felt stripped away, when he looked at her as though she mattered to him. That look had found its way deep into her soul, drawing a longing she'd worked so hard to squelch.

Would she consider marrying Harrison? Assuming he would

speak to her now, and would ever ask for her hand. Could she live as the wife of a local schoolmaster, a man who lived off the land with no wealth or title to his name? Could she forego all she knew and face the scorn of her sisters for her heart's whim?

She remembered his throaty laugh as he'd danced with her, and his crooked grin as he'd teased her. The man riled her, but just as quickly made her laugh. She didn't have to pretend around him. He liked her better when she was herself, crawling in the dirt to play games with the schoolchildren or sloshing through the ocean water as she fished with Max.

She sighed. For someone of her station to marry someone from the working class—it simply wasn't done. She'd be an utter disappointment. Her mother and sisters would never speak to her again, and she would never be able to hold her head up if she returned to England.

But she'd be happy. If all she wanted was to impress her mother and sisters, wouldn't she have given in and married Ashburnham in the first place?

And anyway, her happiness didn't seem like an option now. After the boating incident with Max, Harrison believed her to be the most irresponsible chit on the island. Perhaps in all of the English territory.

And she probably was.

She wouldn't even allow herself to go boating with Max anymore. He'd been entrusted into her care and she fell asleep.

"Ho, there. Georgia."

As if her thoughts conjured him, Harrison's boots thumped on the path behind her. Tiny crabs scuttled back into the cracks of rocks, and she swallowed, steeling herself for a lecture on her reckless behavior. Her emotional state was too fragile for a good set down, even if she deserved it. She didn't turn, but waited for his approach, watching the crabs and wishing she too could hide within the cracks.

"Come away from the edge."

She glanced down at her feet, surprised to find herself so close to the drop-off.

His warm fingers encircled her upper arm and tugged her back a few steps.

"There's something we need to—"

She finally forced herself to turn and face him.

He winced. "—discuss."

He tried to cover it by looking away, but there was no mistaking—his first reaction to her face was shock.

She broke away from his grasp and covered her face with her hands. "God is punishing me."

"It's merely a sunburn."

"No. It's not. Look." She uncovered her face and pointed at her nose.

Harrison's eyes narrowed, and he leaned in closer. Confusion touched his face.

"Freckles." A half-laugh, half-sob erupted from her throat. "My complexion is forever ruined."

He pinched his lips, but a snort of laughter escaped out his nose.

"Go ahead and laugh. I deserve it." She turned and started to walk away. "I was reckless, selfish, and irresponsible, and now God has punished me."

"You were out on the water at midday. That's not God punishing you. That's poor planning."

"It's not simply that. It's everything—my marriage prospects, my family, my looks…" Her voice dropped as she fought against tears. "And now Max."

"Max?" His brows drew together.

She couldn't look at Harrison, so she dropped her eyes to her grip on the parasol. "I don't blame you. I wouldn't let me around him either, but it seems unfair to punish him too. He loved our morning fishing adventures as much as I."

"Georgia…"

She swallowed through the lump in her throat.

"Georgia." He raised her chin with his index finger. "I don't blame you."

"Of course you do. I blame me. I was foolish and—"

"Stop. I don't blame you."

She finally raised her eyes to his face, searching for malice or teasing. He seemed sincere. "You don't?"

"Max told me the whole story. He wanted to prove he could reel in a fish without your help, so he waited for you to drift off to sleep, then pulled up the anchor. He figured he could catch a fish and row back before you woke."

"But I never should have fallen asleep. Not when he was in my care."

"No, but minor lapses in judgment can have worse consequences than we ever anticipated." His eyes reflected a deep pain.

Georgia sucked in a quick breath. The night of his wife's death, he'd wanted to walk home. Surely he didn't blame himself?

"Max told me how your quick thinking saved you both. You were brave and strong, and you saved my son's life."

She searched his face. "You forgive me?"

"I do."

But there was more than that. Her eyes dropped to his boots.

"You don't believe me?" He ducked his chin to see her face, but she didn't look up.

"It's just…all these horrible things keep happening to me."

"Georgia." Her name swept over his lips like the cool ocean breeze. "You're looking for God to alter your situation, but maybe God is looking for a heart change before he changes your circumstances."

He might be right, but how could she do it? "I can't go back to the way I was, and I know I can't remain the way I am, but I can't seem to find a middle ground." Her words sounded like a plea.

He tucked her hand into the crook of his arm and led her further up the path. His eyes rose to the pink parasol, then back to her lavender gown. "In some ways you already have. The Georgia I dragged out of the ocean the first day is not the same person I pulled out of the ocean two days ago."

She couldn't help but chuckle.

He smiled. "Please tell me it's the last time you'll be in need of rescuing."

She eyed him, but couldn't promise anything. "I never meant to be in need of rescuing on the first two occasions."

Harrison's smile broadened.

The path narrowed, and he allowed her to go first. She crested the ridge and stopped at the view of a large sailing vessel anchored in Basseterre Bay. "But all the dreams I've striven so hard for, do they have to change too?"

He stopped alongside her. She peered up at him as his gaze swept over the ship in the distance. "Your dreams to marry an earl you mean."

"Yes... No... I don't know."

He stiffened beside her. "You're still pining for Claremont."

"No."

He sent her a cynical sideways glance.

She summoned the courage to speak the words still so hard to say. "He's not coming."

Harrison didn't respond. He merely returned to stare into the distance.

"Deep down, I always knew he wouldn't, but a letter arrived from my sister confirming it. Turns out, he's now smitten with Miss Cynthia Orville, my closest friend."

He turned to face her, but now it was her turn to stare off into the distance as the sun dropped behind an array of pink clouds.

"I truly believed he was going to propose." She released a long sigh. "He told me he needed to marry, and he wanted me to be his bride. He merely had to get his affairs in order." She hugged her midsection. "I asked him when that would be, and he said a fortnight. He intended to ask for my mother's blessing. I pressed him to come by and get Mama's approval the following afternoon. There would have been time to get his affairs in order while I planned the wedding. But I sailed on the Aberdeen that morning."

A harsh chuckle slipped from her lips. "I realize now I might only have heard what I wanted to hear."

"Claremont has a reputation for playing on a woman's affections."

She shook her head, then lowered it in shame. "Indeed, he wooed me with sweet words before he grabbed my shoulders and pulled me in for a kiss."

She sensed Harrison stiffen next to her. "Claremont is a cad."

"It didn't work out the way he intended." A smile tugged at her lips. "He was so eager in his assault, so intent to steal a kiss. And I was so focused on a proposal, he caught me off guard. I tried to hold my balance, but when he applied more pressure, it was too much. We toppled over the back of the bench into a wisteria vine. Julien landed soundly on top of me and knocked all the air from my lungs." She laughed, but it sounded bitter to her ears. "What a horrid sight we would have made if anyone had passed by. My mouth opening and closing like a fish, unable to make a sound or drag air into my lungs, and his feet hanging over the edge of the bench as he struggled to right himself."

"You deserve better than that lout."

"No, I don't. I was as much to blame. I was so intent on proving myself to my sisters. I only thought of the wedding, not the man I was planning to marry."

"From what Fredrick tells me, you have nothing to prove to your sisters."

She snorted. "Not anymore. I came close enough to smell my wedding bouquet, but then it fell apart." The breeze yanked on her parasol. With a sigh, she closed it and hooked the handle onto the crook of her arm. "Men always leave—Papa, Julien, and they aren't the only ones."

"Your father didn't want to leave."

"I know that now."

"Why do you think the others left?"

"It appears I can attract men, but my personality sends them fleeing faster than a fox during a hunt." She released a self-deprecating laugh.

But instead of laughing with her, Harrison turned her to face him. His hands braced her shoulders in a firm grip.

Dreaded tears blurred her vision, but she couldn't blink them away without letting loose a deluge.

His eyes locked on hers. "Maybe if you let them see the true you. If you didn't push them away."

She shook her head, and the tears slipped down her cheeks. "I don't push them away."

"You do it to me." He handed her a handkerchief.

"That's ridiculous." She wiped the corners of her eyes.

"Every time, I get a peek at the real you. Every time you open up and I get close, like this." He stepped in toward her, and his hand dropped to encircle her waist. "You push me away by bringing up Claremont."

His nearness rattled her, leaving her off balance. Those warm caramel eyes made it impossible to look away. "I didn't…"

She let her words trail off as she recalled the Rousseau house party. Excitement had filled her when she'd seen him across the room, again when they'd danced. It'd been lovely. They'd laughed. They'd teased each other. Then her insecurities welled up, and she'd mentioned Julien, and they fought the rest of the evening.

"If I were a betting man, I'd place high stakes at White's you did the same to Lord Claremont and whomever these other fellows are." His eyes held her captive. "You reject them before they can reject you. You find a way to keep them on the other side of your drawbridge.

"But I've had a glimpse of the princess who resides behind your buttressed walls. She's beautiful, not only in her looks but in her heart. Kind enough to spend time fishing with an eight-year-old boy who misses his mother. Thoughtful enough to hand over an expensive gown for a slave boy's sick mother to wear to the grave. Charming enough to delight in teaching children to read." His voice lowered into an almost-whisper. "And fierce enough to bring this dead man's heart back to life."

His fingers applied gentle pressure to her waist until she swayed in his direction. His eyes deepened to a dark umber.

A heady sensation swept through her, and her fingers curled around his arms for support. *He's going to kiss me. Don't foul this up. Don't make a mess of things as you usually do.*

His mouth hovered above hers.

She didn't breathe. Her lips tingled, ready and eager as she waited.

Instead of kissing her, he drew up and pulled her into his chest.

Her eyes flew open. His familiar scent of spice and coconut enveloped her as she turned her face into his shirt to hide her disappointment. It wasn't a kiss, but it was an embrace. After all she'd done, including her fit about freckles a few minutes ago, she should be thankful he too didn't run from her presence.

"We must head back before anyone comes searching for us," he murmured into her hair.

"Of course."

She pulled away, and Harrison offered his arm. She curled her fingers around his bicep, and he covered her hand with his other and kept it there. A spark of hope flared inside her chest. Did his possessive touch mean something?

He led her back down the path in comfortable silence, even though her world seemed to teeter on the edge of a precipice. She cared for Harrison. There was no sense in hiding the truth. But did he care for her? If he did, why didn't he kiss her?

Once again, the vulnerable girl in pantaloons rose up inside her. Harrison crumbled her walls to dust, and there was not a bit of rubble or even pink muslin to hide her heart behind. Her body started to tremble. She needed cover, like after Eve ate the apple and realized she was naked. Without her façade, would Harrison love her or find her lacking?

"Are you cold?"

"No." She cleared her throat before it clogged with tears. "It's the sunburn. My body's struggling to maintain a normal temperature."

When Harrison walked her up the steps to her father's house, the shadows had already grown long, and the sun hovered on the horizon. He stopped before opening the door.

"I'm afraid I've been putting off telling you some terrible news." He cleared his throat. "I came by yesterday, but you were entertaining company."

Was he upset about Rousseau's visits?

He hesitated, but only concern seemed to furrow his brow. "Booker's mother passed yesterday."

Georgia gasped, and her hand flew to her mouth. "Oh, no."

"It was expected. She had a quiet funeral yesterday. I gave Booker your regards."

"I...I should have been there." Several hot tears slipped down her cheeks, and she wiped them away with her fingers.

"Death happens all the time on Nevis, and with slaves, it's different. Usually, it's only the family that mourns. The other slaves are still expected to work."

"He's a child."

"He's doing well, considering. He knows his mother is in heaven. His aunt will care for him."

She nodded, but ached deep inside for the boy. Her own heart had broken when her father left, but he was still alive. Booker would never again have the opportunity to see his mother this side of heaven.

Harrison stared at her with those warm eyes that penetrated deep into her soul. Her shame no longer had a place to hide, but he didn't flinch, and neither did she.

"I could use your help at school tomorrow if you've recovered."

She nodded. "Of course."

An awkward silence filled the air as they stood there, neither willing to look away. Georgia longed to feel his powerful arms around her once again. She wanted to fling herself into his chest and sob like the weak woman she was.

Harrison opened his mouth as if to speak, but nothing came out. The rhythmic rumble of waves crashing against the shore sounded in the distance. He stood so close she could feel his body absorb the heat that radiated from hers, yet a hundred different reasons blocked them like a glass wall.

He cleared his throat and stepped back. "Max and I will swing by with the wagon tomorrow."

She nodded, her mind not able to summon a response that would make sense.

"Good night then." He turned and traipsed down the steps.

As Georgia watched him go, she cursed her whimsical heart. Somehow, she'd fallen in love with an island schoolmaster, and left herself even more vulnerable than the frightened misfit who flopped her first London season.

CHAPTER 21

...The timing could not be worse. Appeal to the prince on my behalf. Let him know I have every intention of returning. My duty is first to my king, but if there is any way to stall for time, do so. Something unexpected has come up.

—*From the Duke of Linton to Lord Liverpool*

*H*e'd almost kissed Georgia.

Harrison berated himself as he picked his way through the tall grass. A family of land pike scattered, their ear-piercing shrieks alerting him of their displeasure.

He'd wanted to kiss her. There was no denying it.

But how could he betray Laura? How could he love another woman when his heart was buried with his wife's body?

God, help me understand Your will.

He strolled up the walk lined with palm trees that ended at a large bubbling fountain. The great house stood beyond it, the grand entrance welcoming him. But instead of entering, he veered right down a path that led to the house manager's meager quarters and opened the door. The room was clean and tidy, and a blazing fire met him in the hearth.

"Good evening, Mary." He nodded to the servant.

"A letter arrived for you, Mr. Wells. It's in dat tray." She pointed, then bobbed a respectful nod and left through the only door to the servant's entrance of the main house.

He couldn't live in that massive home, but he couldn't let it turn to shambles either. Instead of buying slaves, he'd gone to the auction and purchased their loyalty by giving them their freedom. He offered them room, board, and wages to staff the house and keep it maintained. All but two had accepted his offer. The two who didn't take his offer of work headed to the summit of Mount Nevis, where it was rumored a colony of escaped slaves resided.

The finances that came with his dukedom were both a blessing and a curse. The islanders believed he was an estate manager and the schoolmaster, and he preferred it that way. Very few people would understand the detriments of being a duke, even if he were to admit to the title. He'd left England not only to escape the memories of Laura, but also to protect himself and his son from determined young females and their match-making mamas whose sole desire was to possess his title and fortune.

He grimaced, remembering their attempts to leg-shackle him. They had followed him into the privy. They'd snuck into his carriage. One even crawled into his bed. At least, she'd thought it was his bed. Lady Milton had scared the life out of his poor mother. Each ambitious woman had hoped to wrangle up a scandal and force him into marriage.

Georgia may have been in pursuit of a desirable husband, but who could blame her, when she lived in the shadows of her sisters' good marriages? At first, he'd been disgusted with her antics, comparing her with every scheming female who'd ever tried to manipulate him into matrimony.

But God had opened his eyes to see her insecurities and to

know her heart, and now he couldn't seem to squelch the attraction growing inside him.

She held feelings for him as well. He could see the desire in her eyes. Her lips begged for kissing, and her heart longed for the freedom to be loved. Georgia was not the woman she pretended to be.

But then again, neither was he the man he showed the world. Logic told Georgia he was beneath her as a schoolmaster and wouldn't hold a candle to her mother's expectations. Little did she know, as the Duke of Linton, he was the most sought-after bachelor in all of England. He hadn't meant to be secretive or to toy with her emotions, but he didn't regret his actions. He needed to know if Georgia could love him for him. Not only his title.

"Hello, Papa." Max bounded around the corner of his bedroom. Oscar sat perched on his arm, wings flapping.

"Rawch," Oscar squawked. "Hello."

Max beamed. "He's talking all the time now."

"Lovely," Harrison said in a dry tone.

Max straightened his arm, and the bird flew to the windowsill. "How did your talk go with Miss Georgia? Did she forgive us?"

"Yes, she did. She actually tried to convince me that you shouldn't be punished."

His face lit up. "Really? So, we can fish tomorrow?"

"Sorry, squirt." He tousled his son's hair. "My ruling still stands."

Max's face fell. "Rats."

"It's only a week." Harrison sat on the sofa near the fire and reached for his Bible. "No fishing and a few extra chores won't kill you."

"I know." Max plopped down next to him. "You like Miss Georgia, don't you?" He rested his small chin on his fist. "She makes you laugh and shake your head."

Harrison peered at his son with a crooked smile. "I do like her. She can be frustrating, but she has a good heart."

"I make you angry and frustrated sometimes, but you love me."

"I do. I love you very much."

"Do you love Miss Georgia then?"

Harrison hesitated. "Well, that's complicated."

"Why?"

"I still love your mama."

"I love Mama, too, but I also have enough love in my heart for Miss Georgia." He nudged his way underneath his father's arm and snuggled against his chest. A position Harrison could never get enough of. "Hattie told me that after she had her first baby, she didn't think she could love anyone more. But then she had another baby, and she said more love grew in her heart, more than plenty for both of them."

The fire crackled as silence settled between them. Did his son have any idea how much wisdom was packed into those simple words? Max let out a yawn. "I think Mama would love Miss Georgia."

The words sent a pang through his chest, but he forced himself to smile at his young son. "Your Mama loved everyone."

"Then you should ask Miss Georgia to marry you. She's been real sad and lonely, and I know you've been sad and lonely without Mama. You laugh more now that Miss Georgia is here." He twisted his head to peer up at Harrison. "You know what? I think God sent her to us. God knew we needed her. Will you ask her?"

Max shifted, laid his head in his father's lap, and let out another yawn.

A lump formed in Harrison's throat, making it hard to force out words. "I'm going to have to pray about it some more, son."

Max gave a little shake of his head as his eyes closed. "I've been praying, Papa. Praying enough for both of us."

~

*G*eorgia and Hattie packed enough food to last several weeks—puddings, jams, jellies, pies, breads, cheeses, fruits, dried meats, and more.

"Dis should put some meat on his bones." Hattie handed a basket to Harrison to load into the wagon.

"Booker and his aunt will feast on this." Harrison nodded at Hattie. "Thank you."

"It was all Miss Georgia's idea."

Harrison glanced at her, and his warm, appreciative smile sent a surge of heat to her cheeks. "It was the least I could do." She waved it off, but he continued to grin at her. "Don't smile at me like that."

His smile broadened, deepening the crinkles next to his eyes. "Like what?"

She shooed a hand in his direction. "Like what you're doing. I don't need any more color in my cheeks than I already have."

Harrison settled Max between the baskets of food, then aided Georgia into the front seat. He resumed his spot next to her and spurred the horses in the direction of the school.

They rode in silence, but the thoughts gnawing in Georgia's mind wouldn't let her relax. Finally, she turned to face him. "You said yesterday that God could change me. Do you really believe it? That He can make me into a good person?"

"God can do anything, but I think you misunderstood me."

She braced herself and waited for the lecture. *God can, but you've a lot to atone for...*

He rubbed his forehead before glancing at her. "God knows who you truly are and who you are capable of being. He made you, and He'll help you through when you're ready. It says in Psalm 139 that He knows your inmost being. You are His unique and wonderful creation. He made you special." He exhaled a long breath. "I hate to tell you, but you dishonor Him by pretending to be someone you're not."

"I know that now." Did she dare voice her true fears? Harrison held so much wisdom, and something about him felt safe. Safe enough to trust. She sighed. "In truth, I'm scared. People don't like the real me."

He shook his head "That's where you're wrong. You keep the real Georgia Lennox hiding under a bushel. If you'd let God's light shine through you, you'll find people are drawn to you. Not merely to your outward beauty, but the true beauty you hold inside."

"But I make a mess of things." She wrapped her arms around her stomach. "You said it yourself. I push people away. I foul it up without even being aware."

A smile slid across Harrison's features. "Welcome to being human."

Overhead, a seagull cried as it flew by. The bird veered out to sea, gliding over the ocean. Harrison's rough palm took her hand in his. She stared at his tanned fingers, then at him, and their eyes held for a moment.

"God's grace is more powerful than any mistake you've ever made or ever could make. He will meet you where you are, or if need be, He will pursue you to a far-off island. He's relentless in His desire for you."

Her stomach did a small flip. God desired her?

"I blamed myself when my wife died. If I'd only decided to take the carriage home that day instead of coaxing her into an evening stroll, my whole life would have been different. I was so embittered and wrapped up in guilt that it required me sailing clear across the Atlantic before God could get my attention.

"That's when I met your father. We were both emotionally raw, and we tumbled into God's open arms together. It took time, but eventually, we began to see that not only did God's grace cover our mistakes, but with His help, we could forgive ourselves." He raised his brows. "Have you noticed a difference in your father?"

"Yes." Her response leapt off her lips because the difference was so profound.

"I used to be a lot like the old him—proud, self-sufficient, and indestructible. We both changed. God worked two miracles."

She searched his warm gaze. "Will God change me?"

He didn't back down from her scrutiny. "You have to ask Him."

"That's all?" Georgia blinked. Could that be all? Did she dare hope?

Harrison squeezed her hand. "You simply need to ask him into your heart."

"How?"

Max, who'd been silent thus far, popped up from the back-seat. "It's easy. You pray."

Pray. Ask God to change her. Is that what Aunt Tessa had done, too? A surge of desperation slipped through her. She wanted the peace her aunt possessed. The peace she now saw in her father. And Harrison.

"We'll pray with you." Harrison slowed the wagon to a stop and turned to her, his gaze holding hers steady. "If that's what you want to do."

"Yes." The word slipped out before she realized she'd made a conscious decision. But she had. If God could make her into a better person, she would let Him.

The corners of Harrison's eyes creased in a smile, then he bowed his head. Max did, too, so Georgia followed suit.

"Repeat after me," Harrison said. "Jesus."

Georgia repeated his words. "Please come into my heart. Change me and make me a new person. Forgive me of my past and present sins and make me into Your likeness. Amen."

She opened her eyes and met Harrison's gaze. His smile was warm, his gaze intent. She could get lost in those eyes.

Max tapped her on the shoulder, and she forced herself to look at the boy.

He was beaming at her. "Do you feel any different?"

She was still herself, but a burden had lifted. She felt lighter. She felt...hopeful. She smiled. "Yes, I do. I truly do."

~

They worked side-by-side at the school. On several occasions, Georgia caught Harrison staring at her. It left her giddy, and though she tried to temper her reaction, she couldn't keep the smile off her lips. Only one thing made her frown, and she approached Harrison about it at the end of the day. "Booker didn't come today."

Harrison wiped the chalkboard. "I noticed that too."

"He always comes on his lunch break."

"He was here yesterday." Harrison put down the chalk duster and brushed off his hands. "I hope Rousseau didn't catch him sneaking away. He treats his slaves poorly."

"I know there's animosity between you two, but surely Mr. Rousseau wouldn't hurt a child."

Harrison didn't respond.

"Now, we'll have to carry the food back home. I'd hoped to sit him down and have him eat a meal here. The boy is much too thin." Georgia glanced out the window. "I hope Booker's well. What if he's ill?"

"His aunt will take care of him." Harrison walked over and wiped a smudge of chalk off her cheek.

"Should we ride to his aunt's house to check on him?"

Harrison frowned. "Seeing me snooping around the slave quarters will send Rousseau into an apoplectic fit. I don't want to bring any more trouble upon the boy."

"There must be something we can do."

His amber eyes shown golden with gentle compassion. "I'll see what information I can glean from the servants."

His smooth, marble-like lips moved so close they beckoned her. Her heartbeat tripled its pace. Would those lips feel warm brushing her own?

"I would appreciate that. Thank you." Her voice came out breathy, as if she'd exhaled too much.

She didn't understand the attraction she felt toward Harrison, as if some invisible hand was pulling the strings of a purse, forcing them together. She licked her lips and lifted her eyes to meet his. To her surprise, he'd been studying her. The warm caramel-color of his gaze darkened into deep chocolate pools. Did he feel the attraction as much as she?

His fingers swept along her cheekbone and tucked a stray lock of hair behind her ear before tracing the outline of her jaw.

Heat swept through her body, and she fought to keep her breathing even. Never had anyone caused her heart to jump with a single look or a mere touch.

~

*H*arrison struggled to keep his emotions in check.
God, if this isn't Your will, then remove these feelings from me.

There was a barrage of reasons why he should distance himself from Georgia, but his heart would no longer listen. She was nothing like Laura. She'd proven to be irresponsible and reckless.

But she deserved better than to spend life in second place to his guilt over falling for someone other than his departed wife. More than that, he'd be a cad to play with her emotions, especially when he'd be leaving with the next ship bound for London.

Those reasons faded as he peered at her ripe lips, sweetly offered like a tender fruit. His control began to slip.

His conversation with Max echoed through his mind.

You have plenty of love for both of them.

He should look away, but instead, he trailed his knuckles down the white expanse of her graceful throat.

You're lonely, and she's lonely, Max had said. *I think God sent her to us.*

God, help me.

Max burst through the schoolhouse door with a bird on his arm. "Look, Papa. Oscar followed me here."

Georgia jumped back and spun to face the boy.

Harrison cleared his throat. "How splendid. Go get in the wagon. We'll be right there."

Through the open doorway, he watched Max trudge back to the wagon, while he focused on all the reasons he couldn't be with Georgia. Those reasons were more important than his impulsive feelings.

When he'd made his decision, he turned to face her. "I'm sorry. I didn't mean to mislead you."

The dreamy look in her eyes had cleared, replaced with an ice-blue glare. She raised her chin. "You have nothing for which to be sorry. Despite my lapse in judgment with Julien, I'm not green. I don't become disillusioned and fall in love with every man who stares into my eyes."

She'd done it again. A bitter laugh escaped his lips. "And here I thought you'd be done bringing up his name, but once again—"

"Oh, why do you have to turn everything into an argument? Do you have to be so disagreeable?" She marched out of the schoolroom.

He followed her. "Me? Disagreeable?" *Help me, Lord. This woman is impossible.*

"Not a single gentleman in London infuriates me the way you do, and I've met the whole lot of them."

He should be patient with her. Should set an example for how a Christian should act. But he couldn't seem to hold back his words. "You're too busy batting your eyelashes, and they're too busy drooling over you and vying for your attention, hoping to get you out into the arbor for a secret rendezvous."

She froze and rounded on him, eyes wide. "You think I'm some light skirt?"

"No," he ground out. "I believe you were so desperate to please your mother and sisters by marrying up that you barely heeded the men you had nipping at your heels."

Her jaw dropped open, and she stared at him. Harrison reached for her, but she spun on her heel and climbed up into the front seat. "Take me home." There was a pause before she added, with as much disdain as she could muster, "Harry."

"Fine." He climbed up next to her and added with equal venom, "George." He snapped the reins, and the horses began a fast trot.

"Rawch, George," squawked Oscar.

Georgia swiveled in her seat and swatted at the bird. "Shoo, you stupid bird." Oscar flapped his wings and flew to the back of the wagon.

Max rose to his knees. "Don't get mad at Oscar."

"You taught him to say that." She rounded on Harrison. "To get revenge for the time he called you Harry. That's low, Mr. Wells. Very low."

"I did no such thing."

She scowled at him.

Harrison threw up his hands. "It's a dumb bird."

"Rawch. Dumb bird," Oscar mimicked.

Max giggled until Harrison flashed him a weary look. They rode the rest of the way in silence. Even Oscar seemed afraid to speak. As they pulled up in front of Fredrick's house, guilt ate at Harrison. He'd let his temper get the better of him.

"Georgia." He glanced at her, but she stared straight ahead. "I'm sorry. I shouldn't have raised my voice." He tried for a gentler tone. "I know it's difficult, but you have to choose whom you want to please. Is it going to be God or your mother?"

She turned to face him. Her arms crossed over her chest and her eyes flashing. "Tell me, *Harry*. Why do you care?"

His ire ignited all over again. The woman was infuriating. *Blast it all.* He'd been trying to apologize. He peered into her stubborn, presumptuous face and bit out the first words that sprang to mind. "Because Max needs a Mama who puts God above all else."

Georgia opened her mouth to unleash a retort, but her expression changed from fury to shock to disbelief as his words registered. She turned forward again, staring straight ahead, seemingly frozen.

Harrison blinked, stunned by his own statement. Maybe he'd thought that, but why had he spoken it aloud? A long moment of silence passed. Should he say something? Attempt to take the declaration back?

Suddenly, Georgia hopped from his gig, unaided.

"Wait, Georgia." Harrison leapt after her.

Max passed Georgia the food basket, and a footman approached to carry it for her.

Georgia strode toward the steps, but Harrison stepped into her path and stayed her with a hand on her arm. "Let me explain."

Unshed tears shimmered in her eyes. "Please go. I need to think, and I can't do so in your presence."

Harrison released her arm and stepped aside. Maybe he should make her hear him out, but honestly, he wasn't sure what to say. So he stood there as she rushed up the steps and entered the house. Then, he turned back to the wagon and climbed in.

Max clambered into the front seat next to him. "Papa." His voice was tentative, maybe even frightened. "I don't think that was the best way to ask Miss Georgia to be my mama."

Harrison peered into his son's disappointed eyes and couldn't find his voice.

"Rawch. HarREE," squawked Oscar.

Harrison waved an arm to shoo the bird, his chastisement duly noted.

CHAPTER 22

...I assure you the crystallized sugar from sugar beets grown in Europe will not compare to the pure cane sugar of Nevis. Demand will rise once again. The lower price per pound you've offered is unacceptable.

—From Edward Rousseau to Alexander Allan, Director of the British East India Company

*G*eorgia paced the length of her room. Did Harrison admit he wanted to marry her? She shook her head. No, she shouldn't presume. She'd made that mistake before.

Why did the man vex her one moment and make her heart swirl the next? He cast a spell on her like no other man could. Neither Julien nor her other suitors had ever made her palms sweat or her heart race. They'd never made her want to be a better person or even believe she could. When Harrison's gaze held hers, she felt special. With Harrison, life suddenly held limitless possibilities.

She had to let go of her misgivings. She had to trust him, and more importantly, she had to trust God.

Trust God.

She sank to her knees beside her bed. *Oh God, I don't know what I'm doing. I've made such a muck of my life. Harrison was right. I've fought to prove myself worthy of my mother's affection and sisters' approval. But I'm tired of clawing my way into their good graces. No matter what I do, it will never be good enough.*

Big fat tears dripped onto the wooden floorboards and splashed back up onto her folded hands.

God, forgive me. I just want to be loved.

A calmness spread over her, and though she didn't hear the words, they filled her heart.

You are My beloved.

Could it be true? Could she be God's beloved? Not the pretend Georgia, but the real one?

She wept, but these were grateful tears. Tears of relief. Tears of joy. She had no idea how long she sat there. When she finally crawled up onto the bed, her knees ached, but her heart was full.

She reached for the Bible that had thus far sat untouched on the nightstand, and cracked it open. The name *Joseph* leapt off the page. She read the same story her father had preached several weeks before. This time with new eyes. When she finished, she closed the Bible and prayed.

God, I want to be like Joseph. I want to be confident in how You made me unique and set aside my pride, so I can be open to opportunities where I can serve you. I want to forgive and not hold grudges against my family. Help me to be a part of their healing. Use me to save them as Joseph did.

She rose from her bed. An overwhelming desire to tell someone about what she'd experienced led her to seek out Aunt Tessa. After searching the house and finding no one, she came across Hattie in the kitchen.

"Hattie, have you seen my aunt?"

"The vicar picked her up. Dey went for a shopping trip in town. Dey are quite smitten with each other."

"What about Papa?"

"Oh, he's out with Mista Wells and Maxxy. Dey went to go look at some sugar cane fields dat aren't producin'"

Georgia's shoulders drooped, and she turned to walk away, but then she paused and looked back. "Hattie, you won't believe what happened to me."

Hattie glanced up as she rolled out a pie crust.

"I prayed, and all of a sudden, I was at peace. My heart filled with emotions. I—I can't even explain. I think God might have spoken to me."

A big smile broke out across Hattie's face. "You heard from da Holy Spirit."

"No, I didn't see a dove. This was God."

"Da Holy Spirit isn't a dove. It appeared like a dove when Jesus was baptized. You've heard about da Trinity?"

"Yes, Father, Son, and Holy Spirit."

"Tat's right. The Holy Spirit is God, but in a form dat comes and lives within you once you ask Jesus into yer heart. Tat's who you heard from, the Mighty Counselor hisself."

The Holy Spirit lived in her.

"I'm so happy for you, Miss Georgia. Tat's a wonderful thing. Praise God."

Georgia's eyes fell on the basket of food meant for Booker still sitting on the table. "Hattie, there's no sense in that food sitting for another day, especially if Booker and his aunt need it now. I'll ride over there. I know he lives in the slave village closest to the main house. I can't sit around right now. I'm too happy."

Hattie handed her the basket of food. "Bring Jenneigh with you. I don't trust dat Mr. Rousseau. Lot o' nasty talk about him among my people."

"Oh, I think I can handle the likes of him." She flashed Hattie a coy smile, the one she always used on men.

"Aw, now you be careful, Miss Georgia. Dat man is an oily

239

fish. He can cause an uproar for yer papa. Don't go stepp'n where yer not supposed ta."

~

*G*eorgia stopped the wagon near a village of slave huts at the edge of the sugar cane field. She asked Jenneigh to hold the reins and remain with the carriage while she delivered the basket of food.

Most of the villagers could be seen at work in the fields, or their voices drifted from the boiling houses where they made sugar or rum. A plume of smoke on the other side of the field meant they were busy purifying and curing the sugar.

Dogs and chickens milled about, and the faint smell of dysentery occasionally wafted over from the community outhouse when the wind changed direction. The cramped one-room lodgings were in sorry need of repair. Little fingers and eyes peeked over the cut-out windows, and Georgia lowered her eyes so she wouldn't stare. She couldn't believe people lived in such abject conditions.

An elderly woman, too old to work, sat on her stoop. Her gnarled hands wrapped around a cane resting in her lap. Georgia stopped and asked her where she could find a young boy named Booker. The woman pointed a bent finger to a thatched roof hut about a hundred yards away. Georgia nodded her appreciation and set off toward the shanty.

"Why, Miss Lennox."

Georgia turned to find Mr. Rousseau strolling down the path from the main house. He was dressed in top boots, buckskin breeches, and a Benjamin coat. A large hound sniffed the ground in front of him. A high-polished rifle was tucked under his arm, and a man-servant followed with a large sack.

"You should pay your calls up at the main house. This area

isn't suitable for a well-bred woman like yourself. I wouldn't want you to ruin your gown."

He patted his rifle. "I was about to do some bird hunting, but I can delay my trip." He grinned and slipped his hand under her arm before he swung her in the direction of the hotel.

She pulled back. "Actually, Mr. Rousseau, I came here to deliver food to a child whose mother passed not long ago."

His smile wavered, and a shadow clouded his eyes, but his next words conveyed no such sentiment. "How charitable of you to do God's work. Your kind heart is destined for saint-hood, but I must insist that the conditions of the slave quarters are no place for a proper English woman. There are insects and filth, not to mention the stench. It would be a black mark on my soul if you were to become ill due to my negligence. Come with me. I'll ring for tea and have a footman deliver your basket."

The man-servant unhooked the basket from her arm to carry it for her.

Rousseau tugged harder on her other arm, but Georgia dug in her heels. She curved her lips in a slow, sensual manner and swept her long lashes up to peer at him with an expression meant to dazzle. "I beg your pardon, but I have a special fondness for the boy and would like to deliver the basket personally. I would appreciate your escort. I have nothing to fear in your care." Mr. Rousseau didn't fall for her charm. His eyes narrowed to slits. "How, might I ask, have you made the acquaintance of one of my slaves? Has he been sneaking off for lessons with that provocative schoolmaster?"

The man's tone turned condescending. "I warned you not to associate with the likes of Wells. He'll use a woman's weak mind to his advantage and cause you to fall for the ridiculous idea that slaves should be educated. A woman can't understand the complexities of running a plantation, nor a profitable business."

The man's insults boiled inside her, and she yanked her arm away. "Excuse me, Mr. Rousseau. I, unfortunately, must decline your offer of tea." She turned on her heel and marched toward Booker's dwelling. She almost made it to the door before Rousseau grabbed her wrist.

"Unhand me!" She tried to jerk away, but his grip tightened.

Slaves in the field stopped working to see the commotion.

"Get back to work!" Rousseau yelled. "There's nothing to see here." The slave men and women bent their heads and returned to their tasks. One slave woman dared to hold his gaze, her arms full with a bundle of sugarcane. Still gripping Georgia's arm, he stepped forward and waved his gun at the woman. "I said, get back to work."

The distraction caused Mr. Rousseau to loosen his hold. Georgia, with a quick twist and an upward yank, broke free and stumbled through the doorway of the hut. As her eyes adjusted to the dim lighting, she froze in horror.

Booker lay on the mud floor. A stream of light from the window illuminated his disfigured and bruised face. One eye had swollen completely shut, but the other held a look of sheer terror. She dropped to her knees beside him.

"Booker, who did this to you?" Her hand lifted to stroke his face, but with all the bruising, she stopped herself just in time. The last thing she wanted was to increase his pain.

A crevice of dried blood sealed the split in his lip. His mouth barely moved as he whispered, "My master."

"I'm going to get help. Stay here and don't worry—"

Hands clamped her upper arms and yanked her up before she could finish.

"You beat him." She struggled against Rousseau's vice-like grip. "He's a child, a helpless little boy."

He turned her to face him. "He's a slave who disobeyed an order and needed to be punished."

"What in heaven's name could he have done to deserve *that* sort of punishment?"

Mr. Rousseau's face colored a deeper shade of red. "He refused to work."

"His mother died. Do you not allow them a day to mourn for the dead?"

"If I allowed them a day, they'd want a week."

Her eyes narrowed. "So you beat him, nearly sending him to the grave after his mother. What good would he be to you dead?" Her voice shook with anger. "You're a monster. A monster who preys on the weak so you can feel strong."

Rousseau threw her against the interior wall so hard, tiny sparks of light danced in her periphery. He shifted his rifle and held it across her chest like an iron bar, pinning her there against the rough straw and mud wall.

His eyes held a lethal glare. "You are trespassing on my property."

She stared at the cruel line of his lips as he spit the words in her face. His upper lip curled, and his lower jaw jutted forward like a snarling bulldog, revealing a set of crooked bottom teeth. She struggled for breath and fought to push the gun away with her hands. But she was too weak to budge him.

"You will leave immediately and not repeat what you've seen here, or I'll destroy your reputation *and* that of your father. You may have social status in England, but on this island, you are nothing unless I say you are something. I'm the ruling class here."

God, help me save Booker.

Georgia forced herself to stand firm against the hatred in his eyes and ignore the putrid odor of his breath. She'd been naive to think she could manipulate Mr. Rousseau with her flirtations. He desired power and used intimidation to get it, but his threats against her reputation didn't faze her. By Jove, she'd come back from a disastrous reputation before.

Peace filled her, and her mind focused. If she could get control of his gun, he'd lose his power.

Booker groaned. Rousseau's gaze flicked in his direction.

Georgia acted swiftly. She kneed Rousseau in the groin, and the man howled in pain. His shoulders crumpled, and he pitched forward onto the ground. She yanked the gun out of his loosened grip and quickly spun the barrel around to aim it at his forehead. As she cocked the weapon, she mentally thanked God for her Papa, who'd taught her to shoot during his hunting trips.

Mr. Rousseau scrambled backward on his hands and feet like a crab until he stumbled and landed on his backside.

The slave who'd been following Mr. Rousseau stuck his head in the doorway.

Georgia nodded at the wide-eyed footman. "Get the child and the basket and load them in the wagon."

When he continued to stand there, stunned, she shifted the gun to hover between the slave and Rousseau. The man scrambled into the hut and scooped Booker into his arms.

"The wagon is by the road. Jenneigh will help you once you get there."

"You can't take them," Rousseau barked. "They're my property. That's stealing."

"I'll send your slave back with the rifle, but Booker is staying with me. My father will bring your actions before the town." She sidestepped her way around him, never lowering the weapon, and backed out the door.

"Lennox can go ahead and try," he yelled to her retreating form, "but I own this town. You'll see."

One of them would see, that was for certain. She kept walking backward, pointing the gun in Rousseau's direction. When she was halfway to the wagon, she turned and sprinted the final distance.

"Good Lord, Miss Georgia." Jenneigh climbed in next to Booker in the bed of the wagon and tucked a horse blanket around him.

Mr. Rousseau's footman stood off to the side. Georgia raised the gun again toward him and commanded him to move away. When he was far enough back that she could get a good lead with the horses, she climbed up with one hand into the front seat of the wagon.

"Stay where you are," Georgia yelled to the footman.

With a quick snap of the reins, the horses burst into motion. When they'd gone about ten yards, Georgia half rose from her seat and hurled the gun deep into the tall sugar cane.

The bumping of the wagon caused Booker to moan, but Georgia didn't dare slow the horses until they neared her father's farm.

"Miss Georgia." Jenneigh leaned forward closer to Georiga's ear. "I'm not sure what you've gone and done, but I thank you for it. May God bless your soul."

"Jenneigh, I need you to start praying real hard, because I've gotten Papa and Mr. Wells in a mess of trouble."

CHAPTER 23

…I am not without hope, for I believe our encounter to be God-ordained. I daresay, I flatter myself that you would return the sincerity of my affection for you, or the honesty of my intentions.

—*From Mr. Clark, local vicar in Nevis, to Lady Pickering*

*H*arrison, Fredrick, and Max rested on the back porch of Fredrick's bungalow, enjoying the tropical breeze and a sweet lemonade after inspecting the fields. The thunder of beating hooves and the rumble of a fast-moving wagon sounded in the distance, drawing closer with each second.

"Someone's in a hurry." Harrison rose and strolled to the side of the house to catch a view of the traveler. His pulse jumped as the vehicle came into sight. "It's your wagon, Fredrick."

"Who's—?" Fredrick started to rise.

"Looks like two women driving, and at a breakneck speed." Then one of the figures came into clearer view, and his breath caught. "Georgia's driving. What is she doing?"

Fredrick looked on with his brow furrowed. "I have no idea."

Harrison rounded the front of the house as Georgia jerked the horses to a stop. At the sight of sheer panic on her face, icy fingers of dread wrapped around his chest and squeezed. He raced down the stairs. "What's the matter?"

"It's Booker." She scrambled down from her perch before he could aid her. "Please, help me get him out of the wagon. He's been badly beaten."

Harrison strode to the wagon and peeked over the side. He cringed. The child could barely see through swollen eyes, and his thin arms and legs held gashes and bruises everywhere. Harrison reached into the wagon and gently scooped the boy into his arms.

"Hurry." Georgia led the way up the stairs.

Harrison followed, with Jenneigh, Fredrick, and Max behind him. Booker's face was twisted in pain, but he was responsive and breathing. "We've got you, son," he said. "Everything is going to be all right. We're going to fix you up good as new."

Georgia held the front door open, and Harrison swept past her, but not before he registered the fear etched in her furrowed brow, the worry in her eyes.

She pointed the way. "You can lay him on the sofa in the salon."

Lady Pickering set her embroidery aside and rose when they walked in. "What happened?"

He placed Booker on the cushioned surface, and even though it was soft, the boy still grimaced.

Max peeked his head in between Lady Pickering and Fredrick. "Gosh, he looks awful."

Harrison pointed to the hall, hoping to protect his son's innocence from the horrific injustice done to his fellow class-mate. "Go to the kitchen and ask Hattie to send someone to fetch the physician, then have her bring water and blankets for Booker."

Max nodded and scurried out the door.

"*H*e's been badly beaten." Georgia glanced at Harrison. He wanted to shield her from the scene, too, take her into his arms and reassure her Booker would be all right. But the boy's wellbeing took precedence at the moment.

Georgia wrapped her arms around her midsection, and Harrison's eyes narrowed on the reddish-purple blotches on her skin. Those marks were not from sunburn.

Lady Pickering grabbed a pillow and blanket and began to mother the boy as Fredrick spoke to him in low tones.

Harrison gently pressed a hand on Georgia's lower back and guided her into the library. He motioned for her to sit.

"I don't think I can right now." She paced the perimeter, plucking at the sides of her gown with her fingers.

"Tell me what happened."

Georgia turned to face him. Her eyes were hollow caverns echoing her fear. She bit her bottom lip and hesitated.

"You need to tell me so I can help."

She nodded and inhaled a breath that made her chest rise. "Jenneigh and I went to Rousseau's plantation to deliver the food to Booker."

Fear slammed inside him. "You went where?" Harrison regretted his outburst when she raised her chin and refused to go on. He had to contain his temper and coax her once again into speaking.

Unfortunately, that wasn't the only time he had to fight for control. When she told him how Rousseau pinned her with his gun, his temper threatened to explode like a packed cannon with a lit fuse. His fingers clenched into balled fists, which he hid behind his back so Georgia wouldn't notice. He also carefully veiled his shock as she explained how she turned the gun back on Rousseau.

Harrison's fingers itched to either wallop the chit with a good spanking or applaud her for turning the situation around on a villain. Feelings he'd suppressed flared to life once again, stirring deep inside him as Georgia stood like an avenging angel, eyes flashing and golden strands of hair framing her face. Her pale-yellow gown only enhanced her ethereal appearance.

As she finished her retelling, she released a long gush of air and sank into a nearby chair. Harrison fought to control the clamor of emotions buzzing like hornets in his chest. Her gaze held his, and the avenging angel melted into a frightened girl. Tears welled in her eyes, and her hands shook with tremors. Even her teeth rattled.

Shock. Georgia, who'd so far remained calm under duress, now crumbled from the strain of the trauma she'd faced. Who could blame her after all she'd experienced? Harrison knelt beside her chair and pulled her into his arms. She came willingly, turning her face into his chest and sobbing into his shirt.

He stroked her back, inhaling the blended perfume of the island breeze and English garden that permeated her hair. "You're my brave girl. It's going to be all right."

He wanted to protect her, avenge her, and wrap her in his arms, all at the same time. The fierceness of his feelings pulled the strength from his limbs, and he leaned against the side of a winged-back chair for support. *Thank you, God, for protecting her.*

He held Georgia until her tears stopped and all that remained was the occasional hiccupped sob. Then he drew back and cupped her face in his hands. Though red and puffy, her eyes shown a vibrant turquoise like the Caribbean Sea. He wiped the tracks of her tears away with his thumbs and admired the new sprinkling of freckles across her cheeks and nose. He treasured those freckles. In a way, they were like the markings of a rite of passage. Georgia had changed, inside and out. Her sacrifices had proved it. Her love extended far beyond the superficial.

"I wish you wouldn't have put your life in danger, but you did a good thing. You probably saved Booker's life."

Her eyes teared up once again, and he continued. "Now, I need you to be brave again. Can you do that?"

He waited for her to nod. He wasn't merely saying it. He needed her to be strong. There was no telling how the island would take the news. Rousseau wasn't well liked, and what he'd done to Booker was morally wrong, but he had the law on his side. She'd stolen his property, and at gunpoint to boot. Harrison had some convincing to do and egos to smooth over with the magistrates in the assembly.

Fortunately, some officials were on his side. This wasn't the first time Rousseau had been caught being excessively cruel to slaves.

"I have to settle some things in town. Rousseau, I'm sure, is already there pulling caps with the magistrate and getting the plantation owners all stirred up."

"I should go and explain what happened."

"No." His voice came out firmer than he'd intended, and he hated the way she flinched in response. He softened his tone and slid his hands to her shoulders. "Things could get out of hand. I don't want you in any more danger. There are some adamant opinions on slavery here. Tempers are going to fly."

"But it's going to be your word against his. I could bring Jenneigh to collaborate my story."

He shook his head. "You know they won't recognize a woman's testimony, and definitely not a black woman's."

Her shoulders sagged like a deflating balloon.

"Don't fret. I'm not going to let anything happen to you or Booker. We'll cast our cares on God. It's in His hands, so you are not to worry for even one second, you understand?" His thumbs stroked the creases from her forehead, and he forced a half smile. "They don't stand a chance. If God is for us, who can be against us?"

CHAPTER 24

...I meant no disrespect, Your Majesty. My son and I will sail with the next ship to leave Nevis.

—*From the Duke of Linton to Prince Regent, George IV*

*B*y the time Harrison pulled up to the town square, Edward Rousseau had already gathered Milton Gimbsy, the magistrate, and a handful of plantation owners. Some rested on the low branches in the shade of the banyan tree. Some stood, and others paced back and forth.

Harrison bowed his head and sent up a prayer for wisdom, peace, and understanding. With an *amen* and new-found strength, he sucked in a breath and climbed down from the wagon. "Good day, gentlemen."

"It's because of him." Rousseau stabbed a finger in his direction. "He's the one putting ideas in the woman's head."

Mr. Gimbsy stood. His tanned skin stood out in stark contrast against his sun-bleached hair and white shirt. "Wait a minute. Let's all calm down." He focused on Rousseau with those words. "Why don't you take a seat?"

Rousseau glowered at the man, but perched on a low-set branch of the banyan.

Mr. Gimbsy addressed Harrison. "Mr. Wells, I'm assuming you're aware of the recent event involving Miss Lennox."

"I am, your honor. I've come straight from the Lennox residence, where a boy lays on the brink of death's door."

"That's my slave." Rousseau jumped to his feet. "She stole him from my property, at gunpoint, no less."

Anger flared in Harrison's chest. He crossed his arms to push it down and mentally prayed for strength. "Did Mr. Rousseau happen to mention that the gun was his weapon, wrenched from his hands in self-defense?"

The sounds of gasps and grumbles reached him, but he didn't take his eyes off Rousseau, whose face turned a vibrant red.

"I was hunting and found her trespassing on my property."

"She was delivering a basket of food to the boy, whose mother recently passed away."

"That's what she told you." Little globs of spit flew from Rousseau's mouth as he spoke. "It's a woman's word against mine."

"Trespassing is an offense," a plantation owner shouted.

Harrison turned to the man and kept his expression neutral. "I see. Shall I tell Hattie not to deliver her famous bread pudding to your wife any longer? We wouldn't want her trespassing."

The man squirmed.

"Let's not be hasty," Mr. Gimbsy said.

Rousseau stomped the heel of his boot into the grass. "My property was stolen. I want it back, and I want Miss Lennox punished for her misdeed."

"You punished Miss Lennox enough when you threatened her and pinned her against the wall with your rifle." Harrison wanted to plant his fist into the man's self-righteous face. *God, help me do Your will, not mine.*

"Lies. It's all lies from that woman's mouth." Rousseau's eyes took on a crazed look. "I'm the one who's been wronged."

"Only a weak man hurts a woman, and I witnessed the red marks on her arms from your hands. You attacked a woman who was performing a good deed."

"If I laid a hand on her, it was to stop her from stealing my property."

"Doesn't the Bible tell us to look after the orphans and widows? Miss Lennox was defending the weak." Harrison peered into the faces of the people he'd often sat beside in the same church pew. "Booker recently became orphaned, and it is our godly duty to defend him. The boy was severely beaten, and the blame lies at Rousseau's door."

"There's no proof it was I who beat the child."

"Mr. Wells, we must be tolerant until the full truth is disclosed." The magistrate stepped in. "Though I disapprove of this behavior, Rousseau is a man of much clout. He's beholden to the East India Trade Company, and they have the ear of the king. England wants sugar in their tea, and Mr. Rousseau provides it."

Never before had Harrison been so tempted to give up his identity. All of this would change if they knew he, too, had the ear of the king, and in a much higher position than Edward Rousseau. "Mr. Gimbsy, how can we stand by and allow Rousseau to practice cruelty, mayhap even murder, to our fellow mankind. Merely because England wants three lumps of sugar instead of two?" His gaze swept the gathered crowd. "I daresay, tolerance is a crime when we don't defend those who can't defend themselves."

Murmured grumbles and faint cheers sounded amongst the men.

"I don't like it myself." The magistrate rubbed the stubble on his chin with one hand. "But the boy is Rousseau's property. He must be returned."

Rousseau's eyes narrowed on Harrison, and a smug smile spread across his face.

"Rousseau," the magistrate said, "this is your second offense. You won't be getting a third. Next slave you beat with excessive cruelty will land you in the Nevis jail."

His smile fell.

Mr. Gimbsy turned to Harrison. "Have the boy returned tomorrow."

Harrison locked a lethal gaze on Rousseau. "How much do you want for the boy?"

Rousseau crossed his arms over his chest. "You couldn't pay what I'm asking."

"Try me."

Rousseau's eyes darted around the faces of the other plantation owners. "I don't need your money. I want the land you manage. If you can convince the owners to sell me the deed to their land, I'll give you the boy."

Startled gasps rose at the outrageous price. Several plantation owners, who'd initially argued for Rousseau's side, stood up to protest.

Rousseau stayed them with a hand. "I'm not putting him out on the streets. They can keep the manor. I don't need another home. I'll even throw in the boy's aunt for good measure."

Mr. Gimbsy shook his head. "Now Rousseau be reasonable. You can't expect—"

"I get to name the price." Rousseau interrupted. "Take it or leave it."

Harrison pinned Rousseau with a glare he hoped displayed the proper level of condescension and disdain. He wouldn't typically make a deal when it would profit a man of vile character, but the Holy Spirit nudged him. The land wasn't producing as it had in the past, and besides, he'd love to see the look of relief on Georgia's face when he told her Booker would never have to return.

"Done."

All eyes, even those of Rousseau, turned to stare at Harrison in disbelief.

～

*G*eorgia was nearly frantic by the time Harrison returned.

He joined them for supper, and a single glance showed he was in a somber mood as he entered the room and took his place at the table. Her feet and hands tingled as if tiny ants were crawling under her skin, and her stomach flipped over like the wave that toppled their rowboat.

"What happened?" She leaned forward and pressed her palms on the table. "Is Booker allowed to stay? Was Rousseau there? Did you tell the assembly all that transpired? Did they believe you?"

"Hush, child." Papa raised a hand, ceasing the firestorm of questions spewing from her lips. "Harrison will tell us what happened in good time. Let's not spoil dinner."

She tried to focus on her food, but the twisting of her stomach suppressed her appetite. As she placed her fork down for good, Harrison rested his hand next to his glass and finally spoke.

"Fredrick, would you be able to provide work for Booker and his aunt?"

Georgia rose from her chair. "Really? He gets to stay?"

Harrison nodded, a strained smile growing on his lips.

She couldn't help herself. She reached across the table and scooped up his hand. "Oh, Harrison. Thank you. Thank you."

His fingers squeezed hers, and his thumb gently stroked the inside of her palm. The simple movement radiated waves of heat through her body. From her elation for Booker? Or was this the effect of Harrison's intimate touch? When the moment became too long, she pulled away and glanced at her father, hoping no one would notice the heat in her cheeks.

"That is great news," Papa said as Georgia resumed her seat. "But I'm sure Rousseau didn't let him go without a price."

"The deal cost me my land. The manor itself will remain in my family, but the land is now owned by Rousseau."

"No." Georgia's hand flew to her mouth, and her knees weakened as her stomach anchored itself to her feet.

Harrison's eyes softened and held her gaze, as if to reassure her. "It was for a good cause. There was no way I could send Booker back to Rousseau with a clean conscious." He returned his regard to Papa. "Rousseau has also given his word to leave Georgia alone."

"But how will you survive?" Georgia shook her head, her mind floundering to understand.

"God provides. He has blessed my family. Max and I will not lack."

His words astounded her and, at the same time, deeply touched her heart. Harrison lived to serve God completely, and he did so with great confidence. She admired that, but the injustice left her nerves unsettled. "Wasn't it to be Max's inheritance?"

"Max already has an inheritance from his grandparents in England."

Silence fell over the room. Georgia stared at the custard dessert in front of her. This was all her fault. Her recklessness had cost Harrison his lands. Why had she acted on impulse? Why hadn't she heeded Hattie's warning? Though she'd secured Booker's safety, the cost had been Harrison's livelihood.

Her stomach soured, and she felt the burning of tears in her eyes. She blinked them away and rose. "Please excuse me. I need some fresh air."

~

a light breeze tickled the hair on the back of her neck as Georgia sat on top of a sand dune overlooking the narrows. She watched the pelicans gracefully sail through the evening air. One changed direction, arching downward. The animal folded its wings and plunged into the waters, only to reappear a few seconds later, happily bobbing on top of the waves, a fish in his mouth, an answer for its gnawing appetite.

God, I want to serve you completely, wholeheartedly, but I mess it up. I mess everything up. I want to help, but I don't know how without causing more harm than good. Help me.

Her papa's voice rang out from the recesses of her childhood memories. His breath tickled the hairs on her neck as he steadied her arms for the next shot. *Remember, let God lead.*

She inhaled a deep breath and nodded her head. "All right, Lord," she whispered into the evening air. "I'll let you lead."

Her name sounded behind her, and she glanced over her shoulder. Harrison stood a few feet away, his features unreadable beneath the brim of his floppy hat.

She turned back to watch the pelicans.

He walked up beside her, and she caught a glimpse of his scuffed boots as she scooted over to make room for him to sit. He removed his hat and settled down next to her. His shoulder brushed against hers, and her heart quickened. They sat in silence, watching a large schooner set sail from St. Kitts toward Nevis.

"I'm sorry." She hated that her voice cracked. "I didn't mean to force you to sell your land. I thought I could manipulate Edward Rousseau. I didn't understand what he was capable of." Her chin sank into her chest. "It's not fair you have to pay for my mistakes."

He leaned forward and rested his forearms on his thighs. "You saved Booker, and it was my turn. Besides, it's easier to make sacrifices when you know how much Christ sacrificed for us."

"But I don't deserve it."

"None of us deserves it." He stared at the horizon as the gulls cried a sorrowful song. "Jesus paid it anyway. For me," he shifted to face her, "and for you."

"I've made so many mistakes."

"And Jesus covered them with his blood. The Bible says our sin is removed as far as the east is from the west."

"But the east and the west will never... *Oh.*"

Harrison smiled. "What you did for Booker was a great thing. You risked your life and saved his. The loss of a few fields is nothing compared to how valuable you are."

She wanted to read into his words. *Her worth to God? To Harrison? Both?*

He picked up a shell and ran his fingers over the bumpy surface. "Yes, things have become complicated. They always do, but never forget, you will always be a hero in Booker's eyes."

"But I'm not great. I ruin everything. You said it yourself. I get in my own way."

"You've struggled to impress others, but to be great, all you have to do is serve. That's what Jesus did. He gave his life as a ransom for many. He didn't come to be served. He came *to serve.*" Harrison tossed the shell into a receding wave and looked at her. "You may not realize it, but your heart has already changed. Each time you help teach a child, each time you sacrifice for your ailing father, each time you step up for a beaten slave, you are becoming great, and the kingdom of heaven is rejoicing."

Her vision blurred as warm tears coursed over her cheeks. He brushed them away with the gentle touch of his fingertips, then wrapped an arm around her. She leaned against his side, and they both stared at the vast ocean.

"All of us want recognition. We all desire an 'atta boy' from our fathers and 'atta girl' from our mothers." His hand stroked her arm, sending a chill across her skin. "It's natural. God instilled it in us, and He doesn't condemn us for it. Jesus merely turns it upside down. Recognition comes from becoming a slave to Jesus Christ and serving others. Mark nine says, 'Whoever wants to be first must be the very last and a servant to all.'"

A peace settled around her heart and mind. She longed to be valued. *God, I want to be great because I serve you.*

Georgia shifted to face Harrison. "Is that why God brought you to Nevis? So you could serve Him better?"

He smiled, and the corners of his eyes crinkled. "No, but God can turn all things around for his glory. I came here to run away. England held too many memories and too many expectations. I needed time for God to heal my heart."

She hesitated, unsure if she truly wanted to hear the answer to her next question. Finally, she asked it anyway. "And has He?"

He removed his arm from her shoulder and ran his palms down the length of his trousers. Without his warmth, a chill nipped at her skin.

"I don't think that part of my heart will ever heal."

Georgia's heart sank. "I see."

"But Max taught me that God can grow your heart to have enough love for others."

Her breath caught, and her heart fluttered as if it had grown wings. Could Harrison love her?

"I judged you too harshly when you first arrived at the island." His focus was on a nearby gull, but she knew he was as aware of her as she was of him. "I must apologize for my behavior. You reminded me of the women who sought to take Laura's place." He glanced back at her. "I know now that wasn't your intention. In fact, I've come to appreciate your friendship."

"Thank you." But the words were hollow. She didn't want merely friendship. Her heart longed for something greater, and it made his sentiments hurt all the more. She blinked back tears.

Harrison shifted his weight. He drew one knee up and draped his arm over it. They sat in silence as the sun sank behind a cloud, fanning a crown of orange rays into the sky.

A schooner sailed past on the distant horizon. *Julien could be on that ship.* The thought came without emotion. It emerged purely from habit as it had done for so many ships that had passed before. She blinked and looked away, only to find Harrison watching her.

"Do you still pine after Claremont?" His voice sounded curious, but his eyes scrutinized hers for the truth. "He doesn't deserve it, not if he replaced you so quickly."

She wanted to look away. She wanted to be angry with him for reminding her of her humiliation, but she couldn't. Instead, she shivered, despite the warm evening air. "I had my life all planned. I had a dream, but it was… selfish."

"God will give you a new plan." The golden hue of Harrison's eyes seemed to glow in the fade of the evening light. "His plans are always better."

Harrison stood and reached for her hand, his masculine grip engulfing her small fingers. Her stomach leapt as his thumb rubbed over the top. Did she imagine the intimate touch? Had it been an accident? She stood and peered up at him.

"Georgia." Her name fell from his lips like a caress.

With a tug of her hand, he pulled her to him. Less than a fingertip separated them.

Her head tilted back to hold his gaze, unwilling to let go. A moist breeze fanned the familiar fragrance of coconut, tinged with his spicy masculine scent, swirling the aroma all around her. His other hand reached toward her face, then hesitated.

She waited, praying for his touch.

His fingertips traced her hairline, and her heart strained against the laces of her corset, its beat reverberating throughout her entire body. Every nerve ending heightened its sensitivity until she could feel her breath passing back and forth between her lips, the weight of each fabric fiber against her skin.

"You are not easily forgotten." His voice caressed her, his warm breath fanning her face.

Her stomach flip-flopped like driftwood caught in the surf, swelling and dipping on waves of emotion.

Her mind screamed, *If you lose your heart to him, you'll never be able to look your mother or sisters in the face again. You'll once again be the shame of the family.*

Was she brave enough to face her mother and sisters as the wife of an estate manager? Would she be disowned? *Maybe. Probably.*

Did it matter? *Yes. No.*

Did she love Harrison enough to give up a high society life, to become a member of the working class? *Yes,* her heart begged, but her mind remained frozen in fear.

But her heart didn't care. It plunged into love like the pelican into the ocean. Harrison changed his grip and laced his fingers with hers while his other hand drifted to the small of her back. The heat of his touch spread throughout her body. Her lips parted, and she swayed toward him.

His fingers trailed up her spine, leaving a wake of tingling anticipation. His calloused hand cupped the nape of her neck. Her eyes fluttered closed, helpless against the torrent of emotion welling up within her.

God help her, she loved him. She loved who he was, what he believed, what he valued and stood for. It didn't matter that he held no title. She loved an estate manager. She loved a schoolmaster.

His lips, like warm velvet, molded over her own. Tangled knots of sensation coursed through her stomach, all the way down to her toes. She melted into his embrace, forgetting where she was, forgetting who she was. Her life was this moment.

Harrison's kiss wasn't sloppy like Julien's. His kiss didn't need something from her. His kiss somehow gave, as if sharing a piece of himself with her. She reciprocated in kind.

He drew back and ran his thumb over her lips. "I've never met anyone like you, Georgia Lennox."

Her heart leapt. She lifted his hand and placed a timid kiss on the inside of his palm.

Hunger flashed in his eyes. He crushed her to him and kissed her with an ardor she'd never known. Their arms entangled until she didn't know where she stopped and he began.

This was what it felt like to be in love. Georgia's heart sang. She wasn't certain how long they stayed wrapped in each other's embrace, but a wagon rolled by carrying bundles of sugar cane, and they broke apart. A broad, toothy smile stretched across the driver's face. He tipped his hat with a wink as he passed.

Harrison looped a protective arm around her and pulled her against his side. After the wagon rode out of sight, he kissed her again. Georgia trembled in his arms as a haze of passion immersed her into new depths of longing. Eventually, Harrison released her from the sensual onslaught, and he rested his forehead against hers. "You make me forget myself."

She felt his smile and returned it.

He lifted his head and cupped her face, but his expression grew serious. "There's something I came here to tell you."

Her brow furrowed.

"I've been summoned back to London."

"London? But why?"

"My services have been requested, and Max's grandparents have been pressing for his return. I can't blame them. It's been too long since they've laid eyes on their only grandchild." He cleared his throat. "I also believe God wants to use me in deliberation for ending slavery, both in England and on Nevis."

She put a hand over her mouth and pulled back. Harrison's arms fell to his sides.

God, this can't be happening. I've only begun to understand my feelings. He can't leave.

Her hand lowered. "When?"

"We leave when the Essex sails."

"But the Essex is sailing into port now." The joy she'd felt minutes before flipped into despair. "Can't it wait?"

"I'm afraid not."

I will sail with you.

She pushed the thought away. She couldn't leave her father, and Harrison wouldn't allow her to do so either.

"How long will you be gone?"

"If all goes well, I hope to return in six months. A year at most." He pulled her into his arms and placed a kiss on her forehead. "I never anticipated this."

He's leaving. Just like your father. She shook her head and stepped back out of his reach. *Don't be naïve. He's not coming back. Not for you. You're not worth it.*

Maybe if she asked, he wouldn't leave her. She stared into his eyes. "Please don't go."

"I have no choice." He inched toward her. "I was hoping you'd wait for me."

A loud, steady ringing in her head drowned out his words, and her body began to tremble. She saw herself each night staring out into the ocean, hoping and waiting for his ship to arrive, but it never would. The ringing grew louder. She needed to get away. She needed to run, to scream. *Not again. Not now.* She stepped back.

"Georgia, I don't want to leave you." He stepped forward again. "Believe me. If there was another way, I would take it."

The word *leave* rang in her ears. She retreated another step.

"I will return." His words were soft, and his eyes implored her to understand. But she only saw Papa's back and heard the slamming door as her father left her alone and frightened, hiding behind his office door.

"If you don't return to London in that time..." he continued.

She remembered sleeping in her father's study, watching the door, hoping beyond hope that any moment he'd walk through. She pictured London's dockside as the Aberdeen drifted out to sea, how she had scoured the crowd searching for Julien, hoping he'd received her missive in time. Her heart sinking when he didn't come for her rescue. *He's never coming. You're not worth rescuing.*

"...then I will come back for you."

She turned to go. "I want to believe it, but you won't come for me. No one ever comes." She whispered the words into the night air. "They always leave, but no one ever comes back for me."

She hitched up her skirts and ran.

"Georgia, wait."

$\approx$

*H*arrison chased Georgia a few steps, then stopped and let her disappear among the dunes.

Blast it all. Why hadn't he told her the truth? He kicked at the sand. He was a cad for leaving.

What if the Prince Regent made good on his threat? What if he returned to England only to discover he'd been stripped of his title?

What if all he could offer Georgia was to be the wife of an island schoolmaster? She deserved better.

After Laura's death, Harrison had viewed his title as a nuisance. He'd mocked the label by living the last five years without it.

But now that he needed it, he wasn't certain if he possessed it any longer. If he returned to London straightaway, maybe there would still be time. Hopefully, his last letter hadn't been lost at sea. He prayed it had reached the Prince Regent's hands.

Because only a duke's influence could convince His Majesty to put a stop to Rousseau's cruelty. Only a duke could make the progressive suggestion to parliament that the abolition of slavery would be the way of the future. And only a duke deserved to marry a woman like Georgia Lennox.

CHAPTER 25

...I'm delighted by your returning to London. I notified the servants to prepare your city lodgings. I shall leave for London immediately to care for Maxwell upon your arrival while you meet with the Prince Regent.

—*From Lady Charlotte Weld, Duchess of Linton, to her son, Robert Harrison Weld, Duke of Linton.*

Four days later, Georgia sat on a stool in the library next to Papa. He was tucked in the sofa as she spoon-fed water into his mouth. With each motion, she recited the same prayer over and over. *Lord, please give me more time with him. I've lost so many precious opportunities, and I have so much to make up for.*

This episode was so much worse than the last. Georgia, Aunt Tessa, and Hattie all took turns watching over him. He burned with fever to the point they needed to change his soaked bed clothes every hour. She wrung out a cloth over a small metal bowl and laid it on his forehead.

Harrison had come by at least once a day, but every time she'd been either asleep, having been up all night with her father, or too mentally worn to face the heartache of Harrison's leaving.

Today, he'd come to say a final goodbye, but in an uncharacteristic moment of cowardice, she'd hid in her dressing room. Her emotions were too high, like a pot of tea ready to whistle. If she laid eyes on him, she would break down. She'd beg him to stay, though she had no right. Instead, she selfishly sequestered her heart among her colorful gowns and pretended she could be happy again. Deep down she knew, she'd allowed herself to become vulnerable for the first time since her father left, she'd loved with all her heart, and now her heart would be broken.

"Miss Georgia?" Hattie entered the room, holding out a card with a letter attached. "This arrived for you this mornin.'"

She accepted the letter and flipped the card over. She recognized the slanted script before she read the words. *Lord Julien Greenhill, the Earl of Claremont.* Her brows drew together. The letter didn't look as if it had sailed across the ocean. Was Julien here in Nevis? She broke open the wax seal and unfolded the letter.

Dearest Georgia,

Even on the other side of the Atlantic, you have not been far from my thoughts each day. Mother's health has been lacking, so when she decided it would be good for her bones to try the famous healing springs on Nevis, I jumped at the chance to come and see you. I hope we can continue to further our acquaintance, perhaps allow it to become something more. We are residing at the Artesian Hotel and wish to call upon you this afternoon.

Truly Yours,
Julien

*P.S. As of our leaving, my affairs have been put in order.
Mother has seen to it.*

Her hands dropped into her lap, clutching the letter tight, as she stared across the room at the wall.

Julien was here, in Nevis?

He'd thought about her every day, and he wanted to further their acquaintance?

It didn't make sense. Eleanor said she'd seen Cynthia in Julien's arms. Would her sister lie to her? No. She might tease and belittle, but she never lied. Could Eleanor have misunderstood? That could have been it. Eleanor believed they were in a lover's embrace, but Julien, ever the gentleman, could have been aiding Cynthia. Maybe her hair had gotten tangled in a button, or she'd needed a spot on her neck inspected—*closely.*

Georgia shook her head. Even she couldn't fool herself with that one.

Did it matter? Julien had come for her and he planned to propose. She knew for certain that was what he alluded to by writing that his affairs were in order, but was that what she wanted? To marry an earl? Her mother would be pleased. Her sisters would be jealous. But how did Georgia feel? A month ago, she would have jumped for joy, but so much had changed.

She had changed.

The image of Harrison's teasing smile as he'd held her at the ball flashed through her mind.

I hate to point it out, but you, my dear, are wearing red.

She'd teased back that it was dark pink, and his expression had sobered. His eyes had darkened with what she now understood was passion.

You look ravishing in dark pink.

The dull ache that had tortured her heart for four days intensified. She closed her eyes. Harrison, at this moment, was boarding the Essex to sail back to London. She swallowed a sob.

The pain was too great, but she knew not to hope that he might change his mind and stay.

"Could you help me sit up, dear?" Papa asked.

She opened her eyes and helped raise him with one hand as she used the other to stuff pillows under him for leverage. "Is that better?"

"Thank you, princess. I'm feeling more like myself today."

She smiled at her father. "You look on the mend. Your color is back and the twinkle has returned to your eyes. Praise God."

"Your prayers were heard. God still has plans for this broken body."

"Would you like me to read to you or fetch some of Hattie's soup?"

"No, no. I can read to myself for a bit." He patted her hand as she tucked the blanket under his chin. "Why don't you take the wagon into town? Hattie needs a few things from the market, and I thought you might have something you want to do. A young woman needs to get out and enjoy herself, not waste away caring for a sick, elderly man."

"Papa, you're not elderly."

"Go. Shoo." He flicked his fingers at her. "I need some rest, and I can't fall asleep with someone watching." His lids lowered and he murmured, "Just remember, let God lead."

~

A half-hour later, Hattie pulled the wagon to a stop in front of the market square. Georgia eased herself down and opened her pink parasol to block the sun's rays. "I'm going to walk around and enjoy the sunshine, Hattie. I'll make sure I stay within sight."

"Yes, Miss Georgia."

The older woman scooped up the basket and wove her way around the people milling about the market.

She knew she shouldn't, but Georgia couldn't keep her feet from moving toward the loading docks. Even though her mind listed a slew of objections, her heart longed for one last look of the *Essex* before the ship disappeared on the horizon. She rounded the shops on the ocean side and froze.

The *Essex* was still anchored. Her legs carried her, as if of their own accord, in the direction of the waterfront. She stared up at the railing of the ship, praying for one last glimpse of Harrison.

A pair of arms wrapped around her waist and almost toppled her to the ground.

"I knew you'd come. I knew you wouldn't let us leave without saying goodbye." Max's bright face shone up at her.

Precious Max. She bent down and hugged the boy in a tight squeeze. "I'm so glad I found you. I'm still shocked you're going to leave me all the fish in the Caribbean Sea. How will I be able to reel them all in?"

"I know how we can send secret messages to one another," Max said.

"How?"

"I'll put a message into a bottle, drop it in the ocean, and a fish will swallow it. And then, you can catch it. When Hattie slits its guts, you'll find the message from me. Then you can do the same."

"That sounds like a splendid idea." With gentle fingers, she brushed the hair off Max's forehead and planted a kiss there. "I'll miss our fishing adventures, but knowing there's a message out there for me will help."

He pulled back, and they both blinked away tears. "Yeah, me too."

"Georgia."

Harrison's deep voice reverberated through the marrow of her bones and drew her eyes upward. He looked exactly how he had the first day she'd met him. His buckskin breeches clung in a snug fit to his muscular legs, and his white cambric shirt ruffled in the breeze. He stared at her with a somber expression, but the stormy clouds in his eyes struck her like a hurricane. Her heart squeezed.

She inhaled a steady breath and rose.

He patted Max on the head and told him to wait in the dinghy, then turned back to her. "I didn't think you'd come."

"I tried to stay away." She let out a weak laugh that turned into a half sob. She should have averted her gaze as she blinked back tears, but she couldn't take her eyes off him. "This is hard."

"All aboard."

Georgia cringed at the loud call.

"Last chance to board the *Essex*."

On the ship, men were scurrying about. But when she looked back, Harrison's eyes were still on her.

"Come with me." His eyes widened as if his own words startled him, but then they darkened with resolve. He stepped closer, so close that she had to tip her head back to peer up at him. His fingers fumbled for her hand before enfolding it in a firm grip. The warmth of his skin and his heady scent filled her senses.

She remembered his words on the beach a few days earlier. *You are not so easily forgotten.* She remembered his kiss as if she were the most valuable possession in all the world.

"Come with me." His amber eyes implored her, their small saccades searching the depths of her soul for the answer he sought. "We'll say vows in front of the captain."

Her mind whirled. In the past, she had used all her wiles in an attempt to coerce a marriage proposal out of a man's lips. Now that she'd received one, and from a man she truly loved, she wasn't ready.

Papa still needed her. She couldn't leave him. A few months ago, she never would have considered her family except to use the proposal as a means to brag. But now, she couldn't leave her ailing father. Her breath came in short gasps, and her heartbeat pounded in her ears.

"I can't leave Papa." Her voice came in a mere whisper.

"I know," he brushed his knuckles down the side of her face and his eyes took on a sad smile. "But I figured it couldn't hurt to ask anyway."

～

*H*arrison struggled against the urge to pull Georgia into his arms and place a parting kiss on her soft lips. "Who knew that underneath all those layers of paled pink would lie such a remarkable woman?"

Her face flushed from his compliment, and her eyes lowered, displaying a fan of long lashes against her red cheeks.

A fresh wave of love swept through him, tightening his chest even more. "Your tenderness and passion will be the light that guides me back to you. Don't let them be snuffed out." He touched her chin and forced her to meet his gaze. "I *will* return for you."

He didn't miss the spark of hope that lit within their blue depths, then fizzled. He needed her to believe him, despite the men in her past who told her the same and then broke their word. "Wait for me."

"Prepare to raise the sails." The captain's voice echoed over the water, and they both glanced in the direction of the ship.

He had so much he needed to say and so little time. "I have something I need to tell you. I shouldn't have waited so long, but I wanted to be... "

A hurried passenger carrying a case under his arm brushed past, and Harrison had just enough time to pull Georgia out of his path before the man would have bumped into her.

"All board," shouted a crewman.

"Georgia, I'm not merely a—"

"Papa!" Max's voice shouted. "Come on. They're shoving off."

His gaze flicked to Max as two sailors pushed the rowboat into the water. He couldn't let the boat leave without him, especially with his son on board.

He released her hand and ran toward the dinghy. Before stepping into the water, he glanced back. She raised her hand in a silent farewell. He could tell her strained face was fighting back tears. The same burning that stung his own eyes. Water splashed over his boots.

"Wait for me." He yelled over the sounds of the crashing waves, hoping the noise didn't eat his words.

A man gripped his arm and hauled him into the boat. He sat in the remaining seat in the center of the dinghy next to Max, but he continued to watch Georgia, willing her to say, *Yes, I will wait for you.*

"Miss Lennox." A loud bellow from the shore caused Harrison's head to snap up. Who was calling Georgia's name? He recognized that voice but couldn't place it. He stood as best he could in the rocking boat and scanned the marketplace.

"Miss Lennox."

Harrison's eyes focused on the direction of the sound. A man stood about twenty yards away. He held his cane high in the air, and his other hand tipped the brim of his top hat.

Claremont.

Georgia raised her hand, and utter fear electrified Harrison's blood.

Not now. Claremont couldn't come for her when he was leaving.

Max tugged on his arm. "Papa, you need to sit down."

Harrison strained for a last look at Georgia. Was she excited to see Claremont, or was she still waving farewell to Harrison? The waves blocked his view. He would never know.

∿

*B*linded by tears and out of sheer instinctive good breeding, Georgia half-waved to whoever was calling her name. She stood on her tiptoes and inched to the water's edge for a last look at Harrison. Who knew when or if she would see him again? Her voice scratched her throat with her desperate plea as the rowboat reached the ship. "Please, don't go."

The dinghy was raised, and it became impossible to discern Harrison from among the people lining the deck, waving their scarfs in goodbye.

She strained for an extra lift to see above the waves and was about to take another step forward until a burly man in suspenders blocked her.

"Careful now miss." The man took hold of her arm and pulled her back. "You don't want to be going for a swim."

Georgia peered down into the water lapping at her boots. For a moment, she stared into its rippled barrier, separating her from the man she loved. After giving herself a quick mental shake, she peered back at the man. "Thank you, sir. I forgot myself for a moment. I'm recovered now."

A familiar voice behind called her name again, closer this time, but Georgia was focused on a last glimpse of Harrison or Max. The ship's sails raised and its anchor lifted. The vessel drifted through the waves, intent on its destination. Her chest ached as if she'd been struck by a cannonball. Her hand moved to her breast, and even though she didn't feel a hole, she knew it was there.

Her heart was sailing with the *Essex*.

An exuberant wave reached out to wrap itself around her kid boots as if to pull her out to sea, but Georgia stepped back just in time. The foam retreated. With Harrison gone, who would rescue her this time?

"Miss Lennox."

A hand tapped her shoulder, and she turned. Julien stood beside her in a top hat, coat, and breeches. He reached for her ungloved hand and swept it into his grip.

She couldn't help the surprise that swept through her, even though she knew Julien was in Nevis.

"Georgia." His lips purred her name as he attempted to captivate her with an overly confident smile—part seduction, part manipulation. She'd used the same tactics herself. Funny how she'd never noticed the similar gesture in Julien. "My eyes rejoiced the moment they spied you."

He raised her hand to his lips and kissed the top of her knuckles. She didn't miss the narrowing of his eyes as he noted her uneven nails.

"Lord Claremont. It's good to see you."

He pivoted and tucked her hand into the crook of his arm. "Here, let me escort you back toward the shops. I shouldn't want the sand to ruin our boots."

Georgia stole one last glance over her shoulder at the departing ship and allowed Julien to draw her back to the reality she now faced.

"You are a sight for starving eyes. I've missed you." The glint under his hooded lids used to flutter her heart, but now it turned her stomach.

Now was a good time to place some distance between them. "I hope you bring news from London. How fares Miss Orville?"

His gaze snapped to her face, and she witnessed a flash of guilt before he composed himself. "She... ah, wishes you well but misses your company."

They stepped out of the sand onto the dockside, and he guided her through the hustle and bustle of shoppers and men hauling away cargo. "It was Mother speaking to your friend, Miss Cynthia Orville, that reminded her of our acquaintance. Mother has decided it is time for me to...ah...settle down. She remembered how famously we'd gotten along and was delighted to hear you were in Nevis, for she'd always wanted to visit the infamous springs."

So the idea to sail to Nevis hadn't come from Julien. It was his mother's. He had no desire to become leg-shackled to Cynthia or her, but his mother was forcing his hand. Surprisingly, she wasn't disappointed.

Georgia tilted her head and smiled the way she used to. It all came back so easily, the charm and façade. But the behavior grated. She wasn't this person any longer.

"Let us find a spot in the shade. The heat here is unbearable. Besides, the sun is too strong for your fair complexion."

She cast him a sideways glance as they strolled toward the shade of a cluster of palm trees. Was he inadvertently scolding her for freckles?

"How fares your mother?" she asked.

"Ah, well the trip was horrid for her aches and pains, but she's mended now that she's within the luxury of the Artesian Hotel. She declares that within the few days we've been here, the healing baths have helped regain her constitution. Our stay so far has been delightful. The accommodations are adequate and the food, though unique, has been tasty. Oh, and our host, Mr. Edward Rousseau, is a delightful chap." He glanced down at her. "I'm sure you've made his acquaintance, this being such a small island."

"Yes. We've met." She wasn't willing to elaborate more. *Delightful chap—Ha!*

He stopped and peered down at her. "I'm sorry. I didn't catch that."

She smiled and rolled the end of her parasol with her fingertips. "I want to hear more of London."

His eyes lit up. "Well, you remember the Ingram fellow. It turns out, he…"

While Julien prattled about news of London, Georgia

glanced up at the sun illuminating her parasol. Funny, but it was her last pink item.

Her past behavior now almost seemed comical. When her sister mentioned pink was a feminine color, Georgia had interpreted it to mean that in order to be beautiful, she must wear pink. In her insane desire to outdo her sisters, she took it to the extreme and dressed solely in pink. But what good came of that? Hadn't it merely created more jealousy? Would the cycle of having to outdo one another ever end, or would *top that* be inscribed on her headstone?

"Then the two came to blows. Over Miss Crawford, no doubt..."

What did it matter now what her sisters thought of her, or what her mother thought? They would have to learn to love her for who she was because she wouldn't go back to pretending.

Besides, Harrison found her beautiful.

Harrison. She didn't have to pretend, or bat her eyes, or wear a specific color, in order to be noticed by him. He'd seen her at her ugliest moments, moments when she'd been selfish, conceited, and manipulative. He loved her despite it all. He loved her for who she was, but he'd sailed away.

"The poor bloke was in his cups..."

Her gaze drifted over Julien, dressed as if he'd shopped in Beau Brummel's wardrobe. He associated with royalty and was part of the aristocracy. He lived among the top of the social ladder, but would he love her for who she was?

No.

She stepped back and snapped her parasol shut.

"Got himself leg-shackled." His tone resounded with pity, witnessing to his contempt for the marriage sacrament.

How had she been so blind? A surge of certainty rolled through her, giving her the boldness to speak her mind. "I beg your pardon, but I can't pull off this façade anymore."

He blinked at her and raised his brows.

Georgia didn't care. She shoved the parasol into the earl's chest. He could keep the pink. She didn't want it anymore.

He clutched the umbrella and gaped at her as if she'd taken leave of her senses. "What facade?" He frowned. "Have you succumbed to the heat? The Miss Lennox I knew in London wouldn't be caught dead leaving the house without gloves or having uneven nails. She also listened with rapt attention to my stories and graced me with lovely smiles."

A tingling sensation spread through Georgia's extremities. Her heart swelled, creating an airy lightness that had her feeling as if her feet might float off the ground. *This is what freedom feels like.* A broad smile split her lips.

"There's the delightful smile I remember." He stepped toward her.

She backed away a couple of steps. "I have changed. I'm not the person you remember. God has changed me. He's given me a different dream—a better dream."

Giddy mirth welled up in her throat at Julien's expression of utter confusion. "It's better if I go. Give your mother my regards." She backed away a few more steps. "Oh, and if you come calling, I shall be indisposed." She spun on her heel. "Good of you to pay a visit though," she said over her shoulder as she strode away, sending up a silent thank you for God's saving grace.

She was free. Free from the charade of pretending to be someone she wasn't. God had freed her from the possibility of a loveless marriage, her mother's expectations, her past bitterness...

...and from pink.

CHAPTER 26

…Please mend my broken heart. I fear it won't heal of its own accord.

—*From Georgia Lennox to God (no need to be posted)*

"*P*rincess?" Papa tapped on her door. "May we come in?"

Georgia sniffed and wiped under her puffy eyes. She glanced at the large wet circle on her pillow and flipped it over so no one could see the evidence of her tears. How she wasn't completely dehydrated was a wonder.

The joy of being freed from others expectations had been quickly overshadowed by the realization that, once again, her dream—this time her new dream of a life with Harrison—had sailed away.

After Harrison's parting, she'd wept quietly in the solace of her room. But after two days, Papa and Aunt Tessa probably believed her to be ill. It was time for her to come out of hiding. It was time to make a plan, even if it no longer included Harrison. Inhaling a fortifying breath, she said, "Please, come in." Her voice sounded hollow.

"You haven't been down for breakfast or supper," Aunt Tessa said as she entered the room with Papa in tow.

Georgia pulled herself into a seated position, and they sat on either side of her feet at the end of the bed.

"Hattie said the meals she's sent up have come back untouched." Though his voice was reproving, Papa's gaze was sympathetic.

Her father was up and about, once again his old self. *Praise God.* Aunt Tessa, too, had more life in her eyes, a fact that may have something to do with the vicar.

"I haven't had much of an appetite, but no need to be concerned. It will pass."

"It's my right as a father to be concerned."

She shook her head. "There's nothing that can be done at this point. I made a mistake, and now it's too late to do anything about it."

"Too late to tell Harrison your true feelings?" Papa said.

She tilted her head. "You knew?"

"We suspected." Aunt Tessa smiled in pity.

"It was in your eyes every time you looked at him." Papa rubbed her knee. "It was the same way I used to look at your mother."

Georgia's spirits fell. "And like you and mother, we'll never see each other again."

"Maybe it's time we remedy that."

"What do you mean?" Hope flared in her chest, but she didn't dare consider his meaning.

"If you love Harrison, then you should go after him. Never let him go. Don't do what I did."

"I can't."

"Why not?"

"The *Essex* has already sailed for England."

"There are other ships."

Georgia shook her head. "I can't leave you, not with your illness." She grasped her father's hand. "I lost all those years with you. I don't want to lose any more. Aunt Tessa and I aren't going to leave you."

"I'm not going anywhere." Aunt Tessa flushed and hid a shy smile. "Mr. Clark and I are getting married. I'm going to assist him in the school in Mr. Wells's stead."

A genuine smile crossed Georgia's lips, and she hugged her aunt. "I'm so delighted for you. The two of you make a wonderful match."

"I haven't been this happy since before Robert's passing. Love is a beautiful thing." Her expression grew serious, and she pointed at Georgia's chest. "Which is why you shouldn't let it slip away."

Georgia's shoulders sagged. "But how can I? I don't have a ship or a chaperone."

"Well." Papa straightened and crossed his arms over his chest. "I've booked passage on the *Mayfair*. It's sailing out of Basseterre in two days. I was hoping you'd keep me company on my voyage back to England."

Georgia jerked upright. "I don't understand."

Papa smiled, and the lines in the corners of his eyes crinkled. "It's about time I visited your mother. If she's not going to get up enough nerve to ask me to come back, then I think I'll go there and ask her myself. I don't want to die with unforgiveness between us. It poisons the soul." He nodded at her. "I was hoping you'd join me. I may need a supporter of my cause. Your mother has a formidable will."

Hope surged in her chest as she threw her arms around him. "I can't believe it. We're going home." She pulled away. "But are you well enough to travel? It's a long voyage. What if you have an episode?"

"Then you'll have to nurse me back to health as you've done

before. Besides, I've only just recovered. Usually, there's some time before a relapse. We'll pray for God's protection."

"Oh, Papa. I love you." She squeezed her father tight.

He hugged her back. "I love you too, princess."

The familiar burn of tears stung her eyes. She couldn't believe it. They were going home.

∽

*G*eorgia hadn't grasped just how much Aunt Tessa, Hattie, and Jenneigh had come to mean to her in the past few months until she had to say farewell. There were plenty of tears during their parting, but after that, the voyage proceeded smoothly.

The ship stopped twice for trade, once in Barbados and once in Trinidad. She tried not to let the delays frustrate her, but she strode above deck day after day, rehearsing what she'd say to Harrison once she located him.

Locating him posed another dilemma. She'd questioned Papa repeatedly, but despite their friendship, Harrison was close-lipped about his past. Many of the people on the island were the same way. Papa said it was an unstated rule to give a man his privacy. They came to Nevis to start a new life and forget the past.

When Georgia wasn't sorting through points-in-case, she listed out potential leads on how to find Harrison. She knew he was an estate manager in the countryside surrounding Kent, and had family in London. At least that was something. Her father had encouraged her to leave it in God's hands, but with so much idle time, what else had she to ponder?

Georgia turned her practicing into prayer as she pleaded with God for wisdom for her and understanding from Harrison.

Then one night, the longest night of her life, her prayers shifted focus as her father suffered one of his attacks. Confined to his stateroom, he burned with fever and slipped in and out of consciousness. His words were incoherent and filled with hallucinations.

This was the first time she'd tended him through a sickness without Hattie's help, and she changed the bedclothes and wrung out cloth after cloth saturated in sweat. She replaced them with damp ones on his forehead to keep it cool, but to no avail. One moment, he thrashed about as if on fire, then the next, he lay shivering as if on ice.

In a lucid moment, his feverish lips parted. "Georgia?"

His fingers sought hers, and she raised his hand to her cheek. Tears burned the back of her eyes.

"I thank God for this fever. It's what brought you to me." He caught his breath. "It's the reason I get to look upon your face now." His eyes fluttered closed. "Remember, God is good all the time."

She nodded, even though he couldn't see the response. The tears sliding down her cheeks made it hard to speak.

He dozed off, and she sat by his side, listening to his breathing. Her exhaustion and fear were near to overwhelming, and she raised her face toward Heaven. "God, please don't let him die. This is my fault. Once again, I put my needs first. Even though he wanted to sail, I never should have allowed it. I should have forced him to remain in Nevis instead of consenting to this...this torture."

A sob tore from her throat. She buried her face in the covers and murmured. "Don't let him succumb to the fever, not now, not without any friends or family, except me who put him in this predicament. At least in Nevis, he'd have Hattie and Aunt Tessa. Oh Lord, please get him home. Give him a chance to make amends with Mama, Franny, Eleanor, and Ann."

And then, when the night seemed darkest, and the fever seemed its worst, the Lord's tender presence filled her heart with light. Words of truth replaced her fears.

Do not be afraid, for I am with thee.

God's comforting peace filled her. Theirs was not a hopeless journey. Even if the fever raged, joy would come in the morning.

And it did. Even though the fever didn't break, his hallucinations and nightmares stopped. Papa settled down, and she was able to feed him a couple spoonfuls of fish broth.

Nothing scared her more than watching her father teeter on the brink of death, but God's presence continued to settle her, giving her an anchor upon which to cling. God kept her going night after night, mopping the sweat from her papa's brow and feeding him broth. Nursing him took over her days and nights until mercifully, his fever passed.

She raised more than one prayer of thanks for the miracle. Papa had regained his strength in time for them to arrive in England.

∼

A swirling mist of yellow fog cloaked the docks and streets of London. Georgia filtered out the sounds of pulleys and shouts of men loading the ships for the next voyage. Her ears strained for the clip-clop of horses' hooves signaling the arrival of her mother's carriage. She'd forgotten how tepid the summers were in England and what it was like not to be wiping sweat off her brow. She hadn't seen an ounce of fog in over three months.

A runner had been sent with a note to inform Mama of her return. Georgia had wrestled with mentioning Papa, but decided against it. He agreed with the element of surprise. No need to give Mama time to think up excuses as to why he should go elsewhere.

She glanced at her father, who appeared more nervous than she. He paced the dock, pulling his hands in and out of his pockets. He peered at his watch, then up the street. A seagull cried out overhead, startling him.

She smiled and grasped his hand. "Don't worry, Papa. A wise man once told me to let God lead. Mama will be happy to see you. Maybe not right away, but God will bring her around. You'll see."

His eyes relaxed and a half smile grew on his lips. "When did you become so wise?"

Papa distracted himself from Mama's arrival by engaging in conversation with the sea captain. One trunk sat next to him, which held all their belongings. On the return trip, she'd only filled half the trunk, and it was all she needed. A far cry from the six trunks she'd brought to Nevis, five of which had been lost to the sea. Funny how she didn't miss them at all.

She inhaled the briny air and smiled. There was something about home. Even London's gray skies and slight drizzle were welcome. The oppressive heat of Nevis wouldn't be missed, but she'd grown fond of the bright colors and tropical fauna. It was another world, a beautiful, wondrous world, but London was home.

She scanned the road and couldn't help peering into each passerby's face, hoping to see Harrison. She'd forgotten how large the city was, and her heart twisted at the daunting task in front of her.

But she would not be defeated. Everyone knew the whereabouts of everyone on a small island like Nevis. England was merely a larger island. Besides, she'd sailed across the Atlantic, and God had sustained her. He would help her find Harrison too. She knew it.

It wasn't as if she didn't have a plan. Papa knew the town where he'd worked. She'd start there. Surely, someone would know of his whereabouts. Her family also had social connections. Good estate managers were difficult to come by. Certainly, his name would come up if she put in the right inquiries to the right people.

The Lennox coach, with her family's emblem emblazoned on the side, maneuvered around a bend and rolled to a stop. The footman in their livery stepped down from the rumble seat, lowered the steps, and opened the door. Georgia smoothed her gown with her hands as old insecurities, rose to the surface. Would her mother find her lacking? But Georgia pushed the thought aside and stepped forward.

Her mother descended in a golden day gown that blended with the color of the fog.

Georgia stepped forward. "Mama, you look wonderful." She placed a kiss on either side of her cheeks. Mama appeared as regal as ever with her hair curled under an embellished leghorn hat. "I've missed you."

"I've missed you too, dear. But why have you returned without even penning a letter? Is Fredrick…did he…?"

"Papa is well—"

"And where is Tessa?"

"Aunt Tessa is engaged to be married to a very nice man—a vicar. She decided to remain on Nevis."

"Heavens, Georgia. Where is your chaperone?" She pursed her lips. "Tell me you didn't do something disastrous like crossing the Atlantic without a companion."

"I'm not a duenna." Papa's voice sounded behind her. "But I hope I made a suitable companion."

Mama's eyes widened, and a gasp escaped her lips—her aplomb shaken. "Fredrick."

A grateful warmth spread through Georgia that she hadn't warned mother about Papa. Otherwise, she would have missed the flash of joy and surprise. For a brief moment, the expression restored Mama's youthful beauty.

Mama's hand rose to ensure every hair in her coiffeur remained in place. Her back straightened as she regained her composure and donned a sour grimace. "Are you passing through or have you decided to take up residence in London?" Mama's face remained expressionless, but her voice held a lilt of hope.

She still loved him. Georgia's heart wanted to leap out of sheer delight. She'd known it, but there had been moments on the voyage that she'd worried her assessment of her mother's feelings had been wrong.

"That depends," Papa said, his eyes never leaving Mama's.

A muscle twitched in Mama's temple, and she crossed her arms.

Georgia stepped in before an argument could break out. "It's been a long voyage and we have much to discuss. Papa and I can explain our hasty return in the carriage." She accepted the footman's extended hand and stepped into the coach. She bit back a smile as Papa offered Mama his hand and aided her into the carriage. Her mother's cheeks filled with a faint pink glow.

"To Upper Brook Street," Papa informed the driver before climbing in.

Georgia turned to her mother. "I told him he could stay."

"Merely until I can find other lodging," Papa added.

Mama's face remained impassive. "It's your house."

"I shall not intrude?"

"Stay, don't stay. I don't fancy either way."

Georgia's lips parted. Her mother always had an opinion.

Mama turned to face her and folded her hands. "You have some explaining to do, and I want you to start at the beginning."

Georgia swallowed and began from when the ship arrived at Nevis.

It took her mother some time to get past Harrison being an

estate manager, so Georgia was still telling the tale when they approached Upper Brook Street, and finished as they sat together in the drawing room of their townhome. "And then you arrived at the docks." Georgia chewed on her bottom lip as her mother closed her eyes and exhaled a slow breath.

"A steward?" Her mother questioned once again and impaled Papa with her glare. "I entrust our daughter into your care, and you encourage her to demean herself by chasing a working-man across the Atlantic?"

Papa crossed his arms over his chest. "He's a man of integrity, and she loves him."

"She thought she loved the Earl of Claremont. Of course, she would set her cap for the first handsome man she met. She's an impressionable young girl, but you were supposed to keep some sense about her."

"I know Mr. Wells' character. He was a neighbor, a respectable landowner, and a good friend of mine. They are *in love*, Nora. You allowed Eleanor, Franny, *and* Ann the luxury of a love match. Why can't you extend the same courtesy to Georgia?"

"They were advantageous love matches. Besides, Georgia is too idealistic for her own good."

Papa's voice softened. "Much like you were at her age." He rose and added another log to the fire. "We were a love match."

For a precious moment, the laden words weighed heavily on the atmosphere in the room. And then Mama snapped, "And look where that's gotten us." She turned to face Georgia again. "You mentioned Claremont sailed to Nevis to propose?"

"Only because his mother feels it's time for him to settle down, not because he cares for me. Before I left England, he had an opportunity to propose but used the excuse of having to put his affairs in order. It became obvious from our brief conversation that he was only appeasing his mother."

"I don't see anything wrong with that."

Georgia issued her papa a sideways glance as a plea for help.

Her mother steepled her fingers. "It could be months before Claremont returns to London. It's time for you to seriously consider the Viscount of Ashburnham's suit. Even though the Duke of Linton has returned and Ashburnham won't be handed a ducal title, my preference for the viscount hasn't waned. His mother would be delighted to align our families. Banns could be posted by the end of the week."

"Ashburnham?" Papa walked over and stood in front of Mama, his stance wide in a blatant challenge. "The man is a disgusting lout. I don't care what his mother thinks. I will not allow my daughter to marry the likes of him." He crossed his arms. "And Claremont. Can you honestly tell me the earl is a respectable man of virtue?"

A pregnant pause escalated the tension in the room.

"No." A muscle in Mama's jaw twitched. "I cannot." Her gaze flicked to Georgia. "Don't think I'm unaware of your escapade with him in the garden."

Heat flooded Georgia's cheeks, and she dropped her gaze to the carpet.

Mama crossed her arms and glared at Fredrick. "I don't see how that factors."

"So you'll condemn me to an island for the rest of my life on a smidgen of gossip"—his hands fisted at his sides—"but encourage Georgia to marry a man who'll be known for his indiscretions?"

Mama opened her mouth. "I…" She promptly shut it.

Papa's stance relaxed. "She has my blessing to marry Harrison."

"The steward?" Tears brimmed in Mama's eyes. "What is wrong with wanting the best for your children?"

Papa reached into his coat pocket and pulled out a handkerchief. He unfolded the cloth before handing it to her.

"I merely wanted our girls to marry well so they could maintain a suitable lifestyle." She dabbed at her tears.

Papa knelt by her side and folded her free hand in his. "My love, Mr. Wells can do all that. He has integrity, means, *and* he loves her."

Mama turned to Georgia, her eyes and nose red from tears. "You know that I love you and only want what's best for you. I always have. That's why I've pushed you so hard. You know that, don't you?"

Georgia smiled past the blur of tears in her own eyes. "I do now."

～

*H*arrison strode down the grand staircase of Carlton House, the Prince Regent's place of lodging. His stomach churned with the rich foods and bottomless cups of wine that had been thrust upon him for over two weeks now.

He knew he'd upset Prinny by not rushing home upon the prince's first summons. The prince was more than justified in making him wait for a meeting. Harrison had gritted his teeth and borne the extravagant parties, which began every night and continued into the early morning hours. He'd suffered the willful advances of women, who draped themselves over him like capes and made lewd comments meant to lure him into their beds. He'd had his fill of the debauchery, but had no choice except to suffer through.

He missed Max, who was residing with his grandmother in her London townhome, and he knew each day was another lost before he could return for Georgia—if she hadn't already been lured away by Claremont. She'd never actually told him she'd wait for him, and he berated himself for not waiting for her to say the words—for not making her promise.

Just when he thought he might go mad, Prince George IV

had bid him wait in the anteroom. Five hours later, Harrison had been called into the throne room for a biting meeting with the Prince Regent.

"I thought, all in all, it went rather well," Lord Liverpool stated as he descended the stairs alongside Harrison. "You endured chastisement but regained your title, lands, and parliament seat. A lesson well learned."

"Indeed." Harrison slowed his steps and stopped at the bottom of the stairs where the polished railing ended in an elegant scroll. He turned to the prime minister. "About my request."

"Ah, yes." Lord Liverpool smiled and clasped his hands behind his back. "It's good to have you back, Linton. I've missed your down-to-business demeanor."

They continued to walk through the octagon room lit by overhead windows and a large brass chandelier. Busts of chiseled marble perched on wall-mounted pedestals along decorative panels.

"I received your request, and there are others who support your cause. Let me introduce you to Thomas Clarkson before you return to the countryside for the summer. Good chap and staunch abolitionist."

"Thank you." Harrison shook Liverpool's hand and grinned his first genuine smile since he'd left Nevis. They parted ways, and Harrison climbed into the cushioned seat of his town coach. He tapped on the roof of the conveyance, and the driver snapped the reins.

He couldn't wait to see Max. He even missed that stupid bird that incessantly called out "HarREE." Harrison's lips twitched as he remembered the furious expression on Georgia's face when she'd called him the same name.

His mind drifted to her sunburned face, those eyes that had held his, those lips that had begged to be kissed. Heat stirred within him. He imagined her looking at Claremont in the same manner, and his jaw clenched.

No. He shook his head to clear his mind. He needed to focus, but he could no more remove her from his thoughts than he could remove the echo of the ocean waves from a conch shell.

CHAPTER 27

...I appeal to you for an odd request. I'm in search of an estate manager by the name of Mr. Harrison Wells. If he is in your employment or you know of his whereabouts, please notify me immediately.

—From Miss Georgia Lennox to various lords in the countryside surrounding London

The morning after her return to London, Georgia discovered her mother and father laughing in the breakfast room. Sunlight illuminated the couple as they lounged in their seats while a footman removed their empty plates.

"So, then the parrot proceeds to say"—Papa flapped his arms and gave a fair impression of Oscar—"'Rarwch, dumb bird.'"

Her mother laughed, a melodious sound. But as Georgia entered the room, they sobered. Except for a twitch of her mother's lips, which she firmly pressed together, her expression was serious. However, she couldn't hide the sparkle in her eyes. Georgia barely remembered her mother's laugh, and couldn't recall a time when she'd appeared so young, so...happy.

"Good morning, dear," Mama said. "I'm glad you've finally decided to take my advice and wear colors other than pink."

Georgia glanced at her mint green day gown. "The color pink lost its appeal after I arrived on Nevis."

Papa's eyes sparkled. "May I tell your mother of the events that preceeded this new choice of wardrobe?"

Georgia shrugged with a deep sigh. "If you must."

Her mother leaned in and daintily crossed her arms. "I believe this is a story I must hear."

The tilt of her head reminded Georgia of herself. Could it be? Was Mama flirting with Papa?

Georgia ate her eggs and toast while Papa retold the tale of her trunks being thrown overboard. Her mother half rose out of her chair. Georgia appreciated her mother's indignation, for it had been her own response.

"Thereafter, we couldn't go into town without finding half the natives dressed in pink gowns. I even saw one slave child who'd tied a pair of pink bloomers around his neck like a cape."

Mama's gaze widened, and she covered her mouth with her hand. She blinked at Georgia with horror in her eyes.

Papa continued, "Thanks to Georgia, pink is now all the rage in Nevis. I told you our daughter would be a trendsetter."

Georgia put her fork down. "It's a feminine color."

Crinkles formed at the corner of Mama's eyes, and her shoulders began to shake with what Georgia realized was mirth. She glanced at Papa, who beamed, and a well of giggles bubbled inside Georgia.

"What's so funny?" Her sister, Eleanor, stood in the doorway. Her curious expression quickly turned into one of surprise. "Papa. You're back."

Always one for theatrics, she floated over to their father, who rose from the table. Eleanor kissed the air on either side of his cheeks. Papa held her and examined her at arms' length.

"Eleanor, let me look at you. You've grown more and more

lovely, just like your mother wrote, and she wasn't exaggerating."

Eleanor flushed. As he pulled her into his arms and embraced her, she released a startled yelp. Eleanor's fingertips twitched like she wasn't quite certain where to put her arms, but, after a moment's hesitation, she wrapped them around Papa and relaxed.

Her reaction reminded Georgia of her own the first time Papa had hugged her after Harrison carried her in from the rainstorm. Eleanor's eyes became glassy and brighter blue as Papa released her. Were those tears? It was hard to tell, for Georgia's own vision had begun to mist. How had she not recognized that her sisters longed for their father's love as much as she?

"Let me introduce you to your grandchildren." Eleanor strode back to the door and waved them in. The nursemaid passed the baby to Eleanor. "This is Clinton. He's nine months."

Papa scooped the child into his arms. Clinton blinked his wide blue eyes at his grandfather, and then pulled the glasses off his grandpa's nose.

"He's not afraid to go after what he wants." Papa laughed.

The nursemaid pushed the other two reluctant children into the room.

"This is Calvin." Eleanor put a restraining arm on his shoulder to keep him from pulling his sister's braid. "He's five. And this is Clara. She's four."

Papa pried his glasses out of Clinton's pudgy fingers and passed the baby to his grandma's willing arms. He stepped closer to the children as he cleaned his glasses with the bottom of his shirt. Putting on the lenses, he kneeled, and both grandchildren backed into the safety of their mother's skirts.

"Let me get a good look at you." He peered at Calvin. "My you have a firm stature. I can tell you're going to grow up to be a stately gentleman like your father."

Calvin's little chest puffed, and he nodded at his sister as if to say, *See, that's what I've been telling you.*

"And you, little Clara. You not only have your mother's beauty, but I can tell from the look in your eyes that you have a quick wit about you. I almost feel sorry for the poor blokes who want to make your fancy, because at your coming-out, you're going to leave London on its ear."

A pink stain filled Clara's cheeks.

"Can you spare a hug for your old grandfather?" He opened his arms, and both children stepped into his embrace.

While watching the tender scene, Georgia ate her last bite of toast, then rose from the table. "Well, I have some searching to do."

Papa lifted his head, but Mama said, "I'll go with you. I don't want you traipsing about the countryside unchaperoned."

"I can chaperone." Papa stood. "I might be able to smooth things over with Harrison."

"Who is this Harrison fellow?" Eleanor glanced at each of them.

"It's a complicated story." Georgia turned to Papa. "You stay and enjoy your grandchildren. Mama can catch you up on all the latest happenings."

Fredrick and Nora's eyes met and held, and there was a palpable charge in the air. Eleanor's brows drew together as she watched her parents.

Maybe this would be a chance to extend an olive branch of her own. Georgia turned to her sister. "Eleanor, I could use your help."

Eleanor blinked and turned to Georgia. "You want *my* help?"

"I can fill you in on the carriage ride."

She hesitated. "It might be a nice break from the children."

A smile tugged at Georgia's mouth. "I need some sisterly advice in a matter of the heart."

Eleanor's face lit up. If there was one thing she enjoyed as the eldest sister, it was to offer advice. It would be a welcome change for her, Georgia was sure, to have it solicited this time. Georgia threaded her arm through her sister's.

As they strolled into the front foyer, Eleanor stared at her. "You seem different since you've returned." Her eyes narrowed as she studied Georgia's face closer. "Are those freckles?"

Georgia lifted her chin and smiled. "Indeed, they are."

~

"Stay seated, Thurton." Georgia waved off the footman, who'd fallen from the rumble seat during a particularly bumpy turn and twisted his ankle. "We can handle ourselves this time. Do have that injury looked at as soon as we get home."

"Thank you, Miss Georgia. I certainly will." The footman issued them a grateful smile as they hoisted themselves into the carriage.

"Georgia, I do not believe Mr. Osgood appreciated your grasping his lapel so," Eleanor said, following her into their carriage and taking a seat.

"I don't know what came over me. When the man refused to cooperate. I daresay, I thought I might strangle him." Georgia closed her eyes and slouched against the cushioned seat. "Three weeks of searching and we haven't even found a clue. I don't know where else to look. No one has heard of a steward by the name of Harrison Wells."

"We've tried every manor, estate, and country house in all of Hertfordshire."

"I haven't tried the duke's country home or Tudor Palace."

"Surely, you're not going to knock on the residence of King George himself?"

Georgia sighed. "No, of course not. If Harrison had been working for the king or even a duke, he would have mentioned it. Wouldn't he?" She appealed to her sister for logic, since hers had run out six manors ago.

"Pshaw, of course, he would. Even scullery maids would brag about a position among the king's staff. You may certainly rule those out."

"He did say that it was past time Max saw his grandparents. Maybe he's spending time getting reacquainted with family before beginning his position."

"If that is the case," Eleanor said, "then your only option is to wait. You left each steward and housekeeper with your card. They'll send you a missive if Mr. Wells appears." She patted Georgia's hand. "In the meantime, it will be my mission to make it known to every gentleman of the *ton* that the Lennoxes are in search of Harrison Wells to thank properly for his kindness to our father."

Georgia closed her eyes and fought the sorrow that burned behind her eyelids. "What if we don't find him? What if he vanished, never to be found again? Or what if he returns to Nevis to find me gone?" Georgia's throat clogged with tears, but she continued in a hoarse whisper. "My heart is his. I'll spend the rest of my life peering into the faces of strangers, praying to find him."

"I know I haven't been a godly example for you, but our talks have changed my thinking." Eleanor angled toward Georgia. "Remember you said to lean on Jesus, and he'll make your paths straight? You've got to believe that God will lead you. Never give up hope. Look what he's already done for Mama and Papa. I don't remember ever seeing them this happy. And look how God has brought us together in this search."

Georgia mustered a weak, grateful smile for her sister. "Thank you for all your help. I am truly in your debt."

Eleanor smoothed a wrinkle from her skirt. "Well, I must say traipsing about all over the countryside has been a chore, but the chance to get reacquainted with my youngest sister was lovely." She bit her bottom lip and looked at Georgia. "You were always different. You've always had a purpose. In a way, I was jealous, and not because you were Papa's favorite, but because you weren't afraid to be you."

Her eyes softened. "It's like you rediscovered that self-assurance on Nevis." She laughed. "Look at you. You've brought color back to London."

Warmth soaked through Georgia, buoyed by her sister's kind words.

Eleanor sobered. "I've begun to understand you better these past weeks." She glanced down at her hands. "I know we weren't fair to you when you were growing up." She looked back up at Georgia. "I'm sorry."

"I'm sorry too." Georgia smiled. "For I was a little terror."

Eleanor nodded. "Quite."

"Finding Harrison may look bleak, and I've probably once again made a mull of things, but I'm thankful for you." Georgia rested her head on Eleanor's shoulder. "It demonstrates how God truly can turn all things around for His good."

Eleanor squeezed her hand. "Don't give up, Georgia. We'll find him. I'm sure of it."

❦

Georgia descended the steps of the church into the busy market square. Her time in prayer had helped lift her spirit and given her some direction after her floundering the past few weeks. All her leads on Harrison had fizzled out.

"Care fer an orange, miss?"

Over the ringing of the muffin man's bell, Georgia barely heard the hollow-cheeked girl with a baby slung against her side. Her dirty fingers extended the orange toward her. Georgia accepted it and pressed a farthing into the girl's palm.

"God bless ye, miss." She nodded before moving on.

Georgia sat among the hectic flurry of the open-air market-place, attempting to gather her thoughts. Vendors called out their wares as different scents blended in the air around her. The onion lady passed, and the smell alone burned Georgia's eyes. But the pain was nothing compared to the constant noise of horse hooves clacking, vendors calling out their offerings, and the German band puffing and pounding.

Even though her head throbbed, it had been desperation that led her here. She didn't know what else to do. Over a month had passed since she'd started searching for Harrison, and every trail had gone cold. She'd repeatedly questioned her father for every smidgen of information, anything that Harrison might have said about England.

Papa jogged his memory and mentioned that Harrison had reminisced about a particular cheese that was only sold at the Colton Cheese Shop. So Georgia had stationed herself in front of the cheese shop every day for a full week.

From the café chair, she peered into the face of each gentleman who came and left. She'd even begun to make up names for the regulars who frequented the shop. There was Mr. Gouda, a rotund man who stepped in before low tea each day, and Mr. Havarti, a thin gentleman with a pox-marked face and a genuine smile who always ordered a quarter round. There were others she recognized, men who came and went, but there'd been no sign of Harrison.

Please God, she prayed, as another gentleman—not Harrison—exited the building, *I'm desperate. Please help me find him.* Any reasonable person would have given up long ago, but she couldn't. Something deep within her would not quit until she saw his face again.

What if he returned to Nevis and discovered her gone?

No. She couldn't let her thoughts go there. God would bring them together again. Their reunion was in His hands, in His time. But in the meantime, she would do her part and be diligent in her search.

A boy, the same height as Max with dusty brown hair, inspected the costermonger's cart filled with fruits and vegetables. Georgia perked up and leaned left to get a better view of him. The boy wore his cap low over his face, so she couldn't get a good look. His shoes were caked with mud, and there were holes in the knees of his pants. If this was Max, they must have fallen on hard times. Her heart clenched, and she rose from her seat.

"Stop, thief." The bearded costermonger grabbed the boy by the wrist and suspended him in midair. The boy's legs flailed, but he still clutched a large red apple in his hand. "I don't tolerate thevin.'"

"Put me down." The child's legs thrashed.

The cart owner's eyes scanned the crowd. "Someone fetch the constable."

The boy stilled, the blood draining from his face. Then he squirmed all the harder. "Please, I didn't take the apple. Let me go."

Georgia stared at the boy, but all she saw was the fear on Max's face when their small boat was headed into the large rocks.

She stepped forward. "Fetching the constable will be unnecessary. How much for the apple?"

"I don't believe in a crime going unpunished. What's to stop the lad from trying again? Who's gonna pay fer the apple then? You tell me."

Georgia lifted her chin and stared down the bearded man. "The boy was running an errand for me. He wasn't going to steal the apple. He was going to get my opinion. In fact, upon closer examination, I do believe I'll take that one instead." She pointed at a shiny apple at the top of the pile. "The other seems ready to turn."

The man's eyes swiveled to the apple still held tight in the boy's fist.

"You may hand the child over to me."

The costermonger eyed Georgia, and his gaze roved over her expensive gown and well-made bonnet. Uncertainty shone in his eyes, but he put the child down.

Georgia grasped the boy by the hand, and the youngster peered at her with confusion. She felt him brace as if to run. With the slightest shake of her head and a warning look, she slipped an arm around his shoulder. She turned to the cart owner. "I'd also like a loaf of bread." She passed him a coin, swapped the apples, and took the bread.

She pulled the boy to another set of chairs a bit farther away from the cart and pressed a coin into his palm. "Be a good boy. Run into the cheese shop and purchase a half-round of cheddar and some slices of your favorite cheese."

The child's sunken eyes lit up. "Yes, milady." He darted into the cheese shop.

Georgia watched him through the window. The boy was too thin. He had freckles like Max's, but there were dark circles around his hollow eyes, and his cheeks were concave as if he'd sucked them in. Her heart broke for the child.

He returned and handed her the purchase. His mouth stretched as he chewed on something.

"They 'ave free samples fer people who make a purchase." He spoke around a mouth full of cheese.

She nodded and gestured for him to take a seat. He hesitated as he eyed the loaf of bread, then pulled out the chair and sat next to her. His feet didn't touch the ground, but dangled just above.

"What's your name?"

"John Wesley, but my friends call me Jack."

"May I call you Jack?"

"Fer a slice of that bread you can call me King George."

Georgia smiled. "You are quite the negotiator."

"What's a nego-cee-a-tor?"

"Negotiator." She ripped off two hunks of bread and placed a slice of cheese between them. Jack stared longingly at the food. His lower lip quivered in anticipation, and she could tell his mouth was watering by the number of times he swallowed. She passed him the sandwich, and he tore into it as if he hadn't eaten in days.

"A negotiator is someone who bargains or makes deals." Jack was so intent on his food, she didn't think he heard a word.

He surprised her. "I am a good businessman." He spoke with a full mouth, and she barely made out the words. After swallowing, he said, "Mama has me collect the price for her washin' and mendin' because she knows I'll bring home more coin." He chomped another large bite, devouring most of the bread.

"You must have a mind for numbers."

He nodded.

"I used to help teach children your age, not that long ago when I lived on the island of Nevis."

"You lived on an island?" he asked around the remaining bite of his food. "Did you meet any pirates?" He pushed his hat back to get a better look at her face.

"No, thankfully, I did not."

"Someday I want to be a privateer." He stood and saluted. "Captain Jack of the South Sea. I'd sail the ocean and scour the sea for pirates and the land for buried treasure." His hand extended across the air as if showing her a newfound land. "Aye."

Jack's enthusiasm reminded her of Max. As he continued to demonstrate how he'd command his crew, she felt a pull on her heart to help the child. *But God, what can I do?*

The answer struck her before she'd even completed the thought. She addressed the future Captain Jack. "I'm sure you'll make an excellent privateer, but can you read? In order to be a privateer, you'll need to know how to read."

His face scrunched. "Why does a privateer need to read?"

"To understand the maps, of course. How would a pirate be able to find the treasure if he can't read the clues on the treasure map?"

His little chest fell.

"I will teach you to read."

"You will?"

"Meet me here tomorrow at the same time. We'll sup first, and then I'll teach you."

"Really?" Jack jumped up and down. "Thank you, miss."

"It's Miss Lennox, but you may call me Miss Georgia."

She placed the rest of the bread on top of the half-round of cheese and held it out to Jack. "Take this home to your family."

His eyes lit as if she were offering a chest of gold, and his hands reverently reached forward.

She issued him a stern look. "But no more stealing or the deal's off."

He glanced up at her, his eyes revealing that he believed it was too good to be true.

"Go ahead." She nodded. "Oh and here's an apple and an orange."

His hands were full with the cheese and bread, so Georgia stuffed the apple in one of his pockets and the orange into the other.

He walked to the street's intersection, turned with a smile so broad it showed all his teeth, then disappeared out of sight down a side alley. Georgia laughed despite herself, and a warmth filled her chest.

She may not be able to do for all, but look what she could do for one.

CHAPTER 28

...If you believe the marriage mart has calmed during your absence, you are sorely mistaken.

—*From Lord Liverpool to the Duke of Linton*

The following Wednesday, Eleanor Lennox Hart rubbed her temples as her gaze bounced between her parents. They'd waited until Georgia left with her maid for the market before they sequestered themselves in the office, away from the ears of gossiping servants.

Mama threw up her hands and addressed Papa. "If you could encourage her to attend a few parties before the season ends, then Georgia's affections may be redirected. She can move on with her life, despite this mysterious estate manager. She's wearing herself out on this ridiculous search. If she met another eligible fellow..."

"She's in love." The newspaper Fredrick had been reading crumpled as he dropped it down into his lap. "Some other fop isn't going to do. You don't recover from love as quick as that." His eyes blazed. "I should know."

"Don't bring *us* into this. I'm trying to help our daughter. I can't stand to see her waste away, pining after some steward. A man I'm not even certain exists."

"You are talking about a personal friend of mine, not some imaginary acquaintance we dreamed up."

"A friend who lied about being a steward."

"He's not a liar." Papa's eyes flared.

Eleanor watched as Mama paced back and forth in front of the window.

"Then explain how we've accosted every steward in all of Hertfordshire, Greater London, and parts of Essex and Kent." Mama stopped and put her hands on her hips. "To no avail." She paced again. "I've also sent feelers out to every matriarch in all of London to let them know we're searching for a capable steward who fits Mr. Wells' credentials. No one has heard of the man in all of England."

Papa sat back in the leather chair. "Give it more time, Nora."

"What happens after a year? What about two? She'll be going into her fourth season. Her reputation will be questioned. She'll be put on the shelf."

"She's barely two and twenty, that's hardly on-the-shelf age."

Mama stopped and pressed her hands to her cheeks. "I don't know what to do. Georgia's heart is going to be crushed. She's been putting on a good face, but I can tell she's losing hope."

Eleanor stopped rubbing her temples and sat up straighter in the wingback chair. "I'm with Papa. We can't give up yet. Over the past month, I've seen a different side of Georgia, and I've come to realize I sorely misjudged her. I should have been there for her as her eldest sister. Instead, I either chided her or pretended she didn't exist."

She fought the lump forming in her throat. "Georgia is a stronger person than any of us realized. Did you know she's been sitting outside a cheese shop every day for two weeks because Papa mentioned Mr. Wells prefers a certain cheese that can only be purchased there?"

Mama moved closer to the desk. "I had no idea."

"She's even begun to teach vagrant children how to read the Bible while she waits."

Mama's hand covered her mouth. She shook her head as her eyes misted. "Has she truly?"

Eleanor nodded. "If Georgia's in love, then let's do everything in our power to help her." She chewed her bottom lip. "Maybe he's gone off with the peerage in Ireland. I have connections there. I'll pen a letter to Lady Malahide right away." She reached for the pen and paper on Papa's desk and held his gaze. "Tell me again what Mr. Wells looks like, and don't leave anything out."

Papa described Harrison in detail, then added a description of Max.

Mama tapped the top of the desk with her index finger. "Don't forget about the bird." She glanced at Fredrick. "Didn't you tell me the child had a talking bird?"

"Oh, yes, the parrot." He turned to Eleanor. "Max keeps it as a pet. Its name is Oscar. I imagine they still have the animal."

Eleanor's brows drew together. "Wait a minute. I've heard someone speak of a talking bird recently." Her gaze drifted to the ceiling as she held her index finger against her lips.

She gasped, and her palms dropped to the table with a loud slap. "The Duke of Linton. The duke's son has a talking bird as a pet. I'm sure of it." She stared at her parents. "You don't think…" She reviewed the description of Mr. Wells through her mind, and everything lined up with the brief glimpses she'd seen of the duke at parties over five years ago. Except the duke she'd seen had a beard, but he could have shaved it. "Good heavens, the missing duke." She stared at Papa. "He reappeared several months ago, not long before you. It can't be a coincidence, can it?"

"There's only one way to find out," Fredrick said. "Where is the duke residing?"

Eleanor shook away her stupor. "Ah, let me think." She closed her eyes, then reopened them. "At Ainsley Park in Ashford, I believe. Parliament's session ended a few days ago, so His Grace is probably en route to his countryside home." She sucked in a breath and clasped her hands. "The Dowager Duchess is planning a party to celebrate his return. It's in a fortnight. I might be able to procure us an invitation."

"Nora, have a footman hail a runner." Papa turned to Eleanor with the look of an excited schoolboy. "That's my girl."

Warmth seeped through Eleanor at her father's praise, and she bit her lower lip to keep from smiling. Despite her effort, the corners of her mouth pulled up. She grabbed the quill and began to furiously pen a letter to her friend, the duke's cousin in Ashburnham.

~

"Leave the wool and thick jackets," Harrison instructed his valet as he packed for their return to Ainsley Park. "It will be too humid this time of year." He wasn't looking forward to the welcome home party his mother was planning, but she'd gotten Max excited, and he couldn't disappoint his mother *and* his son.

"That about does it," Harrison said. "I'll leave you to finish. I'll be in my study if anything else comes up."

"Yes, Your Grace." The valet bowed and placed a cambric shirt, neatly folded, into a trunk.

Harrison stepped into the hall and ducked as Oscar grazed his head. The animal flapped its wings and landed on the hand-carved newel post.

"Maxwell," Harrison called. "Come and attend to your bird."

Harrison needn't have bothered, because Max tore around the corner and stopped midway to the stairs. He held out his arm. "Oscar. Come."

The bird stretched, flapped its colorful wings, and landed on Max's raised arm.

Harrison didn't know whether to be impressed or irritated. He'd spoken to Max about keeping the bird caged ever since he discovered bird droppings on the antique chair previously owned by King Louis VI.

"Rawch! HarREE!" it squawked.

Harrison ground his teeth. "Max, put that bird where he belongs."

"But, Papa." Max turned to his father. "He hates the cage. Look how I've trained him." He fed Oscar a treat. "Can't he come out for a bit?"

"You need to prepare his cage for travel."

"Hurrah," Max jumped, and Oscar flapped his wings for balance. "When do we leave?"

"Tomorrow."

Max turned and skipped back down the hall as Oscar flew overhead.

The bird imitated Georgia's screech of his name perfectly. Memories of her shrill voice echoed in his ears, and her irate face filled his mind as if he were once again standing in Rousseau's statuary.

When angered, her eyes would darken to a sapphire blue and flash at him. Her cheeks would burn until they matched her favorite hue of pink. Harrison smiled. Georgia's passion and single-minded determination both attracted and exasperated him. He wanted to kiss her and strangle her at the same time.

How was she faring? The thought pressed a weight on his chest. He pictured Claremont cooing his smooth words in her ear and drawing her into the shadowed sections of Rousseau's statuary. He envisioned her in Claremont's arms when she should be in his. His hands balled into fists. He needed to be on the next ship to Nevis.

"There you are." Harrison's mother approached him. Her

gray-streaked hair was pulled back into a lace cap, and she wore an elegant day gown of twilled French silk. "I've been looking for you. I hoped you'd join me for high tea so we may discuss plans for your return party."

Harrison offered his arm, and they descended the staircase together. "Mother, you know I'm not thrilled at the idea. I want Max to enjoy some peace and relaxation in the country and let his grandparents have their fill of him."

"People want to see you, and a ball is the perfect opportunity. Not to mention efficient, since they'll see you all at once."

Harrison hesitated a step. "Ball? It was supposed to be a few relations visiting. Laura's parents, her sister, and their family." He led her into the drawing room, and she rang for tea.

"You know how difficult it is to leave people out without offending them." She gracefully lowered onto the sofa and spread her skirts around her. "I had to invite your uncle and cousins. And then there's the Lampshires. They're practically family."

Harrison sat in a nearby wingback chair. To his dismay, this was turning out to be a grand affair.

"I've also invited Lord and Lady Carlson. They're bringing their two beautiful daughters, Rowena and Ruth. I'd like you to make their acquaintance."

"This is not to be a matchmaking event."

She softened her voice. "It's time you considered remarrying. It's been six years, and I'd like more grandchildren."

He opened his mouth to tell her about Georgia, but hesitated. What if he returned to discover he was too late and Georgia has betrothed herself to Claremont? His stomach tightened. The longer he remained in England, the more he felt her slipping away.

His mother raised her brows as she waited for an answer.

"You have Max," he stated instead.

"And he is a delight to my soul, but Maxwell needs a mother."

Harrison didn't like where this was headed. "I'll get him a governess."

"A governess isn't a mother." Her lips turned down. "I'm not asking you to marry any chit who comes along. I'm asking that you meet some delightful young ladies and keep an open mind, for your sake and Maxwell's."

As a servant carried in the tea tray, Harrison remembered Max's sleepy face as he spoke of Miss Georgia back in Nevis. *She likes all the same things I do and she looks out for me... She can't take Mama's place, but maybe Miss Georgia could be my earthly Mama until we get to see Mama in heaven? Do you think?*

Harrison sighed as he accepted tea from his mother. "Do *not* get your hopes up."

His mother smiled over her cup. "You'll come around. You'll see."

CHAPTER 29

...We shall be celebrating the return of my prodigal son. It shall be the grandest of affairs. Please extend the invitation to your daughters.

—*From the Duchess of Linton to her distant cousin, Lady Carlson*

The bell chimed on the door of Colton's Cheese Shop. Georgia held her spot with her finger and glanced up from the Bible. *Ah, Mr. Gouda. It must be half past two.* "All right, boys and girls, that was good reading today, but I'm afraid I must be going."

"But, Miss Georgia, you can't stop there." Jack's younger sister, Ava, placed her hand on the Bible's page to keep her from closing it. Her fingernails were caked with dirt, and her big brown eyes melted Georgia's heart. "Does Joseph ever get back to his Papa?"

"Of course, he does." Jack jumped up and swung at the air with a pretend sword. "God helps him, and Joseph goes back and teaches his brothers a lesson."

Georgia chuckled at Jack's enthusiasm. "There were more trials for Joseph to endure, but God was with him the entire

312

time. God had an even better plan for Joseph, but you'll have to come by tomorrow to hear the rest of the tale." She loved stopping during a pivotal part of the story, for the children always returned the following day, ready and eager.

A light tug pulled on her sleeve, and Georgia looked down to see Mary Frances, a neighbor of Jack and Ava's.

"Miss Georgia." She pointed at an approaching patron. "That man looks like the Mr. Wells you told us about."

Georgia's heart lurched, and her gaze pivoted in the direction Mary Frances pointed. She held her breath and scanned the faces. A gentleman with brown hair, well-built and well-dressed, stepped through the crowd. He had Harrison's build and height, but it wasn't Harrison. His nose was too thin and hawk-like. His eyes were too dark, and he didn't walk with the same confident stride that was uniquely Harrison's.

Her heart sank, but she forced herself not to give up hope. He would appear, someday. She just hoped she wouldn't be old and gray.

She smiled at Mary Frances. "You're right. He looks a lot like my friend. Thank you for keeping watch for me." The girl beamed.

A man cleared his throat behind her, and Georgia whirled around to find a middle-aged fellow dressed in homemade clothing, twisting his hat in his hands.

"Milady, I beg your pardon."

"Papa." Both Ava and Jack threw their arms around him, and he knelt and hugged them back. "One moment, children. I'd like to 'ave a word with the lady."

Jack nodded and beamed up at Georgia. "Miss Georgia, this is my papa." He looked at his father. "Papa, this is Miss Georgia…"

"Lennox." Georgia finished for the child. "It's a pleasure to meet you."

"The pleasure is mine, Miss Lennox." His brown eyes darted

back and forth, and he shuffled his feet. "I 'ad to come down 'ere in person to thank you fer all that you've done for me family." The scar on his upper lip zigged and zagged like a snake as his mouth formed the words.

Georgia smiled at him. "You have wonderfully bright children, Mr. Bixby. I enjoy spending time with them. I used to help teach schoolchildren in Nevis and I missed it. Thank you for allowing me to resume the pleasure with Ava and Jack."

"Tis I who is thanking you." He rolled his lips and blinked back tears. "You see, me family doesn't 'ave a pocket to let. With no work and five mouths to feed, the food you've graciously sent home with the children,"—his voice cracked— "it's 'elped us survive."

Tears misted Mr. Bixby's eyes. Jack and Ava wrapped their little arms around his waist.

Ava, too, blinked back tears in her big blue gaze. "Don't cry, Papa."

Jack stepped back and peered up into his father's face. "God will provide for us. Just like the story of Elisha and the widow and the jars of oil."

Mr. Bixby wiped his face with the back of his sleeve and shook his head. "I don't know that one."

Jack's face grew animated as he retold the story. "The widow was going to have to sell her children into slavery to pay down her debt, but she collected a bunch of jars—like Elisha told her —and the oil filled every single jar and stopped at the last one." He turned to Georgia. "It was a miracle from God. Right, Miss Georgia?"

"It was." Georgia smiled, proud of how much Jack had retained.

Mr. Bixby shifted his feet. "That was a long time ago. I don't know if God will—"

"What kind of employment are you looking for, Mr. Bixby?" Georgia couldn't stand to have him dash the children's hopes.

"Any type of work. Before my wife became ill, I used to be a second footman, but now I'd happily work even as a stable boy or gatekeeper."

A slight smile twisted the corners of Georgia's lips. *God is good.* "Mr. Bixby, we happen to be seeking a footman. Ours had a mishap. He twisted his ankle and is on bedrest until he recovers." She reached into her reticule and pulled out a card. "Why don't you clean up a bit, then go and apply for the position." She handed him her card and told him the address.

Mr. Bixby stared at the card and ran his finger along the edge. When he glanced back at her, tears shamelessly dripped down his cheeks. "God bless you, Miss Lennox. Thank you from the bottom of me heart." He squeezed his children. "I'm going to go right now and put on me Sunday best. Thank you, and bless you fer the opportunity."

"I can't guarantee anything." Georgia peered into each of their hopeful faces and lingered on Jack's small features, filled with assurance. "But I believe this was a divine encounter."

CHAPTER 30

...For you darling, I would move mountains, but acquiring an invitation to the duchess's welcome home party is equivalent to moving the Alps. Have no fear, for I shall work my magic. I have not forgotten it was you who introduced me to Lord Macomb.

—From Lady Macomb, the Countess of Amesbury, to Eleanor Hart

"*P*apa, Papa." Max came skidding to a halt outside Harrison's study. The boy tugged at the bottom of his waistcoat, which kept shifting.

Harrison sympathized, for he too missed the loose cotton clothing of the island. The stiff, starched jackets and shirts they were now expected to wear chafed. But he and his son would adapt, in time.

Max entered and plopped into a leather chair next to Mr. Langley, his steward. Max held both sides of the armrests and swung his feet. "Did you know there's a pond on the property ripe for fishing? I bet it's like the pond where Miss Georgia and Uncle Fred used to catch fish."

Harrison put down the stack of correspondences and lifted a brow. "How should you address Mr. Langley?"

Max's head swiveled to Mr. Langley, then he jumped to his feet and gave a formal bow. "Good day to you, Mr. Langley." Then he fell back into the chair.

"Good day, Lord Weld," Langley replied.

Max snickered.

"He's not mistaking you for our Lord and Creator." Harrison prayed for patience. Max was used to the island's relaxed standards. It would take time to teach him proper etiquette.

Max giggled at Mr. Langley. "The islanders pronounced it *Wells*. It's funny to hear people say *Weld*." He added extra emphasis on the *d*. Max leaned forward, and his feet stopped swinging as he peered up at his papa. "Will you fish with me?"

"I can't today."

Max's shoulders drooped.

"I need a day to get settled."

Max slid out of the chair, his chin lowered as he turned away.

All the pressing items that needed tending swirled in Harrison's mind as his son sulked toward the door.

He shook his head and exhaled. Max needed his father. "Tomorrow morning at sun-up."

Max spun around, and his eyebrows practically touched his hairline. "Really, you'll fish with me?"

"I wouldn't miss it." Harrison turned to his steward. "Langley, put it on my calendar. Tomorrow at seven o'clock, a fishing trip with Max."

"Certainly, Your Grace." Langley scribbled it down.

"Will you teach me how to hunt too? Uncle Fred said he taught Miss Georgia, and Miss Georgia told me she was an excellent shot."

Pain ripped through Harrison at the mention of her name. He'd dreamt about Georgia last night. They'd been in separate rowboats. He could see her smile and hear her laughter, but when he reached out for her hand, the boats drifted apart. He called to her, but a fog rolled in, and he could barely make out her shadow.

Then another shadow appeared, and he heard the murmurings of another man's voice. He cried out to Georgia, but she didn't respond. He'd drifted out of their hearing.

Two months had passed, and he hadn't even been able to book passage to sail yet. He'd written to Georgia, telling her of his intent to return. To be safe, he posted three separate letters in hopes she'd at least receive one, but he could never be certain the reliability of sending an overseas letter.

"There you are, Master Maxwell." Mr. Seaton, Max's tutor, filled the doorway. Quite literally since the man stood a good deal over six feet. He pursed his lips and shifted them to the right. It appeared to be a mannerism he displayed whenever he was disappointed. "Pardon my interruption, Your Grace, but Maxwell is supposed to be discussing the works of Plato in the library." He put a restraining hand on the boy's shoulder.

"Time for your lessons." Harrison inclined his head toward Mr. Seaton, but continued to eye Max. "There will be plenty of opportunity for hunting and fishing tomorrow."

"Yes, Papa."

As Mr. Seaton led the boy down the hall, Harrison turned back to his desk. "Where were we?" He picked up the next letter addressed to him, the Honorable Duke of Linton. He broke the seal and read the contents. His distant cousin begged for an invitation so she could introduce him to her three daughters, all of marriageable age.

He wasn't certain who was worse, the young women who threw themselves at him. Or their mothers.

~

*G*eorgia reclined against the cushioned leather seat of their carriage. A week ago when Eleanor had told her about the weekend soiree, she'd thought it might be a good diversion. But as they drew closer, her excitement wore off. Would she be able to put on a good face even though her heart withered inside?

God, be my guide. I'm letting You lead. Sustain me with Your righteous right hand.

Eleanor sat upright and peered out the window at the passing scenery. "My husband was delighted you were willing to accompanying me instead of him. He has an aversion to formal events as much as I loathe joining him on his hunting trips. This works out best for us all, especially since a male escort isn't needed for a house party."

Her hands rested on the edge of the seat and patted the leather in an unrecognizable rhythm. She cleared her throat, wiggled back into the cushions, and glanced at Georgia. "This is the one place we haven't searched, and I have a good feeling about it."

Despite her sister's enthusiasm, Georgia couldn't dredge up the same excitement. She didn't want to get her hopes up. Especially not when they were grasping at the far-reaching prospect that Harrison worked for the Duke of Linton. If Harrison were the duke's steward, surely, he would have mentioned it. One didn't come by such a position easily.

Yes, Harrison was humble, but even he would have dropped the duke's name, if only to put Mr. Rousseau in his place so he wouldn't look down his nose at a *mere schoolmaster*.

"It seems we're drawing near." Eleanor leaned closer to the window for a better look. "Yes, there's the gatehouse now." She turned back to Georgia and pinched her cheeks.

"Ow." Georgia knocked her hands away.

"It's for color. I want you to make a good impression."

She eyed Eleanor. "I'm not here to meet the duke. I'm here to meet his steward."

"Yes, yes, but you want to appear your best when Mr. Wells sets eyes on you."

"The chance of Mr. Wells working for the duke and us not knowing—"

"I told you, I have a good feeling about this one."

"Thank you for helping and allowing me to drag you across half of England," Georgia said, "but I don't want you to be disappointed."

"Never." Eleanor's expression grew solemn. "I could never be disappointed by you." She fluffed Georgia's dress. "I'm sorry I wasn't there for you when you were younger. Mama and Papa were always fighting, and I was trying to make sense of it all in my own mind. I never considered how it made you feel. You were so young and impressionable. How old were you, five and ten?"

"Indeed." Georgia let out a sigh. "It doesn't matter. The past is in the past, and thank God for it." She patted Eleanor's knee. "You're here with me now, and I'm grateful."

Eleanor shifted to look her in the eye. "I wish I could go back in time and change things. I could have protected you. I could have saved you from heartache."

Georgia mulled it over in her mind, then shook her head. "I wouldn't change a thing. All those trials made me who I am. God refined me through it. He showed me that no matter how awful I could be, He still loved me and could use me for His good."

Eleanor flashed her a lopsided smile. "You were beastly, and you always smelled a bit like a swamp."

Georgia laughed. "That's because I practically bathed in it."

Eleanor grimaced. "Thank God you've outgrown that."

"Praise God is more like it."

They both lapsed into silence as the gate raised and they were allowed to pass into Ainsley Park.

"Do you think God would still forgive me?" Eleanor chewed her bottom lip.

A lump grew in Georgia's throat, and she slipped her arm around Eleanor. "Remember the thief on the cross next to Jesus? The one who asked Him to remember him when he came into His kingdom? It wasn't too late for that man, and it wasn't too late for me. Jesus will forgive. All you have to do is repent and ask. Harrison helped me understand that."

Eleanor blotted away tears with the corner of her handkerchief as they pulled up in front of the grand manor house. Across the front, columns with scrolled cornices outlined arched parapets.

"Take a deep breath," Eleanor said. They both inhaled a fortifying breath and expelled the emotion of the moment. Mr. Bixby, with a proudly puffed chest, opened the carriage door and extended his hand to Eleanor. She paused before turning back to Georgia. "No matter what, you're my sister, and I love you."

Eleanor stepped out of the carriage.

"I love you too," Georgia whispered to her retreating frame. God was amazing. While it took Joseph becoming Pharaoh's right-hand man and a famine to bring his family back together, it required sailing across the Atlantic twice and a wild chase after a disappearing steward to bring Georgia's together.

God, if I never locate Harrison, I would still do it all over again, because You are good. Your ways are higher than my ways.

She smiled at Mr. Bixby, who extended his hand to aid her descent from the conveyance. His face was clean, his clothing freshly pressed. "Good day, Mr. Bixby."

He bent into a deep bow. "Good day, Miss Georgia Lennox." He rose with a broad smile that wrinkled the forked creases beside his eyes. "I owe you a debt of gratitude. I am proud to be part of the Lennox household staff. Thank you on my behalf, my wife's, and my children's. You have a saintly heart. God bless you."

Georgia nodded to him and followed Eleanor to the main entrance with newfound warmth seeping into her heart. Saintly, no, but it felt remarkable to do God's work.

The deep ache that had persisted since she'd watched the *Essex* sail lessened a bit. Maybe helping others could overshadow the pain. There was hope. God had a plan, and He would still use her. She had wanted to help others by Harrison's side, but if God intended differently, then maybe she needed to trust that He had a better plan for her life.

She longed to tell Harrison what she'd just experienced. He'd be overjoyed.

The all-too-familiar stab of pain punctured her heart. Would she ever have the opportunity to tell him?

She blinked away tears. All would be well. God rejoiced with her.

Carriages lined the stables, with even more approaching. The three-storied house towered in front of her, its long wings stretching out to the east and west with rows of mullioned windows. Ladies strolled about the grounds like peacocks, all gussied up to attract the eye of the duke.

She knew Eleanor had used her friendship with the duke's cousin to procure them an invitation. However, she didn't esteem the prestigious house party as she once would have. Georgia swallowed and followed in Eleanor's wake, past the massive columns and through the grand main entrance.

"Eleanor, dear." A dark-haired woman approached, dressed in an elaborate gown with enough embellishments to make it weigh at least two stones. She kissed Eleanor on both cheeks, and Eleanor introduced Lady Macomb, the Countess of Amesbury, to Georgia, who bobbed a curtsy.

"James will escort you to your bedchambers to freshen up. Afterward, meet me in the front drawing room and I'll provide you a tour of the house and grounds."

They followed the footman through the reception hall, up an elegant stairway with hand-carved scrolled railings, and down a long corridor to their rooms. He opened both doors and stepped aside.

"That will be all, James." Eleanor dismissed the servant.

They both donned fresh gowns with the help of the ladies' maid provided for them, then joined Lady Macomb in the drawing room for the tour.

As they passed from room to room, Eleanor leaned in and whispered into Georgia's ear. "You keep a lookout for Mr. Wells and I'll keep an eye out for the duke."

Georgia didn't miss the look of determination in Eleanor's eyes or the firm line of her lips. She'd seen the same look on her mother's face whenever she set her mind to something. What was her sister up to? Hopefully she doesn't have a mind to match-make Georgia with the duke.

The tour led to the terrace, which was surrounded by lush perennial gardens and a large fountain. Eleanor pulled Georgia to the outside edge of the cluster of women. They descended the steps, and Lady Macomb pointed to the right.

"Over there is a court for Pall Mall if anyone plays." She waved her hand. "Beyond that lies the steward's house and the woods where the gentlemen fox hunt. His Grace shall be returning from their outing at any moment."

Eleanor grabbed Lady Macomb's arm and pointed back toward the gardens, asking her some nonsense about horticulture. With her other hand, Eleanor shoved Georgia in the direction of the steward's house. Georgia didn't waste a moment. She discreetly slipped around a hedge and down a grassy aisle toward the little cottage on the edge of the wood.

Her heart raced as she approached the door, but she

suppressed her excitement, knowing the chances were slim. In her mind, she ran through what to ask when the duke's steward answered the door. *Sir, I must apologize, but I'm looking for someone. You may have heard of him within your profession...*

CHAPTER 31

...Life as a vicar's wife is grand. Our wedding day was lovely. It seemed all of Nevis attended.

—From Lady Tessa Clark to the Lennox family.

*H*arrison drew to a halt as he breached the woods and stepped into the open yard. He patted Max on the back. "You did well today, son. Next time we'll focus on how to cover your sneeze, so it doesn't scare off the prey. Now run along and get yourself cleaned up. Your grandmother will want you appearing your best in front of her guests."

"Yes, Papa." Max darted off toward the house. Harrison shifted the rifle slung across his back and strolled toward the west entrance. He rounded the outside corner of the garden and spotted a woman, finely dressed, knocking on the door to his steward's home.

His steps slowed. Either Mr. Langley was inappropriately entertaining house guests, or one of them was hopelessly lost. Whichever it may be, Harrison knew it was his duty as host to investigate.

He drew closer, squinted, and stopped. He recognized that

shape. The woman knocked a third time, but there was no answer. If he remembered correctly, Langley was off inspecting the far pasture.

She turned around and glanced about. He advanced a few steps and froze. He must be hallucinating. His heart wanted to see her so badly he was imagining things.

He rubbed a hand down his face. With eyes closed, he told himself he was crazy. It was only wishful thinking.

He opened his eyes.

There, knocking on his steward's door, was Georgia Lennox.

A jolt ran through his body, but logic quickly dampened the effect. What was she doing here? How did she discover he was a duke? What about Claremont? Did she leave him in Nevis, or did they return together?

He resumed his approach. Why was she knocking on his steward's door?

"Georgia?"

Georgia jumped and spun around to face him. Her familiar face stirred his insides in a way he wasn't prepared for. *Lord, she's beautiful.* She always had been, but now, with the small spattering of freckles across her nose, she looked even more appealing, more natural.

Her eyes widened. A multitude of emotions chased across her face—disbelief, amazement, elation, confusion.

"Harrison." Her entire countenance lifted and brightened, illuminating her features in a rosy glow. "It's you." She closed the distance between them. "I am so glad I've finally found you."

His heart lurched, pulsing through his fingers for want of pulling her into his arms. But he needed to know why she was here.

"I made a terrible mistake. I've crossed the Atlantic, searched every property in greater London and beyond, and even posted myself in front of Colton's Cheese Shop to just find you…" Her words drifted off as she caught her breath.

What did Colton's Cheese Shop have to do with anything? He searched her face, then stepped toward her. "How did you get here? When?" *With who?* But he couldn't gather the courage to voice his last question.

She placed a slender hand on his chest, and Harrison's muscles leapt in response.

"I always thought I needed an earl to prove myself, but all I really need is a steward." Her other hand flittered through the air. "My sisters can think what they want, and Mama may always be disappointed in me, but I'll listen to their chastisement for the rest of my days if necessary. I'm in love with a steward, and I want to be his wife and bear his children."

Harrison closed his eyes and gave his head a little shake to clear it. "You're telling me you traveled halfway around the world because you're in love with a steward?"—*my steward?*

"I love you, Harrison Wells. I've loved you since the moment you carried me in your arms out of the raging storm."

As much as her words sent a thrill through him, not everything was making sense. Then a hazy memory surfaced of a time when they sat across the table from one another in Fredrick's villa, and Georgia asked if he managed an estate. He had replied, *something like that.*

She believes I'm the Duke of Linton's steward. He should throw his head back and laugh. Yet his heart was too tied in knots to find humor. "What about Claremont? You didn't arrive with him?"

"Julien?"

Harrison's jaw clenched. He hated her even saying his name.

"Heavens no. I had no idea he was coming to Nevis. I no longer wanted anything to do with him. I love you." She removed her palm from his chest and reached for his hand, squeezing it. "That's why Papa and I sailed from Basseterre."

Harrison blinked. "Fredrick is here?"

"No. I mean yes. Papa is in London. He's becoming reacquainted with Mama. He said it was overdue, but he's not here at this party. My sister Eleanor accompanied me."

"But Claremont came for you. I saw him from the ship. I thought…"

"He sent word as soon as the ship arrived, but I didn't—"

"You didn't speak to him?" His eyes narrowed in disbelief. He'd seen her wave to him from the beach.

"He approached me and babbled on about something." Her brows drew together, and her gaze fell. "I don't remember what. I couldn't go back to being the old Georgia. I'm a new person. I've been made whole, thanks to God." She peered back up at him. "I handed Claremont my parasol—the only pink item I still owned—and walked away. That's the last I saw of him."

Slowly, the tension began to melt from his chest, allowing him a deep inhale.

Georgia was here. She hadn't stayed with Claremont. She'd sailed the Atlantic to find him. Not the Duke of Linton, but Harrison Wells, the steward. Georgia loved him for *him*.

Thank you, Lord, for answered prayers.

She wrapped her slender fingers around his other hand. "I know you asked me to wait for you, but I couldn't wait. I needed to find you."

Harrison peered into eyes so filled with love. His blood raced through his veins, and his heart thundered in his chest. He opened his mouth to say the words, *marry me…*

"Your Grace," a woman called out across the yard. Harrison frowned and glanced over his shoulder to see Miss Ruth Carlson. Georgia still had no idea he was the duke, and Miss Carlson's long strides didn't leave him much time to explain things.

He put his hands on her shoulders, pinning her against the exterior wall. "Georgia, listen to me. I—"

"There you are." Ruth's sister, Lady Rowena Carlson, appeared out of nowhere and peeked around the far corner of the house.

Harrison let go of Georgia's shoulders and rubbed the lower half of his face with his hand. He held up one finger. "Stay here a moment. I'll be right back."

He stalked off in the direction of Lady Rowena and pulled her aside.

"Your Grace," she said, "you promised you'd teach me how to play Pall Mall." She trailed her folded fan down the lapel of his jacket with a demure pout.

"I'm busy at the moment." He grasped her wrist when she didn't remove her fan from his shirtfront. "Another time perhaps." He glanced over his shoulder. Georgia stared back at him with a mixture of hurt and confusion.

"Harrison? Who is she? I thought—"

"Georgia, I can explain."

Lady Rowena turned to Georgia and laughed. "Is she confusing you with someone else?" She hung on his arm. "Don't you recognize our host, His Grace, the Duke of Linton?" She turned back to him and shook her head at such a preposterous notion. "As I recall, your given name is Robert?"

"Robert Harrison." The name slipped from his lips.

"You're a duke?" Georgia's face paled, and her eyes darted back and forth between himself and Lady Rowena. Her gaze slid down to where his fingers encased Lady Rowena's wrist, and her chin trembled.

The look of betrayal in Georgia's eyes ripped a hole through Harrison's heart. He stepped toward her, but Lady Rowena gripped his arm.

Georgia staggered back, then lifted her skirts and sprinted for the house. It took precious seconds to pry off Lady Rowena's fingers, leaving Georgia a fair head start. He chased her across the yard, through an on-going game of Pall Mall, nearly tripping over a rolling ball, and through the garden, brushing past startled guests. Ruth Carlson smiled and blocked his way, but he sidestepped her and kept running. He'd almost caught up with Georgia near the patio, but his mother rose from her group of guests seated at tables and stepped in his path. "Linton, dear. So glad you're finally putting in an appearance. May I introduce you—"

"In a moment, Mother."

He raised his gaze just in time to see Georgia scurry through the North portico entrance and into the house.

"Georgia, wait."

His mother placed a hand on his arm. "Is that the same Miss Georgia that Max speaks of so highly?"

Harrison ignored her and skirted away. Another woman's voice carried the answer, "Miss Georgia Lennox, I believe," as he leapt over a low hedge onto the brick patio. His hunting rifle still slung over his shoulder slammed into his back as he landed.

Harrison charged up the steps onto the north portico. A footman, carrying a tray of glasses filled with lemonade, exited through the doorway at the same time Harrison entered. He tried to shift to the side, but he was moving too quickly. He slammed into the tray. A loud crash ensued, and Harrison found himself drenched in the sticky-sweet liquid.

He reached down, grasped the footman by his wrist and elbow, and yanked the man to his feet. "Dreadfully sorry."

Ignoring the mess, he tried to determine which direction Georgia had gone. A shove pushed him toward the door. He whirled around with clenched fingers to discover a woman who appeared to be an older version of Georgia.

"That way," she said and pointed in the direction of the parlor. "The servants will handle the mess," the woman said. "I'll stall the guests so you two can talk."

Harrison broke into a run, his slick shoes barely gaining traction on the highly polished floor of the solarium. Ladies called his name as he passed, but he ignored them as he dodged a chair and averted a sofa in the back parlor, then rushed into the back hall. His breath came in gasps as he rounded the corner.

The stodgy butler's tone drifted down the hallway. "Calm yourself, miss. We'll bring your carriage around right away."

Harrison skidded into the turn, sliding past the entrance to the reception hall on the marble floors. He grabbed the frame to stop himself, then pulled his body through the doorway.

Georgia gasped. Her stunned face stared at him with pained eyes, glistening with tears.

"Georgia." He was breathing so hard, he almost couldn't get the word out.

Instead of waiting, she pushed the butler out of the way. The poor man stumbled against a side table, almost knocking over a priceless vase, which he managed to save with an inch to spare. Georgia yanked open the door and raced outside.

A crooked smile lifted one side of Harrison's face as he lent a hand to right the butler before chasing after her. He shouldn't have been surprised by her actions. Georgia didn't let anything stand in her way. She'd crossed an ocean for him and turned over half the countryside to find him because she loved him. His poor butler didn't stand a chance.

She slowed to locate the stables, and it was enough of a pause for him to catch up with her. He grasped her arm and spun her around to face him.

Through heaving breaths, he managed to say, "I can explain."

Her eyes were cavernous pools of turquoise blue, the color of the Caribbean Sea, and filled with as much torment. Tears poured down her cheeks and formed dark splotches on her pale lavender gown. She tried to yank her arm out of his grasp, but he held fast.

"You were funning me?" The hurt in her voice made his heart ache. "Did you laugh each time my back was turned? Did my father know? Did I provide you both with enough entertainment?" She squeezed her eyes shut, sending more tears cascading over their brims. "What a naïve, green-girl I am. And to think I loved you."

"Georgia, look at me." He grasped her upper arms and gave her a little shake to get her to open her eyes. A commotion sounded to his right as the footman readied the carriage. "I love you. You must know that." He gently squeezed her shoulders. "I am a duke, but no one in all of Nevis knew. Not even your father. I relinquished my title and sailed to Nevis, not only to avoid the memory of Laura but also to get away from the ambitious women trying to force my hand into marriage."

He willed her to see the truth in his gaze. "I wanted the right woman to be Max's mother. I want that person to be you. You are the only woman for me."

She stopped trying to pull away. However, the skeptical glare in her eyes remained. "But what about the woman you promised to teach Pall Mall?"

"I met her for the first time this morning at breakfast. I mentioned there would be a match this afternoon. She said she didn't know how to play. All I said was there would be plenty of people to instruct her. She is the exact type of woman I ran to Nevis to get away from, scheming and manipulative. There is nothing between us. You and you alone hold my heart."

She swallowed and searched the deep recesses of his eyes.

He could only pray the truth of his words showed on his face.

"I do?" Her expression softened with such optimism that he smiled.

"I love you, Georgia Lennox. Can you love me as a school-teacher *or* a steward *or* a duke?"

She smiled through her tears. "I would love you if you were a rat-catcher."

He chuckled. "Well, let's hope it doesn't come to that." He tucked a loose strand of hair behind her ear and traced the line of her jaw. A horse neighed in the background, and the clip-clop of the animals' hoofs ran in time with the beating of his heart.

"Your coach is nearly here, but please don't leave. I cannot stand another moment without you." He drew her closer. "Marry me. Be my wife and stay by my side until Jesus calls us home."

The rumbling of her coach grew louder.

"Yes," she whispered, then her voice grew stronger. "Yes, I will marry you."

His lips parted as he curled his fingers into her upper back and pulled her into his embrace. "Come here, princess."

"Unhand the lady, you scoundrel." A footman leapt from the back of the carriage and raised his fists to defend Georgia's honor.

Georgia's head whipped around. "Mr. Bixby."

"I saw you runnin' from 'im with me own eyes."

Harrison dragged his gaze away from Georgia. The sooner he ridded them of this distraction the better. He glanced at the man who'd misunderstood Georgia's plight.

He froze.

The footman's eyes widened, then darted back and forth in nervous jerks between Georgia and Harrison. He licked his lips, and Harrison's gaze focused on the scar zigzagging along his upper lip.

This was the face that had haunted his dreams for six years.

Cold fury flowed through his body as he pushed Georgia behind him and whipped his rifle off his shoulder. He cocked the weapon and peered down the barrel at the man's head. There was only one shell left, but he'd make it count.

"No!" Georgia screamed. Before he realized what she was doing, she'd positioned herself between the end of the weapon and the footman.

"Get out of the way, Georgia." He stepped to the side so

Georgia would be out of the line of fire, but she moved with him. "This man murdered Laura."

"It was a mistake." The man's lower jaw began to tremble as if the temperature had dropped to freezing. "God, forgive me. I never meant to kill no one. The gun went off after I lost me grip. It was me one and only robbery. I had five starving mouths to feed. There isn't a day that goes by that my sins don't haunt me. Please, don't shoot. Think of me wife and children."

Harrison stepped to the left for better aim, but so did Georgia.

"Harrison, please, put the gun down. He has a son Max's age. You wouldn't want the boy to live without a father. Who would provide for them?"

"He took Max's mother away from him."

"Killing him won't bring her back."

"Please, sir." Tears slid down the man's cheeks, and he sank to his knees.

Harrison stepped aside and jabbed the barrel of the gun into the man's shoulder. "She was pregnant with our second child. She hugged her stomach as her last breath left her body." He jabbed the end again into his shoulder. This time harder. The man cringed.

"Papa? Miss Georgia?" Max's voice called behind them.

"Stay back, Max." He shot a quick glance over his shoulder.

Harrison's mother took the boy by the hand and held him at bay. He could hear other voices, guests at this party, as people filtered out the front door. He ignored them all.

"Please, Harrison, don't shoot him in front of your son." Georgia's hand gripped the gun's shaft. "I know how badly you hurt, but have mercy. People can change. You told me yourself sometimes little decisions have unintended consequences. Laura's death was a tragic, tragic accident."

She pushed down on the barrel. The gun lowered, but Harrison didn't release his hold. "You showed me forgiveness and taught me I was a new person through Christ." She pushed the end toward the ground. "I'm asking you to extend a bit of that same grace to him. Mr. Bixby claims he didn't mean to shoot her. Please."

Harrison didn't move. Couldn't. This man had killed Laura, and Georgia wanted him to extend grace?

Tears filled her eyes. "If you believe that this man can't be forgiven for his sins, and that he doesn't deserve to be redeemed, then it means you don't truly believe I can be redeemed either. I know our crimes are different, but sin is sin." She implored him with her eyes. "You told me God removes our iniquities as far as the east is from the west. If you truly believe that—"

Harrison's resolve slowly crumbled as the fury seeped from his body.

"—then show him the same mercy you showed me." Georgia presented him a weak smile.

He peered down into the frightened face of the man who'd murdered his beloved Laura. In that moment, God opened his eyes. He saw a man with a family, a man who'd sinned and begged for God's forgiveness, a man whom God had formed inside his mother's womb, a man whom Jesus loved enough to die for. The gun lowered to Harrison's side.

"Thank you." Georgia wrapped her arms around him, and she held him for a long moment. His heart still raced in his chest, but he clung to her, soaking in the sweet scent that was only Georgia's. Doing his best to settle himself.

"Because of you, I've come to know God's love first hand." She rose up on her toes and pressed her lips to his cheek.

She pulled back as the coachman and his groomsmen escorted the badly shaken footman toward the stables.

"Miss Georgia."

Harrison turned toward his son as Georgia opened her arms to Max. The boy ran into her embrace.

"I missed you." Her voice caught, and she kissed Max on top of the head.

He beamed at her. "Does that mean you get to be my new mama?"

She glanced at Harrison. Did she wonder if he would take back his proposal? Or maybe she only questioned when they would tell his son.

He looped an arm around her slender waist and nodded with a smile.

"I knew it." Max danced around them.

After Mr. Bixby was loaded into the carriage and driven away, Harrison focused all his attention back on Georgia.

She bit her bottom lip as she peered up at him, and he could read all the questions in her eyes. He had a lot of explaining to do, but for right now, his only thought was to show her the extent of his longing and punish her with a kiss for staying away for so long.

His mother cleared her throat, but he didn't take his eyes off Georgia. Forget propriety. He didn't care a whit who looked on. This was *his* house, and he was going to kiss the woman he loved in full view. If they didn't like it, they could leave.

He pulled Georgia into a tight embrace, and his mouth devoured hers in the kiss he'd been dreaming of for weeks. It drew gasps from the gathered crowd and an "Ew, yuck!" from Max.

They smiled against each other's lips and drew back slightly. Harrison couldn't pull his gaze away from the swirling depths of her eyes and the love that shone in them. He knew it reflected the love in his own.

Her eyes narrowed, and she tilted her head. "The mysterious Duke of Linton?"

"I can explain—"

"Do you know how many inquiries I sent searching for Harrison Wells, estate manager? I dragged my sister over half of

England looking for you, but no one had heard of anyone by that name."

"The islanders had a difficult time pronouncing the D in Weld, and I gave up correcting them."

"What should I call you, Your Grace?"

His voice softened as a fresh wave of tenderness washed through him. "Love. I want you to call me, *my love.*"

Her eyes sparkled with the same joy that radiated in his heart, and the temptation was too great. He swooped in for another kiss, but when their mouths met, Georgia pulled back and licked her lips. Her brow furrowed as she examined his wet attire. "My love, why do you taste like lemons?"

"No more questions." He claimed her mouth once more.

~

*T*wo weeks later, with the procurement of a special license, Lord Robert Harrison Weld, the honorable Duke of Linton, listened with unimaginable joy as Miss Georgia Evelyn Lennox said "I do" at the little schoolhouse up the road from Ainsley Park in Ashford. Hundreds of people gathered in the yard and up the lane for a peek at the happily married couple.

At the reception afterward in Ainsley Park, Harrison broke off a conversation with Lord Liverpool to find his wife. He scanned the room full of happy guests chatting about the beautiful bride, but he didn't see a trace of her. He tapped his mother's shoulder.

"Pardon me, Mother, but have you perhaps seen where my new wife has run off to?"

"Maxwell led her outside to show her something." She patted his arm. "I told them not to be long. There are guests to entertain."

Harrison would throw the entire lot out on their ears for a few minutes alone with his bride.

He declined a glass of champagne as he strolled out the door to the patio. He scanned the garden. Still no sight of them, but Harrison had a feeling.

He sauntered up to the pond and leaned against a tree, not only to watch, but to support his legs, which grew weak at the sight before him.

Georgia sat perched on a fallen log over the water. Her wedding dress was hitched up, exposing her delicate feet and slender ankles. Max sat beside her and leaned his little head against her arm.

They both held fishing poles.

Harrison's face wasn't broad enough to contain the smile overflowing in his chest.

There were times when life chose for him. There were times when he weighed his options and made the best decision possible. But then there were times, when something he would have never chosen, blessed him in a way he would have never expected. *Praise be to God.*

"And we know that all things work together for good to them that love God, to them who are the called according to his purpose."
Romans 8:28 (KJV)

Did you enjoy this book? We hope so!
Would you take a quick minute to leave a review where you purchased the book?
It doesn't have to be long. Just a sentence or two telling what you liked about the story!

Receive a FREE ebook and get updates when new Wild Heart books release: https://wildheartbooks.org/newsletter

SNEAK PEEK: THE MERCHANT'S YIELD

Here's a sneak peek at the next book in The Leeward Islands Series!

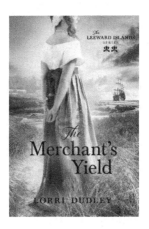

The Merchant's Yield

It was a marriage of inconvenience, but life has a wicked sense of humor.

Charlotte Amelia Etheridge has cowered to her mother's sharp tongue and endless demands for the last time. In a fleeting moment of rebellion, she recklessly asks a foreigner from the Leeward Islands for a dance. But her one courageous act lands her in a compromising position. Forced to wed a stranger, Lottie leaves the only home she's ever known to reside on the isle of St. Kitts.

Nathaniel Winthrop's troubles are mounting, and the rumors of him being cursed are spreading. Due to the dwindling sugar crop, he risks everything to start his own shipping company. The last thing he needs is a wife, especially one with a weak constitution. Yellow fever has already claimed the lives of his mother and siblings. He must guard his heart against falling in love with this gentle beauty, knowing island life will be a death sentence.

No longer under her mother's scrutiny, the newfound freedom of the island rejuvenates Lottie's spirit. If her days on this earth are limited, then it's time she lives life to the full. Now it's up to her to prove that even though Nathan was coerced into marrying her, she's the one he can't live without.

CHAPTER ONE

London, England, May 1814

"Of course, the islander would come."

Charlotte Amelia Etheridge stiffened at Mama's acidic tone. She followed her mother's gaze to the entrance of the Middleton's modest ballroom where guests arrived in hordes of navy and formal black jackets bobbing amid a sea of colorful gowns.

They filled the ballroom with boisterous chatter and a bouquet of expensive perfumes and colognes.

Mama flicked her fan in sharp increments. "Even dressed in English finery, he appears barbaric and uncivilized."

Lottie focused on the landing where Nathanial Robert Winthrop bowed to Lord Gibbons and his wife. His large frame and broad shoulders dwarfed Lord Gibbons's, making the average-height man appear slight in stature. Winthrop's hand tossed back the coattail of his fitted charcoal jacket and tucked into his right pant pocket. He exuded a relaxed, casual self-assurance that uniquely contrasted with the pretentious lords and ladies of the Quality surrounding him. Their grandiose displays sought approval, a favor they would be hard-pressed to receive from her mother, for Lady Etheredge's acerbic tongue could elevate or cut down a person with a single remark.

Winthrop nodded at something Gibbons said, and his teeth gleamed the same bright white as his cravat and shirt front.

Mama nodded in the direction of the gentlemen. "I will make certain Lord Gibbons reserves a dance for you. His mother owes me a favor."

A favor. The jab struck its soft target, but Lottie had numbed to most of her mother's verbal attacks.

"There she is now." Mama stepped away to speak with Lady Gibbons.

Lottie plucked at the sides of her skirt and searched for Priscilla, her closest friend. The large mirrors reflected shimmering light from the overhead multi-tiered chandeliers and exposed her abandoned position. A retreat to the retiring rooms to freshen up might be in order.

Captain Anthony Middleton eyed her.

Lottie paused mid-step.

He weaved through the cluster of people to her side.

This was it. Her pulse leapt. How long had she fancied Priscilla's handsome elder brother and dreamed of this moment?

"If it isn't Little Lottie Ethridge." The deep rich tone of Anthony's voice sent a wave of tingles up her arm.

Lottie fought to subdue a grin she knew would cross the lines of decorum.

The boyishness in his face had disappeared, and he exuded virile sophistication in his navy captain's jacket and highly polished boots. "It has been an age."

She longed to say something witty like how she practiced in front of the mirror while he'd been at sea, but all that came to mind was, "Indeed."

"Green is a lovely color for your complexion." His gaze swept over her like a soft caress. "It also happens to be my favorite color."

Of which she was keenly aware. That, and the fact he despised snakes, took four lumps of sugar in his tea, and sang a little off key. Such knowledge was boon of being close friends with his sister.

"Would you like to—" He glanced away and shifted his feet. "Would you care to—"

"Captain Middleton" Mama drew alongside the two of them. "Your mother is looking for you. I believe she said it was urgent."

Anthony craned his neck toward the entrance. "Perhaps another time." He stole one last glance at Lottie, bowed, and excused himself.

A whimper sounded deep in Lottie's throat as she watched him go. The opportunity had been within her grasp.

"You don't want to dance with the likes of Middleton." Mama frowned at his retreating form.

She gaped at her mother. "Whyever not?"

"He lacks a spine."

"For mercy's sake." Lottie gritted her teeth. "He commands a ship."

"I'm saving you from future heartbreak." Tiny lines framed

Mama's pursed lips. "I have it on the best authority that Middleton dips too deep. I will not abide having a spineless, drunken wastrel as a son-in-law."

"You find fault in everyone." Lottie's fingers curled into tight balls. "Besides, it was only a dance." One she'd hoped turned into courting, and soon after, marriage, but Mama didn't need to know that at the moment.

"You shouldn't be overexerting yourself." Mama fluttered her fan. "The last thing you need is to have another spell."

She hadn't had a fever in over four years. What would it take to prove she was well enough to be like everyone else? If only she could have been able to make her own choice about the dance with Anthony. But once again, her mother had chosen for her. She sucked in a deep breath through her nose to curtail the roiling boil churning inside her.

"You'll find Lord Gibbons has exquisite dance form."

She didn't want to dance with someone instructed to indulge her. She wanted to dance with Anthony.

Mama glanced at Lottie's coiffure and sighed. "I wish you had used powder."

Lottie resisted the urge to put a hand to her hair. "Mama, no one has powdered their hair in a decade."

Her mother's mouth pursed into a thin line. "I'm well aware of the fashion trends, but the powder tones down your color, making your hair a much-preferred strawberry blonde. I daresay blonde is more fashionable than this"—she circled a finger in the direction of Lottie's head—"vibrant red."

Lottie waited for Mama's next line. She could repeat it verbatim.

"Red hair is for opera singers and ballet dancers. Proof of the tainting of our pure bloodline."

Lottie's periphery darkened as the rush of blood filled her ears, blocking out the lively background conversations. She fought to regain a measure of control. Her red hair was a constant reminder she was a disappointment. Not only was she born a girl and not a male heir, but her hair was red. Not a dark Auburn or strawberry blonde, but carrot red. Her mother blamed her father often with a mouthful of venom about the Etheridge line being tainted. Of course, Mama implied that had she known the family's indiscretions, she never would have infected her pure blood with his. It was rumored Lottie's great-grandmother on her father's side had indulged in a fling with an Irishman. In mother's opinion, Lottie's red hair was proof that her grandfather was baseborn.

An ember of hope ignited. If her ancestors had risked for love, then maybe—

just maybe—she might have some of their blood running through her veins.

"He thinks he's one of us." Mama crossed her arm and raised a haughty brow. "As if he can buy his way into the quality."

"Who?" Lottie shook her head to clear her negative thoughts and pivoted to find Nathaniel Winthrop scanning the crowd with a hint of resigned amusement. For a stranger, he owned the room with his subtle manner, as if he didn't care a wit about the pomp and circumstance of the *ton* or its social rankings.

Priscilla said his father had grown wealthy through the sugar trade. Winthrop contributed to his father's legacy by becoming a savvy merchant, trading in sugar and other goods. Clearly he was his own man, and she could picture him standing proudly at the helm of his ship, sailing the vast sea with wind ruffling his hair.

Lottie's eyes drifted closed. What would it be like to hold such freedom? An imaginary breeze pressed against her skin and whipped her undone tresses behind her. Her palms turned out to cup the air.

"Lady Reinhart's daughter danced with him at the Mayfair ball."

Lottie's eyes sprung open, and she dropped her hands to her sides.

"She complained about feeling hardened callouses under his gloves." Mother shivered and a look of utmost disgust deepened the creases around her lips. "You must give him a wide berth tonight."

Lottie withered under the constant weight of her mother's commands. Her lips had parted to offer the expected *yes, mama,* when the islander's gaze met hers from across the room. Their eyes held, and she saw the confidence in their depth, the defiance, as if he were proud of being an islander and not one of them. Deep down within her being, buried under layers of insecurities, a spark of rebellion ignited.

Mama issued her a sideways glance and lowered her voice. "Straighten up, dear. Etheridges do not slouch. You are the daughter of a viscount. Hold yourself with poise in accordance with your station. Hunching isn't going to make you appear less gangly..."

She would never raise herself high enough for her mother's standards, so why should she bother? It was her life, and past time she lived it. Lottie lifted her chin and pulled back her shoulders, but not because of Mama. She ignored her mother's droning and drifted in Mr. Winthrop's direction as if a magnetic force drew her.

"Charlotte Amelia Winthrop?" her mother called.

Lottie weaved through the crowd toward the entrance of the reception hall, her eyes never leaving her target.

He slanted a brow as if to say, *have we met?*

Lord Gibbons touched Mr. Winthrop's shoulder and gestured to Lady Reinhart as if offering an introduction.

The spell was broken.

Lottie froze. What had come over her? Curious stares of other guests bored into her skin, leaving her feeling naked. She pretended to wave to an imaginary acquaintance and hastened to the retiring rooms.

After freshening up, she faced herself in the looking glass. "This can't continue any longer. You are not a puppet. You have your own mind." Her pale blue eyes darkened. "If you want to dance, then you should dance. You're not going to collapse dead on the dance floor as Mama believes." She inhaled a deep breath and, with a curt nod to herself, returned to the ballroom.

Lottie's brother, Gerald, and Anthony, her would-be dance partner, stood on her right with a crowd of their friends. She sidestepped a particularly tall guest and slid next to her brother. "Pardon my intrusion." She dipped into a polite curtsy. "Gerald, I was hoping you would be a dear and allow me some reprieve from…" Her gaze flicked in their mother's direction.

Gerald groaned, and she could practically read his thoughts. If she was here, Mama was bound to follow shortly. "I was about to meet some chaps in the card room."

"Hmm." She leaned closer to Gerald and whispered. "I'd hate to have to retire early due to an oncoming headache, which would leave you to escort Mama home."

Her brother's Adam's apple bobbed. "Let me introduce you to my friends." He nodded to Anthony. "Of course, you know Middleton."

She smiled at Anthony, and he briefly returned it before he flashed a nervous glance in her mother's direction.

Lottie turned toward the other man and stiffened. Her stomach dove for cover. The guest she'd rudely stepped around had been the islander.

Gerald continued. "Lottie, may I introduce you to Nathaniel Robert Winthrop, of the Leeward Island Winthrops. You know, St. Christopher's Island, in the Caribbean."

She winced, for his reference made her appear dimwitted. "I'm conversant with St. Christopher, or St. Kitts, as its natives refer to it."

Winthrop bowed his head.

"Winthrop," Gerald gestured in her direction, but his eyes panned the crowd, "this is Lady Charlotte, my sister. We fondly refer to her as… as… Lottie."

Gerald craned his neck to peer between Anthony's and Winthrop's shoulders. She followed his line of sight to where Mama left her dowager friends and searched the room.

Lottie grasped Mr. Winthrop's sleeve, using his body to shield her from view.

The man's brows snapped into a *V*.

"I-I believe, we've already met." She forced her gaze to meet Mr. Winthrop's assessing one.

"I didn't know you and Winthrop were acquainted." Gerald turned to the Kittitian.

Curiosity and a flash of wonder glinted in the depths of Mr. Winthrop's eyes. He arched a quizzical brow.

"Indeed, I'm sure you remember." She wracked her brain for a plausible explanation.

Mama spotted Gerald and headed toward them.

"Gerald introduced us at the Leicester dinner party. You requested a dance at our next meeting and"—she pleaded with her eyes—"here we are."

Her heart thundered as he studied her for a long moment.

Gerald cleared his throat. "I don't recall attending the Leicester's… Ah." He slapped Anthony in the gut. "Was that the night you brought out that bottle of port? If my mother found out…" His voice faded into the background, for she couldn't tear herself from Winthrop's intense gaze.

"Er—what do you say we finish this conversation in the card room?" The pitch in Gerald's voice raised, and he dashed away. Anthony followed, nodding to guests as he went.

"Pleasure to meet you for the second time." Winthrop bowed slightly.

He moved to pursue Anthony, but she clutched his arm, using his tall frame for cover.

Steely blue eyes locked on her and displayed exactly what he thought of her—a desperate, featherbrained, nitwit who must be nicked in the nob.

"I'm dreadfully sorry. This is very forward of me and completely out of character, but I would love to dance."

She leaned left to see past his large form, only to find Gerald pointing Mama in her direction. Lottie ducked back behind Mr. Winthrop.

He crossed his arms and glared at her with a sharpness that should have chilled her to her core, but her desperation for refuge overshadowed her embarrassment.

The islander's jaw clenched. His nostrils flared. She bit her lower lip and implored him with her eyes.

Her anxiety must have struck a chord somewhere deep down in that statuesque physic, for he nodded and held out his hand.

She released a breath and placed her clammy fingers in his. Thank heaven for the satin gloves that hid her perspiration.

His grip was strong and warm as he pulled her onto the dance floor. The orchestra struck up another song, however, this one had a fast cadence. She hesitated. Did islanders dance? "Do you know the quadrille?"

One side of his mouth drew into a crooked smile. "A bit late to be asking now."

He jerked her into his arms and began to propel her around the ballroom. For a foreigner, he was an expert dancer. He commanded the floor with power, moving with panther-like grace in the waves of rhythm. She held an awareness of Winthrop's every move as if she were an extension of him. The thrill of being whisked around in the brace of such strong hands set her pulse racing. Funny, but Melinda Reinhart had been correct. She could actually feel the roughness of his calloused skin through the thin material of his gloves. Mama would be justified.

Within the safekeeping of his strong arms, Lottie dared to peer into the crowd. Mama's pinched expression and lethal gaze foretold of a future tongue-lashing, not merely for avoiding her mother, but for dancing with someone Mama found beneath her. Not yet ready to surrender, she flashed what she hoped was a coquettish smile at Winthrop.

Perhaps, she'd try her hand at flirting.

Nathan beheld the titian-haired beauty in his arms. Bright copper curls laced with tiny inset pearls crowned a face with skin as smooth as the cream from the coconuts back home.

She moved as one with him, adjusting to the slightest pressure of his hand. For the first time in a long while, he forgot about sugar, trade agreements, and the *Amory's* missing crew, and merely enjoyed dancing with a beautiful woman in his arms.

It was her unguarded openness that drew him. The few women on St. Kitts and at sea were hardened for good reason. To dance with a lady so expressive was refreshing.

She smiled at him, and he bit back his laughter. Miss Etheridge was an innocent, of that he had little doubt, and she had no idea of her allure. He didn't dare allow his gaze to wander down the white expanse above her gown's neckline. Instead, he refocused on the most expressive pair of blue eyes he'd ever seen.

Those bewitching eyes had caused him to relent, despite the fact he should be focused on business with Middleton to obtain British naval escorts for his ships. The merchant company he'd built through his own grit, hard-earned labor, and sugar profits had come under attack of privateers. Now the safety of his crews was his primary concern.

Yet, with one flash of those blue eyes, he'd lost his focus. She had held his gaze, pleading for him to accept her challenge. In that long moment when she hadn't dared to move, and he hadn't dared to answer, he'd sensed her desperation, and it drew out his protective instincts.

He pivoted them into a turn, and she craned her neck once again toward the crowd.

His jaw tensed. "I'll not be used as a pawn to inspire jealousy in a suitor."

"It's not like that."

He maneuvered her around an overzealous couple lacking rhythm. "Really? For I'm completely certain we didn't meet at the Leicester dinner party." He'd attended, but arrived late and sat at the end of the table next to the Leicester's governess. When the meal was over, he joined the men for cigars and solidified a merchant deal with Lord Leicester himself. That had been a fruitful, yet unadventurous, evening. He would have remembered being introduced to Miss Etheridge, if not for her eyes, then for her red hair.

"It's a complicated story." Her gaze continued to rove about the room until it settled on one place.

"Try me. Or, this dance is over."

Her eyes widened. "But the song hasn't ended."

"It has for me." He stilled.

"Wait." Her fingers dug into his sleeve. "I can explain." Her gaze returned to its previous position.

He followed the direction of her eyes to a dower woman scrutinizing them with flared nostrils and a hostile glare. He felt Miss Etheridge stiffen.

"Mama and I are at odds."

Those revealing blue eyes gauged his reaction. "I see." He

forced a deadpan expression. "So, you danced with a lowly islander to upset her."

Her lashes lowered. "I'm sorry."

To her credit, she was an honest chit.

The last note of the music sounded, and everyone clapped, but Miss Etheridge wouldn't release his arm. She shifted direction, like a frightened rabbit, uncertain where to hide.

"Shall we take a turn about the room"—he tucked her hand into his arm—"so we may finish our discussion?"

The tension in her fingers relaxed. "A lovely suggestion."

He turned away from her mother and circled the perimeter of the room. "So your plan is to retaliate?"

"How can I get you to understand?" She sighed. "I walked around with an oversized volume of the History of Scotland on my head for three months to keep myself from growing too tall for Mama's tastes. She reprimanded my embroidery stitches saying they were too large for her liking. I pricked my fingers trying to please her until the handkerchief stained red with my blood. I have powered my hair, for she despises its color."

He paused in his stride, and she turned to look at him.

"It's time I show her that I am my own person." A servant passed, and she plucked a glass of champagne off his tray. "I can make my own decisions."

"And you believe you'll show her by being irresponsible?" He'd once had similar conversations with his younger sister. The familiar pang of sorrow constricted his chest.

"Precisely. No... Well, maybe."

A low chuckle resonated from his throat. "Spirits heighten your emotions and addle your wits." He removed the glass of champagne from her gloved fingers. "Unless you want tomorrow filled with regrets, I suggest refraining." He passed it off to a servant.

Her eyes followed the glass weaving its way through the

crowd back to the kitchens. She rounded on him and narrowed her eyes. "I don't need another person to lecture me."

She gasped and drew a hand to her lips as if stunned by her own words. A becoming rose color spread across her nose and cheeks. He half-guided, half-pushed her behind a potted hibiscus to keep curious eyes from wandering in their direction.

"You haven't lived with her." Miss Etheridge stepped toward him so close her chin tilted up to continue to meet his gaze. "I'm a grown woman, of a marriageable age. Lord willing, I will be running a household soon enough, yet she treats me like a china doll. I'm made of stronger stuff."

Her fingers dug into the sleeve of his jacket. Tomorrow he'd probably find bruises."I'm made of stronger stuff." Her chest heaved against the lace of her gown,

Was Miss Etheridge desperate for an ally? He placed his hand over hers to relax her grip. "I can tell."

A breathy laugh burst from her lips.

He leaned in close enough for any passersby not to overhear. "Be who you are." The heady scent of her hair filled his nostrils. Lilac. "You need not be a puppet, nor go to the opposite extreme to prove otherwise. You are beautiful the way you are."

She drew back. Confusion shrouded her eyes, changing them to the color of an impending storm. Her lips parted in a silent gasp. The temptation to bewilder her further by pressing a kiss on those rosy lips straightened his spine. He was here on business. No time for complications.

He stepped back but continued to hold her gaze. "Pain is unavoidable, but misery is optional."

An array of emotions chased each other across her face— hope, fear, denial, anger. He wished his meaning would absorb into her heart. They hadn't known each other long, but he felt a connection with her, a shared desire to be respected. He admired her passion and vulnerability. Their paths may never cross again, but he wished her well.

He searched the room for Anthony Middleton, but to no avail. The man was probably still relieving his pockets of some coin with Gerald Etheridge in the card room. "Would you like me to return you to your..." Lady Etheridge plowed through the crowd from the far side of the room, her gaze intent on reaching her daughter. "...mother?"

"Heavens, no!" The shrill sound of her voice resonated her panic.

He nodded to a set of doors on their right. "Why don't you convalesce in the retiring room for a spell?"

"Brilliant." She shouted a bit too loud. "I mean... it would be good to freshen up a bit. It was—er—pleasant meeting you, Mr. Winthrop." She bobbed a rapid curtsy and escaped to her place of refuge.

He sighed. It seemed his big-brother instincts hadn't faded over time. Then again, neither had his sorrow.

No more distractions. He'd allowed himself one dance with Miss Charlotte Etheridge. Now back to business. There were too many people counting on him.

He spun on his heel to seek out Capitan Middleton for a meeting, but came face to face with Lady Etheridge instead.

"Who do you think you are?" Her scathing tone afforded no false impressions about how she felt about him. "How dare you dance with my daughter? You haven't been introduced. You haven't gone through the proper channels. Do you have no qualms for etiquette?" She didn't wait for his reply. "Of course not. You're a foreigner who believes money can buy you ranking and the esteem of your peers."

Though he stood a head taller than Lady Etheridge, she still endeavored to peer down her nose at him with the amount of disdain only the true British could muster.

And she wasn't finished. "It is good breeding that gains you respect and admittance to mingle with the aristocracy who are, quite frankly, above your station. It would serve you well to remember that."

"Yet, here we speak, Lady Etheridge, a lowly Kittitian and a highborn, privileged aristocrat."

"What flippant speech from someone here to do business within my sphere of influence."

Nathan's stomach dropped anchor.

Her lips pressed into a white slash, and her eyes narrowed into slits. "Keep away from my daughter. Am I clear?"

His jaw clenched, and he bit out through tight lips, "Quite."

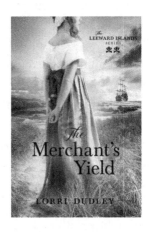

Get The Merchant's Yield at your favorite retailer!

GET ALL THE BOOKS IN THE LEEWARD ISLANDS SERIES

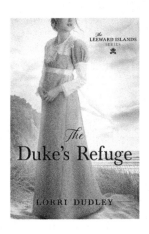

Book 1: The Duke's Refuge

Book 2: The Merchant's Yield

Book 3: The Sugar Baron's Ring

Book 4: The Captain's Quest

FROM THE AUTHOR

Dear Readers,

Thank you for reading *The Duke's Refuge*. I so enjoyed developing Georgia's character. Her brokenness and obsession with the color pink could only be healed by God's unconditional love. However, I must beg your pardon for taking liberties. Pink was not considered feminine during the Regency Era. It would have been more often seen worn by boys because it was a lighter shade of the British military's red coats.

During that era, blue would have been considered daintier, but due to today's standards, I believed that Georgia claiming blue to be feminine would have drawn readers out of the story. I hope those of you who are history buffs, like myself, will forgive my accommodation. Pink as a girlie color is actually a modern development stemming from the 1940s. The trend grew after Mamie Eisenhower wore pink to her husband's presidential inauguration. For more details and source documents please go to Lorridudley.com/the-dukes-refuge-resources.

Love,
Lorri

ABOUT THE AUTHOR

Lorri Dudley has been a finalist in numerous writing contests and has a master's degree in Psychology. She lives in Ashland, Massachusetts with her husband and three teenage sons, where writing romance allows her an escape from her testosterone filled household.

Connect with Lorri at http://LorriDudley.com

ACKNOWLEDGMENTS

First and foremost, I thank God for the opportunity to write. I have seen His fingerprints everywhere in my life, particularly on my writing voyage. He has also blessed me with a wonderful husband and three amazing boys. I can't thank them enough for believing in my dream, for their prayers, and their patience while I finish "one last thought." I love you.

Mom, thank you for being my biggest cheerleader. I'm going to have to add you to payroll for all your networking and proud publicity. Dad, thank you for putting my name on the Sunday School board prayer list and reading my romance writing. I'm so grateful for you both.

I have been (and continue to be) blessed by all the people who have supported me in my writing, especially my blog readers. I'm humbled by the outpouring of love, and appreciative for the encouragement. Many thanks also to my family members, aunts, cousins, and even second cousins, who've been so supportive. May God bless you all abundantly.

Big hugs and kisses to my beta readers, Alissa, Michelle, and Louise. You are the best. I'm also thankful for my wonderful sisters-in-law, especially Liz, who shares the passion for writing. Robyn Hook, my critique partner, you are a godsend, and Robin Patchen, my amazing editor and friend, your talent is incredible, and I could never have gotten this far without you. Special thanks to Misty Beller for your guidance and seeing my potential. And to the Wild Heart Books team, thank you for designing a great cover and for your tremendous editing and marketing wisdom.

Want More?

If you love historical romance, check out the other Wild Heart books!

Marisol ~ Spanish Rose by Elva Cobb Martin

Escaping to the New World is her only option...Rescuing her will wrap the chains of the Inquisition around his neck.

Marisol Valentin flees Spain after murdering the nobleman who molested her. She ends up for sale on the indentured servants' block at Charles Town harbor—dirty, angry, and with child. Her hopes are shattered, but she must find a refuge for herself and the child she carries. Can this new land offer her the grace, love, and security she craves? Or must she escape again to her only living relative in Cartagena?

Captain Ethan Becket, once a Charles Town minister, now sails the seas as a privateer, grieving his deceased wife. But when he takes captive a ship full of indentured servants, he's intrigued by the woman whose manners seem much more refined than the average Spanish serving girl. Perfect to become governess for his young son. But when he sets out on a quest to find his captured sister, said to be in Cartagena, little does he expect his new Spanish governess to stow away on his ship with her six-month-old son. Yet her offer of help to free his sister is too tempting to pass up. And her beauty, both inside and out, is too attractive for his heart to protect itself against—until he learns she is a wanted murderess.

As their paths intertwine on a journey filled with danger, intrigue, and romance, only love and the grace of God can overcome the past and ignite a new beginning for Marisol and Ethan.

⁓

Lone Star Ranger by Renae Brumbaugh Green

Elizabeth Covington will get her man.

And she has just a week to prove her brother isn't the murderer Texas Ranger Rett Smith accuses him of being. She'll show the good-looking lawman he's wrong, even if it means setting out on a risky race across Texas to catch the real killer.

Rett doesn't want to convict an innocent man. But he can't let the Boston beauty sway his senses to set a guilty man free. When Elizabeth follows him on a dangerous trek, the Ranger vows to keep her safe. But who will protect him from the woman whose conviction and courage leave him doubting everything—even his heart?

～

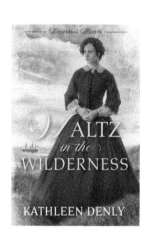

Waltz in the Wilderness by Kathleen Denly

She's desperate to find her missing father. His conscience demands he risk all to help.

Eliza Brooks is haunted by her role in her mother's death, so she'll do anything to find her missing pa—even if it means sneaking aboard a southbound ship. When those meant to protect her abandon and betray her instead, a family friend's unexpected assistance is a blessing she can't refuse.

Daniel Clarke came to California to make his fortune, and a stable job as a San Francisco carpenter has earned him more than most have scraped from the local goldfields. But it's been four years since he left Massachusetts and his fiancé is impatient for his return. Bound for home at last, Daniel Clarke finds his heart and plans challenged by a tenacious young woman with haunted eyes. Though every word he utters seems to offend her, he is determined to see her safely returned to her father. Even if that means risking his fragile engagement.

When disaster befalls them in the remote wilderness of the Southern California mountains, true feelings are revealed, and both must face heart-rending decisions. But how to decide when every choice before them leads to someone getting hurt?